MILLS & BOON

HIGH-SOCIETY
SEDUCTION

BY
MAXINE SULLIVAN

AND

THE
PATE...

BY
MICHELLE CELMER

"If this is unsuccessful, are you still willing to try again?"

"Of course! I'm in this for the long haul." She yawned deeply, her eyes overflowing with tears. "Well, goodness, all of a sudden I feel exhausted."

She must have slept as poorly as he had last night. Plus she'd had that long drive this morning. "Why don't you close your eyes and rest."

"Maybe just for a minute," she said, her eyes slipping closed. Within minutes her breathing became slow and deep and her lips parted slightly. He sat there looking at her and had the strangest urge to touch her face. To run his finger across her full bottom lip...

He shook away the thought. He hoped this was a one-shot deal. He hoped the test came up positive, not only because he wanted a child, but because he wanted to get the emotionally taxing part of the process out of the way. This entire experience was doing strange things to his head.

Dear Reader,

Welcome to book one of my BLACK GOLD BILLIONAIRES series!

I've probably said this before, and at the risk of repeating myself, I just love writing billionaire heroes. But not for the reason you may think. Yes, they're sexy and charming and, yes, they have unlimited resources, but it's more than that. I love that when you peel back the layers, and break down the defenses, they're really just regular guys. They want what everyone wants. Love, acceptance…even if they're too tough or too stubborn to admit it!

That's never been truer than with Adam Blair. He's got it all figured out. He thinks having a child will complete him, fill the hole in his life that has been there since he lost first his mother, then his wife to cancer. What he never counted on was his ex sister-in-law, Katy Huntly, coming into his life. Not only do opposites attract, they practically combust! But how could two people with practically nothing in common, who want totally different things from life, expect to make a relationship work?

I guess you'll just have to read the book to find out…

Best,

Michelle

THE TYCOON'S PATERNITY AGENDA

BY
MICHELLE CELMER

All the characters in this book have no existence outside the imagination of the author, and have no relation whatsoever to anyone bearing the same name or names. They are not even distantly inspired by any individual known or unknown to the author, and all the incidents are pure invention.

All Rights Reserved including the right of reproduction in whole or in part in any form. This edition is published by arrangement with Harlequin Enterprises II B.V./S.à.r.l. The text of this publication or any part thereof may not be reproduced or transmitted in any form or by any means, electronic or mechanical, including photocopying, recording, storage in an information retrieval system, or otherwise, without the written permission of the publisher.

This book is sold subject to the condition that it shall not, by way of trade or otherwise, be lent, resold, hired out or otherwise circulated without the prior consent of the publisher in any form of binding or cover other than that in which it is published and without a similar condition including this condition being imposed on the subsequent purchaser.

® and ™ are trademarks owned and used by the trademark owner and/or its licensee. Trademarks marked with ® are registered with the United Kingdom Patent Office and/or the Office for Harmonisation in the Internal Market and in other countries.

Published in Great Britain 2011
by Mills & Boon, an imprint of Harlequin (UK) Limited,
Eton House, 18-24 Paradise Road, Richmond, Surrey TW9 1SR

© Michelle Celmer 2010

ISBN: 978 0 263 88325 1

51-1211

Harlequin (UK) policy is to use papers that are natural, renewable and recyclable products and made from wood grown in sustainable forests. The logging and manufacturing processes conform to the legal environmental regulations of the country of origin.

Printed and bound in Spain
by Blackprint CPI, Barcelona

Bestselling author **Michelle Celmer** lives in southeastern Michigan with her husband, their three children, two dogs and two cats. When she's not writing or busy being a mom, you can find her in the garden or curled up with a romance novel. And if you twist her arm really hard you can usually persuade her into a day of power shopping.

Michelle loves to hear from readers. Visit her website, www.michellecelmer.com, or write her at PO Box 300, Clawson, MI 48017, USA.

To my dad

One

There was no doubt about it, the man was insufferable.

Yet here she was sitting in her pickup truck in the visitors' lot of the Western Oil headquarters building in El Paso, the ruthless, Texas-afternoon sun scorching her face through the windshield.

Katherine Huntley hadn't seen her brother-in-law, Adam Blair, CEO of Western Oil, since her sister's funeral three years ago. His call asking to meet her had come as something of a surprise. It was no shock, however, that he'd had the gall to say he was too busy to meet on her own turf in Peckins, two hours north, and asked her to come to him. But he was the billionaire oil tycoon and she was a lowly cattle rancher, and she was guessing that he was used to people doing things his way.

But that's not why she agreed to come. She was long past overdue for a trip to the warehouse store for supplies anyway, and it gave her the chance to visit the cemetery. Something she did far too infrequently these days. But seeing Rebecca's grave this morning, being reminded once again that Katy had gone from baby sister to only child, brought back the familiar grief. It simply wasn't fair that Becca, who'd had so much to live for, had been taken so young. That her parents had to know the excruciating pain of losing a child.

Katy glanced at the clock on the dash and realized she was about to be late, and since she prided herself on always being punctual, she shoved open her door and stepped out into the blistering heat. It was so hot the soles of her boots stuck to the blacktop. She swiftly crossed the lot to the front entrance, and the rush of icy air as she pushed through the double glass doors into the lobby actually made her shiver.

Considering the suspicious looks the security guards gave her as she walked through the metal detector, they must not have gotten many women dressed in jeans and work shirts visiting. And, of course, because she was wearing her steel-toe boots, the alarm began to wail.

"Empty your pockets, please," one of them told her.

She was about to explain that her pockets were already empty, when a deep voice ordered, "Let her through."

She looked up to find her brother-in-law waiting just past the security stand, and her heart took a quick dive downward.

Ex-brother-in-law.

Without question the security guards ushered her past, and Adam stepped forward to greet her.

"It's good to see you again, Katy."

"You, too." She wondered if she should hug him, but figured this situation was awkward enough without the burden of unnecessary physical contact, and settled for a handshake instead. But as his hand folded around her own, she wondered if he noticed the calluses and rough skin, not to mention the short, unpainted fingernails. She was sure he was used to women like Rebecca, who spent hours in the salon getting pedicures and manicures, and all the other beauty treatments she neither had time nor the inclination for.

Not that it made a difference what he thought of her nails. But when he released her hand, she stuck them both in her jeans pockets.

In contrast, Adam looked every bit the billionaire CEO that he was. She had nearly forgotten how big he was. Not only did he look as though he spent a lot of time in the weight room, he was above average in height. At five feet nine inches, few men towered over her, but Adam was at least six-four.

He wore his dark hair in the same closely cropped style, although she could see strands of gray peppering his temples now. Of course, as was the case with men like him, it only made him look more distinguished. There were also worry lines at the corners of his eyes and across his forehead that hadn't been there before. Probably from the stress of dealing with Rebecca's illness.

Despite that, he looked good for a man of forty.

Katy was only seventeen when her sister married Adam ten years ago, and though she had never admitted it to a soul, she'd had a mild adolescent crush on her gorgeous new brother-in-law. But neither she nor her parents would have guessed that the charming, handsome man intended to steal Rebecca away from them.

"How was your trip down?" he asked.

She shrugged. "The same as it always is."

She waited for him to explain what she was doing there, or at the very least thank her for making the long drive to see him. Instead he gestured to the shop across the lobby. "Can I buy you a cup of coffee?"

"Sure. Why not?"

Other than the shop employees, everyone seated inside

wore business attire, and most had their nose buried in a laptop computer, or a cell phone stuck to their ear. But when Adam entered, everyone stopped what they were doing to nod, or greet him.

Good Lord. When the man entered a room, he owned it. But he was the boss, and it was obvious people respected him. Or feared him.

She followed him to the counter and he spouted some long, complicated-sounding drink to the clerk, then turned to Katy and asked, "What would you like?"

"Plain old black coffee," she told the clerk. She didn't care for the frou-frou blends and flavors that had become so popular lately. Her tastes were as simple as her lifestyle.

With drinks in hand, he led her to a table at the back of the shop. She had just assumed they would go up to his office, but this was okay, too. A little less formal and intimidating. Not that she had a reason to feel intimidated. She didn't know why she was here, so she wasn't really sure what she should be feeling at this point.

When they were seated, Adam asked, "How are your parents? And how are things at the ranch? I trust business is good."

"We're good. I don't know if you heard, but we went totally organic about two years ago."

"That's great. It's the way of the future."

She sipped her coffee. It was hot and strong, just the way she liked it. "But I'm sure you didn't ask me here to talk about cattle."

"No," he agreed. "There's something I need to discuss with you. Something…personal."

She couldn't imagine what personal matter he might have to discuss with her as anything they might have had in common had been buried along with her sister. But she shrugged and said, "Okay."

"I'm not sure if Becca mentioned it, but before she was diagnosed, we had been having fertility issues. Our doctor suggested in vitro, and Becca was going through the hormone therapy to have her eggs extracted when they discovered the cancer."

"She told me." And Katy knew that her sister had felt like a failure for being unable to conceive. She had been terrified of disappointing Adam. Her entire life seemed to revolve around pleasing him. In fact, Becca spent so much time and energy being the perfect high-society wife that she'd had little time left for her family. Adam's schedule had been so busy, they hadn't even come for Christmas the year before she got sick.

If it had been Katy, she would have put her foot down and insisted she see her family. Even if it meant spending the holidays apart from her spouse. Of course, she never would have married a man like Adam in the first place. She could never be with anyone so demanding and self-centered. And especially someone who didn't share her love for the ranch. But according to her parents, practically from the instant Becca left the womb, she had been gunning to move to the city, to live a more sophisticated lifestyle.

Sometimes Katy swore Becca was a doorstep baby.

"She was so sure she would beat it," Adam continued. "We went ahead with our plans, thinking we could hire a surrogate to carry the baby. But, of course, we never got the chance."

"She told me that, too," Katy said, pushing down the bitterness that wanted to bubble to the surface. Harvesting the eggs had meant holding off on treating the cancer, which just might have been the thing that killed her. Katy had begged Becca to forget the eggs and go forward with the treatment. They could always adopt later on, but Becca knew how much

Adam wanted a child—his own flesh and blood—and as always, she would have done anything to make him happy.

It would have been easy to blame Adam for her death, but ultimately, it had been Becca's choice. One she had paid dearly for.

"I'm not sure what any of this has to do with me," Katy said.

"I thought you should know that I've decided to use the frozen embryos and hire a surrogate to carry the baby."

He said it so bluntly, so matter-of-factly, it took several seconds for the meaning of his words to sink in.

Baby? Was he saying that he was going to hire some stranger to have her *sister's* child?

Katy was beyond stunned…and utterly speechless. Of all the possible reasons for Adam asking her here, that particular one had never crossed her mind. How could he even consider doing this to her family?

She realized her jaw had fallen and closed her mouth so forcefully her teeth snapped together. Adam was watching her, waiting for her to say something.

Finally she managed, "I…I'm not sure what to say."

"So we're clear, I'm not asking for your permission. Or your approval. Out of courtesy—since it's Rebecca's child, too—I felt I should tell you what I plan to do."

He wasn't the kind of man to do things as a "courtesy." He did nothing unless it benefited him. She was guessing that he'd consulted a lawyer, and his lawyer had advised him to contact Becca's family.

"I also thought you could give me some advice on the best way to break the news to your parents," Adam added, and Katy was too dumbfounded to speak. As if losing their daughter wasn't heartbreaking enough, now they would have to live with the knowledge that they had a grandchild out there with a father who was too busy to even give them the time of day? How could he even think about doing this to them? And then to ask her *help?* Was he really so arrogant? So self-absorbed?

"My advice to you would be don't do it," she told him.

He looked confused. "Don't tell them?"

"Don't use the embryos." She was so angry, her voice was actually shaking. "Haven't my parents been through enough? I can't believe you could be selfish enough to even consider putting them through this."

"I would be giving them a grandchild. A part of their daughter would live on. I'd think that would please them."

"A grandchild they would never see? You really think that's going to make them *happy?*"

"Why would you assume they wouldn't see the baby?"

Was he kidding? "I can count on one hand how many times you and Becca came to visit the last three years of your marriage. My parents were always making the effort, and in most instances you were too busy to make the time for them." She became aware, by the curious stares they were getting, that the volume of her voice had risen to a near-hysterical level. She took a deep breath, forced herself to lower it. "Why not get remarried and have a baby with your new wife? You're a rich, handsome guy. I'm sure women would line up to marry you. Or you could adopt. Just leave my family out of this."

Adam's voice remained calm and even. "As I said, I'm not asking your permission. This meeting was simply a courtesy."

"Bull," she hissed under her breath.

Adam's brow rose. "Excuse me?"

"I'm not some simple, stupid country girl, Adam. So please, don't insult my intelligence by treating me like an uneducated hick. I'm here because your lawyer probably warned you that my parents could fight this, and you want to avoid any legal entanglements."

His expression darkened, and she knew she'd hit a nerve. "Your family has no legal rights over the embryos."

"Maybe not, but if we decided to fight you, it could drag on for years, couldn't it?"

His brow dipped low over his eyes, and he leaned forward slightly. "You don't have the financial means to take me on in court."

Not one to be intimidated, she met his challenge and leaned toward him. "I don't doubt there's some bleeding-heart attorney out there who would just love to take on a case like this pro bono."

He didn't even flinch. Did he know she was bluffing? Not only did she know of no attorney like that, she didn't think her parents would ever try to fight Adam. They would be miserably unhappy, but like Becca's defection from the family fold, they would accept it. And learn to live with it. They didn't like to make waves, to cause problems, which is why they allowed Becca to drift so far from the family in the first place. Had it been up to Katy, things would have been different.

Adam's expression softened and he said in a calm and rational voice, "I think we're getting ahead of ourselves."

"What do you even know about being a parent?" she snapped. "When would you find the time? Have you even considered what you're getting yourself into? Diaper changes and midnight feedings. Or will you hire someone to raise the baby for you? Leave all the dirty work to them?"

"You don't know anything about me," he said.

"Sad, considering you were married to my sister for seven years."

He took a deep breath and blew it out. "I think we got off on the wrong foot here."

Actually, what she had done was reverse the balance of power so that now she had the upper hand. It was the only way to deal with men like him. A trick Becca had obviously never learned.

"Trust me when I say, I have given this considerable thought, and I feel it's something I *need* to do. And I assure you that both you and your parents will see the baby. My parents are both dead, so you'll be the only other family the child has. I would never deny him that."

"And I'm just supposed to believe you?"

"At this point, you really don't have much choice. Because we both know that the chances of finding a lawyer who will represent you for free are slim to none. I've been in business a long time. I recognize a bluff when I see it."

She bit her lip. So much for having the upper hand.

"I'm not doing this to hurt anyone, Katy. I just want a child."

But why did it have to be *Becca's* child? "We may not be as rich as you, but we can still fight it."

"And you would lose."

Yes, she would. But she could put up one hell of a fight. And put her parents through hell in the process. Not to mention decimate them all financially.

The sad fact was she had no choice but to accept this. She was going to have to take him on his word that they would see the baby. What other recourse did she have?

"Can I ask who the surrogate will be?"

He was gracious enough not to gloat at her obvious surrender. "I'm not sure yet. My attorney is looking at possible candidates."

She frowned. "How will you know they're trustworthy?"

"They'll go through a rigorous interview process and background check. If they've ever been arrested, or used illegal substances, we'll know about it."

But there was no way to know everything. Katy watched the national news and knew situations like this had a way of going horribly awry. What if the woman smoked, or did drugs while she was pregnant? Or took some other physical risk that might harm the baby? Or what if she decided she didn't want to give the baby up? Would it matter that it was Rebecca's egg?

Or even worse, she could just disappear with Rebecca's child, never to be seen again. For Katy's parents—and probably Adam, too—it would be like losing Rebecca all over again.

"What if you think the woman is trustworthy, but you're wrong?" she asked him, growing more uneasy by the second.

"We won't be," Adam assured her, but that wasn't good enough.

She took a swallow of her coffee, burning her tongue. If she let him do this, she could look forward to nine months of being on edge, worrying about her niece or nephew's safety.

There was only one person she trusted enough to carry her sister's baby. It was completely crazy, but she knew it was the only way. The only *good* way. And she would do whatever necessary to convince him.

"I know the perfect person to be the surrogate," she told Adam.

"Who?"

"Me."

Two

Adam had imagined several possible scenarios of what Katy's reaction would be when he told her his plans. He thought she might be excited. Grateful even that a part of Rebecca would live on in the baby. He had also considered her being upset, or even indignant, which proved to be much closer to the truth.

But not a single one of those scenarios included her offering to carry the baby herself. And as far as he was concerned, that wasn't an option.

Admittedly he had approached Katy first because he figured she would be easily manipulated, but sweet little Katy had an edge now. She was a lot tougher than she used to be. And she was right about his lawyer's advice. If there were a legal battle over the issue of the embryos, he would win. But it could drag on for years. He didn't want to wait that long. He was ready now. And though allowing her to be the surrogate would significantly ease any opposition from her family, he could see an entire new series of problems arise as a result.

"I can't ask you to do that," he told her.

"You didn't ask. I offered."

"I'm not sure if you fully understand the sacrifice it will be. Physically and emotionally."

"I have friends who have gone through pregnancies, so I know exactly what to expect."

"I imagine that knowing a pregnant person and being one are two very different things."

"I *want* to do it, Adam."

He could see that, but the idea had trouble written all over it. In every language.

He tried a different angle. "How will your…'significant other' feel about this?"

"That won't be an issue. I see Willy Jenkins occasionally, but he isn't what I would call significant. We're more like… friends with benefits, if you know what I mean."

He did, and for some ridiculous reason he wanted to string this Jenkins guy up by his toes. To him she would always be Rebecca's baby sister. Little Katy.

But Katy was a grown woman. Twenty-seven or -eight, if memory served. It was none of his business who she was friends with.

Or why.

"The process could take a year," he told her. "Longer if it takes more than one try. What if you meet someone?"

"Who the heck am I going to meet? Peckins has a population of eight hundred. Most of the men in town I've known since kindergarten. If I was going to fall madly in love with one of them, I'd have done it by now."

He tried a different angle. "Have you thought of the physical toll it could take on your body?"

"Look who you're talking to," she said, gesturing to her

casual clothing, the ash-blond hair pulled back in a ponytail. "I'm not like Rebecca. I don't obsess about my weight, or worry about things like stretch marks. And you won't find anyone more responsible. I don't smoke or take drugs, not even over-the-counter pain relievers. I have an occasional beer, but beyond that I don't drink, so giving it up isn't a problem. Not to mention that I'm healthy as horse. And my doctor never fails to point out at my annual physical that I have a body built for childbearing."

She certainly did. She had the figure of a fifties pinup model. A time when women looked like women, not pre-pubescent boys. In his opinion Rebecca had always been too obsessed with her weight and her looks, as though she thought he would love her less if she didn't look perfect 100 percent of the time. Even during chemo she never failed to drag herself out of bed to put on makeup. And when she could no longer get out of bed, she had the nurse do it for her.

The familiar stab of pain he felt when he thought of her that way pierced the shell around his heart from the inside out.

Katy surprised him by reaching across the table and taking his hand. What surprised him even more was the tingling sensation that started in his fingers and worked its way up his arm. Her hands were a little rough from working on the ranch, but her skin was warm. Her nails were bare, but clean and neatly trimmed. Everything about her was very…natural.

Which was more than he could say for this situation, and the odd, longing sensation deep in his gut.

"Adam, you know as well as I do that despite all the back-ground checks you can do, there's no one you could trust as much as me."

He hated to admit it—she was right. Despite their very complicated past and feelings of resentment over Becca, Katy would never do anything to put her sister's child in harm's way. But she could use the opportunity to try to manipulate him, and he never put himself in a position to lose the upper hand. Not professionally, and especially not personally.

Not anymore.

But this was the welfare of his child they were discussing. Wasn't it his obligation as a father to put his child first, to make its health and well-being his number-one priority?

Katy squeezed his hand so tight he started to lose sensation in his fingers, and they were beginning to get curious glances from his employees.

He gently extracted his hand from hers. "Look, Katy—"

"Please, Adam. Please let me do this." She paused, her eyes pleading, then said, "You know it's what Becca would have wanted."

Ouch. That was a low blow, and she knew how to hit where it really stung. The worst part was that she was right. Didn't he owe it to Becca to let Katy do this for them? For the baby? Wasn't he partially to blame for Becca losing touch with her family in the first place?

"Though it's against my better judgment, and I would like to run it past my attorney before I give you a definitive answer...I'm inclined to say yes."

Her expression was a combination of relief and gratitude. "Thank you, Adam. I promise, you won't regret this."

Impossible, since he regretted it already.

Katy left soon after, and Adam headed back up to his office, feeling conflicted.

On one hand he could see the benefits of choosing Katy as a surrogate. In theory, it was an ideal arrangement. But he knew from experience that things did not always go as planned, and what may seem "ideal" one day could swiftly become a disaster the next.

Before he made any decisions, he would speak with his attorney.

His assistant, Bren, stopped him as he walked past her desk to his office. "Senator Lyons called while you were gone. He said he'll be out of the office the rest of the day but he'll call you back tomorrow."

"Did he say what he wanted?"

"My guess would be a campaign contribution. Isn't he up for reelection?"

"You're probably right."

"Also, Mr. Suarez needs to see you when you have a minute."

"Call down to his office and tell him now would be good," he told her. It was doubtful he would be able to concentrate on work anyway. Too much on his mind.

He stepped into his office, stopped at the wet bar to pour himself a scotch, then sat behind his desk and booted his computer.

"Hey, boss."

He looked up to find Emilio Suarez, Western Oil CFO, standing in his open doorway.

Western Oil was in dire financial straits when Adam inherited it from his father, and Emilio's financial genius had brought it back from the brink of ruin. Though he was from a Puerto Rican family of modest means, through grants and scholarships Emilio had graduated college at the top of his class, which was what had caught Adam's attention when he was looking for a management team. Emilio had become an irreplaceable employee—not to mention a good friend—and worth every penny of his ridiculously exorbitant salary.

Adam gestured him inside. "You wanted to talk to me?"

He came in, shutting the door behind him, and stopped to pour himself a drink. "I got an interesting call from my brother today."

"The federal prosecutor, the one in Europe or the other brother?"

The "other" brother was the family black sheep. A drifter who only called when he needed something. Money usually. For bail, or to pay off loan sharks.

"The prosecutor," he said, taking a seat opposite Adam's desk. "And if anyone asks, you did not hear this from me."

"Of course."

"You know Leonard Betts?"

"By reputation only." He was a financial wizard and according to Forbes, the richest man in Texas. It had been said that everything he touched turned to gold.

"You ever invest with him?" Emilio asked.

He shook his head. "He always seemed a little too successful, if you know what I mean. Either he's extremely lucky—and luck can run out—or he's shady."

"You've got good instincts. According to Alejandro, he's been under investigation by the SEC, and it's looking like he and his wife will be arrested and charged for a Ponzi scheme."

Adam shook his head in disbelief. "His wife, too?"

"And her parents. Or at least, her mother. Her father died a few years ago."

"So it was a family business."

"I guess. I just thought I should warn you that, although it's unlikely, there's the slightest possibility that when the media gets wind of this, my name may come up."

Adam sat straighter in his seat. "You've invested with him?"

"No! No, my market is real estate. This is more of personal connection."

Adam frowned, not sure he was liking what he was hearing. It would be in the company's best interest to stay as far removed as possible from this scandal. "How personal?"

"In college, I was engaged to Isabelle Winthrop. Betts's wife."

Adam's jaw nearly fell. Emilio had never mentioned knowing her, much less being engaged to her. Or anyone for that matter. He was so fiercely against the entire institution of marriage, Adam wouldn't have guessed that he would have been planning a trip to the altar with any woman. "I had no idea."

"She dumped me for Betts two weeks before we planned to elope."

"Damn. I'm really sorry, Emilio."

Emilio shrugged. "Honestly, she did me a favor. We were young and stupid. We would have been divorced in a year."

Something in his eyes told Adam he was making light of an otherwise painful situation. But he didn't push the issue. If Emilio wanted to talk about it, he knew Adam was there for him.

"There's no doubt she was a gold digger, but I'll be honest, I never imagined her capable of helping Leonard bilk his clients out of millions of dollars."

"Well, if your name does come up, we'll use Cassandra."

Cassandra Benson was Western Oil's public relations director. For her, media spin was an art form. If properly motivated, she could make climate change sound environmentally beneficial.

"So," Emilio said, leaning back in his chair and taking a swallow of his drink. "What's this I hear about you and a mystery woman?"

"Wow, good news travels fast." He should have taken Katy up to his office. It was just that the coffee shop seemed more... neutral. He should have known better and met her somewhere off campus and far from the building. Like California.

"The CEO can't sit in the company coffee shop holding

hands with a woman no one has seen before, and expect it to go unnoticed."

"Well, she's not a mystery woman. She's my sister-in-law. And we weren't holding hands. We were talking."

"I thought you didn't see Becca's family any longer."

"I haven't in a long time. But something has come up."

"Is everything okay?"

Up until today, Adam hadn't talked to anyone but his attorney and the fertility doctor about his baby plan, but he knew he could trust Emilio to keep it quiet. So he told him, and his reaction was about what Adam would have expected.

"Wow," Emilio said, shaking his head in disbelief. "I didn't even know you wanted kids. I mean, I knew that you and Rebecca were trying, but I had no idea you would want to be a single father."

"It's something I've wanted for a while. It just feels like the right time to me. And since I don't plan to get married again…" He shrugged. "Surrogacy seems to be my best option."

"Why the meeting with Becca's sister…I'm sorry, I don't recall her name."

"Katherine…Katy. I called her as a courtesy, and on the advice of my attorney."

"So, what did she say?"

"She wants to be the surrogate."

One brow rose. "Seriously?"

"Yeah. In fact, she was pretty adamant about it. She claims that she's the only person I can trust."

"Do you trust her?"

"I believe that she would never do anything to harm Becca's baby."

"But…"

"Katy seems very…headstrong. If I hire someone, I'll be

calling the shots. Katy on the other hand is in a position to make things very complicated."

"Correct me if I'm wrong, but if you tell her no, she could make things complicated, too."

"Exactly."

"So you're damned if you do and damned if you don't."

"More or less." And he didn't like being backed into a corner.

"So what did you tell her?"

"That I had to talk to my attorney."

"You hear so many horror stories about surrogacy agreements going bad. Just a few weeks ago Alejandro was telling me about a case in New Mexico. A couple hired a surrogate to carry their baby. She was Hispanic, and halfway through the pregnancy moved back to Mexico and dropped off the map. Unfortunately the law is in her favor."

Adam had heard similar cautionary tales.

"I think, if you have someone you can trust, let her do it," Emilio said.

He would make the call to his attorney, to check on the legalities of it and his rights as the father, but Emilio was right. Choosing Katy just made the most sense. And ultimately the benefits would outweigh the negatives.

He hoped.

Three

What the hell was he doing here?

The limo pitched and swayed up the pitted, muddy gravel road that led to the Huntley's cattle ranch, and Adam lunged to keep the documents he'd been reading on the ride up from sliding off the leather seat and scattering to the floor.

His driver and bodyguard, Reece, would have to take a trip to the car wash as soon as they got back to El Paso, Adam realized as he gazed out the mud-splattered window. At least the torrential rain they'd encountered an hour ago had let up and now there was nothing but blue sky for miles.

As they bounced forward up the drive, Adam could see that not much had changed in the four years since he'd last been here. The house, a typical, sprawling and rustic ranch, was older, but well maintained. Pastures with grazing cattle stretched as far as the eye could see.

The ranch had been in their family for five generations. A tradition Becca had had no interest in carrying on. As far as she had been concerned, Katy could have it all.

And now she would.

The limo rolled to a stop by the front porch steps and Reece got out to open his door. As he did, a wall of hot, damp air engulfed the cool interior, making the leather feel instantly sticky to the touch.

This meeting had been Katy's idea, and he wasn't looking forward to it. Not that he disliked his former in-laws. He just had nothing in common with them. However, if they were going to be involved in his child's life, the least he could do was make an effort to be cordial. According to Katy, the news of his plan to use the embryos had come as a shock to them, but knowing Katy would be the surrogate had softened the blow. And since a meeting with his attorney last week, when he and Katy signed a surrogacy agreement, it was official. With any luck, nine months from her next ovulation cycle she would be having his and Becca's baby.

After months of consideration and planning, it was difficult to believe that it was finally happening. That after years of longing to have a child, he finally had his chance. And despite Katy and her parents' concerns, he would be a good father. Unlike his own father, who had been barely more than a ghost after Adam's mother passed away. Adam spent most of his childhood away at boarding schools, or in summer camps. The only decent thing his father had ever done was leave him Western Oil when he died. And though it had taken several years of hard work, Adam had pulled it back from the brink of death.

"Sir?"

Adam looked up and realized Reece was standing by the open car door, waiting for him to climb out.

"Everything okay, sir?" he asked.

"Fine." May as well get this over with, he thought, climbing from the back of the car into the sticky heat.

"Hey, stranger," he heard someone call from the vicinity

of the barn, and looked over to see Katy walking toward him. She was dressed for work, her thick, leather gloves and boots caked with mud. Her hair was pulled back into a ponytail and as she got closer he saw that there was a smudge of dirt on her left cheek. For some odd reason he felt the urge to reach up and rub it clean.

He looked her up and down and asked, "Am I early? I was sure you said four o'clock."

"No, you're right on time. The rain set us back in our chores a bit, that's all." She followed his gaze down her sweat-soaked shirt and mud-splattered jeans and said apologetically, "I'd hug you, but I'm a little filthy."

Filthy or not, he wasn't the hug type. "I'll settle for a hand-shake."

She tugged off her glove and wiped her hand on the leg of her jeans before extending it to him. Her skin was hot and clammy, her grip firm. She turned to Reece and introduced herself. "Katherine Huntley, but everyone calls me Katy."

He warily accepted her outstretched hand. He wasn't used to being acknowledged, much less greeted so warmly. Adam recalled that the hired help had always been regarded as family on the Huntley ranch. "Reece Wilson, ma'am."

"It's a scorcher. Would you like to come inside with us?" she asked, gesturing to the house. "Have something cold to drink?"

"No, thank you, ma'am."

"If you're worried about your car," she said with a grin, "I promise no one will steal it."

Was she actually flirting with his driver? "He's fine," Adam said. "And we have a lot to discuss."

Her smile dissolved and there was disapproval in her tone when she said, "Well, then, come on in."

He followed her up the steps to the porch, where she kicked off her muddy boots before opening the door and gesturing him inside. A small vestibule opened up into the great room and to the left were the stairs leading to the second floor.

The furniture was still an eclectic mix of styles and eras. Careworn, but comfortable. The only modern addition he could see was the large, flat-screen television over the fireplace. Not much else had changed. Not that he'd been there so often he would notice small differences. He could count on two hands how many times they had visited in the seven years he and Becca were married. Not that he hadn't wanted to, despite what Katy and her parents believed.

"My parents wanted to be here to greet you, but they were held up at a cattle auction in Bellevue," Katy told him. "They should be back within the hour."

He had hoped to get this business out of the way, so he could return to El Paso at a decent hour. Though it was Friday, he had a long workday ahead of him tomorrow.

"Would you like a cold drink?" she asked. "Iced tea or lemonade?"

"Whatever is easiest."

Katy turned toward the door leading to the kitchen and hollered, "Elvie! You in there?"

Several seconds passed, then the door slid open several inches and a timid looking Hispanic girl who couldn't have been a day over sixteen peered out. When she saw Adam standing there her eyes widened, then lowered shyly, and she said in a thick accent, "*Sí,* Ms. Katy."

"Elvie, this is Mr. Blair. Could you please fetch him something cold to drink, and take something out to his driver, too?"

She nodded and slipped silently back into the kitchen.

Katy looked down at her filthy clothes. "I'm a mess. I hope you don't mind, but I'm going to hop into a quick shower and get cleaned up."

"By all means." It wasn't as if he was going anywhere. Until her parents returned he was more or less stuck there.

"I'll just be a few minutes. Make yourself at home."

She left him there and headed up the stairs. With nothing to do but wait, Adam walked over to the hearth, where frame after frame of family photos sat. Adam had very few photos of his own family, and only one of his mother.

In his father's grief, he'd taken down all the pictures of Adam's mother after her death and stored them with the other family antiques and keepsakes in the attic of his El Paso estate. A few years later, when Adam was away at school and his father traveling in Europe, faulty wiring started a fire and the entire main house burned to the ground. Taking whatever was left of his mother with it.

At the time it was just one more reason in an ever-growing list to hate his father. When Adam got the call that he'd died, he hadn't talked to the old man in almost five years.

He leaned in to get a closer look at a photo of Becca that had been taken at her high school graduation. She looked so young. So full of promise. He'd met her only a few years later. Her college roommate was the daughter of a family friend and Becca had accompanied them to his home for a cocktail party. Though Adam had been a decade older, he'd found her completely irresistible, and it was obvious the attraction was mutual. Though it had been against his better judgment, he asked her out, and was genuinely surprised when she declined. Few women had ever rejected his advances.

She found him attractive, she said, but needed to focus all her energy on school. She had a plan, she'd told him, a future to build, and she wouldn't stray from that. Which made him respect her even more.

But he wasn't used to taking no for an answer, either, so he'd persisted, and finally she agreed to one date. But only as friends. He took her to dinner and the theater. She hadn't even kissed him goodnight, but as he drove home, he knew that he would eventually marry her. She was everything he wanted in a wife.

They saw each other several times before she finally let him kiss her, and held out for an excruciating three months before she would sleep with him. He wouldn't say that first time had been a disappointment, exactly. It had just taken a while to get everything working smoothly. Their sex life had never been what he would call smoking hot anyway. It was more…comfortable. Besides, their relationship had been based more on respect than sex. And he preferred it that way.

They were seeing each other almost six months before she admitted her humble background—not that it had made a difference to him—and it wasn't until they became engaged a year later that she finally introduced him to her family.

After months of hearing complaints about her family, and how backward and primitive ranch life was, he'd half expected to meet the modern equivalent of the Beverly Hillbillies, but her parents were both educated, intelligent people. He never really understood why she resented them so. Her family seemed to adore her, yet she always made excuses why they shouldn't visit, and the longer she stayed away, the more her resentment seemed to grow. He had tried to talk to her about it, tried to reason with her, but she would always change the subject.

Elvie appeared in the kitchen doorway holding a glass of lemonade. Eyes wary, she stepped into the room and walked toward the sofa. He took a step in her direction to take the glass from her, and she reacted as if he'd raised a hand to strike her. She set the drink down on the coffee table with a loud clunk then scurried back across the room and through the kitchen door.

"Thank you," he said to her retreating form. He hoped

she was a better housekeeper than a conversationalist. He picked up the icy glass and raised it to his lips, but some of the lemonade had splashed over and it dripped onto the lapel of his suit jacket.

Damn it. There was nothing he hated more than stains on his clothes. He looked around for something to blot it up, so it didn't leave a permanent mark. He moved toward the kitchen, to ask Elvie for a cloth or towel, but given her reaction to him, he might scare her half to death if he so much as stepped through the door. He opted for the second floor bathroom instead, which he vaguely recalled to be somewhere along the upstairs hallway.

He headed up the stairs and when he reached the top step a grayish-brown ball of fur appeared from nowhere and wrapped itself around his ankles, nearly tripping him. He caught the banister to keep from tumbling backward.

Timid housekeepers and homicidal cats. What could he possibly encounter next?

He gave the feline a gentle shove with the toe of his Italian-leather shoe, which he noticed was dotted with mud, and shooed it away. It meowed in protest and darted to one of the closed doors, using its weight to shove it open. Wondering if that could be the bathroom he was searching for, he crossed the hall and peered inside. But it wasn't the bathroom. It was Katy's room. She stood beside the bed, wearing nothing but a bath towel, her hair damp and hanging down her back.

Damn.

She didn't seem to notice him there so he opened his mouth to say something, to warn her of his presence, but it was too late. Before he could utter a sound, she tugged the towel loose and dropped it to the wood floor.

And his jaw nearly went with it. He tried to look away, knew he *should* look away, but the message wasn't making it to his brain.

Her breasts were high and plump, the kind made just for cupping, with small, pale pink nipples any man would love to get his lips around. Her hips were the perfect fullness for her height. In fact, she was perfectly proportioned. Becca had been rail thin and petite. Almost nymph-like. Katy was built like a *woman*.

Then his eyes slipped lower and he saw that she clearly was a natural blonde.

It had been a long time since he'd seen a woman naked, so the sudden caveman urge he was feeling to put his hands on her was understandable. But this was Katy. His wife's baby sister.

The thing is, she was no baby.

A droplet of water leaked from her hair and rolled down the generous swell of her breast. He watched, mesmerized as it caught on the crest of her nipple, wondering if it felt even half as erotic as it looked.

Katy cleared her throat, and Adam realized that at some point during his gawking she had realized he was there. He lifted his eyes to hers and saw that she was watching him watch her.

Rather than berate him or try to cover herself—or both, since neither would be unexpected at this point—she just stood there wearing a look that asked what the heck he thought he was doing.

Why the hell wasn't she covering herself? Was she an exhibitionist or something? Or maybe the more appropriate question was, why was he still looking?

She planted her hands on her hips, casual as can be, and asked. "Was there something you needed?"

He had to struggle to keep his eyes on hers, when they naturally wanted to stray back down to her breasts. "I was looking for the bathroom, then there was this cat, and it opened your door."

"Right."

"This was an accident." A very unfortunate, wonderful accident.

"If that's true, then I think at this point the gentlemanly thing to do would be to turn around. Don't you?"

"Of course. Sorry." He swiftly turned his back to her. What the hell was wrong with him? He never got flustered, but right now he was acting like a sex-starved adolescent. She must have thought he was either a pervert, or a complete moron. "I don't know what I was thinking. I guess I *wasn't* thinking. I was...surprised. I apologize."

"Try two doors down on the right," she said from behind him, closer now. So close he was sure that if he turned, he could reach out and touch her. He pictured himself doing just that. He imagined the weight of her breast in his palm, the taste of her lips as he pressed his mouth to hers....

He nearly groaned, the sudden ache in his crotch was so intense. What the hell was the matter with him? "Two doors down?"

"The bathroom. You were looking for it, right?"

"Right," he said, barely getting the words out without his voice cracking. He forced his feet forward.

Since Becca's death he'd barely thought about sex, but now it would seem that his libido had lurched into overdrive.

"And, Adam?" she added.

He paused, but didn't dare turn back around. "Yes?"

"For the record, if you wanted to see me naked, all you had to do was ask."

Four

Oh, good Lord in heaven.

Katy closed her bedroom door and leaned against it, heart throbbing in her chest, legs as weak as a newborn calf's. The sudden and unexpected heat at the apex of her thighs... heaven help her, she might actually self-combust. It was as unexpected as it was mortifying.

The way Adam had looked at her, the fire in his eyes... she couldn't even recall the last time a man had looked at her that way. Hell, she wasn't sure if anyone *ever* had.

She pinched her eyes shut and squeezed her legs together, willing it away, but that only made it worse. An adolescent crush was one thing, but this? It couldn't be more wrong. Or inappropriate. He was her brother-in-law. Her sister's *husband*. The father of the child she would eventually be carrying.

Not to mention that she didn't even *like* him. He was overbearing and arrogant, and generally not a very nice person.

At least she knew that he wasn't lying about seeing her being an accident. Her bedroom door didn't latch correctly and her cat, Sylvester, was always letting himself in. If she had known Adam was going to be wandering around upstairs she would have been more careful. And maybe making that crack about Adam only having to ask wasn't her smartest move, but she refused to let him know how rattled she was.

Not that she was ashamed of the way she looked. As bodies went, hers wasn't half-bad. She just never planned on Adam ever seeing it. Not outside of the delivery room anyway.

She just hoped he never took her up on her offer.

Of course he wouldn't! He was no more interested in her than she was in him. Not only were they ex in-laws, but they were polar opposites. They didn't share a single thing in common as far as she could tell. Except maybe sexual attraction. But that was fleeting, and superficial. Like her on-again off-again relationship with Willy Jenkins used to be. He was a pretty good kisser, and fun under the covers, but he wasn't known for his stimulating conversation. As her best friend Missy would say, he was nice to visit, but she wouldn't want to live there.

Not that Katy would be "visiting" Adam. She would have to be pretty hard up to sleep with a man she had no affection for. She couldn't imagine ever being that desperate.

She heard a vehicle out front and peered through the curtains to see her parents' truck pull up in front of the barn. Well, shoot! Now she had to go out there and act like nothing happened. Which technically it hadn't.

She yanked on clean jeans and a T-shirt and pulled her damp hair back in a ponytail. As she tugged on her cowboy boots she heard the side kitchen door slam, then the muffled sound of voices from the great room below. She had talked Adam into this visit, so it didn't seem fair making him face her parents alone. And at the same time, she was dreading this. She didn't like to play the role of the mediator. That had always been her mother's thing.

In the week since she had talked Adam into letting her be the surrogate, Katy had been working on convincing her parents that she was doing the right thing, and that they were going to have to trust Adam. She just hoped that seeing him face-to-face didn't bring back a flood of the old resentment.

At first, when they learned that Becca was engaged, besides being stunned that she'd never mentioned a steady man in her life, her parents had been truly excited about having a son-in-law. But from the minute they met Adam it was obvious he came from a different world. And as hard as they tried to be accepting, to welcome him to the family, it seemed he always held something back. Her parents interpreted it as Adam thinking he was better than them, even though he had always been gracious enough not to condescend, or treat them with anything but respect.

At first Katy had given him the benefit of the doubt. She wanted to believe that he was as amazing as her sister described. But when he and Becca visited less and less, and Katy realized just how hard Becca had to work to keep him happy, she'd had to face the truth. Adam was an arrogant, controlling and critical husband.

But Katy wasn't doing this for him. She was doing it for Becca, and her parents, and most of all the baby. Which made what just happened between them seem wholly insignificant. It was a fluke, that's all. One that would never happen again.

She headed down the stairs to the great room. Her parents sat stiffly on the sofa and Adam looked just as uncomfortable on the love seat opposite them. When she entered the room everyone turned, looking relieved to see her.

"Sorry to keep you waiting," she told Adam, and his expression gave away no hint of their earlier...confrontation. Although he might have snuck a quick look at her breasts.

"Your parents and I have had a chance to get reacquainted," he said, and from the vibe in the room, Katy could guess it hadn't exactly gone well.

So as not to be antagonistic and give anyone the impression she was taking sides, she sat by neither her parents nor Adam, but instead on the hearth between them.

The contrast was staggering. Adam looked cool and confident in his suit, like he was ready to negotiate a million-dollar deal, while her parents looked like...well, like they always had. Her father had gotten a little paunchy over the past few years, and his salt-and-pepper hair was thinning at his temples, but he still looked pretty good for a man of sixty-two. And as far as Katy was concerned, her mother, fifty-nine on her next birthday, was as beautiful as she'd been at sixteen. She was still tall, slender and graceful with the face of an angel. She wore her gray-streaked, pale blond hair in loose waves that hung to just above her waist, or at times pulled back in a braid.

She was a perpetually happy person, always preferring to see the glass not only as half full, but the ideal temperature, as well. But now creases of concern bracketed her eyes.

"I was just telling Adam how surprised we were when we heard of his plans," her father said, and his tone clearly said he didn't like it much.

Katy's mom rested a hand on his knee then told Adam, "But we're hoping you can convince us that you've thought this through, and taken our family into consideration."

Katy bit her lip, praying that Adam's first reaction wasn't to get defensive. What had he told Katy that day in the coffee shop? That he wasn't seeking anyone's approval or permission? But he had to expect this, didn't he? He had to know her parents would be wary. That was the whole point of his visit. To set their minds at ease.

Or maybe he didn't see it that way. Maybe he truly didn't give a damn what they thought.

"As I told Katy, I have no intention of keeping the child from you," he assured them, in a tone that showed no hint of impatience, and Katy went limp with relief. "You'll be his or her only grandparents. In fact, I think that spending time on the ranch will be an enriching experience."

"I'm also not sure I like the idea of Katy being your surrogate," her father added, and suddenly everyone looked at her.

"I have my concerns as well, Mr. Huntley. But she wouldn't take no for an answer."

"I think we all know how stubborn she can be," her father said, talking about her as though she wasn't sitting right there. "I'd like to see her concentrate on finding a husband, and having kids of her own."

She was so sick of that tired old argument. Just because practically every other woman in her family married young and immediately started squeezing out babies, that didn't mean it was right for her.

"I'm not ready for a husband or kids," she told her father. Or more accurately, they weren't ready for her. Every time she thought she'd found Mr. Right, he turned out to be Mr. Right Now, then inevitably became Mr. Last Week. She was beginning to suspect that these men who kept breaking her heart knew something she didn't. Like maybe she just wasn't marriage material.

"You might feel differently when you meet the right man," he countered. "And besides, I don't think you realize how hard this will be. And what if, God forbid, something happens, then you can't have kids of your own? You could regret it the rest of your life."

"What if I walk out the door and get hit by lightning?" she snapped. "Do you expect me to stop going outside?"

He cast her a stern look, and she bit her tongue.

"Gabe," her mother said gently. "You know that my pregnancies were completely uneventful. And Katy has always been just like me. She'll do fine. You have to admit it will be nice to have a grandbaby." Moisture welled in the corners of her eyes. "To have a part of Rebecca with us."

"I assure you that Katy will have the best prenatal care available," Adam told them. "We won't let anything happen to her."

The way he hadn't let anything happen to Becca?

The question hung between them unspoken. It was hard not to blame Adam for Becca's death. Though he had done everything within his power to save her. She had seen the best doctors, received the most effective, groundbreaking treatment money could buy. Unfortunately it hadn't been enough.

If she hadn't insisted they harvest the damned eggs…

"What about multiples?" her father asked. "She's not going to be like that octo-mom and have eight babies."

"Absolutely not. The doctor has already made it clear that for a woman Katy's age, with no prior fertility issues, he won't implant more that two embryos at a time. And if Katy is uncomfortable with the idea of carrying twins, we'll only implant one. It's her call."

"But the odds are better if they implant two?" Katy asked.

"Yes."

"So we'll do two."

"You're sure?" Adam asked. "Maybe you should take some more time to think about it."

"I don't need time. I'm sure."

"Could you imagine that?" her mother said. "Two grand-babies!"

"I still don't like it," her father said, then he looked at his wife and his expression softened. "But it wouldn't be the first time the women in this family have overruled me."

"So it's settled," Katy said, before he could change his mind, with a finality that she hoped stuck this time.

"When will this happen?" Katy's mom asked.

"We have an appointment with a fertility specialist next Wednesday," Adam told her. "First he has to do a full exam and determine if she's healthy enough to become pregnant. Then he'll determine the optimal time for the implantation."

"So if everything looks good, it could be soon," Katy said, feeling excited. "I could be pregnant as soon as next month."

"And if it doesn't work?" her father asked.

"We try again," Adam said. "If we do two embryos at a time, we can do three implantations."

"It sounds so simple," her mother said, but Katy knew things like this were never as simple as they sounded. That didn't mean they weren't worth doing.

"And if none of them take?" Katy asked.

"I'll consider adoption."

"We appreciate you coming all the way out here to talk to us," her mother said. "I know it's eased my mind."

Adam looked at his watch. "But I should be going. I need to get back to El Paso."

"But you just got here," Katy said, surprised that after such a long drive he would want to get back on the road so soon. Was he really so uncomfortable there that he couldn't stick around for a couple of hours? What would he do when the baby was born? Would they always be coming to him?

"The least we can do is feed you supper," her mother said.

"I appreciate the offer, but I have an important meeting Monday that I need to prepare for. Maybe some other time."

They all knew those were just polite words. There wouldn't be another time. He wouldn't be coming back if he could possibly avoid it.

Katy rose to her feet. "I'll walk you out."

He said a somewhat stiff goodbye to her parents, then followed Katy out the front door. The moist heat was almost suffocating as they stepped out onto the porch. Adam's driver had taken refuge in the limo and was reading a newspaper, but when he saw them emerge he swiftly opened his door and got out. Katy turned to Adam, thinking that he had to be roasting in his suit and anxious to get back into the cool car.

"Thanks again for coming all the way out here. And thanks for being so patient with my father." It had to be doubly weird for him, trying to convince her parents she would be a good surrogate, when he himself still had doubts.

"It wasn't quite as bad as I thought it would be. Knowing your father holds me responsible for Becca's death, I realize it can't be easy for him to entrust me with the care of his only living child."

"Why would you think that?" she asked, although for the life of her she didn't know why she gave a damn what he believed.

He gave her a "spare me" look. "Not that I blame him. I should have been able to save her."

"Sounds like maybe it's *you* who holds you responsible."

If her words bothered him, he didn't let on. "I've made my peace with Becca's death."

"Your actions would suggest otherwise, Adam."

He looked at her for a second, like he might say something else, something snarky, then he seemed to change his mind.

He turned and walked down the steps. Reece opened the rear car door, but before he got in, Adam turned back to her.

"By the way, I wanted to apologize again, for what happened upstairs."

She folded her arms under her breasts. "You mean when you stared at me while I was naked?"

Reece's eyes widened for an instant, before he caught himself and wiped the surprised look off his face. And if she'd embarrassed Adam—which was the whole point—he didn't let it show. Was he a robot or something? Devoid of human feelings?

"Yes, that," he said.

She shrugged. "It's been stared at before."

"Don't forget we have an appointment with Dr. Meyer on Wednesday at 3:00 p.m."

She snorted. "Like I could forget that."

"I'll see you Wednesday," he said and she could swear he almost smiled. She found herself wishing he would, so he would seem more...human. Maybe he forgot how.

He may have been an overbearing, arrogant, narcissistic jerk, but that didn't mean he deserved to be unhappy. Although he hadn't looked unhappy earlier, when he was standing in her bedroom doorway. He looked like he wanted to throw her down on the bed and have his way with her, which, let's face it, was never going to happen.

He got in the car, and Reece closed the door. Katy waved as they pulled down the driveway. The windows were tinted so she couldn't tell if Adam was watching, but she had the feeling he was. When they turned onto the road and disappeared out of sight, she crossed the porch to the side door around the corner...and almost plowed into her mom, who was pulling on her mucking boots.

Katy squeaked in surprise and skidded to a stop, hoping

she hadn't heard that comment about Adam seeing her naked.

"Going out to the barn?" she asked brightly. A little *too* brightly if her mother's wry expression was any indication.

"Be careful, Katy," she said and it was obvious she *had* heard. "When you fall, it's hard and fast."

Fall? *For Adam?* Ugh. Not in a million years. She had clearly taken what was said *completely* out of context. "It's not what you think. He was looking for the bathroom and saw me getting dressed. It was an accident. What I said just now, that was only to embarrass him."

She didn't look convinced. "I know you always had a bit of a crush on him."

"For pity's sake! When I was a *kid*. Not only do I not have a crush, but I don't even *like* him."

"He's not like us, Katy."

Didn't she know it. "You're preaching to the choir, Mom."

"I just want you to consider this carefully. When you're pregnant, and your hormones are all out of whack, those emotional lines can get…fuzzy."

"I'm not going to fall for Adam. It's not even a remote possibility."

She didn't look like she believed Katy, but she let it drop.

The idea of her and Adam in a relationship was beyond ridiculous. Her mother had to know that.

Or was she seeing something that Katy wasn't?

Five

Adam met Katy at the doctor's office Wednesday as planned. She got there first, and as he walked into the lobby he was a bit taken aback when he saw her. In fact, until she smiled and waved, he didn't even realize it *was* her. Dressed in a white-cotton peasant blouse and a caramel-colored ankle-length skirt, she looked like…a woman. She'd even traded in the her usual ponytail for soft, loose ringlets that framed her face and draped across her shoulders. Even he couldn't deny that the effect was breathtaking.

He had always considered her attractive, but now she looked…well, frankly, she looked *hot*.

It was only the third time in his life that he'd seen her wear anything but jeans and boots. The first was his wedding, and the second Becca's funeral, but neither time had he been paying attention to how she looked. Was it possible that she'd always looked this blatantly sexy and he'd just never noticed?

And today, he wasn't the only one. Heads were turning as she walked past, eyes following her with obvious appreciation. But he knew something they didn't. He knew that as good as she looked in her clothes, she looked even better out of them.

A fact he'd been trying to forget all week.

Katy on the other hand seemed oblivious to the looks she was getting, as though she didn't have even the slightest idea how pretty she was. Or more likely, didn't care either way. He'd never met a woman so casual about her self-image. As evidenced, he realized with a tug of humor, by the fact that under the skirt she was wearing cowboy boots.

He could take the woman out of the country, but not the country out of the woman.

"You're early," he said as she approached him.

"I know, I didn't want to risk being late," she told him, then added, as if she thought he wouldn't notice on his own, "I wore my girl clothes."

"So you did."

"I'm *really* nervous."

"I'm sure everything will be fine." He looked at his watch and said, "We should probably get upstairs."

Though he had resigned himself to the idea of her being the surrogate and had for the most part convinced himself it was for the best, deep down he half hoped the doctor would find some reason to deem her an inappropriate candidate for the procedure. But after a thorough examination, Katy was given a clean bill of health. And like her own physician, Dr. Meyer even went so far as to comment that her body was ideal for childbearing. So there was definitely no turning back now.

It was a done deal.

After a consultation with the doctor in his office, where he explained the procedure in great detail, they made an appointment for the following week to have two embryos implanted.

"Are you nervous?" Katy asked him as they walked back down to the lobby together.

He shrugged.

"Oh, come on, you have to be at least a little nervous."

"I guess." After waiting so long for this, the process did seem to be moving very quickly. "How about you? Are you having second thoughts?"

"Not at all. I'm just really excited. I can hardly believe it's next week. I thought it would take months."

"It won't be a problem, you leaving the ranch for a couple of days?"

"They can get by without me. But I was thinking, because I'll be on bed rest for twenty-four hours after the transfer, maybe you could recommend a hotel."

Did she honestly think he would let her stay alone in a hotel? Not only would that be rude and insensitive of him, he wanted her close by, so he could keep an eye on her and make sure she followed the doctor's orders to the letter. They had three shots at this. He didn't want anything going wrong.

"Nonsense," he told her. "You'll stay with me."

"Are you sure? I don't want to impose."

They pushed out the door into the blazing afternoon heat where his car sat at the curb already waiting for him. "Of course I'm sure."

"In that case, thanks. It's been years since I've been to your house."

Three years to be exact. The day of Becca's funeral.

They stopped on the sidewalk near the limo. He really should get back to work, but she'd driven all this way and the least he could do was feed her.

"Why don't I buy you lunch?"

"I really need to get going," she said apologetically.

"I'll probably just swing into the drive-through on my way home."

She would decline his invitation for something as unpalatable as fast food? Not to mention unhealthy. "Are you sure? There's a café just around the corner."

"I promised my folks I would make a few stops for them on the way home, and I don't want to get back too late. Can I take a rain check?"

"Of course," he said, though her casual refusal puzzled him. When it came to women, he was usually the one declining offers. And lately there had been plenty of them, no thanks to one of his coworkers who thought Adam had done enough grieving and needed to get back into circulation.

Not that Adam considered Katy a woman. In the relationship sense, that is. In his eyes she was a business associate. One who was looking at him curiously.

"What?"

"If it means that much to you, we can go," she said.

"Go?"

"To lunch. You looked…I don't know…disappointed."

Had he? "No, of course not."

"You're sure? Because I can make the time."

"Of course I'm sure."

She didn't look as though she believed him. "I know this has to be tough for you. I mean, as much as you want a child, they're Becca's eggs. It must stir up a lot of feelings." She took a step toward him, reached out and put a hand on his arm. Why did she have to do that? Be so…physical? "If you need someone to talk to—"

"I don't," he assured her, his gaze straying to her cleavage. Probably because there was so much of it, and she was standing so close that it was right there, inches from his face. Okay, more than inches, but still.

"Hello!" she said, snapping her fingers in front of his eyes, until he lifted them to hers. "I'm trying to be nice, and all you can do is stare at my boobs? And people wonder why I dress the way I do."

She was right. That was totally inappropriate. He was acting like he'd never seen breasts before. When not only had he seen breasts, he'd seen hers.

"I apologize," he said, keeping his eyes on her face. "And no, I don't need to talk."

"I just figured you asked me to lunch for a reason."

"I did. I thought you might be hungry."

She sighed heavily. "Okay. But I'm here if you change your mind. Just call me."

"I won't."

"You know, it wouldn't kill you to lighten up a little. You're so serious all the time. That can't be healthy."

"You've never seen me at work. I'm a party animal."

She rolled her eyes. "Sure you are."

"So I'll see you next week?" he asked, anxious to end this nightmare of a conversation. She seemed to have an annoying way of getting under his skin.

"See you next week."

She turned and sashayed to her truck, hips swaying, curls bouncing. Anyone looking at her would know, just from the way she walked, that she had attitude.

And suddenly he was picturing her naked again. Wondering what she would have done if he'd stepped into her room, if he had reached for her...

"Sir?" Reece said, and Adam realized he was standing there holding the door open, and he'd heard their entire exchange. "She's something, huh?"

She was *something* all right. He just hadn't quite figured out what.

"She's really quite beautiful, isn't she?"

"I guess."

Reece didn't say a word, but his expression said he knew his boss was full of it. That any red-blooded heterosexual male would have to be blind not to think she was totally hot. But the last thing Adam needed was for his driver to think he had a thing for his surrogate. Not that he didn't trust Reece implicitly, but there were certain lines a man did not cross, even hypothetically.

This was definitely one of them.

Katy assumed the week would crawl by, but before she knew it, she was on her way back to El Paso. Adam had called a few days earlier, suggesting she come to stay the night before, so she wouldn't have to make the two-hour drive before the appointment, but she told him no. As nervous and excited as she knew she would be, sleeping would be tough enough without being in an unfamiliar room, in a strange bed. And for some reason, the thought of sleeping in the same house with Adam made her nervous. Not that she thought he would try something. It just felt…weird. But tonight she didn't have a choice. She physically couldn't drive home.

Her mother had offered to drive her to El Paso and stay for the procedure, then drive her directly back. She wasn't too keen on Katy staying at Adam's place, either. But the doctor said bed rest, and she couldn't exactly sack out in the truck bed for the two-hour drive.

Adam still lived in the sprawling, six-bedroom, seven-bath, eight-thousand-square-foot monstrosity Becca had insisted they needed. They could have had a whole brood of children and still had space to spare. And though she loved her sister dearly, and was sure that she had been a very accomplished interior designer, her personal tastes were excessive to say the least, and bordering on gaudy. She didn't seem to understand the concept of less is more.

Katy pulled up the circle drive and parked by the front

door, next to the concrete, cherub-adorned fountain, realizing how utterly out of place her truck looked there.

She grabbed her duffel from the front seat, climbed out and walked to the front entrance, but before she could ring the bell the door swung open. Standing there was Adam's housekeeper, whom Katy vaguely remembered from the day of Becca's funeral, an older woman with a gently lined and kind face.

Though Adam seemed the type to insist his staff wear a formal uniform, she was dressed in jeans and a Texas A & M sweatshirt.

She smiled warmly. "Ms. Huntley, so nice to see you again! I'm Celia."

Katy liked her immediately.

"Hi, Celia."

"Come in, come in!" She ushered Katy inside, taking the bag before she could protest. The air was filled with the scent of something warm and sweet. "Can you believe how hot it is and it's barely 10:00 a.m.? Why don't I show you to your room, then I'll get you something cold to drink. Are you hungry? I could fix you breakfast."

"I'm fine, thanks." She'd been too nervous to force down more than a slice of toast and a glass of juice before she left home. "Is Adam here?"

"He went into the office for a few hours. He's sending a car for you at ten-thirty."

She'd been under the impression they would ride to the appointment together, but she should have known he would squeeze in a few hours at the office first. Hadn't that always been Becca's biggest complaint? That Adam worked too much. Which begged the question, when would he have time to take care of a baby? But it was a little late to worry about that now.

Celia led Katy across the foyer and either Katy had a

skewed recollection of the interior, or Adam had made changes to the decor because it wasn't nearly as distasteful as she remembered. Considering she had only been here twice before, it was difficult to be sure. In any case, it was very warm and inviting now.

They walked up to the second floor and Celia showed her to one of the spare bedrooms. If Katy was remembering right, the master was at the end of the hall not twenty feet away. She didn't like that Adam would be in such close proximity, but what could she do, ask to sack out on the living-room couch? At least Celia would be there to act as a buffer.

Besides, she was being silly. She was only staying there because it was convenient. And because, she suspected, Adam didn't completely trust her to follow the doctor's instructions, if left to her own devices. She had to admit that being flat on her back for twenty-four hours sounded like the worst kind of torture. She was not an idle person. She didn't have the patience to sit around doing nothing. But this time she didn't have a choice.

"This is nice," Katy said, looking around as Celia set her bag down on the floral duvet. The room was tastefully decorated in creamy pastels. Feminine and inviting without being too frilly.

"There are fresh towels in the bathroom. And if you need anything, anything at all while you're here, don't hesitate to ask. I think it's a very generous thing you're doing for Adam. Since he decided to do this, it's the happiest I've seen him since he lost Becca. He would deny it if you asked, but the last few years have been very hard on him. I was starting to believe he would never get over her."

If he loved her that much, why did Becca have to work so hard to keep him happy? she wanted to ask. Why was she always terrified that he would grow bored and leave her for someone else? Maybe Celia wasn't seeing the whole picture, or hadn't known Adam long enough to realize what he was really like.

Katy sat on the edge of the bed. "How long have you worked for Adam?"

"Ever since his father passed. But I've known him most of his life. I practically raised him. When he wasn't off at boarding school, that is."

"Oh, I didn't realize you'd been with the family that long."

"Going on thirty-two years now. Since Mrs. Blair, Adam's mother, took ill. I lost my own boy in the Gulf War, so Adam has been like a son to me."

"I'm so sorry," Katy said. Losing a child was a sorrow her parents knew all too well.

"I still consider myself blessed. I have two beautiful daughters and five grandchildren between them."

"What do you think of Adam having a child? If you don't mind my asking."

Celia sat down beside her. "I think Adam will be a wonderful father. He lets my grandchildren come over and use the pool, and he's so good with them. He's wanted this for a very long time."

Celia was probably biased, but Katy wanted desperately to believe her. Although, wanting a child, and being good with someone else's grandchildren, didn't necessarily make someone a good parent.

"When you get to know him better, you'll see," Celia assured her.

"But how am I supposed to get to know him when he's so closed off. So uptight."

"That's just a smokescreen. Though he doesn't let it show, he feels very deeply. He's been hurt, Katy. It takes him time to trust. But he's a good man." She laid a hand on Katy's knee. "I know it's been hard for you and your parents. And probably nothing I can say will totally reassure you. But I promise you, Adam would never do anything to deliberately hurt anyone. Especially family."

"I want to believe that." But she didn't. Not for a second. Because that would mean everything her sister had told her was a lie. And believing that wasn't an option.

Six

On a normal day, Adam was an active participant at the informal weekly management team briefing they held in his office, but today he couldn't stop looking at the clock.

Nathaniel Everett, their Chief Brand Officer was explaining the new campaign his team had been developing to promote their latest, ecologically friendly practices. Groundbreaking upgrades that would not only keep them in line with future federal guidelines, but no doubt result in record profits.

On a normal day that would have filled Adam with a thrilling sense of accomplishment, but today his heart just wasn't in it. In fact, for a while now, six months at least, work didn't hold the same appeal as it had in the past. And that fact hadn't escaped his team.

At first he'd written it off as a temporary slump, but when he didn't go back to feeling like his old self, he began to suspect it was something deeper. Clearly something was missing. There was a void in his life, in his very soul that work would no longer fill. It was when he knew it was time to have a child.

"So, what do you think?" he heard Nathan ask, and realized he had completely zoned out.

"Good," he said, hoping he could fake his way through.

Nathan smiled wryly. "You haven't heard a damn thing I've said, have you?"

He could lie, but what was the point? "Sorry. I'm off my game today."

"Rough night?" Nathan's brother, Jordan, their Chief Operations Officer, asked, his tone suggestive. He'd been asserting for months that Adam's major problem was he needed to get laid. And while Adam wouldn't deny he'd been...*tense* lately, random sex with a woman he barely knew was Jordan's thing, not his. In fact, common knowledge of Jordan's sexual prowess was what had endeared him to the roughnecks on the rig. Despite his Ivy League education, they related to him somehow. Looked up to him even. He managed to fit in, yet still hold his own in the boardroom without batting an eye. He was like a chameleon, changing color to suit his environment.

Adam envied him that sometimes.

"Only because I didn't sleep well," he told Jordan. "Maybe we can reschedule for tomorrow."

Jordan shrugged. "Fine by me."

"I have a meeting with Cassandra anyway," Nathan told him, rising from his chair. "Should we say 10:00 a.m.?"

Everyone agreed, then gathered their things and left. Emilio, who had been quiet through most of the meeting, hung back.

"Everything all right?" he asked. He obviously didn't buy that a simple lack of sleep could leave Adam so distracted.

"Katy and I have an appointment today. In fact, I have to leave soon or I'm going to be late."

"The fertility doctor?" he asked.

Adam nodded. "She's having the embryos transferred today."

"I didn't realize it would be so soon. Congratulations."

"That doesn't mean it will work, but Katy is young and healthy and the doctor seems hopeful."

"I'll keep my fingers crossed for you. I guess I don't have to ask if you're nervous."

It took a lot to set him on edge, but today the pressure was getting to him. "It shows, huh?"

"Hey, who wouldn't be? This is a big step you're taking."

Adam looked at his watch. "And I have to meet Katy."

Emilio turned to leave, but stopped in the doorway. "I meant to ask the other day. This is probably none of my business…."

"What?"

"Well, since Becca had cancer, and that can be genetic…I just wondered if that would put your child at risk. It runs in my family, too. On my father's side."

"I've spoken to a geneticist and the fact that cervical cancer doesn't run in either of our families reduces the risk of predisposing the baby."

Emilio grinned. "So you've done your research. That's what I figured. Well, good luck."

When he was gone Adam grabbed what he needed and headed down to the parking garage. Since Reece had gone to get Katy, he took the company limo to the doctor's office. When he got inside, she was already there in the lobby waiting for him. And this time he had no trouble spotting her. She stood by the elevator bank, her face flush with excitement, dressed in her "girl" clothes again. This time it was a yellow sundress with a fitted bodice and A-line skirt, and instead of boots she'd worn strappy, flat-soled sandals.

Though he would never admit it to anyone, she looked sexy as hell. And if she were anyone but his sister-in-law, or his surrogate, he just might put an end to his three-year dating freeze and ask her out to dinner.

But no matter how attractive he found her, she was who she was, which kept her strictly off-limits. Not that she would agree to go out with him if he did ask. Knowing her, she would refuse on principle alone, just to irritate him.

"Early again, I see," he said as he approached her.

"You can thank Reece for that. He was worried about traffic."

He stabbed the button for the second floor. "Did you get settled in at the house?"

"I did, and Celia seems wonderful."

"She is."

"She really adores you, you know. You're lucky to have someone like that in your life."

She didn't have to tell him that. After his mother died, and his father took a permanent emotional vacation, Celia was the only "parent" he'd had. She wasn't just his housekeeper. She was family. He couldn't imagine what his life would be like now if it hadn't been for her.

"How can you look so calm?" she asked as the doors slid open and they stepped in. "I don't think I've ever been so nervous in my life."

"I don't do nervous." Katy must have put on perfume, too, because she smelled really nice. Flowery and feminine, but not overpoweringly so. In fact, the scent was so faint, yet so intoxicating, he had the urge to lean in closer and breathe her in. Bury his nose in the silky curls tumbling like silk ribbons across her shoulders.

Silk ribbons? Jesus, he needed to get his head examined.

"How could you not be nervous?" she said, clearly unwilling to let the subject drop.

"Okay, I'm a little nervous. Happy?"

"Well, if you are, you sure don't look it. I guess you're just really good at hiding your feelings."

"That comes as part of the outdoor plumbing package." The doors slid open and they stepped out, but when he turned to Katy she had a funny look on her face. "What?"

"Did you just make a joke?"

"I guess so. Is that a problem?"

"The ability to joke suggests you have a sense of humor. Adam, I had no idea."

He tried to looked indignant, but the corners of his mouth twitched upward.

She gasped. "Oh, my gosh! You just smiled! Do you know that since I met you at Western Oil that day I haven't seen you smile a single time? I didn't even realize you still knew how."

In spite of himself, he smiled wider. "All right, you've made your point."

She gave him a playful poke. "Better be careful, or God forbid, people might start to think you have feelings."

What she didn't realize was that he felt very deeply. Too much for his own good, in fact. And look where it had gotten him.

Which is why he expended so much effort to feel as little as possible now. Or at the very least, not let it show.

They walked down the hall to the fertility suite and were immediately shown into the doctor's private office for a quick consultation, in case they had any last-minute questions—a courtesy Adam was sure he reserved for only his special patients. In other words, the ones with the thickest wallets. Dr. Meyer had a fund for lower-income couples with medical conditions preventing them from conceiving, and understanding their pain, not to mention the perks it would include, Adam had donated generously.

After a brief chat, they were taken to the room where Katy would change into her gown.

"I guess this is it," Adam said. "I'll see you afterward."

"Afterward?" she asked, looking confused. "You're not going to come in for the procedure. I thought you would want to be there."

"I do. I just…I thought it would make you uncomfortable."

"Call me old-fashioned, but I believe a father should at least be in the room when his child is conceived. Even if he's not actually…you know…doing the work."

Leave it to Katy to be absolutely blunt. "If you're comfortable with it, then sure, count me in."

"The doctor knows the situation. I'm sure he can be discreet. And if not…" she shrugged. "It's not like you haven't seen me naked. And you'll be seeing it all again when the baby is born. Right?"

He had hoped she would allow him to be in the delivery room, but he figured he would wait until later in the pregnancy to ask. Now he didn't have to worry.

He didn't doubt that if he'd hired a surrogate, a stranger, she might not be as open to him being so involved in the entire process. And he appreciated it. More than Katy would ever know.

"Well, I better go change," she said. "Don't want to keep the embryos waiting."

"Thank you, Katy."

She smiled, then she did something totally unexpected. She rose up on her toes and pressed a kiss to his cheek.

Her lips were soft and warm and just the slightest bit damp. And though it didn't last long, just a second or two, something happened. Something passed between them, although he couldn't say for sure what it was. If it was physical or emotional. But whatever it was, he felt it straight through to his bones. And clearly, so did she.

She stepped back, looking puzzled, lifting a hand up to touch her lips. And something must have been wrong with him because his first instinct was to take her in his arms and draw her against him, bury his face against her hair and just…hold her. He wondered what she would do if he tried.

But he didn't, and after a few seconds the moment, whatever it was, seemed to pass.

"I guess I better go," she said, glancing back to the nurse who was waiting for her, looking apprehensive, as if the gravity of what she was about to do had suddenly taken hold. "You'll be there?"

Maybe she just didn't want to feel as though she was in this alone. "I'll be there," he assured her, and realized that his heart was beating faster. Maybe he was more nervous than he'd thought. Or could it have been something else?

She started to turn, and before he realized what he was doing, he reached out and grabbed her arm. Startled, she turned back to him, looking at his hand as though she was surprised he would touch her. And honestly, he was a bit surprised himself.

"You're sure you want to do this," he said. "It's not too late to back out."

The apprehension seemed to dissolve before his eyes and she smiled. A really sweet, pretty smile that he was sure he would remember for the rest of his life.

"I'm sure," she said, placing her hand over his. "I want to do this."

He let his hand slip out from under hers and fall to his side.

"You can sit in the procedure waiting room," the nurse

said, pointing it out to him. "They'll call you in when she's ready."

The waiting room was blessedly empty, but after twenty minutes passed he began to worry they had forgotten about him. He was about to get up and ask someone what was taking so long when another nurse appeared in the doorway. She led him to an exam room where Katy was already in position with her feet in the stirrups, ready to go. And other than a bit of bare leg, she was very discreetly covered.

She looked relieved to see him.

"Is everyone ready?" the doctor asked, looking from Katy to Adam.

Adam nodded. Katy took a deep breath, exhaled and said, "Let's do it."

She reached for his hand and he took it, holding firmly as the doctor did the transfer. The procedure itself seemed pretty simple, and if Katy's occasional winces were any indication, involved only minor discomfort. Within ten minutes it was over.

"That's it," Dr. Meyer said, peeling off his gloves. "Now comes the hard part. The waiting."

Per his orders Katy had to lie there for two hours before she would be allowed home, so after the staff cleared the room Adam pulled a chair up beside her and sat down.

"I think it worked," she said, looking contentedly serene. "I can almost feel the cells beginning to divide."

"Is that even possible?" he asked.

She shrugged. "Probably not, but I have a good feeling about this."

He didn't want to get his hopes up, but he had a good feeling about it, too. Something about the day, the entire experience felt...special. Like it was meant to be. Which was strange, since he'd never been superstitious.

She looked over at him and smiled. "If someone had told

me a month ago that I would be here today, having fertilized embryos injected into me, I would have told them they were insane."

Boy, could he relate. He always knew that someday he would use the embryos, but not with Katy as the surrogate. "If it's unsuccessful, are you still willing to try again?"

"Of course! I'm in this for the long haul." She yawned deeply, her eyes overflowing with tears. "Well, goodness, all of the sudden I feel exhausted."

She must have slept as fitfully as he had last night. Plus she'd had that long drive this morning. "Why don't you close your eyes and rest."

"Maybe just for a minute," she said, her eyes slipping closed. Within minutes her breathing became slow and deep and her lips parted slightly. He sat there looking at her and had the strangest urge to touch her face. To run his finger across her full bottom lip...

He shook away the thought. He hoped this was a one-shot deal. He hoped the test came up positive, not only because he wanted a child, but because he wanted to get the emotionally taxing part of the process out of the way. This entire experience was doing strange things to his head.

He sat there for a while, checking messages and reading email on his phone. Then he played a few games of Tetris.

After an hour, when she was still out cold, he decided to make a few calls. Careful not to disturb her, he stepped out into the hall and called Celia on his cell, asking her to have lunch ready when they got back, then he checked in with his secretary and returned a few other calls that couldn't wait until he got back to the office. When he finally returned to the room, Katy was awake.

"Oh, there you are," she said, looking anxious. "I thought maybe you'd left."

Did she really think he would just up and leave her there

alone? "Of course not. I just had a few calls to make and I didn't want to disturb you." He reclaimed his seat. "Did you have a good nap?"

"Yeah. I must have gone out cold. All the stress probably. At least now, if we have to do it again, I'll know what to expect." She touched his arm. "I wish it could have been Becca here with you."

Emotion caught in his throat. "Me, too."

There was a knock at the door, then the nurse stuck her head in. "You can get dressed and go now."

"Already? I guess I slept longer than I thought."

"And don't forget, strict bed rest for the next twenty-four hours," she said sternly.

"Like I could forget that," she muttered, sitting up.

Adam waited in the hall while Katy put her clothes on, then they went to the reception desk to make an appointment for her blood test in ten days.

"Can you believe that ten days from now we'll know if I'm pregnant?" she said excitedly as they walked down to the limo. His only concern right now was getting her home and back into bed. Although he was sure, the next ten days might just be the longest of his life.

Seven

It was official. Katy was starting to dislike Adam a lot less.

She had just assumed that when they got back to his place he would get her settled, pat her on the head and say good job, then motor off to the office for a shareholders meeting or something equally important sounding. In reality, he had barely left her side all day. She watched television and Adam sat in a chair beside the bed with his laptop.

He must have asked her a hundred times if there was anything she needed, anything he could do for her. And here she had honestly believed the only person he cared about was himself. He'd even smiled a few times.

And that kiss back in the doctor's office? What was up with that? It had been an impulse on her part. After all, what they were doing was pretty personal. It just seemed like the right thing to do. She'd never expected to *feel* it. Although to be honest she still wasn't sure what it was exactly that she'd felt. It was an odd sort of…awareness. Not sexual exactly, but not completely innocent, either. It was as if some deeper part of each of them had risen to the surface and collided, causing a sort of cosmic friction or interference or something. And she could tell, by the look on Adam's face, that he'd felt it, too.

It had been a weird, but not unpleasant experience. In fact, it felt sort of nice. But that didn't mean she wanted it to happen again. Unfortunately the more she tried to forget it, forget how smooth his cheek felt, the tangy scent of his aftershave, the more it consumed her.

She couldn't help sneaking looks his way, wondering if he was thinking about it, too. But she wasn't being as sneaky as she thought because he finally looked over at her and asked, "Is there a reason you keep looking at me?"

"Am I?" she asked, as if she'd had no clue. "I didn't realize. I guess I must be doing it unconsciously."

"Okay," he said, although he didn't look as though he believed her. But he didn't push the issue, either. And she was glad. She made a conscious effort not to look at him again.

Around six when Celia brought them supper on a tray, it was a relief to be able to sit up for a while. Celia set her tray over her lap, then gestured Adam to the opposite side of the bed.

"You, sit," she ordered.

"I am sitting."

"Now, *niño pequeño,*" she said sternly. "Little Boy." A holdover nickname from when he was small, Katy was guessing.

"Why can't I eat here?" He sounded like a little boy arguing with his mother.

"Because I said so, that's why. Now move, before your supper gets cold."

"You're seriously not going to let me eat here? In a chair, I might add, that I *own?*"

"And you honestly think I'm going to let you eat spaghetti on *Persian silk?* Becca would roll over in her grave."

He seemed to get that it was a losing battle, because he shoved himself up from the chair and mumbled, "The way you boss me around, a person would think this was your house."

He rounded the bed, kicked off his shoes and climbed on, sitting cross-legged next to Katy. "Happy now?"

"Good boy," Celia said, setting his tray in front of him, stopping just shy of patting his head. He looked more than a little annoyed, which Katy was guessing was the whole point. He may have *owned* the house, but Celia was clearly in charge.

It was one of the sweetest, most heartwarming things she had ever seen. The big powerful billionaire was really just a pussycat.

"Can I get you anything else?" Celia asked.

"A double scotch if it wouldn't be too much trouble," Adam said.

She smiled and said, "Of course. Katy?"

"Under the circumstances, I should probably lay off the booze. But thanks for asking."

"I didn't mean…" She sighed and shook her head, as if they were both hopeless. "Heaven help us, you're just as bad as he is."

She walked out mumbling to herself.

"Niño pequeño?" Katy asked, unable to stifle a smile.

"I swear sometimes she thinks I'm still ten years old," he grumbled, but there was affection in his eyes. He loved Celia, even if he didn't want to admit it.

"I think everyone needs someone to boss them around every once in a while," she said. "It keeps you grounded."

"Well, then, I should be pretty well-grounded, because she bosses me around on a daily basis."

And she could tell that though he wanted Katy to believe otherwise, he wouldn't have it any other way.

Celia returned several minutes later with his drink, then left them to eat. Katy just assumed that when they were finished, Adam would sit in the chair again. Instead he fluffed the pillows and leaned back against them. It was probably the most laid-back she had ever seen him. In fact, she'd never imagined he could be so relaxed.

She couldn't help but wonder if it had anything to do with the scotch. Maybe the alcohol had lowered his inhibitions. She recalled Becca telling her once, a long time ago, that if she wanted something, all she had to do was give him a drink or two and he was about as staunch as a wet noodle. And while Katy didn't necessarily believe it was ethical to take advantage of an intoxicated person, if it made him open up to her a little…well, what was the harm?

When Celia came back for their dishes, Katy asked her for a glass of orange juice. "And I think Adam could use another drink."

He looked at his watch, then shrugged and said, "Why not?"

Around nine, after he'd drained his second glass and was clearly feeling no pain—he'd even laughed during one of the shows—she used the bathroom and changed into her pajamas, then climbed back into bed. The program they'd been watching had just ended, so she switched off the television, rolled on her side to face him and asked, "Adam, can we talk?"

He looked down at her and frowned. "Is something wrong?"

"Oh, no, nothing," she assured him. "It just only seems

right that I should get to know the father of the baby I'll be carrying. Don't you think?"

His brow dipped low. "Oh, you mean you want to *talk*."

"What have you got against talking? It's how people get to know each other."

He looked uncomfortable. "That wasn't part of the deal."

"Maybe it should be."

"You know, my life isn't really all that interesting."

"I doubt that." She gave him a playful poke. "Come on, tell me something about you. Just one thing."

"Let me think. Oh, I know. I don't like talking about myself."

She laughed. "Adam!"

"What?" he said with a grin. "You said one thing."

"Something I don't already know. Tell me about…your father."

He shrugged. "There isn't much to tell."

"Were you close?"

"There were times, when my mom was still alive, that he would occasionally notice me. But then she died, and he checked out."

That was the saddest thing she'd ever heard. If they were all the other had, they should have stuck together. They could have leaned on each other. The way she and her parents supported each other when Becca died. She supposed that sort of tragedy could either pull a family together, or rip them apart.

"You must have been very lonely."

He shrugged again, "Celia was there for me."

He said it so casually, but she had the feeling that losing his mother had scarred him deeper than he would ever admit. How could it not?

"How did your mother die?"

"Cancer."

Which must have made learning about Becca's cancer all the more devastating. And scary. "How old were you?"

"Young enough to believe it was my fault."

She sucked in a quiet breath. That was probably the most honest thing he had ever said to her. Her heart ached for him. For the frightened little boy he must have been.

He looked over at her. "Everyone has bad things happen to them, Katy. You get through it, you move on."

Was he forgetting that she had lost someone dear to her, too?

"Have you?" she asked. "Moved on, I mean." She knew the instant the words were out, as the shutters on his emotions snapped closed again, that she had pushed too far. So much for getting to know one another.

He looked at his watch and frowned. "It's getting late."

He got up and grabbed his shoes from the floor.

"You don't have to go," she said. "We can talk about something else."

His expression said he'd had just about all the conversation he could stand for one night. Maybe a dozen nights. Maybe he was only in here to keep tabs on her. To be sure that she followed the doctor's instructions. "You need your rest and I have an early meeting tomorrow. I probably won't see you in the morning, but Celia will get you whatever you need."

Like the turtles she and Willy used to catch in the grass by the riverbank when she was a kid, he'd sensed danger and retreated back into his shell. God forbid he let himself open up to her, let himself *feel* something. Would it really be so terrible?

He hesitated in the doorway, like he might change his mind, but instead he said, "Have a safe trip back to Peckins," then he was gone.

Adam had actually started acting like a human being today, which she couldn't deny intrigued her. And now that she'd had a preview of the man hiding behind the icy exterior, she wanted to dig deeper. She wanted to know who he was.

But when had this ever been about getting to know Adam better? And why would she bother? When it was over, and the baby was born, they would just go back to being strangers. Seeing each other occasionally when he brought the baby around.

She laid a hand gently across her belly, wondering what was going on inside, if the procedure had worked and the embryo was attaching to her womb. Her tiny little niece or nephew, she thought with a smile. Even knowing that there was only an average 10 percent success rate, she had a good feeling about their chances.

She switched off the light and lay in the dark, thinking about everything that had happened since she left Peckins that morning. The ease of the procedure, and the way Adam had stayed with her all day. She thought that they had shared something special, that they were becoming friends, but it was clear he didn't want that. And for some stupid reason the idea made her inexplicably sad.

It had only been seven days since the procedure, and would be three more days before she would even know if she was pregnant, and Katy had already determined that she agreed to have a child with the most demanding and obstinate man on the face of the earth.

Adam had called her about a *million* times.

Okay, so it was more like fifteen or twenty, but it sure felt like a million. She had only been back to Peckins an hour when he phoned to check on her, which, in light of his cool attitude the night before, she found sort of touching. He reminded her that the doctor said to take it easy for several days, meaning no heavy lifting or strenuous activity. Which she, of course, already knew. She assured him she was following the postprocedure instructions to the letter, and he had nothing to worry about.

Thinking that she'd made herself pretty clear, she was surprised when later that evening he'd called *again*.

Was she eating right? Drinking enough water? Staying off her feet?

She patiently assured him that she was *still* following the doctor's orders, and when they hung up shortly after, assumed that would be the last she heard from him in a while. But he called again the next morning.

Had she gotten a full eight hours sleep? She wasn't drinking coffee, was she? And since country breakfasts were often laden with saturated fats, she should consider fruit and an egg-white omelet as a substitute.

She assured him again, maybe not quite so patiently this time, that she knew what to do. And she was only a little surprised when he called later in the day to say he'd been doing research on the internet and needed her email address so he could send her links to several sites he thought contained necessary information about prenatal health. And had she ever considered becoming a vegetarian?

If he was this fanatical before there was even a confirmed pregnancy, what was he going to be like when she was actually pregnant? Two to three calls a day, *every* day, for nine months?

She would be giving birth from a padded room in the psychiatric ward.

It wouldn't be so bad if the phone calls were even slightly conversational in tone. As in, "Hi, how are you? What have you been up to?" Instead he more or less barked orders, without even the most basic of pleasantries.

On day seven, he called to say that he'd been giving their situation considerable thought, and he'd come to the conclusion that he would feel more comfortable if she came to stay with him in El Paso for the duration of her pregnancy. So he could "keep a close eye on her."

It was the final straw.

"I will not, under any circumstances, drop everything and move two hours from home. The ranch is my life. My parents need me here. And all the phone calls and emails…it has to stop. You're *smothering* me and we don't even know that I'm pregnant yet."

"But you could be, so doesn't it make sense to start taking care of yourself now? This is my child we're talking about."

"It's also my life."

"If you were here with me I wouldn't have to call. And you wouldn't have to do anything. Celia would take care of you."

She liked Celia, but honestly, it sounded like hell on earth. She wasn't an idle person. Most days she was up before dawn and didn't stop moving until bedtime. "I *love* working, Adam."

"But obviously you'll have to quit."

"Why would I do that?"

"Because you'll be pregnant."

Oh, he did *not* just say that. "What century are you living in? Pregnant women work all the time."

"At a desk job maybe, or as a clerk in a store. I seriously doubt there are pregnant women out there roping cattle on horseback and mucking stables."

"Is *that* what you think I do?"

"It's not?"

"Not *just* that. And, of course, I wouldn't do those things when I'm pregnant. Do you really think I would be that irresponsible? And for your information, I spend a *lot* of time behind a desk."

"I didn't mean to imply that you're irresponsible. And I

guess I just assumed your responsibilities were more physical in nature."

"So you assumed I got a business degree just for the fun of it?" she snapped. "Next you'll be telling me that I'm wasting my education staying on the ranch." As if she hadn't heard that enough from Becca over the years.

"I'm just worried about the health of my child."

"We obviously need to get a few things straight here. One, I am *not* moving to El Paso. There is no reason why I can't have a perfectly healthy pregnancy in Peckins. And two, I am definitely not quitting work. My parents depend on me, not to mention that I love what I do. I understand that you're worried about the baby's health, but you're just going to have to trust me. And lastly, if you insist on calling to check up on me, could you have the decency to not treat me like a…a *baby factory*. Maybe we could even have a conversation. You do know what that is, right?"

"Yes," he said curtly. He obviously didn't like what he was hearing, but when she signed the contract to be his surrogate, nowhere did it say she had to comply to his every demand.

Move in with him? Was he nuts?

"Even though Becca is gone, we're still family. Would it really be so terrible if we were friends?"

"I never said I didn't want to be your friend."

"You didn't have to. I'm sure you've heard the phrase, *actions speak louder than words*. And maybe you haven't considered this, but if you get to know me a little better, it will be easier for you to trust me."

"I suppose you're right," he said grudgingly.

At least it was start. But she had the sinking feeling that it was going to a really *long* nine months.

Eight

Since their phone conversation three days ago, Adam had cut off all contact with Katy, and it had been surprisingly difficult. Since the procedure he'd been thinking about her almost twenty-four/seven. The more he read up on pregnancy, the deeper home it hit just how many things could go wrong with not just the baby, but Katy, as well.

He had accepted responsibility for Becca's death, and learned to live with the guilt, but the idea that her sister's life was now in his hands had him on constant edge. It was his responsibility to make sure she was healthy.

It was something he should have considered before he put this baby plan into motion. But it was too late now. Katie was due to arrive any minute so they could go for her blood test. In a few hours they would know if the procedure worked.

He was both excited and dreading it. Hopeful but conflicted. From his home office, where he'd been working while waiting for her to arrive, he heard the doorbell. Even though he was sure it was Katy, he let Celia answer it.

After a minute, Celia knocked on his door. "Katy is here, and I think something is wrong. She ran straight upstairs to the spare bedroom. And it looked like she'd been crying."

He bolted up from his chair, his heart in the pit of his stomach.

With Celia close behind Adam rushed up the stairs to the spare room. The door was open, so he stepped inside. The door to the bathroom was closed. He knocked softly and asked, "Katy, are you all right?"

"Give me a minute," she called.

He walked back over to the bedroom door to wait with Celia. After several minutes the bathroom door opened and Katy emerged. She was in her girls' clothes, and her red-rimmed eyes said she probably had been crying.

Ridiculous as it was, his first instinct was to take her in his arms and try to comfort her, which was exactly why he didn't.

"What's wrong?" he asked.

"I had some light cramping this morning before I left, but I thought it might just be a fluke." She sniffled and swiped at the tear that had spilled over onto her cheek. "But it wasn't."

The disappointment was all-encompassing. "You're not pregnant?"

She bit her lip and shook her head. "I was so sure it worked. I really expected to be pregnant."

Celia crossed the room and gathered Katy in her arms, and Adam couldn't help thinking that it should be him comforting her. But he was glad Celia had stepped in for him.

"You'll have more chances," Celia assured her, rubbing her back soothingly. "I know it's disappointing, but it will happen." She looked over at Adam and gestured to the box of tissue on the nightstand.

He plucked one out and brought it to her. Celia took it and

pressed it into Katy's hand. "Why don't I make you a soothing cup of chamomile tea?"

Katy sniffled and nodded.

Celia turned and gave Adam a look, then jerked her head in Katy's direction, as if to say "Console her, you idiot." But he couldn't seem to make himself do it.

Katy stood there dabbing her eyes. "I was so sure I was pregnant."

"The doctor said it could take a few times."

"I know, but I had such a good feeling." She took a deep, shuddering breath. "I'm so sorry, Adam."

"Sorry for what?"

"I feel responsible."

She looked so damned...forlorn. And Katy never struck him as the kind of woman to cry on a whim. He recalled that even at Becca's funeral she'd held it together. And how could he just stand there, like a selfish bastard, when he was the one who put her in this situation? Had he really grown so cold and unfeeling?

Or was it that he felt *too* much?

"I'm sorry," she said in a wobbly voice. "I'm acting stupid."

Another tear spilled over and rolled down her cheek, and he cringed. The gene all men possessed that made them wither at the sight of a crying female kicked into overdrive. Besides, if he didn't do something, she would probably just interpret it as him being mad at her, or something equally ridiculous.

Feeling he had no choice, he stepped closer and tugged her into his arms. She came willingly, leaning into the embrace, hands fisted against his chest, head tucked under his chin.

There it was again, just like when she'd kissed his cheek, that feeling of awareness. As if every touch, every sensation was multiplied tenfold. The softness of her body where it pressed against his. The flowery scent of her hair. The flutter of her breath through his shirt and the warmth that seemed to seep through her clothing to his skin.

His body began to react the way any man's would. Well, any man who hadn't been this physically close to a woman in three years. Or intimate in closer to four. Until recently he couldn't say he'd missed it. He'd barely given any thought to sex. It was as if his body had been in deep hibernation, unable to feel physical pleasure.

But he sure as hell could feel it now. And if he didn't get a hold of himself, she would feel it, too.

"I'm sorry," she said again.

"Would you *stop* apologizing."

"I just feel like, maybe if I had done something different, if I had been more careful."

Beating herself up over this wasn't going to change anything. "It was nothing you did."

"But you only have embryos for two more attempts. What if those fail, too?"

"I knew going into this that there was a chance it wouldn't work. I do have other options."

"But then the last of Becca will be gone forever."

"Katy, look at me." She didn't move, so he cradled her chin in his palm and lifted her face to his. Big mistake. Her eyes were wide and sad, and so blue he could almost swim in their depths, and when they locked on his, the sensation was so intense he felt it like a physical blow. Whatever it was he'd been about to say to her was lost.

Her lips parted, like she might speak, and his eyes were drawn to her mouth. Though he knew it was wrong, never had the idea of kissing a woman intrigued him this way. And clearly whatever craziness was causing this, it was doing the same to her. He could tell, by the sudden shift in her demeanor, by the look in her eyes, that she was going to kiss him again. And he wasn't entirely sure he wanted to stop her.

Not only did he not stop her, but as she rose up, he leaned in to meet her halfway.

Their lips touched and whatever was left of his common sense evaporated with their mingling breath. His only coherent thought was *more*. Whatever she was willing to give, he would take.

So thank God Celia chose that exact instant to call up from the base of the stairs, "The tea is ready!"

Katy pulled away from him, eyes wide with the realization of what they had just done.

"We'll be down in a minute," he called to Celia.

"Oh, my God," she whispered, reaching up to touch her lips. "Did you *feel* that?"

Feel it? His heart was about to pound out of his chest. And he couldn't stop looking at her mouth.

He needed to get a hold of himself.

"Okay, this is not that bad," she said, trying to rationalize a situation that was completely *ir*rational. "We're both disappointed, and upset. That's all. This doesn't mean anything. Right?"

Leave it to Katy to take the situation and blow it wide open.

"Right. We're just upset." He didn't know if he actually believed it, but it seemed to be what she needed to hear. Why couldn't she be one of those women who was content to pretend everything was fine. Like Becca. It had been like pulling teeth to get her to admit when there was a problem, or she was upset about something.

Of course, that had been no picnic, either. Was there no happy medium?

"We need to call the doctor's office," Katy said. "Find out what we should do."

He was glad one of them was thinking clearly. Because the only clear thought he was having right now was how much he'd like to see her naked again.

They had opened a door, and he couldn't help wondering if it was only a matter of time before someone stepped through.

She had kissed Adam. On the mouth.

One minute Katy had been racked with guilt that the procedure hadn't worked, and the next she was practically crawling out of her skin, she was so hot for him. And thank God for Celia and her timing, or who knows what *might* have happened. The possibilities both horrified and intrigued her. Though Becca was gone, he would always be her brother-in-law. Her sister's husband. To Katy *and* her parents, who would kill her if they had any clue what had just happened.

Sure, she'd hoped she and Adam could get to know each other, but she'd never meant in the *biblical* sense. Talk about going from one extreme to another.

Like her mom had so eloquently put it, he wasn't like them. So whatever was causing these weird feelings was going to have to stop.

Despite the fact that they both seemed determined to forget it happened, their trip to the doctor's office later that afternoon had been tense. But at least the appointment with Dr. Meyer had been encouraging. He assured her that she'd done nothing to cause the implantation to fail. He wrote her a prescription for hormone shots that she would begin taking a week before the next scheduled implantation. He explained that it could make her womb more hospitable and increase their chances for success.

She wasn't sure what the shots were actually doing for her womb, but as she drove back to El Paso the morning of the second procedure, her emotions were in a hopeless tangle.

What if things were completely awkward between her and Adam? He had emailed her a few times in the past week to check on her, but they hadn't actually talked since her last visit.

Like last time, she drove straight to Adam's house, then Reece took her in the limo to the clinic. She assumed Adam would already be waiting in the lobby, and she was so nervous about seeing him again her hands were trembling. But he wasn't there yet. She waited in their usual spot by the elevator, wringing her hands. He sent her a text message a few minutes later that said he was running late, and to go on up without him.

What if he didn't make it on time? Would they wait for him? The idea of doing this alone made her heart race.

She took the elevator up to the clinic. She checked in, hoping they would make her wait this time, but the nurse called her back right away. She took her time changing into a gown, her anxiety mounting, waiting for a reply saying that he'd arrived. But when the nurse took her to the procedure room, she had no choice but to leave her phone in her purse.

He wasn't going to make it, she realized. Was he really held up at work, or avoiding her? Had that kiss done more damage than she'd realized? This was starting to become a familiar cycle for her. Get close to a man, let her guard down, then inevitably drive him away. What other conclusion could she draw, but that there was something seriously wrong with her? She was like a human deflector. Men got close, then bounced off the surface.

Most of her friends were already married and starting families. And here she was having a baby for someone else, because she was so unappealing, so unlovable no one wanted her.

The nurse got her situated on the table and ready for the

transfer. She must have sensed Katy was upset because she put a hand on her shoulder and asked, "You okay, honey?"

Tears welled in her eyes. "I don't think Adam is going to make it."

"Mr. Blair is already here, in the waiting room."

"He is?"

She nodded and smiled. "I was just about to go get him."

She was so relieved, if she hadn't been lying down, her knees probably would have given out.

The nurse slipped out into the hall, returning a minute later with Adam. She was so happy to see him she had to bite down hard on her lip to keep from bursting into tears, but they started leaking out of her eyes anyway.

Looking worried, Adam grabbed a chair and sat down beside her. "Katy, what's the matter? Why are you crying?"

"I thought you weren't coming," she said, her voice wobbly.

"I told you I'd just be a few minutes late."

She wiped her eyes. "I know. I don't know what's wrong with me."

"It's probably the hormones you've been taking," the nurse said, handing her a tissue. "It makes some women weepy."

In that case she hoped it worked this time, so she didn't have to take this emotional roller-coaster ride again. For someone who barely even suffered PMS, this was the pits.

"Is there anything I can do?" Adam asked, looking so adorably helpless, she could have hugged him. Or kissed him. He was sitting awfully close. If she just reached up and slipped a hand around his neck, pulled him down...

Ugh. Had she really just gone from weeping, to fantasizing about jumping him? As if things weren't weird enough already.

She really was a basket case.

The door opened and Dr. Meyer came in, asking cheerfully, "Are we ready to make a baby?"

Katy nodded and held her hand out to Adam. He took it, cradling it between his, holding tight while the doctor did the transfer. Just like the last time it was quick, and mostly painless.

"You know the drill," the nurse told them when it was over. "Two hours on your back."

The nurse stepped out into the hall and it was just the two of them. Alone. Last time Adam had let go of her hand as soon as the procedure was finished, but not now. Maybe he didn't think she was so terrible after all.

"I'm really sorry about earlier," she said. "I *never* cry. Not even when I was thrown from a horse and busted my collarbone. But it seems as though every time I see you now I'm blubbering about something."

"Katy, I understand."

"I just don't want you to think I'm a big baby." Because that's sure what she felt like.

"I don't. The same thing happened to Becca when they were getting her ready to harvest the eggs. Then they found the cancer and, well, suffice it to say that didn't help matters."

It was hard to imagine Becca crying about anything. Even the cancer. She had always been so strong, so determined to beat it. Even near the end, when all hope was lost, she was tough. Around Katy and their parents anyway.

"Sometimes I feel guilty that I don't miss her more," she said. "That we drifted so far apart."

"It happens, I guess."

"It's really sad. She was my sister for twenty-four years, but I don't think she ever really knew me."

That seemed to surprise him. "In what way?"

"She always thought that by staying on the ranch with

our parents, I was settling—giving in—or something. She must have told me a million times that I was wasting my education. And my life. She said I should move to the city, try new things. Meet new people. And no matter how many times I told her that I loved working on the ranch, that it was what made me happy, she just didn't seem to get it. If it wasn't good enough for her, then it wasn't good enough for anyone. It was so...*infuriating*."

"What she thought shouldn't have mattered."

But it did. She had always looked up to Becca. She was beautiful and popular and sophisticated. Of course, she could also be self-centered and stubborn, too.

"I felt as though she never really saw me. The *real* me. To her I was always little Katy, young and naive. I think she expected me to be just like her. And not only did I not give a damn about being rich and sophisticated, I could never pine for a man the way she did for you. It's like she was obsessed. Everything she did was to keep you happy. To keep you interested. It just seemed...exhausting."

Adam frowned, and Katy felt a stab of guilt. What had possessed her to say something so insensitive?

"Oh, shoot. Adam, I'm sorry." She squeezed his hand, wishing she could take the words back. "I didn't mean to imply—"

"No, you're right. She was like that. But for the life of me I could never understand why. She didn't need to work to keep me interested. I loved her unconditionally. She was so independent and feisty."

Katy smiled. "She was definitely feisty. Full of piss and vinegar, my grandma used to say."

"She lost that. I don't know why, but after we got married, she changed."

"Maybe she loved you so much, she was afraid of losing

you. Maybe she was worried that once you were married, you would get bored with her."

"That's ridiculous."

"When she met you, she seemed truly happy for the first time in her life. She was never happy at home. She never came out and said it, but we knew she was ashamed of where she came from. You'll never know how much that hurt my parents."

He surprised her by turning his hand and threading his fingers through hers. "I tried to get Becca to visit more. I told her I would make time. I had no family, so I knew how important it was. She just…" He shrugged helplessly.

That should have hurt, but mostly Katy just felt disappointed. Especially since Becca had led them to believe that it was Adam who never had time for them.

"It was like that with the fertility treatments, too," he said. "They found the cancer, and wanted to do the surgery and start treatment immediately. She flat-out refused. She wanted to harvest her eggs. I begged her to reconsider, but she knew it was our last chance to have a child that was biologically ours. There was no reasoning with her. The doctors warned her that she had a particularly aggressive strain, but she wouldn't budge."

Becca had always led Katy and her parents to believe that Adam had been the one to make that decision, that he insisted they wait and harvest the eggs first, and they had believed her. Had it all been a lie, to shelter herself from her parents' disapproval?

Why did she portray him to be so unreasonable and demanding?

"You want to hear the really ironic part of all this?" Adam said. "I don't think she really even wanted kids."

It was true Becca had never been much of a kid person. Katy had been a little surprised when she mentioned they were trying to get pregnant. But when it didn't happen right away she'd been devastated. Because when Becca wanted something, she didn't like to wait. After that, it was as if she was obsessed. "For a year that's all she talked about," she told Adam.

"Because she knew it was what *I* wanted."

"Why wouldn't she want kids?"

"I think...I think she was afraid that if we had a child, I might love it more than her. She wanted to be the center of my universe, and I think she believed that the baby would replace her."

Was she really that insecure? She was smart and beautiful and talented with a husband who loved her. Why couldn't she just be happy? Why did she have to make everything so complicated?

"I loved Becca," Adam said, "but I don't think I ever completely understood her. But that wasn't her fault. I should have tried harder, made more of an effort. I'll regret that for the rest of my life."

It occurred to her suddenly that she and Adam were talking. Having an honest conversation. And she hadn't even been trying. It just...happened.

She and Adam were from totally different worlds. So why, at that very moment, did he feel like an equal? Not a billionaire oil man, but just a man.

Nine

Something was off.

Katy jolted awake and opened her eyes, expecting to be in her bed at home, but as her eyes adjusted she realized she was in the spare room at Adam's house.

For a second she was confused, then she remembered they'd had the embryos implanted that morning.

She must have fallen asleep during the movie they were watching. She would check the time on the digital clock on the dresser, but that would necessitate her rolling over, and she was too comfortable to move. She must have conked out a while ago because the television had gone into sleep mode. She wondered why Adam hadn't switched it off when he left.

She usually slept pretty light, so she was surprised she hadn't felt him get out of bed. He'd sat there beside her almost the entire time they had been back from Dr. Meyer's office. She hadn't even cared that he'd spent part of the time working on his laptop. She was content to just sit beside him reading the novel she'd brought with her. She even told him it was okay if he would be more comfortable working in his office. His reply was that they were in this together, and if she had to lie around all day, it was only fair he did the same. He was turning out to be a lot nicer than she ever expected. Still a bit dark and mysterious, but at least he'd opened up to her a little today.

She thought about her mother's warning, how Katy always fell hard and fast. Maybe she did have the slightest bit of a crush on Adam, but she knew better than to think it would amount to anything. She was finished with one-way relationships. And men like Adam didn't get serious about women like her. They had absolutely *nothing* in common.

Was she attracted to him? Of course. When they kissed had she practically burst into flames? She sure had, but all that meant was that they were attracted to each other.

And was she tempted by the thought of taking that attraction out for a quick spin? *Hell, yes!* But she knew that would only lead to getting her heart crushed, and who needed that? The trick was to keep herself out of temptation's way.

And what was the point of lying here in the dark obsessing about it when what she needed was a good night's sleep?

She closed her eyes, willing herself to relax. She was just starting to drift back off when she felt the bed move. If she were at home she would just assume Sylvester had jumped into bed with her. But as far as she knew Adam didn't have a cat.

Maybe it had been her imagination.

Curious, she reached back, patting the covers behind her, her hand landing on something warm and solid. She yanked it back and looked over her shoulder. The reason she hadn't felt Adam get out of bed was because he never had!

Oh, good Lord.

Was it a coincidence that she'd just been thinking about avoiding temptation, and here it was, lying right beside her? Maybe it was fate. Or a sign.

It was a sign, all right. A sign that she needed to wake him up and get him the hell out of here.

She rolled over. He was lying on his side facing her, one arm under his head. She reached out to shake him awake, then stopped just shy of touching his arm. He was so serious all the time. Even when he smiled there was an undercurrent of tension, as if he was always plotting, always planning his next move. Now he looked so…peaceful.

As if it possessed a will of its own, her hand moved to his face instead, but until she felt the rasp of his beard stubble against her fingers, she didn't think she would be bold enough to actually touch him. And now that she had, she couldn't seem to make herself stop.

There was a small white scar just below his lip where the skin was smooth and she couldn't resist tracing it with her finger. The mouth that sometimes appeared so hard and unrelenting looked soft and tender while he slept. She wanted to touch that, too. With her fingers. And her lips.

The idea of actually doing it, touching her lips to his again, made her scalp tingle.

This is a bad idea, she told herself, but knowing that didn't stop her. In fact, it made doing it even more exciting. Because honestly, when did she ever do anything that was bad for her? As long as she could remember, she'd been the good girl. The obedient daughter. Didn't she deserve to take something for herself? Just this once?

Heart pounding, she leaned close, touching her lips to his chin. He didn't wake up, didn't even stir, so she moved up a little, to the corner of his mouth, and pressed her lips there, quickly, then pulled back to check his face. His eyes were still closed. The man slept like the dead.

Trembling with anticipation, she closed her eyes and very gently pressed her lips to his...and almost moaned it felt so nice. And there it was again, that curious feeling, just like before. *Awareness.* Like a magnet pull, drawing her closer to him. She wanted to curl herself around his body, sink into his warmth. She would crawl inside his skin if she could.

She realized her lips were still pressed to his, and without meaning to, she'd gotten a little bit carried away. She opened her eyes, to make sure he was still asleep, but Adam's eyes were open, too, and he was looking right at her.

She sucked in a surprised breath, and backed away, sure that she must have looked like a deer in headlights.

She waited for him to berate her, to ask her what the hell she thought she was doing. Instead he blinked several times, eyes foggy from sleep and asked in gravelly voice, "Did you just kiss me?"

Okay, so maybe he wasn't as awake as he looked. Maybe she could lie and say it had been an accident. She had just leaned too close and accidentally bumped lips with him. He would buy that, right?

He was asleep, not stupid.

"Katy?" he said, waiting for an answer.

"Yes," she choked out, shame burning her cheeks. Not only for what she'd done, but for the fact that she wanted to do it again. "I'm sorry. I don't know what I was thinking."

She braced herself for the anger, but instead Adam touched her face...so tenderly that shivers of pleasure danced along her spine. Then he looked her right in the eye and said in a voice thick with desire, "Do it again."

He *wanted* her to kiss him?

Katy was too dumbfounded to move, but Adam apparently didn't want to wait, because he leaned in and kissed her first.

She discovered the instant their lips touched that it was

a heck of a lot more fun kissing him when he was actually participating. It was exciting and terrifying and confusing and…wonderful. And it was obvious, after several minutes of making out like sex-starved teenagers, when he rolled her over onto her back and tugged her pajama top up over her head, this was going way beyond kissing. She may have started this, but it was clear that Adam intended to finish it.

What are you doing? the rational part of her brain demanded, that part that wasn't drowning in estrogen and pheromones. *This is* Adam, *your* brother-in-law. *Your* sister's *husband. This is wrong.*

But it was hard to take her rational self seriously when Adam was kissing her senseless and sliding his hand inside her pajama bottoms. She moaned as his fingers found the place where she was already hot and wet.

Already? Who was she kidding? Since she started the hormone shots she'd been walking around in a near-constant state of sexual arousal. It wasn't unusual for her to feel heightened sexual awareness when she was ovulating, but this was horny times fifty.

Maybe this had been inevitable. And maybe it made her a lousy sister, or just a terrible person in general, but she didn't care. She wanted him. She had never done a truly selfish thing in her life, but she was going to do this.

And she would *not* fall in love with him.

She fumbled with the buttons on Adam's shirt, her fingers clumsy and uncooperative, until she got fed up and just ripped the damned thing open. If he cared that she'd just ruined his shirt he didn't say so. Of course, he was a little preoccupied driving her crazy with his fingers and his mouth.

She shoved the shirt off his shoulders and down his arms, her eyes raking over his chest. Swirls of black hair circled small dark nipples then narrowed into a trail down the center of his lean stomach, disappearing under the waistband of his slacks.

Breathless with excitement, she put her hands on him. His skin was hot and she could feel the heavy thump of his heart. She wanted to touch him everywhere.

She half expected him to be as controlled and closed off as he always was. Hadn't Becca confided to her that sex with Adam was "nice," but sometimes she wished he would be a little more passionate, more adventurous? But Adam must have changed, because if he were any more passionate than he was now, they would set the sheets on fire. He was reckless and impulsive and…crazy.

They kissed and touched, tore at each other's clothes. There was barely a second when his mouth wasn't somewhere on her body. Her lips, her breasts, the column of her throat. He licked and nibbled as if he wanted to eat her alive. Until the sensations all started to run together, and her entire being quivered with the need for release.

And when she didn't think she could stand much more, when she felt she would go out of her mind if he didn't *take* her, he said, "I have to make love to you."

Not he *wanted* to, but he *had* to. As in, he wanted it so badly, he couldn't stop himself. And she felt exactly the same way.

As he centered himself between her thighs, his strong arms caging her, she considered fleetingly that maybe they shouldn't be doing this, but as he thrust inside her, her brain could do nothing but feel. Feel his hands and his mouth. Feel the slow, steady rhythm of his body moving inside of hers, connecting in a way she had never imagined. It felt as if she had been working up to this moment her entire life. Every man who had come before him…they hadn't come close to making her feel what she did now. Excited and humbled and terrified all at once. And as she cried out with release, felt

Adam shudder and then go still inside of her, she was terrified that no one ever would again.

Because as earth-shatteringly wonderful as this had been, this was Adam, her brother-in-law. He was a billionaire oil man and she was a rancher. He wore thousand-dollar suits to work and she spent her days wading through cow manure.

They were worse than oil and water. They were gasoline and a lit match. And she could tell, by the way he rolled over and lay silently beside her, the only sound his breath coming in sharp rasps, he was probably thinking the same thing. He was probably afraid that she had just fallen head over heels in love with him, and was wondering how he was going to let her down easy.

Well, he didn't have to worry about her. She was firmly rooted in reality.

She took a deep breath, blew it out and said, "Despite what you're probably thinking right now, this was not a big deal."

Not a big deal?

Adam lay beside Katy, trying to catch his breath, after what was by far the best sex of his entire adult life.

Despite the fact that it was over *way* too fast. But it had been almost four years since he'd been with a woman, so the fact that he'd lasted more than thirty seconds was, in his opinion, a small miracle.

Then he had a thought, one that just about stopped his pulse. "Were we supposed to do that?"

"Well, given the nature of our relationship—"

"No, I mean, was that on the list?"

"List?"

"The things you're not supposed to do after the embryo transfer."

He heard her inhale sharply, then she jolted up in bed. "I don't know."

"I don't recall the doctor mentioning anything about sex, but I could swear there was something on the list." He might have thought of it sooner, but when he woke to discover her kissing him, his brain must have shorted out.

"Do you still have the list?" she asked. "I think I left it here the last time."

"I think Celia put it on my desk."

She swung her legs over the side of the bed and he grabbed her arm. "You're on bed rest. I'll go."

She looked at him like he was an idiot, since she was probably thinking that the damage had already been done. But technically she was still on bed rest, and since she hadn't actually gotten out of bed, maybe they were okay. He switched on the lamp, blinking against the sudden bright light. He found his pants on the floor beside the bed and yanked them on. Then he turned and saw Katy sitting there naked, fishing her panties from between the covers, her skin rosy, her breasts covered with love bites, and almost took them back off again.

He actually paused for a second and reached for his fly, then thought, *What the hell are you doing?* They shouldn't have slept together the first time, but once could at least be written off as sexual curiosity. Or temporary insanity. The second time, though, showed intent. It implied a relationship, and he sure as hell didn't want that.

He didn't care how fantastic the sex was. There was no way it was going to happen again.

He left Katy wrestling with her undergarments and headed down to his office. He found the list buried under a month's worth of miscellaneous papers. He switched out the lights and took the stairs two at a time up to the bedroom.

Katy was sitting in bed, wearing her pajama top and panties, looking anxious.

"Got it," he said, sitting beside her.

"What does it say?" she asked, leaning close to read it with him.

He saw it right away, at the bottom. He pointed to the line. "No intercourse or orgasms."

She closed her eyes and cursed. "So what does this mean?"

"That it might not work, I guess."

"And if it did work, could what we did have hurt the baby?"

"I don't know. I wouldn't think so. We'll just have to wait and ask, I guess. I wonder, though, maybe intercourse alone isn't that bad, maybe if you didn't..." He looked at her hopefully.

She looked confused, then she realized what he was implying. "Of course I did! You couldn't *tell?*"

He shrugged. She wouldn't be the first woman to... embellish. "I thought it couldn't hurt to ask."

"I'm so sorry," she said miserably, drawing her knees up to her chest and hugging them. "This is all my fault."

"No, it isn't."

"I started this. If I hadn't kissed you..."

Why did you? he wanted to ask her, but he had the feeling he'd rather not know. Besides, it didn't even matter. It happened. The damage was done. "I could have stopped you, but I didn't."

She buried her face in her hands. "How could I let this happen?"

"It's been an emotional couple of weeks for both of us. We made a mistake."

"We definitely can't do this again," she said.

"I agree."

"I mean, it was great, but…well…you know."

He was a little curious to know what she meant. What he was supposed to know. If for no other reason than to see if they had the same reasons, but at this point it didn't seem to matter.

They sat there in awkward silence for a minute or two. What was left to say at this point? "I should leave you alone, so you can get some rest."

She fidgeted with the edge of the blanket. "I do have a long drive tomorrow."

He got up and grabbed his shredded shirt from where it had landed on the floor. "Try not to worry. If it doesn't work, we'll try again."

"And we're never doing *this* again," she said, gesturing to the bed, as if he wasn't already clear on that point.

"Like you said, it's not a big deal. It doesn't change anything. It happened, and it won't happen again."

He couldn't tell if she looked relieved or disappointed, and the truth was, he really didn't want to know.

Ten

The next ten days were the longest in Katy's life. She tried to keep herself busy with work, but even putting together the ranch's quarterly taxes wasn't enough to distract her from the guilt that she might have completely blown their chances to conceive. And she didn't care what Adam said. It was her fault. He never would have made the first move.

Though she tried to put on a good face for her parents, they could tell she was upset. She told them she was just worried that it wouldn't work, but she didn't tell them why. How could she?

By the way, Mom and Dad, did I mention that I seduced and slept with my dead sister's husband? They would never forgive her. And she couldn't blame them. She wasn't even sure if she could forgive herself.

She did try to talk to her mom about Adam, and how he wasn't the man they thought he was, and her mom got that, "Oh, no, here we go again, Katy has a crush" look, so she didn't even bother. Maybe because she was too ashamed to admit that her mom had been right. Although it was obvious by how readily Adam agreed it was a mistake, that he hadn't spontaneously fallen madly in love with her.

She wished she could say the same. But that was her own fault. Still, he was all she could think about lately. She probably wouldn't have minded him inundating her with calls and emails this time, but he seemed to know instinctively that it was better to back off. He'd text messaged her a couple of times, to see how she was feeling.

She kept waiting for some sort of sign, to start *feeling* pregnant.

"I knew right away," her best friend Missy told her as she fixed a bottle for the three-month-old strapped to her chest, while balancing a toddler on one hip and dodging the groping hands of the three- and five-year-olds. "My mood changed and my hair started falling out. Not like I was going bald," she added at Katy's look of horror. "But it got thinner during all my pregnancies."

"I don't feel anything," Katy told her.

"Oh, sweetie," she had said clucking sympathetically. "I'm sure it will work. And if it doesn't, you'll just try again. The doctors can only do so much. You have to trust your body to do the rest."

But she had betrayed her body. She didn't give it a chance to do the rest. And talking to Missy only made her feel worse because she was even more convinced that she wasn't pregnant. Because she didn't feel *any* different than before. Other than the crushing guilt that she had set Adam's baby plan back at least a month, not to mention that he only had two more viable embryos. Then the only thing left of her sister would be gone forever.

How would she live with herself if she had ruined this for him?

This had been so much easier when she didn't like him. When she thought he was a cold, arrogant jerk.

The morning of their next appointment, Katy drove to El Paso feeling like she had a boulder in her chest, convinced the transfer didn't take. If it had, she would have felt something by now. Some subtle sign that her body was changing. But there was nothing. Not a twinge or a flutter, no weird food cravings or morning sickness. She was so sure her period would start she almost hadn't bothered to come, but it would be her only chance to see Adam for at least another few weeks, when they did the final transfer.

And if that didn't work? Well, there was a good chance she might never see him again. And who knows, maybe it would be for the best.

She had herself so worked into a lather that when she stepped through the doors to the lobby of the medical building and saw Adam standing by the elevators waiting for her, she immediately burst into tears. Mortified beyond belief, she turned right back around and walked out.

She heard the door open behind her, and hurried footsteps in her direction, then she felt his hand on her shoulder. "Katy, what's wrong?"

She shook her head, unable to speak.

His arms went around her, pulling her against his chest. And even though she knew she was only torturing herself, she sank into him. Clung to him. Why did she do this to herself? Why did she fall for men who didn't want her?

He stroked her hair, her back. "Talk to me, Katy. What's wrong?"

Only *everything*.

"I'm not pregnant," she said miserably, burying her face against his chest.

"You started your period?"

"No, but...I just know. It didn't work."

"You don't know that," he said patiently.

"I do, and it's all my fault."

"Listen to me. You have to stop blaming yourself. And what's the point in getting so upset if you don't even know for sure?"

"I told you, I just know. I don't *feel* pregnant."

"That doesn't mean you aren't." He took her by the shoulders and held her at arm's length. "Calm down, and let's go inside and get the test. Then we'll know definitively if you are or aren't."

"And if I'm not?"

"Let's worry about that when the time comes, okay?"

She nodded and wiped her cheeks.

With a hand on her back, as if he thought she might try to make a run for it, Adam led her back through the door and up to the clinic.

They had to sit in the general waiting room this time, with half a dozen other couples, several of whom were clearly expecting. Happy couples who loved each other. Which of course only made her feel worse.

When the nurse finally called them back Katy was on the verge of tears again. Adam must have realized because he took her hand and gave it a reassuring squeeze. The nurse drew blood, slapped a bandage on, and said, "I'll send this right to the lab and we'll call later this afternoon with the results."

"How much later?" Adam asked.

"Usually between three and four. Sometimes earlier. It just depends how busy they are."

"That's it?" Katy asked. "We don't see the doctor?"

"Not until after you get your results."

They stopped at the front desk on their way out, and Adam was able to get them an appointment for seven that evening, so she wouldn't have to make the long drive out again.

"I'm not letting you drive home that late," Adam said when they met back at his house and she mentioned leaving straight from Dr. Meyer's office. He opened the front door, disengaged the alarm, and gestured her inside. "You can stay with me."

"I'm not sure if that's a good idea."

"You don't trust me?"

She didn't trust herself. Especially not when he'd been so touchy-feely with her. Hugging her and holding her hand. It was torture. What would he do if she made the first move again? Would he give in and make love to her? Or would he push her away this time?

She wouldn't be finding out, because the possibility that he would reject her would be more than she could bear.

She followed him into the kitchen. "It's not that I don't trust you," she said. "It'll just be…awkward."

He stopped and turned to her. "Katy, if we're going to make this surrogacy thing work, we have to get past what happened. If you can't do that—"

"Of course I can." It was obviously just a little harder for her than it was for him. "You're right. I'll stay here."

He pulled two bottles of water out of the fridge and handed her one. "So, what would you like to do until the doctor's office calls?"

"Don't you have to go back to work?"

He leaned against the edge of the counter. "Nope. I'm yours all day."

Oh, didn't she wish.

"We could go for a swim," he said.

"I didn't bring a suit." Or pajamas, or clothes for the next day, she realized.

He shrugged. "Who needs bathing suits? It's not like I haven't seen it before. Right?"

Her heart slammed the wall of her chest. She was too

stunned to reply. Hope welled up inside of her, then fizzled out when she saw the corner of his mouth tip up and realized that he was kidding.

"That was a joke," she said.

"Yeah. It was a joke."

Not only did he have a sense of humor, but it was warped. And he obviously had no idea what he'd just done to her. Why would he? She was the one who'd said it meant nothing. Right? He had no idea how conflicted she felt. And she intended to keep it that way.

"Celia has a whole cabinet full of bathing suits in the cabana. There's bound to be one that will fit you."

Since they didn't have anything better to do, and they could take their cell phones with them by the pool, why not? But of course she found out *why not* when she walked out of the cabana, in the modest one-piece she'd found in her size, to find Adam standing by the pool, bare-chested, his bronze skin glistening in the sun, making him look like a Greek Adonis. He looked *really* good for forty. In fact, he could totally put to shame most of the twenty-something guys she knew. His body was truly a work of art. And she was stuck looking at it for God only knows how long.

Hey, it could be worse, she thought. He could be wearing a Speedo.

Since she didn't want to be away from her phone, she only waded around for a few minutes, then she laid back in one of the lounge chairs, sipping iced tea and watching Adam do laps. She recalled Becca telling her once that he'd been on the swim team in college. He'd been so good that later he had a shot at making the Olympic team, but had to drop out when his father died so he could take over Western Oil. She would have to ask him about that some time.

Or not. Probably the less she got to know him, the better. Why make it harder on herself?

Around one Celia brought out a tray of cheese enchiladas and homemade tamales, and though Katy was hungry, and the food was delicious, she was too nervous to eat much. She kept looking at the cell phones sitting side by side on the table, willing them to ring. And at the same time she was dreading it.

An hour later Celia left to do some shopping, and at three Katy and Adam had had enough sun and decided to go in. She was in the kitchen refilling her iced tea, and he was about to go take a quick shower, when his cell phone started to rumble on the counter. Then it started to ring.

For a second they both just stood there looking at it, as though it were some deadly venomous insect neither wanted to touch. Then Adam sighed, grabbed it off the counter and answered.

"Yes, this is he," he said to the caller, and though she could hear someone talking, she couldn't hear what they were saying. She stood there with her heart in her throat, waiting. He said, "uh-huh" twice and "we'll be there," then he hung up.

She was gripping the edge of the counter, hands trembling, and her heart was thumping out about a thousand beats per minute. "Well, what did they say?"

Adam shook his head, looking shell-shocked, and her heart plummeted. She was right. It hadn't work. They blew it. Then he said, "Positive."

It took a second to process, then she repeated, to be sure she hadn't heard him wrong, *"Positive?"*

He nodded.

"This isn't a joke? It's really positive? It worked?"

A grin spread across his face. "It worked. You're pregnant."

All the stress and grief, and every other emotion that had been building for the last ten days welled up like a geyser and erupted in a whoop of joy that her parents probably heard all the way in Peckins.

In one minute she was across the room, and the next she was in Adam's arms and he was hugging her tight.

"I guess you're happy," he said, and though she couldn't see it, because she was plastered against him, she could hear the smile in his voice.

More than just being happy that she was pregnant, that at least one of the embryos had attached, she was relieved that she hadn't screwed things up for him. She could stop feeling guilty. She could stop thinking back to that night and berating herself for kissing him in the first place, and for not stopping him when he kissed her back, and started undressing her.

Touching her.

Sort of like right now, she realized, as she became aware that her breasts were crushed against his bare chest, that his hands were on her bare back. He smelled like chlorine and sunblock, and his skin felt hot to the touch. And it took exactly two seconds to realize that hugging him had been a terrible mistake.

But why wasn't he letting go? And why were his hands sliding farther south, dangerously close to her behind.

"Um, Adam?"

"Yeah?"

"Maybe you should, you know…let go of me."

"I probably should," he said, nuzzling the side of her throat.

Oh, good Lord.

"Okay…*now,*" she said, but he didn't let go. But to be fair, neither did she. Then she felt his lips on her neck and her legs nearly gave out.

"Katy?"

"Huh?"

"I think I have to kiss you again."

There it was again, that "have to" line.

"I really wish you wouldn't," she said, but his hands were already sliding up her back, tangling through her hair.

Oh, hell, here we go again, she thought as he eased her head back and crushed his lips down on hers. It was so hot she was sure she would melt into a puddle on the kitchen floor.

Did the man have to be such a good kisser.

"Hey Adam, are you two—oops!"

They both jumped a mile and swiftly untangled themselves from each other. Celia stood in the kitchen doorway, her arms filled with reusable canvas grocery bags.

"I'm sorry," she said, looking embarrassed. "I didn't mean to…interrupt."

Everyone seemed at a loss for words, so Katy said what she could to fill the awkward silence.

"We just heard from the doctor's office." As if that brought logic to their passionate embrace. "I'm pregnant!"

Eleven

According to the ultrasound Dr. Meyer performed at their appointment later that evening, she was pregnant with a single embryo.

After a brief examination, he showed them to his private office and explained just about everything she and Adam needed to know about her pregnancy—she was honestly, truly *pregnant!* What changes to expect in her body, and the things she should and shouldn't eat. The kind of activity that was safe and what medications weren't. And her due date, which they learned was early the following spring.

But now the appointment was almost over and neither had mentioned the one thing they both needed to know. It was the huge pink elephant in the room. And since Adam didn't seem inclined to ask, it was up to her to put it out there.

"If you have any other questions for me—" the doctor started to say, and Katy said, "I have one."

She looked over at Adam and he had a slightly pained look

on his face. "Suppose, *hypothetically,* that a surrogate were to have sex right after the transfer. Could that hurt the baby in any way?"

The doctor looked up sharply from the notes he'd been jotting in her file. "You didn't, did you?"

His reaction startled her.

It couldn't be that bad, could it? "Even if we did, the embryo latched on," she rationalized. "So no harm done. Right?"

"Successful implantation is only part of the reason. For surrogates like yourself, who have no known fertility issues, there's also the problem of conception."

"But didn't we want her to conceive?" Adam asked, before she had the chance.

"In all likelihood, because the embryos were implanted at the most fertile stage in her cycle, her body also released its own healthy and viable egg. And I'm sure I don't have to explain to either of you what happens if you introduce sperm with an egg."

Katy's stomach bottomed out, and Adam went pale.

The doctor looked from Adam to Katy. "Gauging by your reactions, should I assume this might be the case?"

"So what you're saying," Adam clarified, as if it wasn't crystal clear already, "is that it could be Katy's own fertilized egg, and not one of the embryos."

"It could be."

Katy felt sick to her stomach. This could not possibly be happening.

Under the circumstances, Adam sounded unusually calm and detached when he asked, "Is there any way to tell?"

"Only though a DNA test. Either after the birth, or through amniocentesis."

"How soon could the amnio be done?" Adam asked.

"At the earliest, fourteen weeks, but I do have to warn you that there are risks involved."

"What kind of risks?"

"Infection, miscarriage."

Katy stared at him, slack-jawed, feeling as though she had just taken the leading role in the world's most horrific waking nightmare.

"So what kind of odds are we looking at?" Adam asked. How could he be so *calm?* Panic was clawing at her insides. It was all she could do not to get up and pace the room like a caged animal.

"Of course, I can't be certain, but I would put the odds at somewhere in the ball park of five to one."

She felt a slight tug of relief. As far as odds went, that wasn't *too* bad.

"Five to one that it was one of the embryos?" Adam clarified.

"No. That it was Katy's own egg."

Oh, crap.

Katy felt light-headed, like she might faint. What the *hell* had they done? Having her sister's baby was one thing, but to have her own baby, and with Adam of all people? This was crazy!

She wasn't ready to have a child yet, especially not with her sister's husband! A man she loved, whose only interest in her was to produce his offspring.

She had a sudden and disturbing vision of her family up on the stage during a *Jerry Springer* episode.

Her family. Oh, God. How was she going to explain this to her parents? They had been so excited when she called to tell them the good news earlier. They would be furious enough if they knew she had slept with Adam, but to learn she could be having her own baby, not Becca's? They might never speak to her again.

Adam put his hand on her arm. She looked up at him and he gestured to the door. She realized, the appointment was over. There was nothing else the doctor could do for them at this point. From now on it would just be a waiting game. At least twelve more weeks.

It sounded like a lifetime.

Her legs felt unsteady as Adam led her out. She only half heard him as he stopped to make next month's appointment, then he ushered her out of the office and to the elevator. He was taking this awfully well.

"I can't believe this is happening," she said, as the elevator doors slid closed. "This is all my—"

"If you say it's your fault one more time, I swear to God I'm going to make you *walk* home," he said sharply, his eyes flashing with anger.

Whoa.

So much for him taking it well. Apparently he was as freaked out as she was. He was just better at hiding it.

He took a deep breath and blew it out. "I'm sorry. I didn't mean to snap. I just think that blaming each other, or ourselves, isn't going to get us anywhere. It's happened, and now we have to figure out the best way to deal with the situation."

She nodded.

Reece was waiting for them when they walked out of the building. After they got in the limo, Adam asked, "Would you like to stop someplace and get dinner?"

The thought of food made her stomach roil. "I'm really not hungry right now."

"You've hardly eaten a thing all day. It's not healthy to skip meals."

Nor would it be healthy to eat a meal, then barf it back up, which is what would probably happen. "I'll have something later. I promise."

They were silent for the rest of the drive back to his place. She figured they would talk later that evening, after they'd each had a chance to process it, but as they walked inside she was hit with a wave of fatigue so intense she knew she needed to rest first. She was so exhausted she tripped on the foyer step and would have fallen on her face if Adam hadn't caught her by the arm.

"You okay," he asked, brow creased with worry.

"Just really tired. I think I need to lie down."

"You know we need to talk."

"I know. And I'm not trying to avoid it. Maybe if I sleep for an hour or so, I'll feel better."

"Of course," he said, leading her upstairs to the spare room.

"Would you possibly have an old shirt or something that I can sleep in? I didn't know I would be staying over so I didn't bring extra clothes." She felt uncomfortable enough sleeping here, where this nightmare of a situation had been conceived, she couldn't imagine doing it in her underwear.

"I'm sure I can dig up something." He left for several minutes, then reappeared with a long-sleeved, button-down silk pajama top. "Will this work?"

"That's perfect. Thanks."

"I'll be in my office if you need me." He hesitated by the door, like he wanted to say something else, then he left, closing the door behind him. A second later she heard the muffled sound of him walking down the stairs.

It took all the effort she could muster to change into the pajama top, and though it was way too big for her, it was cool and soft against her skin. And even though it was freshly laundered, it smelled like Adam. That might have excited her if she hadn't been so dead on her feet. It was as if it was all just too much to take in and her body was shutting down.

She crawled into bed, under the covers, and must have been out before her head even hit the pillow.

She woke later, feeling drugged and disoriented, not sure where she was, or if it was day or night. She recalled the doctor visit and for a second thought maybe it had all been a terrible dream.

But she was at Adam's house, and it hadn't been a dream. It was very, very real. She looked over at the digital clock, blinking to clear the sleep from her eyes. It read 1:15 a.m.

One-fifteen? She shot up in bed and swung her legs over the side, instantly awake. She and Adam were supposed to talk. He was waiting for her!

Then she realized, he had probably gone to bed already, and their conversation, critical as it would be, would have to wait until morning. She was disappointed, but at the same time relieved. She needed time to think this through, to wrap her head around it, and knowing Adam, he would want to make a decision right away. He would want to begin planning their next move.

She got up and used the bathroom, then brushed her teeth with a spare brush she found in the cabinet. Since she would have to wear the same clothes tomorrow for the drive home, and there was nothing she hated more than not feeling fresh, she washed her panties in the sink and hung them on the towel bar to dry.

She was about to climb back into bed when her stomach let out a hollow rumble, and she realized that she was famished. She recalled how delicious the enchiladas were that they'd had for lunch and wondered if there were any leftovers. She should really eat something. Because as Adam had pointed out, she shouldn't be skipping meals. Cliché and silly as it sounded, she was eating for two now.

She opened the door and peeked out into the hallway. The house was quiet and dark, just as she'd suspected. She felt her way down the stairs and tiptoed through the living room to the kitchen.

"Going somewhere?"

At the unexpected voice she let out a squeal of surprise, and whipped around. Adam was sitting slumped down on the couch, holding something…a drink, she realized. He was sitting in the dark drinking. Not that she could blame him. If alcohol wasn't bad for the baby, she would be drowning in it by now.

"I woke up hungry," she said. "I was going to get something to eat."

As her eyes adjusted, she could see that he was shirtless, and wearing what looked like a pair of pajama bottoms.

Oh, my.

"I though you'd gone to bed," she said.

"Couldn't sleep."

Well, that was understandable. She wondered if he was upset, or even angry with her. It was too dark to see his individual features so she really couldn't get a read on him.

"I'm sorry I slept for so long."

"S'okay."

"I wasn't trying to avoid you."

"I know."

She took a step closer. "Are you okay?"

"What do you think?"

Fair enough. "Do you want to talk?"

"Actually, I think I'd prefer you take off your clothes."

She actually jerked backward. Was that another joke? "E-excuse me?"

"I want to see you naked."

"N-naked?"

"You said before that if I wanted to see you naked, all I have to do is ask. So I'm asking."

She may have said it, but she didn't actually *mean* it. And never in a million years did she believe he would actually ask. It had to be the alcohol talking. "You're drunk."

"So what if I am?"

"So, you're clearly not thinking straight."

"Isn't that the point of drinking?" He downed the contents of his glass and set it on the table beside him. "Besides, it's not like I haven't seen you naked before."

"Yes, but don't you think it will inevitably lead to something else?"

"Again, that's kind of the point."

Her heart started to hammer. "But we said we wouldn't."

"We said a lot of things, and look where it got us. So get naked, now."

He was only doing this because he was upset and intoxicated. He didn't really want her. Not the way she wanted him. "No. I'm upset, too, but this isn't going to solve anything."

"No, but it'll feel good, and that's enough for me right now. Don't you want to feel good?"

Maybe feeling good wasn't enough for her.

But what if it was? Maybe she could have him just one more time.

No. Bad idea.

"Adam, I'm serious. Stop. We can't do this. I don't want to do this."

"Making love to you again is all I've been able to think about," he said, and his words warmed her from the inside out. Even though she knew he was only saying them because he'd been drinking and his inhibitions were compromised. And even if he had been thinking about it, it was just sex to him. It had nothing to do with love. That's the way it was for men.

The men she knew anyway.

"We shouldn't," she said, but with a dismal lack of conviction. He was starting to wear her down.

"Come here, Katy," he said, in a low growl that set every one of her nerve endings ablaze.

He reached out to grasp her wrist. She put up only the slightest bit of resistance before she let him pull her down into his lap. She was straddling his thighs, his silk pajama pants feeling unbelievably erotic on her bare bottom. Then he kissed her, tangling his fingers through her hair. Tenderly, his lips soft, his mouth sweet and tangy as his tongue slid against hers.

Wait a minute...*sweet?*

She broke the kiss and pulled back to look at him. Where was the alcohol taste? She grabbed the glass he'd been drinking out of and sniffed it. "What was this?"

"Orange juice."

"With vodka?"

"Nope. Just plain old orange juice."

"But...you said you were drunk."

"No, *you* said I was drunk. I just didn't correct you."

"But I thought—"

He didn't let her finish. He covered her lips with his and kissed away whatever she'd been about to say. He stroked and caressed away her doubts, until there was nothing left but raw need. When he pulled the pajama top up over her head and saw that she wasn't wearing panties, he growled low in his throat. "I think you forgot something."

"I didn't have a clean pair for tomorrow, so I washed them out in the sink."

"Lucky me," he murmured as he dipped his head to take her nipple in his mouth. Her entire being shuddered with ecstasy.

Adam lifted her off his lap and laid her down on the cushions, settling beside her, then he was kissing her again. Her lips and her throat, her breasts. He tortured her with nips and love bites, until she was burning up with need. He worked his way downward, across her stomach, then lower still.

She was no stranger to oral sex, although she wasn't usually the one on the receiving end. And on the rare occasion she'd been in the hot seat, the truth is it hadn't really been that fantastic. More clumsy and awkward than arousing. But as Adam slipped down onto the floor beside her, spreading her thighs to make room for himself, as his tongue lashed out to taste her, she was so close to unraveling she couldn't see straight.

Then a light switched on in the kitchen, dimly illuminating the room. She and Adam froze as they heard Celia shuffle out of her room. The couch was facing away from the light, so the only way she would know they were there was if she walked into the living room, which wasn't entirely impossible.

She heard Celia get a glass out of the cupboard, and fill it with water. She was frantically trying to recall where Adam had thrown the pajama top when she felt his tongue on her again. She was so surprised she gasped, slapping a hand over her mouth to smother the sound. What the heck was he doing? Did he *want* to get caught?

Getting caught kissing was one thing, but this? This would be absolutely mortifying.

She tried to push his head away, to close her legs, but that only seemed to fuel his determination. He pressed her thighs open even wider, devouring her. Could this possibly be the man her sister claimed wasn't *adventurous* enough? And maybe it was the element of danger, or the sheer stupidity of what they were doing, but the more she tried to fight it, the more turned on she was getting. Then Adam entered her with his fingers, thrusting them deep inside of her, and her control shattered. She buried her face in the cushion to muffle the moan of pleasure she couldn't suppress.

She'd barely had a chance to catch her breath when the light suddenly went out, and Celia shuffled back to her room behind the kitchen.

The second Katy heard the door close she gave Adam a good hard whack on the top of his head.

"Ow! What was that for?" he said, ducking away from a possible repeat attack.

"Are you crazy?" she hissed, sitting up. "She could have walked in here and seen us."

He was grinning. "But she didn't. And you can't deny that the idea of being caught was arousing as hell."

No, she couldn't deny it. But it wasn't a chance she was willing to take again. "Maybe we should move this party upstairs."

"That's probably not a bad idea."

No, it was. This whole thing was a horrible, horrible mistake. But it was too late now. He'd pleased her, and it was only fair to reciprocate. Right?

And if they were going to do this, they might as well have fun. And worry about the consequences in the morning.

She located the pajama top on the floor and pulled it on, just in case, then turned to Adam, grinning wickedly, and said, "Last one there is a rotten egg."

Twelve

Katy darted up the stairs, and Adam took off after her, catching up just outside the bedroom where she'd been sleeping. He hooked his arms around her waist, trapping her against him, and tugged in the direction of his bedroom. She pulled away from him, looking hesitant.

Confused, he asked, "What's the matter?"

"Where are we going?"

"My bedroom."

"Not there."

Because it wasn't just his bedroom, he realized. It was Becca's.

He didn't try to explain that while it was Becca's room, too, the bed itself had to be replaced due to her illness. And that even before that, he and Becca hadn't exactly shared a lot of passionate nights there.

But he didn't want to make Katy uncomfortable, so

when she took his hand and led him into the spare room, he let her.

She pulled the pajama top off and walked backward toward the bed, summoning him with a crooked finger. And when he got there he shoved him backward onto the mattress. The sheets were cool against his skin and smelled like her. He tried to pull her down beside him, but she straddled his legs instead. Her skin was flush with arousal, her nipples puckered tight. Her hair hung down in mussed curls that grazed the tops of her breasts. He'd never seen anything so sexy in his life.

She ran her hands down his chest, raking his skin with her nails. "I want to see you naked."

"All you had to do was ask," he said with a grin, and she tugged his pajama bottoms down and off his legs. Then she just stared at his erection in awe, as though she'd never seen one before.

She must have noticed his curious expression, because she said, "I didn't get a good look the other night." She reached out and wrapped her hand around him, slowly stroking from base to tip, then back down again. "I've never seen one this big. Not that I've seen a lot of them. Only three, besides yours."

That surprised him. Not that he thought Katy was the kind to sleep around, but she had a way about her that was blatantly sexual. Like the way she was casually running her thumb over the head of his erection, making it really tough to concentrate on the conversation. "That's not many," he said.

"You know, I didn't lose my virginity until I was nineteen."

Another surprise. "Really?"

"I had done a lot of fooling around before then, but I

planned to wait until I was married to actually seal the deal."

She gave him a gentle squeeze and his breath caught. "So why didn't you?"

"Because it occurred to me around then that it could take a long time to find Mr. Right, and I figured if fooling around felt good, actual sex would feel even better."

"Did it?"

She shrugged. "Not at first. But then sometimes it did, depending on who I was with. But that never really mattered because I'm completely capable of taking care of my own needs if necessary."

He didn't know who these men were she was sleeping with, but it would be a cold day in hell when he let a woman he was with "take care of her own needs."

"Is it weird that I'm telling you this?" she asked.

"Oddly enough, no." Even though he was having an increasingly difficult time concentrating on what she was saying. His gaze was fixed on her hand, sliding slowly up and down his shaft.

"When did you lose your virginity?" she asked.

"I was sixteen."

"Seriously?"

"She was eighteen."

"Ah, an older woman. Did it last?"

"About fifteen seconds."

She laughed. "I meant the relationship."

"That *was* the relationship." And he wouldn't last much longer than that now if she kept stroking him that way. "We hooked up at a party. I never saw her again."

"I've never had a one-night stand. Unless you count ten days ago." Letting go of his erection, she ran her hands up his stomach, over his chest. "But I guess after tonight we'll have to relabel it. Is there such a thing as a two-night stand?"

He didn't see any reason to slap a label on it. It was what it was.

She gazed down at him, lids heavy, cheeks rosy. "I like talking to you. And I like that you're willing to open up to me. I know that's not easy for you."

Not only did she like it, he realized that talking like this was turning her on. Like verbal foreplay.

A woman who got off on conversation. Who would have imagined? But he needed more. Less talk and more action. He needed to get his hands on her body, to be inside of her. It was all he'd been able to think about since that first time ten days ago. Looking back on it now, he should have realized that this was inevitable. That once was never going to be enough. "Why don't you make love to me," he said.

Her honey-dipped smile said she thought that was a pretty good idea. "Like this? With me on top?"

"However you'd like." On top, on the bottom. Upside down or sideways, he didn't really care.

She rose up onto her knees, flush with anticipation and centered herself over him, then she sank down, taking him inside of her, inch by excruciating inch, until he was as far as he could go. She was hot and wet and tight.

She looked down at him, and smiled. "Hmm, that's nice."

She took the words right out of his mouth. She started to move, riding him slowly, as though she had all the time in the world. Her eyes drifted closed, head rolled back. She looked completely lost in the sensation, and he was so fascinated watching her, his own pleasure seemed almost insignificant. He was content to let her use him as long as she wanted, stroking everything he could reach. Her thighs, her stomach, her breasts. Every part of her soft and feminine.

She took one of his hands and guided it between her legs, where their bodies were joined. He rubbed her there, and she started whimpering, making soft breathy sounds. She began to tremble all over and he knew she was almost there. Then her body clamped down hard around him, clenching and releasing. Watching her come was the most erotic thing he'd ever seen, and just like that he lost it. It was sexual release like he'd never felt before, hot pulsations that robbed him of the ability to do anything but feel.

Katy crumpled into a heap on his chest, curling herself around him. He could feel her heart hammering just as hard as his own. As much as he hated to admit it, sex with Becca had never been like this. She had always been too uptight, too worried that she would disappoint him to just let loose and have fun. And when they were trying to get pregnant, sex became a job. Then she was diagnosed and that put an end to their sex life altogether.

Maybe he should have felt bad comparing the two, and guilty knowing that, as much as he loved Becca, Katy was everything he'd always hoped his wife would be in the bedroom. But he didn't. Everything else was so screwed up, this seemed to be the only thing that made any sense. Even though it made no sense at all.

Maybe this was wrong, and he would regret it someday. All he knew was that for the past three years since Becca died he'd barely been able to look at another woman. Not a day passed that he didn't ache from missing his wife. But when he was with Katy he could forget for a while. He finally felt…at peace.

It was too bad that it had to end.

Katy woke the next morning and reached for Adam, but he wasn't there. She sat up and looked at the clock, surprised that it was almost nine-thirty. She was usually up at the crack of dawn. Of course, it had almost been the crack of dawn when Adam finally let her go to sleep.

The man had an insatiable sexual appetite, not to mention the stamina of someone half his age. After the third time she even started to wonder if he'd swallowed a couple of Viagra. Until he mentioned that, before their first night together, it had been *four* years, and suddenly it made sense. She didn't even know men could go that long without sex. She had just assumed he'd been with women since Becca died. But he was sure making up for lost time.

Now it was that dreaded morning after, and as exciting and, for lack of a better word, *magical,* as it had been, they had to face reality. Not to mention the situation with the baby.

She rolled out of bed and took stock of the room. Blankets askew, sheet pulled off the mattress in one corner. Celia was going to walk in and know instantly that they'd had wild sex all night. Of course, they hadn't exactly been quiet, so it was possible she'd figured it out for herself already.

Just in case, Katy spent a few minutes straightening things up, then took a long, hot shower. She half hoped that Adam had gone to work, even though she knew delaying the conversation they needed to have wouldn't make it any easier. But he was sitting at the kitchen table drinking coffee and reading the *Wall Street Journal.* She'd expected him to be dressed for work, but he was wearing chinos and a polo shirt with the Western Oil logo on it. His hair was damp, so he must have gotten up not long before she did. It was the first time she had seen him wear anything but a suit or slacks and a dress shirt. In fact, she had begun to question whether he even owned any casual clothes. Apparently he did, and damned if he didn't look delicious in them.

When he heard her enter the room he looked up and said, "Good morning."

"Mornin'."

"There's coffee," he said.

"I can't. You know, the baby."

"I made decaf."

"Oh. Thanks."

"Sit down. I'll pour you a cup."

She took a seat across from his, while he got up and poured her coffee. She couldn't tell if she should be uncomfortable or not. She was having a tough time reading him.

He set a steaming cup of black coffee in front of her and asked, "Are you hungry? I could make eggs or something."

"I didn't know billionaire oil men cooked."

"They do if they're hungry and their housekeeper is running errands. Or if you don't trust my cooking, I could take you out."

"I think maybe we should just talk instead."

He sat across from her. "Okay, let's talk."

She sat there for a minute and realized, they had so many things to cover, she wasn't even sure where to begin. "Where should we start?"

"Why don't we start with us."

She grimaced. She had really hoped that was the one part they wouldn't have to talk about. And she knew that as much as she wanted there to be, there was no "us."

"I think we both know that this has the potential to get very complicated," he said.

It already was. "Look," she said. "Last night was great, but it never should have happened. Things are just so…jumbled up. We let our emotions get the best of us."

He looked relieved. "I'm glad you feel that way."

She knew he would be. She was letting him off easy. Giving him an out. Of course he would take it.

"But I want us to be friends," he said.

The "let's still be friends" speech. How many times had she heard that one? She gazed into the inky depths of her cup, so he wouldn't see how much this was hurting her.

And let's face it, even if he suddenly decided that he wanted a wife, that he wanted *her,* she would never cut it as the future Mrs. Adam Blair. He was way out of her league. Not to mention that he was here, and she was in Peckins. It was an impossible situation.

"Katy?"

"We could be having a baby together. That means we're more or less stuck with each other."

He arched one brow. "You make it sound pretty awful."

Because for her it would be. For a while anyway. But it was imperative he didn't know that. Because then he would feel guilty, and things would get uncomfortable. That was the last thing she wanted.

She forced a smile. "That's not what I meant. And of course we'll be friends."

"After talking to Dr. Meyer, I think we have to face the fact that it probably is ours."

"I know I said that I wasn't ready for a child of my own, but now that it's a possibility…I could never just hand it over to you."

He reached across the table and curled his hands over hers. She wished he would stop doing that. Stop touching her. He was only making it harder. "Katy, I would *never* expect you to do that. If it's our baby, we'll figure out a way to make it work."

Our baby. Hearing him say that gave her shivers.

She pulled her hands from his, before she did something stupid, like throw herself in his arms and *beg* him to love her. To at least try.

"What about the surrogacy agreement?" she asked.

"Null and void, I guess. We'll have to work out some kind of custody agreement and child support. But I don't want you to worry. Financially, everything will be taken care of."

Custody and child support? What a nightmare.

"I don't want to wait for the birth for the DNA test," she told him. "I want to do the amnio. As soon as possible."

"The doctor said there are risks. Is it really that critical to know so soon?"

Not for him, maybe. But it was for her. "I need to know what to feel."

He frowned. "I don't understand."

"Either way, this is your baby. You're the father. But what am I? The baby's mother or just the aunt? I can't bear spending nine months thinking I'm going to have my own child, only to find that I have no maternal rights."

"I guess I never thought of it like that. Of course we'll do the amnio."

And until then she would just have to try to stay partial, try not to get too attached. Just in case. Because having her heart broken again so soon would be more than even she could bear.

"I also think we shouldn't talk about this with anyone but the doctor," she told him. "Not until we get the results. I can't put my parents through that."

Although, ironically, they were in the same situation as Adam. Whether it was Becca's baby or Katy's, it was still their grandchild. Only Katy's dilemma was unique.

"Whatever you want," Adam said. "I know this isn't what either one of us signed on for, but we'll make this work, Katy. Everything will be okay."

Eventually, she hoped.

She looked up at the clock, saw how late it was getting and said, "I really need to get home."

"You don't have to run off."

Oh, no, she did. The longer she stayed here, the more her heart hurt. "I have to get back to the ranch, and you probably have to get to work."

"I have been taking a lot of time off lately."

She took a swallow of coffee then got up and dumped what was left in the sink.

Adam got up, too. "I'll walk you out."

It was another scorcher, and she found herself looking forward to the cooler weather of autumn. She opened the truck door and turned to say goodbye, and Adam was right behind her. Startled, she stumbled backward and hit the front seat with the small of her back. He stepped closer, caging her in, and suddenly she couldn't breathe, couldn't think straight. And he knew it.

"One last kiss?" he asked, but he was already leaning in, taking charge.

No, no, please don't do this, she begged silently, but then his lips were on hers, and Lord help her, she couldn't deny him. His arms went around her, crushing her against the solid wall of his body. His fingers tangled in her hair. And she melted.

"Come back inside with me," he whispered against her lips. "Just one more time, and I promise I'll never ask again."

She wanted to, more than he would ever know. But she couldn't. Her heart was already splitting in two. He thought they'd had really awesome, no-strings-attached sex. But the strings were there, invisible to the naked eye, and she had to back away, before she became hopelessly entangled.

Adam watched Katy drive away, feeling...conflicted. Which was not a familiar feeling. He didn't want her to leave, and at the same time, he knew it was for the best. He cared about Katy. And though she was trying to hide it, he could see that she had pretty strong feelings for him. The last thing he wanted to do was hurt her. Especially now.

"I hope you know what you're doing."

He spun around to find Celia standing in the front doorway watching him. "Your note said you were running errands."

"I was. Then I got home."

Great. "You could have said something."

"But then I wouldn't have been able to eavesdrop, would I?"

At least she wasn't shy about admitting it. "How long have you been here?"

She folded her arms across her chest. "Long enough."

Long enough to hear something that was putting that disapproving look on her face. The look that, since he was a small boy, always preceded a firm lecture.

He really wasn't in the mood.

"I assume you don't plan to marry her," she said.

"That would be a correct assumption. We don't even know for sure that the baby is hers."

"And if it is?"

He wouldn't marry her then, either.

She stared at him, tight-lipped.

"Don't do that," he said, walking past her into the house. "I'm not a kid any longer."

She slammed the door. "Then stop acting like one."

Wow, he hadn't seen her this angry in a long time. Not since the time he stole the headmaster's keys, took his Beamer for a spin, then crashed it into a tree. His father, whose attention he'd been trying to get, had been too busy to come get him, so he'd sent Celia. And boy was she pissed. Just like now.

And for what?

"I really don't see why you're so upset," he said.

"I'm upset because I like Katy, and you're breaking her heart."

"That's ridiculous." He walked to the kitchen and she followed him. This had nothing to do with Katy's heart. "She's understandably upset. It's a complicated situation."

"She's upset because she loves you, *estúpido*. And

you're too much of a chicken to admit what you know is the truth."

He took a sip of his coffee, but it was cold, so he dumped it in the sink. When he turned back to her, she was staring at him. He sighed. "Okay, I'll bite. What *is* the truth?"

"That she could very well be the best thing that has ever happened to you! She's your soul mate."

An unexpected surge of emotion had him turning toward the window. "I buried my soul mate three years ago."

She stepped up behind him, touched his shoulder. "You buried your wife," she said softly, "but not your soul mate."

That wasn't the way he saw it.

"How long are you going to keep her up on a pedestal, pretending everything was perfect? I cared for Becca, and I know you loved her in your own way, but you were never half as happy with her as you are with Katy. You have this light in your eyes when you talk about her, and you probably don't realize it, but you talk about her a lot. And when you're with her...it's just so obvious that you two are meant to be together."

Celia was obviously seeing things that weren't really there. It was no secret that she hadn't been crazy about the idea of him marrying Becca. She never thought they were a good match. But she had been good to Becca nonetheless. Even when Becca sometimes hadn't been so nice to her. Becca wanted to be his entire universe and she'd been jealous of his relationship with Celia.

And yes, they'd had difficult times, and marital troubles, and instead of facing them he'd buried himself in work instead. But that wasn't her fault. He hadn't given their marriage a chance to be better.

And if he had, if they'd had a perfect marriage and had been blissfully happy, losing her would have been even more unbearable.

"I won't bury another wife," he told Celia.

"You don't get to choose who you love. The question is whether or not you accept that love."

"I'm content with my life just the way it is, and when the baby is here, it will be perfect."

"You really believe that?"

"I *know* that." He looked at his watch. "Now, I need to get to work."

She frowned and shook her head, as if she was thoroughly disappointed in him. But the last thing he needed was her playing matchmaker.

Did he have feelings for Katy? Of course. Could he love her? Without a doubt, but that didn't mean he should allow it. He wouldn't make that mistake again.

Thirteen

Though he planned to hold off until their regular manager's meeting, Adam couldn't wait to announce his good news. And after speaking with the rest of the board of directors, it was agreed that the sooner he set things in motion, the better. Though it meant shuffling a few meetings around, he gathered everyone in his office later that afternoon.

"I have a bit of good news," he said, then added, "Personal news," gaining the rapt attention of everyone. "I'm going to be a father."

Emilio grinned, while Nathan and Jordan just looked stunned.

"I wasn't even aware you were seeing anyone. Much less seriously enough to father a child," Nathan said, obviously anticipating a public-relations nightmare on the horizon. "Tell me she isn't the daughter of anyone important. Or, God forbid, underage."

Adam laughed. Leave it to him to expect the worst. "There's no scandal here. It's mine and Rebecca's child."

Nathan blinked. "Oh."

Jordan looked confused. "How is that possible?"

Adam told them about the embryos, and Katy's offer to carry the baby. For now, that was all they needed to know.

A lot of backslapping and handshakes followed, but he wasn't finished yet.

"There's something else. Something I'll be announcing formally in a few months. But I wanted to tell you all first. After the baby is born, I'm stepping down as CEO of Western Oil."

Three mouths fell open in unison.

"Stepping down?" Nathan asked. "You live for this company."

"I'll still be on the board. I just won't be as involved in the day-to-day operations. I want to be there for my child."

"Had you considered hiring a nanny?" Nathan asked.

"I could do that," Adam said. "But I promised myself a long time ago that when I had children, I would be there for them. Not a ghost, like my father. Especially since I'm raising this child on my own."

"Which raises the question, will you look outside the company for a replacement, or promote from within?" Emilio asked, getting to the heart of the matter.

"I've already spoken to the board. It was agreed that we would promote from within."

The three men exchanged glances. That meant that for the next eight months they would be under a veritable microscope, their every decision and act used to judge them. Three friends—two of them family—in competition for the brass ring. It had the potential to get very ugly. How they all handled the stress would be a determining factor to the board's decision.

"So who would you choose?" Nathan asked, knowing that the board would most likely follow Adam's lead.

"I won't make a choice until the board votes," he told them. "Until then everyone has an equal shot at the position. In essence, my choice will depend on your performance for the next eight months."

"No pressure there," Jordan said wryly.

"This position *is* pressure," Adam told him. "And as you all know I have a lot vested in this company. We all do. If not for each one of you, it wouldn't be what it is today."

"I think we all know who will get it," Nathan said. "You and Emilio are good friends. He's obviously got the advantage."

"This is business," Adam said. "Friendship has nothing to do with it."

"Not to mention that I'm going to leave you guys in the dust," Jordan said smugly, with a smile that said he was as good as in. His brother glared, but was smart enough to keep his mouth shut.

"Any questions?" Adam asked, but everyone seemed pretty clear on the way things would be until the decision was made.

When the meeting was over, Emilio hung back. "I just wanted to say congratulations again. I know this is something you've wanted for a long time."

Adam gestured for him to close the door. He'd promised Katy he wouldn't tell anyone the truth, but Emilio was one of his closest friends. He knew he could trust him to keep their secret.

Emilio shut the door and sat back down.

"What I said about the baby being mine and Becca's, that might not be the case."

He frowned. "Whose is it, then?"

"Mine and Katy's."

"You slept with her?"

"The day the embryos were transferred the second time. The doctor says there's a five-to-one chance Katy's egg was fertilized."

Emilio shook his head and muttered something in Spanish. "Maybe this was inevitable."

Inevitable? "What do you mean?"

"A man doesn't talk about a woman constantly unless he's attracted to her."

Had he really talked about her so much that both Celia and Emilio took notice? Without even realizing it?

"What are you going to do now?" Emilio asked.

"The only thing we can do. Have a DNA test, and if it is Katy's, share custody."

"You won't marry her?"

Emilio had no business lecturing him on marriage. "I'm surprised you would even ask that. Especially when you're so against marriage."

Emilio shrugged. "I'm not the marrying type. You are."

He *was*. But not anymore. "You know damn well I'm never getting married again."

"I know you've said that."

"But you obviously don't believe it."

"I believe you have a responsibility to the child. And its mother."

"And if you were in my position? Would you ask her to marry you?"

"Of course."

Adam was stunned. "You don't believe in marriage."

"No, but in my culture it's a matter of pride for a man to take responsibility for his actions," he said, then added sheepishly, "And if I didn't, my mother would probably disown me."

"So you think I should marry her."

"What I think doesn't matter."

Then why all the unsolicited advice? What the hell was with everyone lately? First Celia, now Emilio?

"This is getting really complicated."

"You slept with your deceased wife's sister and you're having a baby. At what point did you think it *wouldn't* be complicated?"

He had a point.

"Look," Emilio said. "You've had a rough couple of years. I just think that you deserve to be happy." He looked at his watch and pushed himself up from his chair. "And speaking of being happy, I have a date with a lovely *older* woman."

"Older?"

"My mother," he said with a grin.

"You have my sympathies." Monthly trips to the opera was one part of his marriage Adam didn't miss. Becca insisted they keep box seats. He used the time to either check email on his phone, or take a nap.

Emilio chuckled. "Not all men hate opera."

No, but he was betting more than half were only there for their wives. Although he had come to suspect that Becca favored the social aspect of the experience over the actual performance. She was big on flaunting their wealth, and always obsessed with wearing clothes from whichever up-and-coming designer was in favor at the time. She routinely spent the entire day in the salon getting her hair and nails and makeup fixed. He could never figure out why she couldn't be content to just be herself. Like Katy.

He did not just think that. Maybe he *was* too preoccupied with her.

Emilio was at the door when Adam asked, "Before you go, can I ask you a question?"

"Of course."

"Before Becca got sick, did I seem happy?"

Emilio frowned. "I'm not sure what you mean."

"Did you think we had a good marriage?"

He considered that, as though choosing his words carefully. "I recall thinking that if you were happy, you would have spent less time at work, and more with your wife."

"You work as much as I do."

"But I don't have a wife at home."

Another good point.

"Out of curiosity, why do you ask?"

"Celia said something this morning…" He shrugged. "You know what, never mind. Have fun tonight."

Emilio looked like he wanted to say more, but he knew Adam well enough not to push.

When he was gone, Adam glanced at the phone. Talking about Katy made him want to pick it up and call. She'd text messaged him earlier to say that she had gotten back home safely, so he really had no reason to call her. Maybe all he wanted was to hear her voice.

Which was exactly why he didn't do it.

Adam managed to hold out a week before he stumbled across a legitimate excuse to call Katy. He was reading an article on the internet about prenatal DNA testing, and a safer, less invasive method was mentioned.

He called her cell but it went straight to voice, so he tried the ranch phone instead. Katy's mom answered.

"Well, hello, Adam. What a pleasant surprise. How have you been?"

"Good. Busy."

"You know, we didn't get a chance to congratulate you. We were so pleased to hear that it worked the second time. I did some reading on the subject online and it sounds as though you and Katy were quite lucky."

Not as much as she might think.

"Is she there?" he asked.

"She's out running errands for her father, but she has her cell with her. Do you have the number?"

"I tried her cell but it went right to voice mail." He hoped the errands didn't involve any heavy lifting. She had to be careful not to overexert herself.

"There are a lot of holes in the service out here. She was probably driving through a dead zone."

What was the point of even having a cell phone if there was no reception? What if she got into an accident, or broke down? He would have to look into getting her a satellite phone.

"Don't forget, we still owe you that supper," she told him. "We'd just love it if you came up to see us. It's only right we celebrate together. We could make a day of it."

"I'd like that," he said, surprised by the realization that he actually meant it.

"You're welcome anytime. You know we don't stand on formality here. You just jump in your car and head up whenever the mood strikes."

"I'll do that."

"You're family, Adam. Don't ever forget that."

He had a sudden and unexpected lump in his throat. Her parents had every reason to think the worst of him, yet they still considered him one of them.

It was sad that Becca never understood what an extraordinary family she had, and he regretted not insisting she make more of an effort to keep in touch.

He regretted a lot of things about their marriage, and only recently had he begun to realize that.

"When Katy gets in could you tell her I called?"

"Will do, Adam. You take care."

He hung up and tried her cell again, this time leaving a message. "Hey, Katy, it's me. I found some interesting information about DNA testing that I want to discuss with you. Call me when you get this."

He answered a few emails while he waited for her to call him back. But after an hour passed, he began to wonder if she'd gotten his message. He dialed her cell, once again getting her voice mail.

"Me again," he said. "I just wanted to make sure you got my last message. Call me."

She was probably on the road, he figured, and wouldn't check her messages until she got home. Which was fine, since she shouldn't be driving and talking on her phone at the same time anyway. No point in taking chances.

He immersed himself in work, and before he knew it, it was nearly five o'clock. Katy hadn't called yet, but he was sure she had to be home by now. He tried her cell, but again it went straight to voice.

He dialed the ranch, and her mother answered again. "She's here, Adam, but she's out in the north pasture with her father. As soon as she gets inside I'll tell her you called. It shouldn't be more than an hour."

He waited one and a half, then he got caught up in an overseas call that ate another hour. When he was finished Bren buzzed him.

"Ms. Huntley called."

"Why didn't you tell me?" he snapped, and realized he'd just bit her head off unjustly. She had strict instructions that unless it was a dire emergency she was not to interrupt overseas calls.

"Sorry," he said. "Long day."

He picked up the phone and called Katy back again.

"You mean she didn't call you?" her mother said, sounding surprised. "I gave her your message."

"No, she did. But I was on an overseas call. Is she there now?"

"No. She left about ten minutes ago. She went to see a movie with her friend Willy."

Willy? "Willy Jenkins?"

"That's right."

He felt his hackles rise. She was with Willy "Friends-with-Benefits" Jenkins? The idea of what they might do after the film made his blood pressure skyrocket.

"I'll probably be asleep when she gets in, but I'll leave a message that you called."

Meaning she was expecting Katy to be late. "I'd appreciate that," he told her, jaw tense. He hung up and shoved himself back from his desk. As long as she was pregnant with *his* child she had no business sleeping with *anyone*. Who knows what kind of diseases or viruses this Willy person could have contracted? The way she made it sound, he wasn't one to turn down a casual roll in the hay. He could have slept with dozens of women.

He distinctly recalled that when she offered to do this for him, she agreed to practice abstinence.

The only exception to that particular rule was if the man she was sleeping with was *him*.

After playing phone tag for the better part of the next day, Katie finally got a hold of Adam around seven. Her parents were outside so she curled up on the couch with the cordless phone.

Though she had tried hard to keep him off her mind, she'd missed him. Missed hearing his voice.

"Hi, it's me," she said when he answered.

"Well, you're a tough woman to get a hold of," he said sharply.

She was so taken aback she was speechless. And hurt. They hadn't talked in almost a week, and when they finally did he was a jerk. He was clearly upset with her, but she couldn't imagine what she'd done.

"I've been calling you for two days," he said. "I guess you've been busy."

"Busy?"

"Going on dates with Willy Jenkins."

Dates? Is that what this was about? Her mom must have mentioned she went to the movies last night when she talked to him. Although she would hardly call it a date. "You have a problem with me going to the show with a friend?"

"I do if you're sleeping with him."

Sleeping with him? Where the heck had that come from? Her mom sure hadn't told him *that.* "Who told you I was sleeping with him?"

"You did."

"I did? When?"

"That day in the coffee shop. You said you were 'friends with benefits.'"

Yes, but that was years ago, and... Oh, good Lord. She slapped a hand over her mouth to stifle a giggle.

Was he jealous? Of *Willy?*

The billionaire oil man was threatened by a lowly ranch hand? Adam must have been sitting around all day stewing in his own juices.

It was such a ridiculous notion, and he had himself in such a lather, she couldn't resist poking the lion with a stick.

"What makes you think it's any of your business *who* I sleep with?" she asked him.

"As long as you're pregnant with my child, it's my business."

"How do you figure?"

"We had an agreement that you would practice abstinence while you were pregnant."

They did? She didn't recall agreeing to that. But since

she'd had no plans to sleep with *anyone*—not even him—it never seemed relevant anyway. "So I should be practicing abstinence, unless I'm having sex with you? Is that it?"

There was a pause, then he said, "That's different."

Behind her someone cleared their throat, and she snapped her head around to find her mom standing in the kitchen doorway. The woman was stealthy as a damned cat. And it was clear, by her expression, that she'd heard what Katy said about sleeping with Adam.

Well, damn it all to hell.

Fourteen

"Adam, I need to call you back," Katy said.

"Why?" he demanded.

"Because I do."

"We need to discuss this," he barked, like he was issuing an executive order.

"I know we do. It'll just be a few minutes."

"What's so important you can't talk to me right now?"

At the end of her patience, she said, "Willy is here for a quickie, that's what!"

She hung up on him and dropped the phone on the couch beside her.

Her mom stood in the kitchen doorway, arms folded, shaking her head. "That was real mature."

Not one of her finer moments, but he was sort of asking for it.

The phone immediately began to ring. Her mom walked over to the couch, picked it up and answered. "Well, hello,

Adam." She paused then said, "She's not feeling too well. Morning sickness, I'm afraid."

Another pause, then she said, "Yes, I know it's not morning. They just call it that, but it can happen anytime of day. I'll have her call you back when it passes."

She hung up and sat down beside Katy.

"I fell hard and fast, just like you said I would," Katy admitted. "So go ahead, say I told you so."

"Would it make you feel better if I did?"

She sighed and collapsed back against the couch cushions. "Probably not."

"Are you...*seeing* him?"

"He didn't want me." She shrugged, suddenly on the verge of tears. "What else is new, right?"

"Oh, honey." She gathered Katy in her arms and hugged her.

"I guess I should have listened to you."

"At least now I know why you've been moping around for a week." She paused, then asked, "Did he...seduce you?"

"He was a perfect gentleman," she admitted, as if she wasn't ashamed enough. "This was my fault. I don't know what I was thinking. I guess I *wasn't* thinking."

"It'll be easier after you have the baby. You won't have to see him at all if you don't want to."

Now that her mom knew about the affair, not fessing up to the rest of it felt like lying. "Actually, I might be stuck seeing him a lot. For at least the next nineteen years."

"What do you mean?"

"There's a pretty good chance that my own egg was fertilized."

She braced for the fireworks, but instead her mom hugged her tighter. "Oh, Katy. Why didn't you say something?"

"I thought you would be angry. And I was embarrassed that I screwed things up so badly."

"How does Adam feel about this?"

"He's been wonderful. Besides breaking my heart, but that isn't his fault. I know how you and Daddy feel about him, but he's not the person you think he is. Rebecca lied to us, Mom. About a lot of things."

"Katy—"

"I know you don't want to believe it. I didn't, either. But Adam told me things, and he has no reason to lie."

"I don't find that so hard to believe," she said, sounding sad.

"We don't have to tell Daddy about the baby, do we?" Katy asked.

"Your father and I don't keep secrets."

"He's going to be furious. And he's going to want to kill Adam."

"Give him a little credit. He may be upset at first, but he'll be reasonable. I do think it will be easier to swallow coming from me."

She was so relieved she felt limp. "When are you going to tell him?"

"I'll talk to him tonight, when we go up to bed. That way he'll have all night to mull it over before he talks to you."

She threw her arms around her mother and hugged her. "Thank you. For being so understanding. I thought you would be so disappointed in me."

"Oh, sweetheart, you've been the best daughter a mother could ask for. It would take an awful lot to disappoint me."

Katy rested her head on her mother's shoulder, breathed in the scent of her perfume. Avon Odyssey. She'd worn the same fragrance as long as Katy could remember. It was familiar and comforting.

"So, does Adam know how you feel about him?"

"What's the point? Even if he felt the same way, it would never work. We're too different."

"Different how?"

"He's rich and sophisticated, and I'm not."

"So, you think he's better than you?"

"Not better, but we want different things out of life. Not to mention that he's in El Paso. And I'm happy right here, where I am." She sat back and looked at her mother. "Aren't you the one who told me that he's not like us?"

"I guess I did." She touched Katy's cheek. "I just don't like to see my baby unhappy. And like you said, maybe he's not the man we thought he was. He must be pretty special if you fell for him."

"Well, it's all a moot point because Adam said himself that he'll never get married again. And even if he did, if he wanted me, I would always feel as though I was competing with Rebecca. I don't think she had a clue how lucky she was."

"Probably not. Your sister took a lot of things for granted."

She sat snuggled up to her mom, like she had when she was little, and found herself wishing she could go back to those days. When things were so much less complicated, and her life actually made sense.

"You should probably call Adam back," her mom said.

Yeah, and she should probably apologize for the "quickie" remark. In all fairness, if their roles were reversed, she wouldn't be too keen on the idea of the mother of her child sleeping around.

It wasn't Adam's fault that she'd fallen for him, so it wasn't right to take out her frustrations on him.

"I'll call him right now."

Her mom gave her one last firm squeeze, then got up from the couch. Katy hit Redial, expecting Adam to be fuming by now, but when he answered he sounded humbled.

"Are you okay?" he asked.

"I'm fine."

"I owe you an apology," he said, totally stunning her. "I overreacted. I'm used to being in charge, being in control, and with you so far away, I'm feeling a little...well, helpless, I guess."

She knew that hadn't been easy for him to admit. "I'm sorry, too. That remark about Willy was uncalled for. Of course you have every right to be concerned. And for the record, I'm not sleeping with him or anyone else. Nor do I intend to."

"I don't suppose you would reconsider moving here until the baby is born."

Good Lord, what a nightmare that would be. As if this wasn't complicated and heartbreaking enough. "I can't, Adam."

"Just thought I would ask."

"And, just so you know, I wasn't sick. My mom overheard what I said about us sleeping together, and I could tell she wanted an explanation."

"How much did you tell her?"

"Everything."

She could practically feel him grimacing. "I thought you wanted to wait until we knew for sure."

"I did, but not telling her started to feel like lying. And she took it surprisingly well."

"What about your dad?"

"She's telling him tonight. He may not take it so well."

"He doesn't happen to keep firearms around?"

She smiled. "Yeah, but he hasn't pulled his rifle on anyone since I was sixteen and he caught me behind the stable kissing one of the ranch hands."

"You are kidding. Right?"

"Nope. Not only did the guy get fired on the spot, I think he had to go change his shorts."

"I guess I should watch my back, then."

"Nah. If my dad was going to take you down it would be in the chest. Or if he really wanted you to suffer, the gut."

"Now you *are* kidding," he said, but he sounded a little nervous.

She laughed. "Yeah, I'm kidding."

"So, you've been feeling okay?"

"I've been feeling great."

They eased into a conversation about her pregnancy, and he told her about the test he'd read of on the internet. They made plans to bring it up at her next appointment in three weeks. They ended up talking for almost an hour. She lay in bed later, replaying the conversation over and over, wishing things were different. Both anticipating and dreading her doctor appointment. Sometimes she missed Adam so much, the feeling sat like a stone in her chest. She knew seeing him face-to-face would only make it worse. Yet she longed to be close to him again. And she was terrified that if he got too close, if he wanted to make love again, she wouldn't be able to tell him no.

She tossed and turned all night and woke so late the next morning she missed breakfast, but Elvie kept some scrambled eggs and bacon warm for her. After she ate she went searching and found her mom in the chicken coop.

"Sorry I slept in."

"That's okay. Your body is changing. You need more rest than before. I used to get exhausted in my first few months."

"Is there anything you need me to do before I lock myself in the office?" It was her day to do the payroll and order supplies.

"Nothing I can think of."

Katy turned to leave and her mom added, "I talked with your dad last night."

Katy's heart gave a resounding thud. She had completely forgotten that she was going to break the news. "So, what did he say?"

"He said he sort of had the feeling something was up with the two of you," her father said from behind her. Katy swung around to find him leaning in the coop doorway. "And he said that while he'd prefer to see you married and settled down, a baby is a blessing. No matter whose it is."

"Thank you, Daddy," she said, and all of a sudden she was on the verge of tears.

Then he came over and hugged her and she did start crying.

She felt terrible for thinking he would be angry, and expecting the worst. As far as parents went, hers were pretty darned wonderful. It made her wonder, as she had so many times before, how could Becca have taken them for granted?

As long as she lived, it was a mistake she would never repeat.

The day of Katy's appointment couldn't come fast enough.

Adam told himself it was because he was eager to learn about the baby's progress, but the truth was, he'd missed her. Since their phone conversation, when he'd accused her of sleeping with her friend Willy, they'd been talking a lot more often. Usually in the evenings, after he left work and she finished her chores. He had never been much of a talker. He was more the silent-observer type, but that turned out not to be a problem, because Katy did enough talking for the both of them. And the more they talked, he found himself opening up to her.

It was astounding how different she and Becca really were. While Becca had been complex and at times intractable, Katy was so...uncomplicated. And honest. If she said something, she meant it. There were none of the games women seemed to like to play. He found himself calling more often, making up excuses to talk to her, just so he could hear her voice.

Though he'd known many women in his life, he'd never actually been friends with one. Sadly, he realized, not even Becca. They used to talk when they were first dating, but now he wondered if she was only telling him what she thought he wanted to hear. Katy in contrast didn't pull any punches. If she felt strongly about something, she wasn't afraid to speak her mind. At times quite passionately. But he liked that she challenged him. Because in all honesty, given his position of power in the corporate sector, not many people stood up to him.

He considered her more of an equal than most of his "rich" friends and colleagues.

The day of the appointment, when Reece pulled the limo into the lot at the fertility clinic and saw her truck already parked there, Adam experienced an anticipation that he'd not felt in a very long time. He didn't even wait for Reece to get out and open his door. And when he walked inside and saw her standing near the elevator, something deep inside of him seemed to...settle. Followed promptly by the yearning to pull her into his arms and hold her.

She smiled brightly when she saw him, her skin glowing with good health and happiness. Just the way he imagined a pregnant woman should look. She was dressed in her girls' clothes, and though she looked sexy as hell, he knew she would look even better wearing nothing at all. But the last thing either of them needed was to complicate this situation, and sleeping with her would do just that.

But damn, what he wouldn't give to take a quick nibble of her plump, rosy lips.

"Hi, stranger," she said as he approached her, rising up to

give him a quick hug and a peck on the cheek. It took all his willpower not to turn his head so it was his lips she kissed instead. There was an energy that crackled between them. The same sensation of awareness he'd felt when they kissed the first time.

"You look fantastic," he said.

"Thanks. I feel great. My friend Missy is jealous because by this point in all four of her pregnancies she was sick as a dog."

The elevator opened and they stepped inside. He touched her back, to guide her, and electricity seemed to arc between them. And he knew, from the soft breathy sound she made, the slight widening of her eyes, that she felt it, too.

When they signed in at the doctor's office they were called back immediately to an exam room. Adam waited in the hall while she changed into a gown, and he was only in the room a minute or two when Dr. Meyer knocked.

"So how have you been feeling?" he asked Katy. "Any morning sickness?"

"None at all. I feel great. A little tired sometimes, but I just go to bed earlier."

The doctor smiled. "Sounds like a reasonable solution. You've been taking the vitamins I prescribed?"

"Every morning. And our cook has been filling me up on vegetables and whole grains."

"Excellent."

He asked her a few more questions, then took her blood pressure and pulse.

"I need to do an internal exam," he said, looking from Adam to Katy, as if he wasn't sure Adam would be staying or not. And frankly neither was Adam. But Katy smiled and said, "That's fine."

It wasn't as if he hadn't been up close and personal with

every conceivable inch of her body anyway, but the doctor was still very discreet.

"Everything seems to be progressing well," he said when he was finished. "Why don't you get dressed and meet me in my office."

After he stepped out of the room, Adam said, "Thanks for letting me stay."

"I'll bet seeing that makes you pretty happy to be a guy," she joked.

"Men have their own indignities to endure," he said, but spared her the gory details. "I'll wait in the hall for you."

Katy emerged a few minutes later and they walked down the hall to Dr. Meyer's office.

"Do you have any questions for me?" he asked when they were seated.

"We've been reading up on DNA testing," Adam told him, and asked about different options. His opinion was that if they wanted to do the test as soon as possible, the safest way would be through amnio.

"I have a question, too," Katie said. "My mom was telling me how fast her labors were, and since I'm two hours away, I'm wondering what that could mean for me. So far my pregnancy has been just like hers were. I'm afraid that if I go into labor and have to drive all the way to El Paso, I might give birth in the truck."

"I didn't realize you lived so far from here," the doctor said, looking concerned. "Do you have a regular ob-gyn closer to home you could see?"

"I've been seeing Dr. Hogue since I was twelve, and he delivered both me and my sister."

"I know Dr. Hogue. He's a very competent physician."

Adam wasn't sure he liked that. "Shouldn't she be seeing you?"

"Honestly, as long as her pregnancy remains uneventful—

and I have no reason to believe it won't—I see no reason why Katy shouldn't see her regular physician. I'm sure he'll have no problem keeping me apprised of her progress."

Meaning Adam would be driving to Peckins for her appointments instead of Katy coming here.

"Are you upset?" Katy asked him when they left the office and walked down the hall to the elevator.

"Not upset. I wish you would have discussed this with me first."

"I know, and I would have, but it was something my mom brought up this morning before I left. And while I like Dr. Meyer, I think I'll be more comfortable seeing Doc Hogue. He knows me."

Adam could object, and insist she see Meyer, but why? What was his justification?

It would be an inconvenience for him. Though no more than it was for her. And since she was the pregnant one, wasn't it safer if he did the traveling? And she had a valid point about getting to the hospital. "If that's what you want, then of course."

She took his hand and squeezed it, smiling up at him. "Thank you, Adam."

Their eyes met, then locked, and he felt it like a fist to his gut. His palm buzzed, then went hot where it touched hers. He wanted to kiss her. No, he *needed* to. And he was 99 percent sure she was thinking the same thing.

As if caught in a magnetic pull their bodies began to move in closer, her chin tipped upward, and his head dipped....

Then the damned elevator door slid open and people stepped out. Katy jerked back, breaking the spell.

He cursed silently as he followed her on and they rode it down to the first floor. They walked though the lobby and out the door. It was overcast, and thunder rumbled in the distance. The weathermen had been predicting rain.

"Sounds like there's a storm headed this way," he said.

"I better get going," Katy said. "So I beat it home."

"But you just got here. I thought we could spend some time together."

"I really have to go."

Reece pulled up to the curb to meet him, but Adam gestured for him to wait, and followed Katy to where her truck was parked.

"You could at least let me take you to lunch."

"I don't think so." She seemed in an awful hurry to leave, and she wouldn't look at him.

He took her by the arm and turned her to face him. "Katy, what's wrong?"

"I just really need to go."

"Why?"

She glanced around, like she worried someone might be listening. "Because you almost just kissed me, and if I stay, you *will* kiss me."

"Would that be so terrible?"

"Yes, because after you kiss me you'll make up some stupid excuse why I should come to your house, and I will, because at this point my brain will have completely shorted out. And we won't be there thirty seconds before we're naked and…well, you know the rest."

"Would *that* really be so terrible?"

"I'm not a yo-yo. You can't say one minute that it would complicate things, then try to jump me the next. It's not fair."

She was right. He was sending mixed signals like crazy. He cared for her. More than any other woman he'd been involved with, maybe even Becca, but this relationship had no future. Not a romantic one anyway. To let himself love her, to care that much, would make it that much more unbearable if he ever lost her.

Though he wished it were possible, he couldn't give her what she wanted. What she deserved. A man who would love her, and marry her.

"You're right. I'm sorry."

A bolt of lightning arced across the sky to the south.

"I really have to go," she said.

"You'll call me and let me know when you make your appointment."

"Of course."

"And let me know that you got home safely."

"I will." She hesitated, then rose up to press a kiss to his cheek, lingering a second before she turned and climbed in the truck, and as he watched her back out and drive away, he could swear he saw tears in her eyes.

Fifteen

As soon as Katy got home from El Paso she called and made an appointment with Doc Hogue, then she texted Adam with the date and time, because frankly she was feeling too emotional to talk to him. It took everything in her not to sob all the way home. The way he looked at her...for a minute she let herself believe that he wanted her. As close as they had become lately, she thought he was going to tell her that he'd made a mistake, that he loved her.

Why did she keep doing this to herself? Even if he did love her, there was no rational way to make it work. They could try a long-distance relationship, but that would only last so long before they grew apart. She'd seen it happen before to friends who had boyfriends in the rodeo and the military.

When she chose to be with a man, she wanted be *with* him. Not one hundred and fifty miles away. Not that she could be with a man who didn't want to be with her. But she was happy that she and the father of her child—if it *was* her child—would be good friends. Still, she was almost relieved when he called her a week before the doctor appointment to say that he had to fly out of the country and wouldn't make it back till two days after her appointment.

"It's imperative that I go," he told her.

"It's okay," she assured him. "Things happen. Besides, it's only my third month. I seriously doubt anything exciting will happen."

"I wanted to meet the doctor."

"So you'll meet him next month."

But next month didn't happen, either. Two days before her appointment Adam caught a nasty flu virus.

"You sound terrible," she said when he called to tell her, dousing her disappointment.

"I feel terrible," he croaked, his throat so raw and scratchy he could only speak in a coarse whisper.

"Do you have a fever?"

"One hundred and one. Celia won't let me out of bed and she's been force-feeding me chicken soup."

"Good. It sounds like what you need is rest."

"I'm sorry, Katy," he rasped.

"For what?"

"I feel terrible for missing another appointment. Not to mention the amnio. I wanted to be there with you."

And she had wanted him there. She didn't like feeling that she was in this alone. But he couldn't help that she was sick.

"I've heard it's really not that big of a deal. They'll numb me so I won't feel a thing. And, no offense, but I wouldn't want to go anywhere near you right now. The last thing I need is the flu. Just take care of yourself and you'll be better in time for the next appointment."

Her mom went with her to her appointment, and after her checkup, it was off to the hospital for the amnio—which really wasn't all that bad. Doc Hogue had already warned her that it usually took six to eight weeks to get the results—in some cases even longer, and she knew the waiting would be torture.

When she called Adam to tell him the test went well, he sounded relieved. "Nothing will stop me from making the next appointment. I promise."

She hoped that was true. And not just because she wanted to see him, but things were progressing faster than she'd anticipated. Her mom had always said that she started showing early in her pregnancies, so Katy shouldn't have been surprised when, in the last week of her fourth month, she woke up one morning and couldn't fasten her jeans.

"Isn't that supposed to happen?" Adam asked when she called him later that night to complain. "And didn't you tell me that you're not worried about the physical repercussions of pregnancy."

"I don't care about that," she told him. "But there's nothing more I hate than shopping!"

He laughed and called her "unique."

Delaying the inevitable, she wore her jeans with the button unfastened, but after a couple more weeks, when she couldn't get the zipper up more than an inch, and the buttons on her shirts were stretched to the limit, her mom dragged her to the maternity shop for a new wardrobe.

With her next appointment only a week away, Katy felt torn in two. On one hand, she was anxious to see Adam, on the other, she was dreading it. They talked on the phone almost daily now, but seeing him face-to-face…she was afraid it would be a stark reminder of everything she couldn't have. Would *never* have. And though she had never come right out and told Adam how she felt, she was pretty sure he already knew. She also knew that if he was going to have a change of heart, he'd have had it by now. Losing his mother, then Becca, had done something to him. It had cut him so deeply she didn't think he would ever completely heal. He would never come right out and say it—he was too tough for that—but she knew he was afraid of being hurt again.

The Friday before her five-month checkup, Katy had finished up in the office for the day and was taking an afternoon nap when she woke to the sound of her mom's voice. She stood in the bedroom doorway.

"Wake up, honey. We have a visitor."

She sat up and yawned, rubbing her eyes. "Who?"

"Come down and see for yourself," she said, wearing a smile that made Katy suspect she was up to something.

Katy rolled out of bed and peeked out the window. There was a sporty little red car parked in front of the house. Who did they know who drove a sports car? She stretched to look out toward the barn and saw her father standing by the fence with a man Katy didn't recognize. Not from the back anyway at this distance. He was tall and broad-shouldered, wearing jeans, cowboy boots, a plaid flannel shirt and a black Stetson.

Puzzled, and anxious to meet the mystery man, she quickly dragged a comb through her sleep-matted hair and brushed her teeth.

She grabbed a sweater and headed downstairs, and as she glanced in the family room on her way out the front door she noticed a duffel bag next to the sofa. Whoever it was, it looked as though they were there for an extended stay. Maybe it was some long-lost cousin or uncle that she didn't know about.

She stepped out onto the porch, checking the car out as she walked past. The plates were Texas, but the car looked totally unfamiliar. And very expensive.

So it was a *rich* long-lost relative.

She crossed the yard to where her father stood with the mystery man, and he must have heard her coming because he suddenly turned in her direction. "There you are, Katy! Look who came to visit."

The man beside him turned, his head lowered so that his face was hidden by the brim of his hat. Then he lifted his chin, and when his face came into view, her heart did a somersault with a triple twist.

"Hello, Katy," Adam said.

Her first instinct was to throw herself into his arms and just hold him, but she restrained herself. Especially with her dad standing there. "What are you doing here? Our appointment isn't until Tuesday."

"I figured if I came early I would be guaranteed not to miss it this time. And your mom is always telling me I should come and stay for a few days. So here I am."

"Well," her dad said, looking from her to Adam. She could tell he was wary of Adam's presence, but he restrained himself from butting in. "I better head in and…see how dinner is coming along."

They both knew that the only part of dinner he ever participated in was eating it, and he was just making an excuse to leave them alone. But she was grateful.

When he was gone, Adam looked her up and down, eyes wide, and said, "Wow, you look…"

"Pregnant?" she finished for him.

He grinned, and it was so adorable her knees actually went weak. She'd missed seeing him smile. Missed everything about him. "I was going to say fantastic. Pregnancy definitely agrees with you."

She laid a hand on her rounded belly. "Doc Hogue said he's never had a patient who took to it so well. If it wasn't for my belly getting bigger, and the fact that some days I need an afternoon nap, I wouldn't even know that I was pregnant."

He nodded to her belly. "Can I feel?"

This was the part she dreaded. Well, one of the parts. He talked a lot about being anxious to touch her belly, and feel the baby move, and she knew darned well what happened when he put his hands on her. But she couldn't tell him no. Not when it meant so much to him.

"Sure," she said, trying to sound casual, when in reality her heart had begun to pound.

His hand was so big it practically dwarfed her tiny bump, and the warmth of his palm seeped through her shirt to warm her skin. "Have you felt the baby move?"

"Little flutters, but the book says those could just be muscle spasms. No kicks yet. But Doc Hogue said probably soon."

The feel of his hand on her belly was making her go all soft inside, and the energy building between them was reaching a critical level. She knew if she didn't back away soon she was going to do something really dumb, like throw her arms around his neck and kiss him, but Adam didn't give her a chance. His arms went around her, tentatively, as if he thought she might object to being held, and said, "I missed you, Katy."

She couldn't have fought it if she wanted to. She wrapped her arms around him and squeezed, tucking her head under his chin, breathing him in. "Me, too."

It was wonderful, and awful, because she managed to fall in love with him all over again. Not that she'd ever really stopped. But being apart for so long made her forget a little.

What if she *never* got over him?

The dinner bell started clanging and her mom called from the house, "Come on, you two. Time to eat!"

Though she didn't want to, Katy let go of Adam, and decided right then that there would be no more hugging and touching while he was here. It seemed he could turn his feelings on and off like a lightbulb, but for her it wasn't so easy. A few more days of this and her heart might never recover.

Something very weird was happening.

In the past, whenever Becca brought Adam over it was always awkward, the conversation stilted. Probably because Becca herself was so uncomfortable, as if being back home would rub off on her somehow and tarnish the new life she'd built with Adam. But now, everyone was happy and relaxed and seemed to genuinely enjoy each other's company.

After supper, while her dad took Adam out to the stables, Katy and her mom sat out on the porch swing.

"As much as I hate admitting I'm wrong," her mom said, "You were right about Adam. He's a good man. Maybe if your sister had been more comfortable here, he would have been, too."

"I've given up on trying to figure out why Becca did the things she did. Maybe if she'd lived, she would have eventually come around."

"Maybe," her mom said. They were quiet for several minutes, then she said off-handedly, "I noticed Adam couldn't keep his eyes off of you at dinner."

Katy had noticed that, too. Adam sat across from her, and every time she looked up from her plate he was watching her. And each time their eyes met she would feel this funny zing through her nervous system, and her heart would skip a beat. She'd barely been able to choke her dinner down. "What are you suggesting?"

Her mom shrugged. "Only that a man doesn't look at a woman that way if he doesn't care about her."

Whether or not Adam cared about her wasn't in question.

"But for me, that just isn't enough. I want the whole package. I deserve that. And, Adam, well, he's not available."

"Things change."

"Not this."

She might have argued further but Adam and her dad walked up, putting the conversation to an abrupt end.

They all sat out on the porch and watched the sunset until ten, when a chill set in the air. It was hard to believe it was fall already. The time seemed to fly by lately.

Her parents settled in front of the television to watch their favorite sitcom and her mom told Katy, "Why don't you get Adam settled in the blue room." When Katy cut her eyes sharply her way, she added, "It's the nicer of the two."

It was also right next door to, and shared a bathroom with, her own room. The green room was at least across the hall. Although, if he were staying with the men in the bunk house it would be too close as far as she was concerned.

Her mom wasn't trying to set them up, was she? Did she think proximity would make Adam change his mind? She wanted Katy to be happy, but she was making her miserable instead.

"This way," she told Adam, leading him up the stairs. He grabbed his duffel and followed her up. The heavy thud of his boots on the steps seemed to vibrate up through the balls of her feet to twang every single one of her nerves.

As soon as she hit the top step Sylvester darted out from his hiding spot behind the artificial palm tree and tried to wrap himself around her legs, so she toed him out of the way.

"The homicidal cat," Adam said.

"Homicidal?"

"He did that to me the last time I was here. I almost fell down the stairs."

"He can't help it. He got kicked in the head by a horse a

few years back and he hasn't been right since. He mostly just stays up here and hides."

"And opens doors," Adam said with a grin, and she didn't have to ask what he meant. If it hadn't been for Sylvester opening her bedroom door, Adam never would have seen her naked, and maybe this entire mess might have been avoided.

She doubted it, though. With sexual attraction like theirs, sleeping with him had been inevitable.

"Here it is," she said, stepping into the spare room. "I know it isn't the Ritz, but the linens are fresh and there are clean towels in the bathroom cabinet. But if you flush the toilet and it keeps running just jiggle the handle and that should fix it."

The door snapped shut behind her and she whirled around to find Adam leaning against it. He had a look in his eyes, as if he was about ten seconds from devouring her.

Oh, Lord, give me strength.

"Don't look at me like that," she said.

His duffel landed with a thud on the floor beside him. "Like what?"

"Like I'm the main course on the buffet table."

He grinned. "Is that how I look?"

"I can't, Adam." But she wanted to. She wanted to slide her hands under his T-shirt, up his wide, muscular chest. She wanted to feel his bare skin against hers.

He took a step closer and her heart started to hammer. "I was just going to ask if I could feel the baby, that's all."

She didn't believe him for a second. Once he got his hands on her, her belly wasn't the only thing he would touch. And she would probably let him, because she wanted him so much she could hardly see straight.

"Maybe tomorrow," she told him. "I'm going to turn in for the night."

"It's barely ten."

"And I have to be up at five."

"How about a kiss goodnight, then?"

Why was he doing this to her? "I don't think so."

"Why?"

At the end of her rope, she asked, "Adam, what do you want from me?"

He shrugged. "I just...*want* you."

Isn't that the way it always was? They wanted her...until they didn't any longer. Well, she wanted forever, and he wasn't a forever kind of man. Not anymore. "That's not enough for me."

His expression was grim. "You want more."

"I *deserve* it."

"You do. And I'm being selfish." He opened the bedroom door. "I'm sorry. I'll back off."

"Do you need anything before I turn in?"

He shook his head. But as she walked past him to the door he caught her arm and pulled her to him. And heaven help her, she couldn't resist wrapping her arms around him.

Though it was packed with emotion, there was nothing sexual about the embrace. He just held her, and she held him. But it wasn't any less heartbreaking.

"I wish I could be what you need," he whispered against her hair.

She nodded, because if she tried to speak she would probably start blubbering. Besides, they'd already said all they needed to say.

Since he'd popped in unannounced, Adam felt it was only fair to do his share of work while he was visiting, so when Gabe invited him to ride along while he repaired fence posts, he went with him. It was tiresome, backbreaking work, but it felt good to be out in the fresh air and not cooped up in an office behind a desk for a change. Since Becca's death he'd become something of a shut-in. Now he was even thinking it was time to start living again.

They had finished replacing several busted fence posts when Katy's mom brought them lunch on horseback. Thick barbequed beef sandwiches, a plastic bowl full of potato salad and cold sodas. They sat in the truck bed and ate. Adam was so famished he wolfed down two sandwiches and a huge pile of salad.

"Don't they feed you in El Paso?" Gabe asked with a wry grin.

"I don't get this hungry sitting behind a desk," he admitted.

"Out here you earn your appetite. When I think about sitting at a desk day in, day out…" He shook his head. "Being outdoors, that's my life."

"You never considered doing anything else?"

"Nope. I know every inch of this land. It's who I am."

"It sure is beautiful."

He pointed to the east. "See past that fence line? That's ten acres of prime land, some of the prettiest around here. It used to be a horse farm but it went belly-up last fall and the property went into foreclosure."

"I'm surprised no one was interested in buying it."

"Times are bad. I thought about purchasing it and expanding the east pasture, but with this economy it's too much of a gamble. It would be perfect for a young couple, though. Build a house, raise a family. Maybe keep a horse or two."

Adam couldn't help wondering if he was talking about Katy. Was it possible she was she seeing someone? No, she would have told him. But realistically she wasn't going to stay single forever. She was going to find a good man. One willing to give her everything he couldn't. What she *deserved*.

"I understand you should be getting the DNA results

soon," Gabe said, balling up the plastic from his sandwich and stuffing it in the paper sack from their lunch. "What do you plan to do if it's Katy's?"

The question put him on edge. Up until now they had avoided talking about Adam's relationship with Katy. But it was bound to come up. "I want to assure you that I'm going to take care of her and the baby. They won't ever want for anything."

"You know, it makes sense in a weird way. You fell in love with one of my daughters. I guess it's not so unusual you'd fall in love with the other one."

Love? Did he think…did he think Adam was going to *marry* Katy? "Katy and I…we don't have that kind of relationship."

"Is that why you two talk on the phone for hours practically every night?"

"Gabe—"

"And you can't keep your eyes off of her?"

"No disrespect to you or to Katy, sir, but I don't want to marry anyone."

"You've got something against marriage, son? I know Becca could be a handful, but—"

"Becca was a good wife. And the day I buried her, I swore it was something I would never do again."

Gabe took a swallow of his soda, then said, "So you'll spend your life alone instead? Sounds like a pretty miserable existence."

Not alone. He would have his child. "I don't see it that way."

Gabe shrugged, like it was no skin off his nose. "We should get busy. We have a lot to get done before supper."

He didn't want Gabe, or Katy's mom, deluding themselves

into thinking he was going to whisk Katy off her feet and carry her into the sunset. They would just have to get used to the idea of him and Katy being good friends.

Sixteen

Katy barely made it to three o'clock when she was so exhausted she had to lay down. And though she only planned on sleeping an hour or two, when she woke to the sound of the water running in the bathroom, it was almost six.

Her dad must have given Adam quite a workout if he needed a shower.

She knew she should get up, but she was so comfortable she didn't want to move. She curled in a ball, the tops of her thighs pressed against her belly. She was just starting to drift off when she felt it. A soft bump.

Her eyes flew open. Could that have been the baby kicking?

She lay there very still, waiting to see if it happened again. Then she felt it, a distinct kick. Maybe those flutters she'd been feeling had been the baby moving after all.

Nearly bursting with excitement, she rolled onto her back and pulled her shirt up so she could see her belly. It only took a few seconds before she felt another kick, and it was so hard this time she could actually see her stomach move!

She lay there frozen, afraid that if she moved the baby might stop, and she wanted Adam to feel it, too.

She heard the shower shut off and the sound of him tugging open the curtain.

"Adam! Get in here!" she called. "Hurry!"

Only a few seconds elapsed before the bathroom door swung open and Adam appeared, fastening a towel around his waist, hair mussed and still dripping. When he saw her lying there he must have thought the worst because all the color seemed to drain from his face. "What's wrong?"

"Nothing." She gestured him over. "Hurry, it's kicking."

He was across the room in a millisecond, and perched on the edge of the mattress. "Are you sure?"

"Just watch," she said. "Right below my navel."

They waited several seconds then there was another quick bump-bump. "Did you see that?"

Adam laughed. "Oh, my God! Can I feel?"

She nodded, and he very gently placed his hand over her belly. His hand was warm from his shower and still damp. And there it was again, a soft little jab, as if the baby was saying, "Hey, I'm in here!"

She had been trying so hard to stay disconnected, to not think of it as *her* baby. But in that instant, feeling the baby move, she fell hopelessly in love. And she wanted it to be hers, so badly her heart hurt.

"What does it feel like to you?" he asked.

"Just like you would think. Like someone is poking me, but from the inside. I should call my mom in here so she can feel it."

"She's not here. She and your dad went out. She said they were going to catch a film in town and they would be back late."

They hardly ever went to the movies, so odds were good they were just giving Katy and Adam some time alone. They both seemed to have it in their minds that Adam was going to have a change of heart and suddenly decide that he loved her. What she didn't think they realized, what she hadn't realized until last night, was that he *did* love her. Even if he couldn't say it, she could see it in his eyes. And knowing that made his rejection a little easier to swallow for some reason. She wasn't damaged Katy, whom no one could love. Someone finally did. It just sucked that he was afraid to acknowledge it.

"It stopped," he said, sounding disappointed, but he didn't take his hand from her belly. And the fact that she was lying in bed wearing nothing but a shirt and panties, and he was only wearing a towel, started to sink in. Suddenly she felt hot all over and her heart was beating double time.

She would never know what possessed her, but she put a hand on his bare knee.

Dark and dangerous, his eyes shot to hers. "That's *not* a good idea."

Probably not. But for all the energy she'd spent convincing herself that this was never going to happen again, it didn't take much to have a total change of heart. And though she knew it was a mistake, and she was asking for heartbreak, she wanted him so much she didn't care what the repercussions would be.

She stroked his knee, scratching lightly with her nails.

"You're sending some pretty serious mixed signals," he told her, his voice uneven.

"Then let me be 100 percent clear." She slid her hand under the towel and up the inside of his thigh. He groaned and closed his eyes.

"I can't let you do this," he said, but he wasn't making an effort to stop her. And when her fingertips brushed against the family jewels he sucked in a breath and said in a gravelly voice, "Katy, stop."

"I can't. I want you, Adam. Even if it's just for a night or two."

He still wasn't ready to give in, so she took his hand that was still resting on her belly and guided it downward, between her thighs. "Touch me," she pleaded, and that was his undoing. He leaned over and kissed her. And kissed her and *kissed* her, and it was so perfect, she wanted to cry. He tugged the towel off and slid under the covers beside her. She expected it to be urgent and frenzied, like the night after she found out she was pregnant, but Adam took his time, kissing and touching her, exploring all the changes to her body, telling her she was beautiful. She'd never felt so sexy, so attractive, in her life. And when he made love to her it was slow and tender.

Afterward they lay curled in each others arms and talked. About work, and the baby, and the ranch—anything but their relationship.

Around ten she threw on her robe and went down to the kitchen to get them something to eat while Adam checked his phone messages. When she came back up with a plate of leftovers, Adam was dressed and shoving clothes into his duffel bag.

"You're leaving?" she asked.

"I'm sorry," he said. "I had a message from my COO. There's been an accident at the refinery."

"What kind of accident?"

"An explosion."

She sucked in a breath. "How bad?"

"Bad. At least a dozen men were hurt."

Katy's heart stalled. "How seriously?"

"Second- and third-degree burns."

"Oh, Adam, I'm so sorry."

"Since I took over, safety has been my number-one priority and we've had a near-spotless record. Not a single accident that required more than the need for a small bandage. Injured employees means negative press and lawsuits and OSHA investigations."

"So this could be bad?"

He nodded. "This could be very bad. But my main concern right now is making sure those men are being taken care of."

"What caused the explosion?" she asked.

"We're not sure yet." He sat on the bed to pull on his socks and boots. "They're still trying to put out the blaze. Jordan said they had just completed a maintenance cycle and were bringing everything back on line when something blew. Which makes no sense, because everything had just been thoroughly inspected." He rose from the bed and grabbed his duffel. "Katy, I am going to try like hell to be back in time for your appointment, but I just don't know if I can."

"Adam, don't even worry about that. If you can make it, fine, if not, there's always next month."

"Yes, but I've been saying that for two months now. I *want* to be there."

She smiled. "I know you do. That's why it's okay if you're not."

He dropped the duffel, gathered her up in his arms and planted a kiss on her that curled her toes and shorted out her brain. And if he didn't have to leave, man would he be in trouble.

"What was that for?" she asked when they came up for air.

"Because you're being so understanding."

"That's what you do when you love someone," she said.

It wasn't until she saw the stunned look on Adam's face,

that she realized what she'd just said. How could she have just blurted it out like that?

And he obviously had no clue how to respond. It might have been amusing if she wasn't so mortified.

"Wow," she said, cheeks flaming with embarrassment. "I did not mean to just blurt that out."

"Katy—"

"Please," she said holding up a hand to stop him. "Anything you say at this point will only make it worse, and I'm humiliated enough. Just, please, let's pretend it never happened."

If there was any hope that he might have ever returned the sentiment, it died with his look of relief. "I really have to go."

"Go," she said, forcing a smile.

"We'll talk about this later." He gave her another quick kiss, then grabbed his duffel.

No, they wouldn't talk about it, she thought, as she listened to his heavy footfalls on the stairs, then the sound of the front door slamming. She resisted the urge to get up and watch him drive away. It would just be too hard, because it was a symbol. A symbol of the end of their relationship as she knew it. Not just their sexual relationship, but their friendship, as well.

Remaining friends after this would just be too…awkward. She didn't doubt that he knew she had strong feelings for him, maybe even loved him. But knowing it, and actually hearing the words were two very different things. He had no choice but to shut her out. She just hoped he would always be there for the baby.

And it occurred to her, as close as they had become these last few months, not only did she just lose her lover, but she'd also lost her best friend.

It never ceased to amaze Adam how, when his company did something positive, like adopting new and innovative

environmentally friendly practices, he was lucky to get an
inch on page twelve of the business section. But toss in a
suspicious inferno, a few injured workers and an OSHA
investigation and they'd made the front page of every national
newspaper in the country. He personally had been hounded
by the press at the office and even outside his home.

They had gone from being praised as having the most
impressive safety record in the local industry to being labeled
a deathtrap overnight.

Already they had been served with lawsuits by six of the
thirteen injured men, the ones whose burns had been the
most severe. The board, on the advice of their attorneys,
had already agreed to settle the suits. It would set them back
financially, but Adam was steadfast in his belief that it was
the right thing to do. He was just thankful that no one was
left permanently disabled, or, God forbid, killed.

Since the refinery had been in maintenance mode, the
number of men on the line had been reduced by nearly half.
The majority of the damage had been to the infrastructure.
And now, every day they had to remain off line while the
equipment was checked and rechecked, they lost hundreds
of thousands of dollars in revenue.

Monday afternoon Adam called an emergency executive
meeting in his office. OSHA had begun their investigation
and it was beginning to look like the accident really wasn't an
accident after all. If they ruled that it had been a case of gross
negligence on the part of the men on the rig, the company
would be slapped with a hefty fine.

Jordan, loyal to the death to his men, refused to believe
they could possibly be responsible.

"My men work damned hard," he said, wearing a bare
spot in the oriental rug with his pacing. Unusual considering
he was by far the most laid-back of the four. "I would trust
most of them with my life. There's no way they would be so

careless. Not to mention that the entire line in question had just been thoroughly inspected. It doesn't make sense."

"Something about this does smell fishy to me," Nathan said. He sat in the chair opposite Adam's desk, looking troubled.

"You suspect foul play?" Adam asked.

"I say we shouldn't rule anything out. It would have to be an inside job, though."

Jordan stopped pacing to glare at his brother. "Impossible. Our people are loyal."

"Who then?" Nathan asked.

Jordan looked as though he wanted to deck him. "*Not* one of mine."

Adam didn't like the idea that one of his own employees could be responsible, but they had to know for sure, before there was another accident. "I think we need to hire our own investigator."

"We'll have to keep it quiet," Emilio, who had been standing by the window quietly observing, finally said. "If it was sabotage, and someone on the line is responsible, if they find out we're digging, any possible evidence will disappear. If he thinks he got away with it, he may be careless."

"Nathan," Adam said. "I want you in charge of this one."

"Why him?" Jordan scoffed, outraged. "I'm the one who understands the day-to-day operations. Those men trust me."

"Which is exactly why I'm assigning it to Nathan. It's going to get out eventually and you should have a certain degree of deniability. Not to mention that you're biased."

Jordan knew he was right. "Fine. But I want to be kept in the loop."

"Of course. If we do have suspects, you'll be in the position to keep a close eye on them, so this doesn't happen again. And

I suppose it goes without saying that until this is resolved, I won't be stepping down as CEO. However long that takes. But that does *not* mean I won't be watching all of you."

"How is the pregnancy going?" Nathan asked.

"Great. In fact, I have to be back in Peckins tonight. Katy has her five-month checkup tomorrow." And he and Katy were long overdue for a serious discussion about the future of their relationship.

"Wait a minute," Jordan said. "You're actually leaving town? After everything that just happened?"

"I'll only be gone a day or two."

"What if we need you here?"

Jordan's reaction was understandable. Six months ago Adam wouldn't have dreamed of leaving town during a crisis. Not for a couple days. Not for five minutes. But his priorities had changed. Hell, his whole life had changed, and he had Katy and her family to blame. Or thank.

He kept thinking about what Gabe said, about how spending his life alone would be a miserable existence. Well, Adam *had* been miserable. For three years now. Until he got tangled up with Katy, he had genuinely forgotten what it felt like to be happy. To have something to look forward to.

Calling and asking her to meet him was one of the smartest things he'd ever done.

"We'll manage," Emilio said, sending Jordan a sharp look. "Can you two give me and Adam a minute?"

Nathan and Jordan left, and Emilio sat on the corner of Adam's desk.

"Okay, what's up?"

"What do you mean?"

"Jordan is right. You never leave during a crisis."

Emilio was going to find out eventually, so why not tell him now. "Something happened the other day when I was in Peckins. Something…unexpected. When I heard about the accident, I told Katy I had to leave, and said I might have to miss her appointment."

He winced. "You've missed two already."

"I know. And you know what she said?"

"I'm guessing it can't be good if it has you rushing back there."

"She said it was fine. That I could just go to the next one. She said knowing that I want to be there is good enough. And when I thanked her for being so understanding, she said that's what you do when you love someone."

Emilio's brow lifted. "She told you she loves you?"

He laughed. "Yeah, she just kind of blurted it out. And my first instinct, after I got over the surprise of her saying it, was that I love her, too."

"So did you tell her that?"

"I didn't get a chance. She got really embarrassed, and asked me to forget she said anything. I had to go. It didn't seem right to throw it out there, then leave."

"So you're going to tell her when you get there?"

"At this point, considering everything I've put her through, I don't think telling her is good enough, so I'm going to show her, too." Adam pulled the ring box out of his desk drawer and tossed it to Emilio.

Emilio laughed. "Is this what I think it is?"

Adam grinned.

He opened it and gave a low whistle. "I thought you were never getting married again, never taking the chance on burying another wife."

"It wasn't losing Becca that had made getting over her so hard. It was the regrets. The things we *didn't* say. And I can't go on pretending that we didn't have problems. Almost from the start."

"So why have kids?"

"I guess I thought that having a baby would fix everything.

I thought it would bring us closer together. But honestly, it probably would have just made it worse. Neither one of us was very happy. If she hadn't gotten sick, I don't doubt we would be divorced by now."

He knew now that Celia was right, Becca *wasn't* his soul mate. She wasn't the love of his life, and he was pretty sure she sensed that.

"It's never easy admitting our mistakes," Emilio said.

"It's different with Katy. She's unlike anyone I've ever known. She couldn't care less about my money. And if she thinks I'm acting like an ass, she isn't shy about saying so. She's everything I could possibly want or need in a wife. I can't even imagine my life without her in it."

"So what are you still doing here?" Emilio asked, tossing the ring back to Adam.

"It's only three."

"Yes, but you have a long drive ahead of you. Besides, we can handle things without you."

Emilio didn't have to tell him twice.

They weren't expecting company, so when Katy pulled up the driveway after a quick trip to the bank, she was surprised to see a car there. Before she got a good look she thought it might be Adam, but this was a dark sedan. A Mercedes, or BMW or something similar. And she knew Adam drove a red and sporty car.

She parked by the barn, thinking maybe they really did have a rich uncle. But she didn't have time to worry about that. She had a letter in her jeans pocket that could very well change the rest of her life. She got out and walked to the house, wondering who it could be. She went through the kitchen, the scent of home-fried chicken making her mouth water.

"Smells delicious, Elvie."

"That man is here," she whispered.

"What man?"

She nodded to Katy's belly. "The baby's father."

"*Adam* is here?" Elvie had to be mistaken.

She nodded, wide-eyed, and crossed herself. She was convinced, because Adam was so tall and dark and handsome, that he was *el Diablo* in the flesh.

She pushed through the kitchen door to the great room, expecting to see some man who looked like Adam sitting there with her parents, but it actually *was* Adam. And the instant she saw him, she knew all that stuff about them not being friends anymore was just bull.

When they heard her come in everyone turned in her direction.

She thrust her hands on her hips and asked Adam, "Exactly how many cars do you own?"

He grinned at her, then turned back to her parents and said, "I think that about covers it."

The three of them stood and her dad shook Adam's hand. Why would he do that?

"What's going on?" Katy asked them.

"Let's take a drive," Adam said.

"Why?"

"So we can talk."

"But it's almost suppertime."

"We won't be long."

Whatever he had to say must have been pretty bad if they had to leave the ranch. "Where are we going?"

"Not far." He crossed over to where she stood and took her hand, leading her to the front door. She looked back at her parents, but their expressions didn't give anything away.

Would he hold her hand—and in front of her parents—if he was about to tell her something awful? Or did he think it would soften the blow?

He opened the passenger door for her and she slid into the soft leather seat. He walked around and got in the driver's side, saying, as he started the engine, "Buckle up."

He waited until she was fastened in, then put the car into gear. It felt a little weird being in a car with him while he was actually behind the wheel. In the past it was always Reece driving. Not that she expected him to be a terrible driver. It was just...different.

"How many cars do you own?" she asked as he made a left onto the road.

"Just the three."

They drove about a half a mile, then Adam made a sharp left and pulled up the road to the abandoned horse farm next door.

"What are we doing here?"

"I'll explain," he said cryptically.

The house and stables were in disrepair and the property overgrown, but it used to be a beautiful piece of land. And had the potential to be again someday. Her dad had talked about buying it, and she'd been disappointed when he changed his mind. Though she had never admitted it to anyone, she had even considered purchasing it. She had enough for a down payment in the bank. She just didn't like the idea of living alone.

Adam parked in a clearing by the stable and they got out. The sun was just beginning to set and there was a chill in the air.

"Are you warm enough?" he asked.

She nodded. He took her hand again and they walked slowly toward the stables. "Does this mean you're staying for my appointment tomorrow?"

The question seemed to surprise him. "Of course. Why would I drive all this way and not go?"

She shrugged.

"What do you think of this land?" he asked her.

"It's nice. Perfect for a small horse farm."

"What would you think if I said I bought it?"

She stopped in her tracks. "What? Why?"

He grinned. "So I could build a house here. And probably a new stable."

"You're serious?"

"Yep."

Well, if the baby was hers, and he was going to be visiting a lot, didn't it make sense that he had somewhere to stay? But they weren't even sure yet.

They started walking again, past the stables and along the corral fence, the overgrown grass and weeds grabbing at her pant legs. "I think that sounds like a good investment."

"So you wouldn't mind living here?"

Living here? He was going to build a house for *her?* Did he know something she didn't? Had the lab sent him a letter, too, and had he read it? After they agreed they would look at the results *together.*

"Adam, what's going on?"

They stopped where the corral turned, near an apple tree that had probably been there longer than the house. "This should do," Adam said.

"Do for what?"

"There are a few things I have to tell you, Katy."

She swallowed hard, bracing for the worst, her hands clammy she was so nervous.

"We had to launch an investigation into the accident at the refinery, and as soon as it's resolved, I'm leaving Western Oil."

For a full ten seconds she was too dumbfounded to speak. And when she found her voice, it was uncharacteristically high-pitched. "Leaving? As in quitting?"

"I'll still be on the board, but I'm stepping down as CEO."

"W-why?"

"It's time. I want to be around to see my child grow up."

"That's wonderful," she said, wondering what that meant for her, if it meant anything at all.

"Remember the other night, when you said you love me?"

She cringed, still mortified that she had actually done something so stupid. "I thought we agreed not to talk about that."

"You issued an order, and I didn't agree to anything."

It was obvious he wasn't willing to let it go. He was going to torture her. "Okay, what about it?"

"I'll admit I was a little stunned—"

"You were way more than stunned. And I don't blame you, Adam. It was wrong of me to put you on the spot like that."

He took a deep breath and exhaled. "Can I finish?"

She nodded, even though she knew she wasn't going to like what he had to say.

"I was in a hurry to leave, but if I'd had more than thirty seconds to think about it, I would have told you that I love you, too."

He heart climbed up into her throat. She had never expected him to admit it, to say it out loud.

"Aren't you going to say anything?" he asked.

"I...I don't know what to say."

"You could say that you love me, too."

Unable to look in his eyes, and see the sincerity there, she looked down at the ground instead. "You already know that."

"I *need* you, Katy."

For now. But what about a month from now? He didn't want to get married, and she couldn't accept any less than that.

She wanted forever.

Adam bent down on one knee in the weeds. She thought he was going to pick something up off the ground, then she saw that he already had something in his hand.

"What are you doing?"

"Something I should have done months ago." He opened his hand and sitting on his palm was a black velvet box. It actually took her several seconds to figure out what was happening. Then she started to tremble so hard she wasn't even sure her legs would hold her up.

Adam opened the box to reveal a stunning diamond solitaire ring. He looked up at her and grinned, "Marry me, Katy?"

"You're serious?"

"I've never been more sure of anything in my life."

"But…Becca—"

"Is gone. Becca was my wife, and I loved her, but I didn't need her the way I need you. You're my soul mate. I don't want to go another day, another minute, knowing you aren't going to be mine forever."

She'd imagined this moment so many times in her head, but none of her fantasies compared to the real thing, and she'd be damned if she was going to give him even a second to change his mind.

She threw herself in his arms so hard that they lost their balance and tumbled backward in the weeds.

He laughed and said, "Should I take that as a yes?"

"Definitely yes," she said, kissing him, wondering if this was a dream. Was it even possible to be *this* happy?

Adam sat them up and pulled her into his lap. "Would you like this now?" he asked, holding up the ring box.

She'd almost forgotten! "Will you put it on me?"

He took it from the box and slid it on her finger. It was

a perfect fit. "I have *huge* fingers. How did you guess the size?"

"I didn't. I asked your mom."

"When?"

"Sunday morning."

Katy's mouth fell open. "She's known about this since *Sunday?*"

"I didn't tell her why I needed it, but I think she had a pretty good idea."

Suddenly it made sense why he was sitting there with her parents when she walked in, and why her dad shook his hand. "Oh, my gosh, did you ask my parents' *permission?*"

"I thought it would be a nice touch, since I kind of missed that step last time. I figured they deserved it."

She threw her arms around his neck and hugged him, the baby pressed between them. That's when she remembered the letter in her pocket. They were together now, and no matter whose baby it was, she would be raising it. But he deserved to know the truth.

"I have to show you something," she said, pulling the letter out. "This came in today's mail."

"The DNA results?"

She nodded.

He took the letter from her, and for a minute he just looked at it, then he looked up at her, shrugged and said, "I don't care."

"You don't care?"

He took her hands. "What difference do genetics make? This is *our* baby, Katy. Yours and mine. Either way, it's a miracle. So unless you really need to know—"

"I don't," she said. "Though I tried to be impartial, and not get attached, I've felt like this baby has been mine pretty much from the day it was conceived."

With a smile on his face, Adam ripped the envelope in

two, then into fourths, then he kept on ripping until there was nothing left but scraps, then he tossed them in the air.

Katie couldn't help wondering, though…would she ever be curious? Someday would she want to know?

But the following spring, when Amanda Rebecca Blair was born—a healthy eight pounds seven ounces—and Katy held her daughter for the first time, she knew without a doubt that it would never matter.

* * * * *

"You want me to pretend to be your mistress?"

"Companion," he corrected. *For now.*

"Why me?"

"You're different."

Her eyes watched him. "So if I agree to this, you'll do what you promised to do? You'll investigate my claim?"

"Regrettably, you'll have to wait."

"Don't you trust me to keep to my word?"

"Never trust a woman with a grudge."

Was it a trick of the light or did she somehow look vulnerable? It made him wonder what fool had given her up. Then again, some men could only take so much of that deliciously smart mouth.

And some men liked to live dangerously.

Dear Reader,

Welcome to the next book in my Roth series, set around the second brother in this rich and powerful Australian dynasty. This story is about loyalties to family…between friends…and between lovers. Strong emotional ties link them all, yet it's those very ties that put love to the test.

And if anyone has been tested by love it's handsome widower Adam Roth. He knows how easy it is to love and to lose, so having Jenna Branson cross his path and insist that a member of his family cheated her brother has Adam stepping in to shield his remaining loved ones.

Jenna Branson simply wants the money owed to her brother. She certainly doesn't want to get emotionally involved with one of the Roths, but she finds herself unable to deny a growing attraction to a man who clearly has his own family's best interests at heart. Just as she does.

Being a hero or a heroine isn't just about loving each other. When you love, the urge to protect your loved ones is incredibly strong. You do all you can to help, even if it means divided loyalties. How heartbreakingly humiliating it would be, then, to discover those loyalties had been misplaced, and at a terrible price, too.

To win, one of this pair will need to lose. I hope you cheer for Jenna and Adam as they fall in love and seek a way to *both* come out winners.

Happy reading!

Maxine

HIGH-SOCIETY
SEDUCTION

BY
MAXINE SULLIVAN

Published in Great Britain 2011
by Mills & Boon, an imprint of Harlequin (UK) Limited,
Eton House, 18-24 Paradise Road, Richmond, Surrey TW9 1SR

© Maxine Sullivan 2010

ISBN: 978 0 263 88325 1

51-1211

Harlequin (UK) policy is to use papers that are natural, renewable and
recyclable products and made from wood grown in sustainable forests. The
logging and manufacturing processes conform to the legal environmental
regulations of the country of origin.

Printed and bound in Spain
by Blackprint CPI, Barcelona

The *USA TODAY* bestselling author **Maxine Sullivan** credits her mother for her lifelong love of romance novels, so it was a natural extension for Maxine to want to write her own romances. She thinks there's nothing better than being a writer and is thrilled to be one of the few Australians to write for the Desire™ line.

Maxine lives in Melbourne, Australia, but over the years has travelled to New Zealand, the UK and the USA. In her own backyard, her husband's job ensured they saw the diversity of the countryside, from the tropics to the Outback, country towns to the cities. She is married to Geoff, who has proven his hero status many times over the years. They have two handsome sons and an assortment of much-loved, previously abandoned animals.

Maxine would love to hear from you. She can be contacted through her website at www.maxinesullivan. com.

Special thanks to fabulous Desire™ editor Shana Smith
for her cheerful assistance and behind-the-scenes
help over the years.

<u>One</u>

"And this is Jenna Branson. She's one of our up-and-coming jewelry designers."

Jenna heard her boss's words, thankful that at least she'd had time to recover from her shock. Having Adam Roth walk into the Conti corporate box at Australia's Flemington Racecourse a few minutes ago had stunned her.

Oh, God! she'd thought. Here was the middle son of Laura and Michael Roth, iconic owners of Roth's, the luxury-goods department stores. His family was Australia's aristocracy. The crème de la crème of Australian society. She'd never wanted to meet any one of them. Not after what Liam Roth had done to her brother.

She watched in silent horror now as this Roth family member lowered his tall, lean body onto the chair opposite. His gaze came straight at her across the table, homing in like she was the only person in the room. She hid a small gasp as his pair of blue eyes trapped hers for a heart-stopping moment in time.

"It's a pleasure to meet you, Jenna," he murmured, his gaze taking in her lustrous, shoulder-length brown hair, then the details of her face, before sliding down to the soft floral dress she knew looked good on her. For the first time ever, she actually wished she *didn't* look quite so feminine.

Jenna tried to smile, but she wasn't sure if she managed it. "Yes, you, too," she somehow said, hoping she sounded sincere but almost choking on the words. Why, oh, why had she given in to pressure and come here today? If only her boss, Roberto, and his charming wife, Carmen, hadn't been so insistent. She would have much preferred to spend her Saturday relaxing in her apartment.

"Have you backed any winners yet?" Adam asked in a smooth voice that was as cultured as it was deep.

She tried to settle her heart back in place. "Not so far."

He smiled the confident smile of a man who knew women. "Then perhaps your luck will change."

If he thought *he* was going to change her luck, he was in for a surprise. "Perhaps."

Just then her boss's son returned to the table and sat down next to her, almost making her shudder, giving her something else to worry about. Marco had been asking her out for months. Now he thought he'd worn her down. Nothing could be further from the truth.

"You didn't bring a date?" he said to Adam, after a short greeting.

"No. Not this time."

"That's not like you, *amico mio,*" he joked, but he slid his arm along the back of Jenna's chair as if silently staking a claim.

A note of awareness docked in Adam's eyes, sending an

odd ripple of apprehension shooting down her spine. She didn't want either man thinking she was here with Marco. Nor did she want either one thinking she was available for some sort of dalliance.

Unfortunately, as the afternoon wore on, she was fully aware of Adam surreptitiously watching her every movement. She tried her damnedest not to react, but his interest was a living thing. It made her uneasy, though not in a sleazy way like with her boss's son. Adam Roth was a playboy. A sophisticated master playboy, despite being a widower whose wife had died in a car accident over four years ago. She had no doubt he knew all the right moves.

One thing saved her. Her brother. Remembering what Stewart had been through gave her the advantage. She knew what this man's family was capable of, and that helped put up an invisible barrier to deflect any attempt at intimacy.

By the time they'd finished eating a late lunch, she was more than ready to make an escape to the powder room. Thankfully, Marco was involved in watching the next race with another woman and her generous cleavage. So while everyone was occupied Jenna grabbed her purse to slip out of the room, her heartbeat stuttering when she saw Adam notice her leaving.

Once in the corridor she hurried along the plush carpet to find the ladies' room. She had a feeling he would follow. That he was about to ask her out. She didn't want that, she decided as she found what she was looking for just ahead. She reached for the door handle...started to open it...

"Jenna."

She stilled, tempted to ignore him and go inside the room but suspected he would merely wait for her to come out. Taking a deep breath, she dropped her hand and turned around to face him.

Adam was right behind her, his proximity surprising

her, causing her knees to wobble. He reached out to cup
her elbows and steady her. At his touch the sound of the
race caller outside wound down to a mere whisper, and
the excitement of the guests cheering their horses along
the final stretch muted to low volume, making her forget
everything else for a moment.

Then his eyes warmed and his firm lips spread into a
sensual smile that promised to take her places she'd never
been. "I think you'll find that's not what you want," he
drawled, his voice a hot whisper along her spine.

She blinked. "It…isn't?"

He indicated the sign on the door. "That's a storeroom."

"Oh." In her hurry, she hadn't noticed. Her mind had
been focused on getting away from him. She pulled back
and he dropped his hands. He was still too close.

If she'd had time to think, she would have felt foolish
for rushing and making such a mistake. As it was, she half
turned to take a quick look down the corridor hoping to
see the ladies' room and still make her escape in the next
few seconds.

But then a thought flashed through her mind. Wasn't she
crazy to walk away when she had a Roth right here in front
of her? Wouldn't swallowing her pride and confronting this
man be a small price to pay? She'd been praying for a way
to help her brother and now she had it. Heck, she had to do
something to help Stewart.

Taking a deep breath, Jenna opened her mouth to speak,
but shut it again as a young woman walked by. A hallway
wasn't the place to talk about a private matter.

Instead, she gestured to the storeroom. "Do you think I
could have a word alone with you?"

The oddest gleam entered his eyes. "In there?"

"Yes." She had to talk to him. Now. If she wasn't quick enough, the opportunity would pass. "Please."

Adam didn't move. He had a strange look about him. As if he were...*disappointed* in her.

He shook his head. "Sorry, beautiful. You're stunning, and I must admit I'm very tempted, but a quick grope in a broom cupboard isn't my thing. I prefer to wine and dine a woman first."

She gaped at him. "Wh-what?"

He assessed her with a touch of regret. "No doubt many a man would be pleased to make you their own on such short acquaintance, but I find a little romance is more... satisfying." He went to turn back to the function rooms. "I was going to ask you out, but—"

She pulled herself together in time to grab his arm. "You think I'm after *sex?*" she hissed, totally insulted. "I can assure you that's the last thing on my mind."

His gaze darted down to her hand on his sleeve, then up again but she refused to let go in spite of feeling the muscle beneath her palm.

"I really do need to speak to you. I prefer we do it in private...." She swallowed, then dared to threaten, "But I can do it just as well in front of an audience."

A cool look entered his eyes. "Seeing how we only met a few hours ago, I can't imagine you'd have anything of importance to say to me."

She continued her grip on his arm. "Then you'd be wrong."

There was a measured silence. "Did you engineer this meeting today?"

"No. But that doesn't mean I don't have a valid complaint about your family."

"My family?" he said, stiffening.

"Perhaps you'll let me explain in private."

There was a pause. He inclined his head. "Very well."

At his reluctant acquiescence, she finally dropped her hand, letting out a silent sigh of relief, but aware this was only the first step.

Adam reached past her and pushed open the door, indicating she should precede him into the room. He was all business now, making it clear he had nothing else on his mind. Once inside he closed the door and positioned himself in front of it. "Okay, talk."

She realized her mistake in not getting him go first into the room. She had no escape now, only a large frosted window that gave a false impression of freedom—and a short distance between her and her inadvertent captor. Oh, God, what on earth was she doing?

Then she made herself remember her brother's anguish. And that gave her the courage to press onward. She drew back her shoulders. "I want you to give my brother the money your brother Liam conned out of him."

He froze, then, "Rewind that and play it again. Slowly this time."

Oh, this man was good at keeping his cool—very good—but he'd probably had plenty of experience covering up for his late brother. Many times he would have had to lie to the people Liam Roth had duped over the years.

"I expected you to deny it. The Roths stick together." Stewart had told her that and she had no reason *not* to believe him. The rich and privileged always seemed to get away with everything. Her ex-boyfriend, Lewis, had been the same, though he was nowhere near equal to the Roths. He'd thought his money had entitled him to do whatever he liked—including cheating on her.

Adam Roth's eyes flickered with annoyance. "I can't deny something if I don't know the details," he said curtly, bringing her back to the present. His brows jerked together. "Who's your brother anyway?"

"Stewart Branson."

His expression gave nothing away. "Am I supposed to know him?" He didn't give her time to answer. "I'm afraid you're talking to the wrong guy, sweetheart. My family has nothing to do with this."

She was annoyed by his instant dismissal. "I know what my brother told me."

His jaw set. "I'd like to hear exactly what he said."

Jenna let out a slow breath, relieved he was at least willing to keep listening. "Six weeks ago there was a segment on the news about your parents attending an Australia Day dinner. They showed footage from Liam's funeral." Adam's younger brother had died from a terminal illness in early December.

He didn't move. "Go on."

"Stewart had dropped by my apartment. He looked terrible. I was just about to ask him what was wrong when he looked at the television and saw the funeral procession and broke down. He said your brother had tricked him into giving him a large sum of money he could ill afford." She could still remember how appalled she'd been at what she'd learned.

"Liam wouldn't do that."

"I'm afraid he did," she said with total conviction.

"He had his own money. He didn't need anyone else's."

She tilted her head. "Didn't he invest in a failed theme park up north?" It had been in all the papers recently. She even remembered Liam's name in particular because of his death.

Now, *that* appeared to get Adam Roth's attention.

"Go on."

The air was tight with tension, but Jenna couldn't let trepidation get to her. "Around two years ago Stewart met Liam at a function and—"

"What function?" Adam fired at her.

She tried to think, but it was hard with him staring her down like this. "I don't know. Stewart didn't say."

Adam's brows drew together, then he murmured, "That's around the time my brother found out he was sick."

"I know," she said quietly, feeling bad for bringing all this up again. "But that doesn't change anything. Your brother still took the money."

His mouth flattened. "I'm not convinced."

Jenna hated this. As far as she was concerned she shouldn't have to convince him of anything. It just *was*.

"I believe they discussed the theme park venture and Liam assured him it would be no risk. Foolishly, Stewart used his house as collateral and gave him three hundred thousand dollars."

Adam gave a harsh laugh. "Three hundred thousand? And he handed it over without question?"

"Stewart trusted your brother," she said, her teeth setting on edge. "I mean, he's a Roth, right? Your family's integrity is supposed to be beyond question."

"It *is* beyond question." His whole demeanor said she'd offended him.

"So where's my brother's money then? They were supposed to start building the theme park six months ago, only there were delays on top of delays. Finally the company went bust, as you would know." It was in the media. No one could have missed it, nor the fact that Liam had been one of the investors, notwithstanding being terminally ill at the time. "My brother believes that Liam took the money under false pretenses, and so do I. Your family owes it to Stewart to repay the full amount."

His gaze sliced over her. "Where's your brother now?"

"He's an architect. He's gone off to the Middle East to try and earn some fast money so he won't lose his family home. Fortunately, he's managed to keep up his house payments until recently, but now…" Her heart constricted with pain. "*And* he's got a wife and two small children who are missing him badly. They want him home, but he won't return until he has enough to keep the bank happy and to stop him from losing the house."

The worst thing for Jenna was not being able to talk to anyone about this. She'd been keeping it all to herself. Both her parents and Stewart's wife thought he'd simply gone overseas to pay off his house sooner. Poor Vicki had no idea she was at risk of losing their gorgeous family home of which she was so proud.

"Why didn't he come to me himself?" Adam asked. "Surely you shouldn't have to do your brother's dirty work for him?"

She didn't appreciate his tone. "Stewart said it was no use talking to your family about it because you'd close ranks anyway." She studied his hostility. "I see what he means." Stewart had been a total mess that day at her place, and she wouldn't have him worrying over her involvement in this now. She'd get it sorted first.

He fixed her with an intense stare. "There's a legal system in place to protect him. Has he started proceedings?"

"How can he do that? He doesn't have the money. And besides, he had to find a way to stop his wife and children from being thrown out on the street *now*. Once he gets that sorted, you can bet he'll be back to take you to court." Her lips twisted. "Not that it would do him much good. No doubt your legal team will find a way to evade paying up in the end."

A muscle ticked in his cheekbone. "I don't take kindly to insults to my family."

"That's a shame," she mocked, then felt a twinge of conscience. Usually she didn't have a nasty bone in her body, but after what this man's late brother had done to Stewart, she knew she couldn't back down.

"What do you want me to do about it?"

She steeled herself. "Give him his money so he can come back and be with his family."

"I'm expected to hand over three hundred thousand dollars on the word of you and your brother?" He gave a terse laugh.

"It would save a lot of trouble...and embarrassment for your family."

He shot her a chilled look. "Don't try and blackmail me, Ms. Branson."

He could be as formal as he liked, but it didn't change anything. "It's not blackmail. It's a promise."

She'd never suspected she would have the heart, but if she had to, she would find a way to take this to his parents or to his older brother, Dominic, who'd recently married Liam's widow, Cassandra. She prayed she didn't have to. Yet thinking about it, she knew Adam was definitely the one most approachable over such a matter, regardless of the ice-cold look he was giving her at this precise moment.

"If you do anything to upset my parents," he warned, sending a shiver under her skin that had nothing to do with the coolness of the room, "I'll make you pay and pay dearly."

She held her ground. "Then why not *pay* my brother back his money and save everyone the hassle?"

"I don't do business that way."

"Obviously."

He watched her in silence, then his look turned as sleek

as silk. "I see Roberto and Carmen think highly of you." His tone was idle, but she knew better.

"Yes." All at once she could feel her control of the situation slipping away, but had no idea how to get out of it.

"And Marco wants you."

"That's not my problem."

"I see." He offered her a sudden, satisfied smile that didn't reach his eyes. "I wonder if Roberto would be interested in knowing one of his employees is taking advantage of his hospitality today for her own purposes?"

She glared at him. "*Now* who's blackmailing whom?"

His shoulders rose and fell. "I'm just saying that if I let it be known I'm not happy, then you'll lose your job. I doubt you'll get another one with such a prestigious company."

A lump wedged in her throat. "I get your point, but it doesn't change a thing. If you don't do right by my brother, *I* won't do right by you and your family."

A hint of admiration entered his eyes. "I like your style. You don't back down much."

She angled her chin at him. "I'd like to think I don't back down at all."

His lips twitched, then he sobered. "I need time to investigate this claim of yours to see if it's bogus or not."

"It's not bogus."

"Then humor me and let me go through the motions." He considered her with slow deliberation, and something stirred inside her. "In the meantime you could do me a favor."

She stiffened. "*Me* do *you* a favor? I don't see how I could do that, and I don't see why I should anyway."

"Let me finish," he chided, a warning light in his eyes. "I need a…female companion."

She looked at him in utter disbelief. "You want me to

become your *mistress?*" She'd heard of things like this happening, but—

"No, I want you to be my companion for a few weeks."

The thought still staggered her. "No, absolutely not."

"No?"

"I won't do it. I'd rather go to the media and let them sort you out."

"Don't forget there are always two sides to every story, Jenna. I have family I love and so do you, apparently. We don't want to see them hurt any more than they have been." He assessed her with narrowing eyes. "Do we?"

She released a shaky breath. "No, we don't."

"Then let's make a truce," he said, looking pleased by her answer. "I'll look into the situation about the money, but you've got to promise me a few weeks of your time."

She blinked. "Why me?"

"That's a fair question…." They heard voices outside in the corridor as people walked past. "But not one I want to talk about right now. Are you free for dinner this evening?"

"I suppose so," she said, but her stomach was dipping as if she was on a roller coaster.

"What a refreshing attitude."

"Get used to it."

He ignored that as he handed her a business card. "Call that number on the back and give them your address. A driver will pick you up at eight and bring you to my apartment."

"I have my own car. And I'd prefer to go to a restaurant if you don't mind."

"And I'd prefer to talk in the privacy of my own home." He reached for the door handle. "My driver's available. Use him." Then, giving her one last look, he left the storeroom, closing the door behind him again.

She stood there for a few minutes, catching her breath and thinking over what had just occurred. Somehow he'd turned the tables on her and now she had to consider his ludicrous proposition. His companion for a couple of weeks? He said it wasn't as his mistress, but was she being naive? Surely he knew other women who would be better suited to such a task. Some would probably even see sex as a free perk.

Why her?

Truth be told, she was intrigued and a little flattered, but she still didn't intend to take him up on such an outrageous offer. She'd go to dinner if that's what he wanted. She'd even listen to what he had to say, if it was the only way she would see any of Stewart's money, but that was all she'd do.

Looking down at the card in her hand, she realized too late she'd have to use his car service tonight after all. He hadn't given her his address and she wouldn't be able to get there otherwise. It galled her that he'd think she would easily do his bidding, but needs must.

Her resolve firmly in place, she left the storeroom and took a few steps to go back to the corporate box, but decided she couldn't face any of them a moment more this afternoon. She already had her purse, so she left a message at the hospitality desk thanking her hosts but telling them she had a headache and it was best she go home. Her boss and his wife should understand, and she doubted Marco would even realize she'd gone.

Something told her that Adam Roth wouldn't be so forgiving in his place.

Two

Adam finished dressing, then glanced at his gold watch as he slipped it back on his wrist. Seven-thirty. Jenna Branson would be here soon.

She hadn't come back to the corporate box after their discussion in the storeroom, yet he knew she had gumption, that one. Beautiful and a sexy challenge, he would enjoy spending the next month with her, but it had been her unrelenting attitude this afternoon that had him conceiving an idea to sort out a major hassle in his life. With his best friend's wife showing clear signs of having "the hots" for him, he was becoming increasingly concerned. How long before Chelsea gave herself away in front of Todd? He couldn't let that happen, not for his friend's sake, nor his own.

Right now he needed someone like Jenna. Someone who could stand up for herself, but not get emotionally involved. Someone who at the end of the month would leave without having to be asked. Oh, yeah, she would definitely be happy to walk away from him. She was so unlike some of the women he knew, who preferred to simper and do his bidding at the click of his fingers and were more a pain in the butt than not.

Of course, not all the women he knew were like that. There were some he admired, like his sister-in-law Cassandra, who reminded him very much of his mother. Both women had the same sense of compassion and integrity, yet fought for what they believed in. Both women put their family first. He liked that in a person whether they were male or female.

Family was family.

And keep your enemies close, he reminded himself, as he left his bedroom and went into the open-plan living room. Jenna Branson was the enemy, when all was said and done. She could cause immense anguish for his parents if she pursued the avenue that Liam had conned her brother out of a large sum of money.

The problem was that he *wasn't* sure Liam hadn't done such a thing. He missed his younger brother terribly, and heaven knew Liam hadn't deserved to die so young, but if anyone had gone through life taking what he wanted, it had been Liam.

That wasn't to say his brother would have conned this Stewart Branson out of his money. Liam hadn't been a con man. But he *had* tried to get others to invest money in the theme park, unable to see it hadn't been a good investment. Along with Dominic, Adam had tried to convince their brother not to go ahead with it. It had been just before the diagnosis of his illness, but as far as he knew, Liam had still invested in the theme park, though thankfully it had only been a quarter of a million dollars, not the half a million he'd originally planned on.

And all that left a question unanswered, settling a hard knot in his stomach. Who was to say Liam hadn't convinced Jenna's brother to invest money, as well? And the fool may well have gone and done it. Until *he* discovered the truth he wouldn't rest.

Jenna Branson needn't know that.

Just then the concierge phoned to say Jenna was on her way up to the penthouse, and Adam felt a kick of excitement as he went to meet her at the private elevator. Curbing his desire while keeping her close was certainly going to be a challenge. One he would enjoy.

The elevator doors slid open with a soft ping and inside stood a stunningly lovely woman in a black dress, her long legs tapering down to high-heeled shoes. With her hair back in a chignon and her exquisitely smooth features, she was even lovelier than he remembered. He made a decision then. He didn't need to pressure any woman into being his mistress, but if this willowy brunette wanted more, he wouldn't say no.

"You obviously had enough time to make yourself beautiful," he murmured, as she stepped onto the plush carpet inside his apartment.

The hint of a blush enchanted him as she came closer.

She gave a thin smile. "You should save the compliments for the real women in your life, Adam."

"You're not real?" He liked the sound of his name on her lips.

She stopped a few feet away. "I'm your worst nightmare."

Laughter escaped from him. "No woman's ever told me that before."

"Just goes to show there's always a first time."

He let his amusement slide, then paused deliberately. "I've got to agree there. The first time is *always* special."

Something wavered in her eyes before she stepped past him. He caught the captivating scent of her perfume as she moved. Midnight Poison, if he wasn't mistaken. Its seductiveness…its name…suited her.

"Nice place you have here," she said a few moments later, glancing around the luxurious surroundings, giving him glimpses of her back view that were equally as eye-catching as her front. "Very tasteful." She turned and shot him a wry look. "I'm surprised though. I thought you'd at least have an *Arabian Nights* theme. For your harem, that is."

He chuckled. "This is my nonharem apartment." He saw her lips curve up at the corners. "Good. You can smile."

Her smile instantly disappeared. "Don't get used to it. I usually only smile for the people I like."

"Then you must like me," he mocked, enjoying verbally fencing with this woman. *Really* enjoying it. She was a breath of fresh air.

Her mouth quirked some more but she turned away and placed her purse on the coffee table. When she looked back, she was serious again. "Shall we get down to business?"

"Let's have a drink before dinner." He headed for the bar. "White wine okay?" he said over his shoulder.

There was a tiny silence. "Um…yes, thank you."

He could feel her eyes on him. He knew the effect he had on women, but this woman's mixture of coolness and reluctant responsiveness wasn't something he'd previously encountered. He was intrigued.

Carrying two flutes of wine toward her, he handed her one. "Come outside and look at the view."

"I've seen it before."

He cupped her elbow with his free hand, her skin soft beneath his palm. "Not from my balcony you haven't."

On the balcony he pointed out places of interest. "There's

the Royal Botanic Gardens over there," he said, moving closer, feeling her inch away, oddly pleased by her reaction. "And the Dandenong Ranges way over there." He moved closer again.

"Stop testing me, Adam."

She was astute, this one. "Is that what I was doing?"

"You know very well you are. And I don't appreciate it," she said, a pulse hammering at the base of her throat. Yet she didn't move away. Jenna stood her ground and he realized she meant it. He sensed there was a part of her that wanted him, but she wasn't going to take it further. It was a new experience for him. Not even Maddie had—

The old pain kicked in. Maddie was long gone. Nearly five years in fact. Their child would have been four, if their unborn baby hadn't died along with its mother.

He shoved aside his thoughts. His world had moved on. "Let's eat," he rasped, twisting on his heels and going back inside the apartment, putting one foot in front of the other like he always did when the grief got to him. He heard her follow him, but he concentrated on going into the kitchen, getting the first course that his housekeeper had left in the refrigerator.

By the time he carried two plates of chicken and mango salad into the dining area, he was back in total control. Soon he was sitting opposite her at the table while they enjoyed their meal. Well, *he* was enjoying it. She was picking.

"You don't like the food?"

"It's fine." She cast him a candid look. "I just don't like being here, that's all."

Adam felt a flash of irritation. Her reluctance was beginning to wear a little thin. Women usually clambered over each other to get an invitation to his apartment.

And into his bed.

He took a sip of wine. "Tell me about your family."

Her eyes flashed at him as she put down her fork. "I'd prefer you tell me why you want me to be your...companion for a month. That *is* why you asked me here tonight."

"It might help me get a clearer picture of your brother," he pointed out, used to setting the pace.

She pressed her lips together, but relented. "My parents are alive and well and have just retired. Then there's Stewart and me. Stewart's older by five years. He and his wife, Vicki, have two little girls."

As always, he had to ignore a squeezing of inner pain at the mention of someone else's children. "How old are they?"

"Five and three." She gave him a cutting stare. "Old enough to miss their father."

"I don't doubt it." He wondered if Stewart missed his kids as much as they missed him. Did the man know how lucky he was to even have them? *He* sure as hell wouldn't be leaving his own kids for months on end.

Not that he planned on having any.

Not now.

The only child in his life was his year-old niece, Nicole, whom they'd recently learned was Dominic's child through artificial insemination, and not Liam's. She was a cute little thing who adored her father, and the feeling was reciprocated. It would cut out Dominic's heart to leave her for any length of time.

And that was the reason Dominic and Cassandra had taken Nicole with them on an extended honeymoon to the family vacation home in the tropics in Far North Queensland. It was the reason *he* was now officially staying here in Melbourne to help his father run Roths, instead of traveling around the country checking on their department stores and sorting out any problems, like he usually did. He had to admit it actually felt good to stay in one place this time. Before he'd felt restless and needed to move around, but lately it hadn't seemed to be enough.

The telephone rang from across the room, jerking him from his thoughts. He didn't move. Whoever it was could call back, and if it was who he thought it would be, then she'd definitely call back.

"Aren't you going to answer it?"

"No."

It gave another ring.

Jenna looked at the phone, then at him. "Don't let me stop you."

"I won't." He couldn't help but be abrupt. He was sick to death of these phone calls. He shouldn't have to put up with it. If it wasn't for—

Just then the answering machine clicked on and a husky female voice came over the line. "Adam, this is Chelsea." There was a pause. "I'm looking for Todd and I thought he might be with you. If you could phone me back when you get in, that would be great." Another pause. "I'll be waiting," she said, almost breathlessly, then hung up.

Silence settled over the room, then Jenna arched a brow. "You didn't want to talk to her?"

"*She's* the reason I need a companion."

She tilted her head at him. "I don't understand."

Right. It was time to tell her why he needed her help. He didn't like giving a stranger information that could ruin his friendship with his best friend, but on the other hand, Chelsea was trying to ruin it anyway. He had nothing to lose. Besides, if Jenna tried to use this against him, he'd destroy her and her family. No question.

He put down his fork and leaned back in his chair. "Chelsea's married to my best friend. Todd and I have known each other since we were kids. I was best man at

his wedding last year and he was my best man when I...
got married."

"You're a widower, aren't you?"

So she knew about that. Then he grimaced inwardly. He
supposed it would be hard *not* to know it. Nothing about
his family stayed out of the media long.

"Yes. I'm a widower." He hated that term. Loathed it,
in fact. It made him sound like a damn victim. He wasn't.
He'd suffered a loss. A massive one, but he'd picked himself
up. He'd moved on.

"So, what's the problem with this Chelsea?"

He renewed his focus on the present. "Think about it.
You didn't hear anything...*personal*...in her voice just
now?"

"Of course I did. She wants you."

He grimaced. Jenna made it sound like this was an
everyday occurrence. "And she's doing everything in her
power to try and get me into bed."

She seemed to pause, then sent him an intent look. "How
long has this been going on?"

"Nothing's *going on,*" he snapped. "Not on my part
anyway."

She waved a dismissive hand. "On her part then."

Dammit, Chelsea was beginning to drive him to distraction. And not in a pleasurable way, either.

"I didn't notice anything unusual until about six
weeks ago when she suddenly started coming on to me.
I did nothing to encourage her. I'm still doing nothing
to encourage her, but it doesn't seem to be helping." He
expelled a long breath. "Trouble is I really liked her before
that, too. I thought she was good for Todd."

"She's attractive?"

"Yeah, she's attractive but she's my best friend's *wife,*

Jenna. I certainly don't find the prospect of cheating on my friend to be desirable, either."

A curious look passed over her face. "I'm surprised. I thought—" She broke it off there.

"What? That I'm the type of man to break up a marriage?" His lips twisted. "Thanks very much," he said in disgust.

"You *do* have a reputation for being a playboy."

"With single women. I stay away from the married ones. That's my policy."

"Good policy," she said, and he wasn't sure if she was being sarcastic or not. "But Chelsea might not know that."

"She should," he snapped. "I've made it more than clear that I only date single women."

"You may *think* you have but—"

He scowled. "Whose side are you on anyway?"

She set her chin in a defiant line. "No one's. Not this Chelsea's and certainly not yours."

Tension gripped his shoulders, but he forcibly made them relax. "Okay, that's obvious. But getting back to the point, Chelsea hasn't come right out and said anything to me yet but she's definitely on the prowl. I need to stop this before it goes much further. I don't want her doing something she'll regret."

She acknowledged his words with a dip of her head. "Does Todd know any of this?"

"Hell, no. It would rip him apart. He really does love his wife. If I tell him what I suspect she's up to, she'll just deny it and then I'll be the one who loses a damn good friend."

She appeared to soak that up. Then her eyes narrowed. "So you want me to pretend to be your mistress for a few weeks?"

"Companion," he corrected. *For now.* "And make it a month."

Her eyes widened. "A month?" She immediately shook her head. "No way. Besides, being your companion won't work. No woman in her right mind would have a platonic relationship with *you*. Chelsea knows that. She'll suspect something's amiss."

"Fine, you can be my pretend mistress then," he said, pleased whatever way she called it. "If she thinks I'm involved with you, she might back off."

"And if she doesn't?" Jenna challenged.

"Either way, I lose." And that wasn't something he was familiar with. "If she continues to make a pest of herself, then Todd is going to realize it sooner or later, and part of him is going to blame me even if he knows I had nothing to do with it. I don't want it to get to that stage." Todd was the only one to eventually get through to him after Maddie's death. "He helped me a great deal when I needed him. I wouldn't repay him by doing the dirty on him and sleeping with his wife."

Their eyes met but Adam didn't look away. He wasn't one to talk about it, but he wasn't ashamed of needing his friend, either. Not after losing a loved one. *Two* loved ones, he thought, including the loss of his unborn child.

Jenna picked up her glass, took a sip of wine, then her gaze settled on him. "I'll ask the question I asked this afternoon at the races. Why me?"

He'd be disappointed in her if she hadn't asked the question again. "You're different. There's no emotional involvement between us." She went to speak and he held up his hand. "Except maybe dislike on your part," he mocked.

"True."

He gave a thin smile. "And at the end of four weeks, we don't have to worry about seeing each other again."

"And you don't have to worry about running into me," she mused, half to herself.

"There is that," he conceded.

Her eyes watched him, a hopeful light in them she was trying not to show, unsuccessfully. "So if I agree to this, you'll do what you promised to do? You'll investigate my claim?"

He leaned back in his chair and nodded. "Just as soon as we make an appearance together at the Mayoral Ball next Friday night. The month starts from then."

Her eyes went wide. "But today's only Saturday. That's a whole week away."

"Disappointed?"

She made a derisive sound. "Only because I want to get started straight away."

He shrugged. "Regrettably, you'll have to wait. I'm flying to Sydney tomorrow for a three-day conference, and I won't be back until Thursday morning." This was one conference he had to attend to keep on top of things with their competitors. His father would hold down the fort here, though his parents needed to go to Brisbane Thursday afternoon, leaving *him* to represent the family at the ball on Friday night.

"So you won't start the investigation before then?" she asked matter-of-factly, but he knew otherwise. "Don't you trust me to keep to my word?"

"Never trust a woman with a grudge."

"I've found you should never trust a man. Period."

He lifted one brow. "Someone I know?"

Her eyes took on a wary look. "I doubt it."

Was it a trick of the light or did she somehow look vulnerable? It made him wonder what fool had given her up. Then again, some men could only take so much of that deliciously smart mouth.

And some men liked to live dangerously.

Three

Jenna spent the next few days wondering what she'd gotten herself into by agreeing to be Adam Roth's pretend mistress. She didn't know how she was going to do this. It would mean spending a small amount of time in private with him, and a whole lot of time in public. Standing close. Touching him. Smiling. Acting like she was enamored with him.

Fat chance!

Dammit, there was already something between them that she didn't want to recognize. An awareness of each other that greatly disturbed her peace of mind. It distracted her when all she wanted to do was focus on the very reason they were together.

He'd just better keep to his end of the bargain or he was in for a big shock. He would deserve everything he got after that. She would take this to the media if necessary. She prayed she didn't have to. She didn't like being the bad guy in this, not when that title belonged to the late Liam Roth.

Yet her curiosity was piqued by all this with Chelsea and Todd. Adam had to be stuck between a rock and a hard place or he wouldn't have confided in her. He wouldn't risk her knowing such a thing. That at least gave her the confidence to believe he would do as he said.

Actually, she was amazed he had any scruples at all, and especially when it came to his best friend's wife. No doubt it was the *only* scruple he had, she mused, then decided that wasn't quite fair of her. He clearly loved his family. She could even understand him protecting his dead brother and the family name. She just didn't like that it was at *her* family's expense.

Of course there *was* one man she knew who definitely had no scruples at all, and she faced him at work on Monday morning, after apologizing to his father for her abrupt departure at the races. Roberto had been fine about it, but she had a hard time convincing Marco Conti that she'd left because of a headache and not because she'd seen him chatting up another woman and had been jealous. The man's ego was colossal, making it difficult to refuse his invitation to go to dinner with him the following Friday night. In the end, she had to tell him she already had another engagement, and for those few minutes she was thankful that was true. It was the only time she wanted to thank Adam Roth for anything.

And then Friday evening arrived and it was seven o'clock and her apartment doorbell was ringing. She hurried to check through the peephole before answering it, thinking it was Adam's driver come to escort her down to the car.

It wasn't.

It was Adam himself.

Her heart picked up pace as she patted her chignon, then

smoothed her hands down her evening dress and checked herself in the hall mirror. It would be her little secret that she'd found this dress tucked away in a secondhand store. She hadn't the money to buy a fancy new dress, not after what she'd spent on a dress for the races. And the two evening gowns she owned from when she dated Lewis weren't suitable, either. One was more for winter and the other had a wine stain on the bodice the dry cleaner hadn't been able to remove. Thankfully, dry-cleaning this secondhand dress had really brought out its depth of color.

Taking a deep breath, Jenna opened the door. She hadn't seen Adam since last Saturday night, and in his black tuxedo he looked superb and even more attractive than she remembered, if that were possible. Pictures in the newspaper hadn't done him justice, and neither had the color ones in magazines. In the flesh, the man had a serious case of handsome.

Then she realized he was standing there, his masculine appreciation spilling over her in the off-the-shoulder chiffon gown the color of deep blue sapphires. She knew she looked nice and she was pleased with that, but her aim had been to hold her head high next to Chelsea, not to draw this man's attention to herself.

Unsettled, she swung away to the living room. "I'll get my purse," she said, hoping her voice sounded even. She didn't invite him inside. She would only be a moment.

"Well, that's another first," he drawled as he followed her into the apartment and closed the door.

"What's that?" Heart thumping, she continued over to the coffee table.

"You didn't allow me to compliment you on your appearance."

She picked up her clutch purse, feigning indifference. "Was I supposed to?"

"Most women do."

"I'm not most women."

"I'm beginning to believe you're right." He paused. "But let me compliment you anyway," he murmured, his eyes darkening. "You really do look lovely tonight."

Her cheeks grew warm, but she had to remember he wasn't being nice out of the kindness of his heart. He had a motive for everything he did. "Thank you." She stepped toward him, feeling the need to get out of the apartment before—

"Did you design that necklace?"

The question stopped her in front of him, her hand going to the jewelry at her throat. "Yes. It's one of my own."

He nodded. "You'll definitely be a hit with Chelsea then. She loves jewelry."

"I'm so pleased we'll have something in common," she mocked. "Apart from you, that is."

He didn't smile.

His eyes said come closer.

Without warning Adam slipped his arm around her waist and brought her up against him, those eyes filling with purpose. "Here's one thing she *won't* have in common with you," he murmured, and brought his head down to hers.

Shock tingled through her veins and she opened her mouth, thinking to speak, but his tongue took advantage of the moment and silkily plunged inside. Her breath caught, then looped around her throat, but she couldn't seem to break free. His tongue savored the softness, the hollows, skillfully sapping her of strength until she felt like a swizzle stick swirling round and round, until she had to reach out and cling to him to stop from sinking to the ground.

He broke off the kiss and slowly peeled back. "We

needed to look like lovers," he said, his voice husky but in control.

Reality kicked in. It was clear he had enjoyed the kiss, but it hadn't shaken him up like it had her. God, his kiss had relegated every other kiss she'd ever had to the back of her mind, but he didn't need to know that. He might suspect it, but she'd never admit it. She had her pride.

Gathering herself, she quickly moved back out of reach. "You didn't need to kiss me for that. There's no one around."

"Didn't I?"

Another of his little tests, she realized, aware this really was more about him taking what he wanted than him wanting to give the impression they were lovers. Needless to say though, the hint of red lipstick at one corner of his mouth wouldn't go astray, she decided cynically, tempted to rub it off with her finger, but she didn't dare.

She raised her chin. "You're a good kisser, I'll grant you that," she said, trying to come across as worldly-wise and experienced, while totally ignoring her complete and utter meltdown in his arms.

"I'm glad you think so," he said smoothly, looking confident, arrogant and very self-satisfied.

Oh, he knew all right.

"No doubt you've had plenty of practice."

"I aim to please."

"How nice," she said sweetly, taking a step around him.

He moved in front of her, forcing her to stop. "What about you, Jenna?"

"Me?" Was he asking if she aimed to please? Please who? *Him?*

"Have you had plenty of practice kissing a man?" he

asked, clarifying, though she wasn't sure which question was more dangerous.

"That's *my* business." Suddenly the slight sting of her ex-boyfriend's comment about her "lacking" in some areas came to mind. "Why are you asking? Wasn't I any good?" she said without thinking, then could have kicked herself for giving anything away.

His eyes held a gleam of speculation. "You were superb," he assured her.

A shade of relief washed over her. Not for his sake, but for hers. "Good. I'd hate to think you were disappointed in my performance."

He considered her, and this time the gleam was a definite curiosity. "Why? Has someone been disappointed in your... performance before?"

She stiffened. "That's a very personal question."

His gaze intensified, then as if it didn't really matter, he shrugged. "Forget it." He looked at his watch. "We'd better get going," he said, all businesslike now, but she was sure he saw more than he was letting on.

All at once she felt like she was up against Goliath in the sexual stakes. She brushed past him toward the door, needing to get out of the apartment, where a sort of magnetic energy appeared to be bouncing off the walls. No, make that *magnetism*. The word summed up Adam Roth to perfection.

In the back of the limousine, Adam apologized before answering a call on his cell phone, saying it was important. Jenna didn't mind. She was merely grateful they didn't need to talk. That kiss back there had turned her upside down and she was still stunned by her reaction to a man she'd only recently met. It had been an excuse to create a sense of intimacy, but it had worked too well.

Trying to put it from her mind, she stared through the

side window and blocked out Adam's voice. She wasn't thrilled about being here, but at least her family was delighted, she mused. Telling them about her date tonight hadn't been something she'd wanted to do, but she'd had to preempt them seeing her picture in the papers with Adam over the next month. That meant earlier in the week she'd told her parents and her sister-in-law how he'd asked her to the Mayoral Ball, deciding she would field any future questions about him only as required. Unfortunately she couldn't do anything about them getting their hopes up over what was merely a smoke screen.

She'd had a very specific reason for telling them, of course. Stewart would have a heart attack if he suspected what she was doing on his behalf, so she'd asked them not to mention anything to her brother about Adam, asking them to keep it all low-key in general. She'd pointed out that Stewart was protective of her and how he'd worry if he knew she was dating another playboy. Her brother had certainly been vocal enough about her involvement with Lewis, and it hadn't been too hard for them to believe this would upset him.

Adam ended the call just as they arrived. He apologized again, this time with a charming smile that in the confines of the car pronounced his magnetism even more.

Jenna searched for something to say. "Are your parents going to be here tonight?"

"No, I'm attending on their behalf. They had a previous commitment."

"I suppose one Mayoral Ball is the same as another," she said unthinkingly.

"It does get a bit like that," he agreed, with a ghost of a smile. Then a worried look entered his eyes. "Regrettably my uncle needed to go for some medical tests. My parents thought their time better spent in Brisbane supporting him."

She winced at her own prejudgment. "That's very good of them."

"He's family," was all Adam said as the limousine glided to a stop near the Town Hall.

Luckily the Lord Mayor and Lady Mayoress's arrival ahead of them had the small media contingent focusing there, and Jenna was pleased when she and Adam were able to blend in with others and make their way inside the building without anyone taking notice.

The Melbourne Town Hall was a magnificent building well over a hundred years old, and it had taken her breath away the few times she'd been here. Every inch of it was regal and majestic, from the grandeur of the main staircase, marble foyer and glorious stained-glass windows, to the soaring ceilings crowned with chandeliers. The centerpiece of the building was the richly carved wood pipe organ that was the largest in the southern hemisphere.

The Main Hall had been decorated magnificently for the glittering event tonight, so it didn't matter that there was a slight delay in being shown to their table. But as she and Adam were being guided to the front of the room shortly after, Jenna could have groaned when she saw where they were sitting. She hadn't given it any thought before now.

"You okay?" Adam murmured in her ear.

"I didn't expect to be sitting with the Lord Mayor of Melbourne and the Lady Mayoress," she hissed.

"Don't be nervous."

"I'm sorry, but I'm not used to attending such a posh affair."

He gave a crooked smile. "They might look posh on the outside, but believe me, on the inside they're just like you and me."

"I doubt that," she muttered, then somehow managed a smile for the guests ahead.

Introductions were made to the dignitaries, though there were still a couple of vacant chairs. They were probably reserved for the Prime Minister, she thought with wry cynicism. So much for keeping a low profile. She wasn't used to quite such exalted company. For all Lewis's connections, his family would barely reach the coattails of these people.

As drinks were served, Adam leaned in close under cover of the conversation. "If it makes you feel better, just think of everyone here in their underwear," he whispered for her ears only. "We're all equal in our skin."

She moved her head back a little, and her gaze drifted up from his firm lips and into his blue eyes. Suddenly, equality took a dive. This man *had* no equal.

"Are you picturing me in my underwear yet?" he murmured, a gleam in those eyes, his head still close to hers, his cool, clean breath floating over her.

Her stomach quivered. "I—"

"Hey, Adam," a male voice interrupted. "Stop monopolizing the lady and introduce us."

Relieved at the interruption, Jenna glanced up to see a couple taking a seat at their table. The man was handsome and vaguely familiar, and the attractive blonde next to him was trying to hide her curiosity as she looked at Jenna. There was also something in the other woman's eyes...

"Hey, you have your own lady to monopolize, Todd," Adam joked, casually slipping his arm around Jenna in a proprietary gesture. So this was Todd and Chelsea. Adam appeared to be relaxed, but Jenna could feel the sudden tension in his body, and she realized this was his way of keeping the other couple at a physical distance. No doubt he didn't want to encourage Chelsea by kissing her hello, either.

But Chelsea took it into her own hands. "Adam, how *are* you?" she said, leaning down and giving him a kiss on the cheek. His lower cheek. Nearer his mouth. Jenna felt his arm tighten against her back.

He introduced her then, and Jenna became conscious of who these people actually were. Ordinary people? Not on your life. Todd was the son of a well-known real estate giant, and Chelsea's father was in steel. Wealth dripped from their family trees like liquid gold.

Good God, what had she gotten herself mixed up in? She'd known the Roths were a part of the upper classes, so she should have expected his best friends would be, as well. Now she had to pretend she was one of them. Could she do it? She glanced at Chelsea and saw that gleam in her eyes, and Jenna knew she'd give it a darn good try.

Thankfully, she didn't have to sit next to the other woman. Unfortunately, the round table gave them a clear view of each other and didn't put half as much distance between Chelsea and herself as she'd like.

After that, talk at the table was limited as a constant stream of people who came up to chat with the dignitaries. This was followed by a delicious three-course dinner, interspersed by speeches, some long, some short, some downright boring.

And polite society was…well…polite.

"So, Jenna," Chelsea said, as all the fanfare died down. "Do you live here in Melbourne?"

Jenna was just finishing the last of a dessert she didn't know how to pronounce but that was out of this world. Her appetite lost now, she nodded and kept her face blank as the inquisition began. The band had started up in the background with soft dance music but not enough to put a stop to any conversation.

Chelsea tilted her head. "I haven't seen you around before. What do you do?"

No doubt in Chelsea's crowd, a person usually *did* things that didn't involve employment. In *her* world, a person worked to survive. "I'm a jewelry designer."

"Oh?" Chelsea's gaze flicked to the necklace, but all she said was, "How lovely. Anyone we know?"

"I'm afraid not." No need to tell her she worked for Conti's. The less Chelsea knew about her, the easier things would be. Besides, it was obvious now that the other woman wasn't about to admire her design in front of the men.

Meoww…

Chelsea gave a false laugh. "Silly me. I guess if we knew your designs, then I wouldn't need to ask who you work for."

Todd looked on his wife with affection. "You're not silly, darling. You're very sweet."

"Oh, Todd," she murmured, but Jenna noticed she didn't actually look him in the eye.

Todd winked at Adam. "Don't you think my wife is sweet, Adam?" There was nothing in his glance that said he suspected anything amiss between his wife and his best friend.

Adam smiled. "Very sweet, Todd." Then he stood up and held his hand out to Jenna. "Excuse me, but I want to dance with my lady," he said, before leading her out to the middle of the floor, where he gathered her up against him, his hard body melding her curves.

Her pulse gave a rapid thud and she drew back, pretending to look up into his face but mainly needing to *not* be quite so close. "She's got it bad for you, Adam."

"Thanks. Just what I *didn't* need to hear."

"Sorry, but that woman is saccharine sweet."

"Yeah, and I'm definitely not into sweet things." One corner of his mouth lifted. "It's why I like you so much."

She had to smile. "You say such nice things to a girl."

He chuckled, his blue eyes amused. "Keep smiling, Jenna."

She reminded herself this was merely for their audience. "Like this?" she said, flashing him a brilliant smile.

He looked down at her. "Not quite. Make it dreamier. Like you mean it."

"Ahh, playacting, you mean?"

"*Now* you're getting the hang of it."

They shared another smile. A warm one this time. Then without warning his gaze slid downward and trailed along the cleave of her breasts like slow-moving fingertips. She could feel herself blush as her smile dissolved.

"Good. That's very convincing," he murmured. "Now you're acting like we're sharing an intimate moment."

She stiffened. "Am I?"

"Relax. You're spoiling it."

Her head went back farther. "*Me?* You're the one who's taking this to another level."

He pressed his hand against her upper back, guiding her head closer to his shoulder. "Shh. We look like we're arguing. Pretend you're whispering sweet nothings in my ear."

She didn't care what they looked like right then. This wasn't about acting for the others. This was about him taking advantage of the moment. "I'm not sweet, remember? And I don't *do* sweet nothings."

"Chelsea's watching us," he said softly.

"Tough."

A second ticked by before he warned silkily, "Don't forget our deal, Ms. Branson."

She caught her breath. "Don't forget Stewart" was what he was really saying. It was on the tip of her tongue to remind him of his own brother, Liam, but tit for tat wouldn't wash with him right now. It would be unwise of her not to take heed. She had to look at the bigger picture and not spoil all they'd accomplished this evening.

Somehow she forced herself to relax as she looked over his shoulder at the other dancing couples.

"That's better," he said, after a minute or two.

She immediately pulled back her head to look at him, not wanting him to think she was a timid little mouse who did what he told her to do. "By the way, why didn't you tell me who Todd and Chelsea were? I didn't know I'd have to deal with such affluent people."

He looked surprised. "I didn't think it mattered."

"It doesn't," she lied. "But it would have been nice to have been forewarned."

"You're doing well. Don't let them intimidate you." He leaned his head back to look down at her. "Remember the underwear trick," he said, giving a devilish smile.

She rolled her eyes, but she was trying *not* to think about Adam stripped down to his underwear. She automatically knew he wouldn't wear boxer shorts. No, this man would wear men's briefs, unashamedly revealing to a woman how much he could want her. The thought made her feel warmish and light-headed.

The music ended right then, and they returned to their table. She suspected her flushed cheeks would tell the others how Adam affected her, but thankfully his attention was diverted by another couple.

Jenna grabbed her purse and headed for the powder room, needing some breathing space for herself. Her cheeks had cooled by the time she sat on a stool and tucked some loose strands of hair back into her chignon. She was refreshing her lipstick in the large mirror when Chelsea entered the room. She smothered a groan. This was just what she didn't need.

The woman smiled at her as she slid onto the stool next to Jenna and started to fluff up her hair. A few more seconds then, "You and Adam look like a pair of lovebirds," she said casually, her gaze sliding across to Jenna in the mirror.

Jenna put her lipstick away as she fought to keep her expression happy. "Do we?"

"I must admit I was surprised to see you with him." Chelsea tidied another strand of her hair. "He's been going out with another woman for quite some time now."

Jenna managed to hide her surprise. Adam could have at least prepared her for that. "These things happen." She picked up her purse, about to get to her feet.

"How long have you known him?" Chelsea asked, applying some blusher now.

Jenna stayed sitting, all at once curious how far this woman was prepared to go. "Long enough," she said, giving a private little smile, seeing a flash of dismay in the other woman's eyes. "And you? How long have you known Adam, Chelsea?"

Chelsea recovered quickly. "Almost a year," she cooed. "We're still just getting to know each other."

Jenna was slightly taken aback. If she *had* been involved with Adam, she'd be quite upset by this woman's intimations. "What does that mean?" she said coolly, telling herself she was only playing a part but determined not to let this woman run roughshod over her anyway.

Chelsea blinked. "Er...nothing." She seemed horrified, almost as if she hadn't expected to be caught out. And that was probably more true than not. Who would challenge an heiress very often?

Jenna watched her pick up her purse and hurry into one of the cubicles, closing the door behind her, but she had to wonder why the woman hadn't known she was being obvious—to other people if not to her husband. Was Chelsea's world totally without accountability?

After that there was more socializing, with other people dropping by their table. Chelsea was quieter than before, and she avoided talking directly to Jenna, though her eyes would sneak to Adam whenever she thought no one was watching.

The evening slowly wound down and Jenna found she was tired of being constantly on show. She wasn't sure she'd like this life.

"Would you like to go home now?" Adam said quite loudly during a break in conversation, and though relieved, she knew he wanted others to think they were going "home" together.

"Oh, you can't!" Chelsea exclaimed, before Jenna could reply. "Come back to our place for a drink, Adam. Please."

Todd nodded. "Yes, good idea. You both should come back to our place for a nightcap. Or we can go to the casino for a few hours, if you like."

Jenna swallowed a groan. No, she didn't like. She wanted to go home to her own bed. To sleep. And to forget about these people, if only temporarily.

Adam shook his head. "Thanks, but it's getting late and Jenna and I have a full weekend coming up." He smiled at Jenna like she was the be-all and end-all of his existence.

"Oh, but—" Chelsea began.

"Darling," Todd said, putting his hand on his wife's arm. "They want to be alone."

Chelsea's face went blank. "Oh."

Todd laughed. "Don't tell me you've forgotten how that

feels?" He smiled musingly at the others. "How soon they forget."

For the first time, Jenna had the feeling that Todd was putting on a show. She didn't know why. His smile was as bright as before, his attitude as easygoing. There was just a hint of something...something deep in his eyes perhaps....

They all got up from the table together, then left in separate limousines. As they drove off, Adam pressed a button and the screen slid open. "Harry, go straight to my place," he instructed, putting his hand on Jenna's arm to silence her when she went to speak.

"Yes, Mr. Roth." The screen slid shut.

Her stomach fluttered. "I want to go home, Adam," she said firmly. This wasn't part of the deal.

"Chelsea and Todd are behind us."

"What!" She sat up straighter and twisted around. The white limousine was behind them. "Are they following us?"

"No. Their path home goes right past my apartment building. It's just our bad luck that they left at the same time as we did."

She glanced at him suspiciously in the passing street-lights, but he didn't seem to be hiding anything. "I'll catch a cab home from your place then."

"Harry will take you after you have a nightcap."

"I'd prefer to go straight home as soon as we get there." Was he up to something after all?

His eyes fixed on her. "Are you scared of coming up to my apartment?"

"No."

"Scared of me?"

"No." And if she was, she would never admit it.

He studied her, then appeared to accept her answer.

"Look, Chelsea and Todd are night owls. They could be driving around looking for someplace to go. I don't want them to see you in a cab, and I don't want to risk them seeing you inside this limo alone, either." She opened her mouth. "Yeah, even with tinted windows. It's best you wait at my place for a while. Give them time to get settled somewhere."

"Are you making this up as you go along?"

He chuckled. "No." Then he sobered. "I wish the hell I was. I know it all sounds unlikely, but just humor me this once."

She thought about that. It really was no use taking a risk, no matter how slight. And while she didn't like to think Adam would go back on his word, he might well decide to do nothing just yet about the money for Stewart. Not until she'd "paid" her dues.

In full.

She inclined her head. "I suppose I could have a small nightcap with you."

"Good."

They drove awhile. It was almost midnight and being a Friday night, St. Kilda Road was still flowing with traffic and people strolling along the streets, but she and Adam may as well have been the only ones around. Jenna could feel him on the seat next to her…could see the length of his thighs beneath the dark trousers…could inhale the scent of his aftershave…. His presence disturbed her.

She glanced at him, needing to break the silence. "Chelsea said you've been seeing another woman."

His lips firmed into a straight line. "It was over a few weeks ago."

It was hard to tell if he was annoyed with *her* for mentioning it, with Chelsea for telling her or with the other woman. Probably all three.

"She needs to get up-to-date then," Jenna reflected.

"She needs more than that," he muttered, for a moment looking like a man who'd had more than enough. His face hardened again. "Chelsea befriended Diane, who won't admit it's over between us. Unfortunately, Diane—that's the lady I was going out with—unwittingly keeps her informed. Diane has no idea Chelsea is using her for her own purposes."

She tilted her head back. "Boy, your life is a real mess, isn't it?"

He grimaced. "Yes, but not through any fault of my own." Then he gave a shrug. "All this goes with the territory, I'm afraid."

"Territory? Being a Roth, you mean?"

"Being a man," he drawled, his sense of humor reappearing.

She laughed, then suddenly a car horn blasted a good-night from Todd and Chelsea, making Jenna jump, and the white limousine went zooming past just as they arrived at the front of Adam's apartment building.

"Make yourself comfortable while I pour us that nightcap," he said, once they stepped out of the private elevator upstairs.

Jenna put her purse down on the couch and strolled onto the balcony. She wasn't planning on making herself too comfortable, certainly not in the way he might mean.

He followed her soon after, and they stood there sipping brandy and looking out on a warm autumn night that still held strong traces of summer. The building wasn't particularly high, but it was prestigious and on the main thoroughfare. From what she could tell the last time she was here, the whole of the top floor was his penthouse, with a sweeping panoramic view of the city, the bay and the mountain range in the distance.

Of course the last time she was here on the balcony, Adam had been standing much too close for her liking. She looked at him now and found him watching her with a flame flickering in those dark depths. Her breath caught high in her throat. He'd loosened his tie and he looked incredibly sexy.

"That color suits you," he murmured.

Nervously, she said the first thing that came to mind. "Vinnie's has some great things."

A crease formed between his eyebrows. "Vinnie's? I don't think I've heard of them."

She couldn't help herself. She laughed. "St. Vincent de Paul. You know, they run a lot of the secondhand stores."

His expression faltered. "You're wearing a *used* dress?"

"Unheard of in your world, no doubt," she said, oddly not taking offense. He really didn't know any better. "It's clean and they have some great stuff. Seriously, lots of people buy secondhand goods from them. It works out well all around. People have decent clothes to wear that they might not be able to afford, and the money goes back into charity."

He stood there looking at her as if she was speaking another language, and she laughed again at his confusion. This guy had no idea of the real world. Not everyone could afford caviar and champagne.

Out of the blue, his gaze intensified on her face, then dropped down to her lips. The flame returned to his eyes. She could feel her smile slip away as he slowly brought his head toward her. She couldn't seem to move, not even to put aside the glass she cradled in her hands.

He placed his lips on hers and stilled, and it was the most incredible thing she'd ever experienced. He didn't touch her with anything but his mouth, yet he was oddly touching her in other ways she didn't want to think about. How was this happening?

And then his brandy tongue nudged her lips open. She didn't resist. She couldn't, and he began long, mesmerizing slides over her. He did it in right measures too, not to tease, but exploring her...just right...so right...mouth-to-mouth as his warm breath shimmied through her, holding her suspended in time...until the moment she'd be able to take a breath on her own again.

He slowly drew back, a watchful expression about him. She took that first breath then, aware something had clicked between them. A blink later, his eyes filled with male satisfaction. Jenna stiffened, not wanting him to get the wrong impression here. She wasn't available for long kisses that lingered.

"I should slap your face."

"Mmm, kinky."

Her chin rose. "Just because I *didn't* slap your face doesn't mean I'll let you get away with it again."

Challenge flared in his eyes, then banked, his sensual mouth curving upward. "In other words, you don't want to be my mistress and I'd better not expect you to be?"

"Exactly."

"Fair enough."

She managed a snort. What the hell was he playing at?

He arched a brow. "You look surprised."

"I am. I didn't expect you'd give up so easily."

"Who said I had?" He smiled...but a moment later it was gone. "Stay the night."

"Wh-what? Didn't we just agree—"

"It's getting late. You can sleep in the spare room."

She searched his face, not sure what she was looking for precisely. "Is all this really necessary, Adam?"

"Unfortunately, yes. It's only just occurred to me, but I

wouldn't be surprised if Chelsea appears on my doorstep tomorrow morning to see if you're still here."

Unease rippled through Jenna. "There's a name for this. It's called stalking."

"It's beginning to appear that way, yet I really have no proof of anything. Every time she calls me, or even if she were to come here tomorrow, she has Todd as her excuse. Nothing she does right now would hold up in court." He grimaced. "Not that I want it to get that far."

"Maybe you might need to say something to Todd?" She wasn't sure why, but she didn't mention her suspicions that Todd might be aware of something going on with Chelsea.

"Not yet. Hopefully having you around will make her come to her senses."

"And if it doesn't?"

"I'll worry about that if it happens."

All at once, any arguments for going home didn't seem so important. She put her glass down on the small table. "I think I'd like to go to bed now," she said, then schooled her features, trying not to show how intimate that sounded.

He merely nodded, looking pleased that she was staying. "I'll find you something to sleep in."

"Thank you." She waited for him to comment, surprised when he didn't take the opportunity to make some sort of sexy remark.

"But do me a favor," he finally said. "Don't put the light on in the bedroom, just in case."

She lifted a brow. "In case?"

"In case Todd and Chelsea see it. They know the penthouse. They can see it from the road." A pulse ticked in his temple. "Bloody hell! I hate living like this."

In spite of everything, she had to have some sympathy

for him. He was used to living in a media fishbowl, but no doubt he'd always been able to rely on his close friends.

Until now.

Now his closest friend and wife were the very ones he had to keep at arm's length.

It was strange having a woman spend the night in his apartment and not in his bed, Adam mused, returning to the balcony after showing Jenna to the spare room and pouring himself another small measure of brandy. In the darkness he took a seat on the lounger until his skin cooled under the late-night breeze. It was no use going to his room and undressing. Not yet. Not with thoughts of Jenna slipping his T-shirt over her head and down her delicious body, as she would be doing right this minute.

Groaning, he told himself to push the thought to the side, but it was darn hard pushing any thoughts about Jenna to the side. She was so beautiful and had looked gorgeous in that gown tonight, whether it was secondhand or not. She'd been such an asset at the ball, holding her own with everyone, including Chelsea...including *him*. He hadn't had such an enjoyable time with a woman for a long time, especially at these affairs, where everyone was someone and no one fully relaxed from being on show.

And yet being around Jenna could never relax a man. Not unless it was in the aftermath of making love to her, and even then he suspected he'd want her again immediately too much to relax. Hell, after kissing her twice tonight, and after dancing with her, he didn't just suspect it. He *knew* he would want her again right away. No question.

God, he'd better stop thinking about her or he'd never get to bed. He needed all the sleep he could get, not just because she was in his apartment tonight, but with her being in his life for the next month. He had the feeling he was going to be sleep deprived from now on. Whether he was sexually deprived, too, was up to Jenna.

And at least there was one thing. Jenna was keeping his worries about Chelsea at bay. And that meant she was serving her purpose.

He'd chosen well.

Four

Jenna had undressed by the light of the city last night as Adam had asked, so she awoke the next morning to the full sun streaming through the glass panes. It was Saturday, but this wasn't like her usual Saturdays. She normally didn't wake in an unfamiliar bed in the apartment of a man she barely knew, wearing that man's shirt. A man it was wise to keep at a distance.

The very thought had her tossing back the blankets and sliding out of the sheets, the T-shirt she'd slipped into last night after Adam had left the room grazing her thigh. He hadn't commented on the balcony, but as he'd handed her one of his shirts, the look in his eyes said he was fully aware of what she'd be wearing to bed.

Warmth stole under her skin at the memory.

Then she spotted her evening gown draped over a chair, and reality returned. There was nothing worse than waking up and realizing you had to dress in yesterday's clothes.

At least she'd had the forethought to wash out her panties before going to bed last night, and they were now wearable again.

In the guest bathroom she showered, then brushed her teeth with a new toothbrush she found in the vanity cabinet. Thankfully she had some makeup in her purse, and she began to feel more human as she slipped her own clothes back on. After that she went to look for Adam in the main living area. If he wasn't about, she'd leave a note and take a cab home. She rather hoped he'd gone out.

It was interesting that she didn't see any photographs of Adam's late wife around the place. As much as he was in the public eye, she was discovering he was a very private person. Of course grief was a very private thing after all, she thought. She remembered hearing of the accident and thinking it a tragedy, but never in a million years would she have believed she'd meet the man, let alone pretend to be his mistress and wake up in his apartment. Life had certainly taken a turn she hadn't expected.

Nor needed.

Adam was at the breakfast bar, eating cereal and fresh fruit. He looked fresh enough to eat himself, and so damn handsome, but she pretended not to notice as she placed her purse on the coffee table.

He looked up, observed her deep blue evening dress, and furnished her a lazy smile. "Ahh, the morning after."

"Exactly," she said with a grimace.

"Yet you still manage to look gorgeous."

"A little bleary-eyed this morning, aren't we?" she mocked.

He laughed. "Did you sleep well?"

"As well as could be expected." It was amazing she'd slept at all, considering the circumstances.

"I hope you didn't feel the need to lock your door?"

"Actually, no, I didn't." She figured that if he'd been going to make a move on her, he would have pressed for more during that kiss on his balcony.

God help her, but she'd never drink brandy again without thinking of it. Of him. She was doomed to forever remember.

"Did Chelsea turn up, by any chance?" she asked. It *had* been the reason he'd asked her to sleep here last night.

His whole face became hard-edged again. "No, thank heavens. She's the last thing I need." Then he visibly forced himself to relax with a smile. "And now…about today. Are you doing anything special?"

She was suddenly wary. "It depends."

"I have to go to the Carlton Gardens this afternoon. My family is sponsoring a gardening exhibit at the Melbourne International Flower and Garden Show and I said I'd drop by while my parents are out of town. I'd like you to come with me. We can take a walk around the gardens afterward. It's quite something."

Jenna could see her leisure time over the next month being swallowed up by him and his engagements. "You didn't think to mention this before?"

His brow furrowed. "Don't you have anything to wear? We'll stop by one of the boutiques."

She made a dismissive gesture. "No, that's not the problem."

"You don't like flowers?"

"I love flowers, but that's not the point. I didn't think all this was going to take up so much of my time."

His mouth tightened. "No, the point is that it's a good idea to be seen together again after last night. It'll put us in other people's minds as a couple."

His words sank in and she sighed heavily. "I guess so."

"Your enthusiasm becomes you," he drawled.

She ignored that as her eye caught sight of the newspaper beside him. "Is there anything in that about the ball?" she said a little anxiously as she moved a few feet farther toward him.

"No. There's some pictures, but we managed to miss out this time."

"Good." Her parents and her sister-in-law might have known about her date last night, but she was still glad not to have her and Adam's picture splashed across the papers. She really wasn't interested in that kind of notoriety.

He frowned. "I assume your question means you haven't told your parents about me then?"

"I told them," she said, disabusing him of the idea. "But only about the ball. They don't know about Stewart and the money." She realized instantly her mistake in saying too much. She pulled a face. "Darn. I shouldn't have told you that."

A hint of steel momentarily glinted in his eyes. "We're in the same boat, remember. My parents don't know about it, either."

"That's true," she said, clamping down on her anxiety. They might be able to destroy each other's families, but in an odd twist, their only guarantees in protecting them were each other.

All at once he lifted his foot and drew the stool out from beside him. "Come and eat some breakfast," he said, and suddenly the focus was back on the moment again.

On them.

She looked at him, looked at the stool. If she sat down he would be right next to her. "Thanks, but I'm not really hungry."

"You'll need something in your stomach for the after-noon. You don't want to be light-headed and faint. Then you *will* be in the papers," he joked, but she had the feeling he knew why she didn't want to sit beside him.

She slid onto the stool, determined to show he didn't frighten her. "Perhaps I'll just have some fresh fruit."

"Help yourself." He indicated the platter of sliced fruit then lifted the coffeepot in a silent gesture.

She nodded. "Thanks. Did you fix all this yourself?" Somehow she couldn't see him in a kitchen peeling and slicing fruit for too long. This man belonged in the boardroom—her pulse fluttered—and the bedroom.

"No. I have a housekeeper."

Jenna concentrated on forking slices of mango and pineapple onto her plate, but she was wondering if the housekeeper had known there was someone sleeping in the spare room last night.

"Yes."

She blinked, then glanced up at Adam. "What?"

He shot her an amused glance. "Yes, my housekeeper knew someone was sleeping in the other bedroom. I had to leave her a note so she wouldn't disturb you."

He'd read her mind again. Was he clairvoyant, or was she being too obvious? She hoped it wasn't the latter.

"That would have been a novelty for her then. I'm sure the spare room doesn't get used too often around here."

He laughed softly. "Oh, yeah, you're right about that."

She couldn't help it. A smile pulled at her lips. "A novelty for you too, I imagine."

"Double 'oh, yeah.'"

She chuckled and so did he. And then his eyes snagged hers. She felt like she was being pulled into them…willingly drowning….

"Er…" She dragged herself back from the brink. "Where's your housekeeper now? Is she still here?" She'd concentrate on this.

He took a moment to answer. "She's gone to Vic Market. She wanted to get some fresh food."

Queen Victoria Market was the premier open-air market, brimming with Old World charm, but right now Jenna was having trouble getting past the husky *charm* of this man's voice.

She took a breath and focused. She assumed the woman didn't live here. That would definitely cramp Adam's style.

And then a sudden thought struck her.

"How well do you know her, Adam? I mean, if Chelsea got to Diane then she could probably get to your housekeeper. Then she might tell Chelsea we didn't sleep together last night. She could do it inadvertently."

He was shaking his head before she'd finished speaking. "No, that wouldn't happen. Sheryl has been with me for ten years. I trust her implicitly." His voice said he was firm on this. No doubts at all.

She held his gaze. With his family being in the limelight it would be hard to trust people. For him to trust his housekeeper was saying something. "I'm glad."

After they finished breakfast, Adam had to take a couple of calls and she knew it was a good time to leave. He phoned his driver to come and get her.

"Be ready at one," he said. "Harry will collect you then."

Jenna was ready as planned, dressed in a sleeveless linen dress topped with a summery jacket. She told herself it wasn't like she was the queen or anything. This was just a business event, just like her dealings with Adam were business when it came right down to it.

Still, she was nervous. If she hadn't been with Adam, she'd have worn her good pair of jeans and sneakers and roamed around the gardens with a girlfriend. Maybe she'd have even taken Vicki and the girls, or gone with her parents. Her mother and father both liked this sort of thing.

Adam must have sensed her anxiety. "Don't stress out," he whispered, as he walked her along one of the many paths in the Carlton Gardens, through an explosion of colorful exhibits and displays, toward the historic Royal Exhibition Building.

She was grateful for his arm inside the Great Hall as quite a few high profile people stopped to talk to him. The one thing she did notice now—as she had last night—was that people treated you differently when you were with a Roth. No wonder the Roth men thought they were God's gift to women. No wonder Liam had thought he was beyond reproach.

It was late afternoon before they could leave to take a walk around the outside exhibits spread over the glorious gardens. Thankfully she'd had the sense to wear comfortable, low-heeled yet stylish shoes, but trust a man not to think about her walking in high heels, she mused, as they strolled through a world of flowers and scents, past historic fountains and ornamental lakes. She glanced at him and saw him walking with his jacket thrown over his shoulder. He looked like a model for a magazine advertisement.

He caught her eye and she looked away. "The weather's perfect today," she said, pretending to admire the creativity of the exhibits, pretending *not* to notice how terrific he looked or the arm that snaked around her waist and pulled her close even as they walked. It was for show, she told herself.

"Are you glad you came?" he asked, smiling down at her.

She nodded. "Yes, I am actually." Now the formalities were over, she meant it. The fresh air, the warm sunshine and the man beside her were potent stuff. She wasn't silly enough to let down her guard completely, but for the moment, the stroll in the afternoon sunshine was making her feel pleasantly lazy.

Later as they were finally leaving the gardens, he said, "How about we go for a drink at the casino? We could have an early dinner in one of their restaurants after that."

It sounded wonderful but… "I really should go home."

"Why?"

"Do I need an excuse?" she asked, but her voice lacked conviction.

"Yes."

She smiled and he smiled back, and suddenly she knew she was in danger of completely letting her guard down today. She couldn't afford that.

She gave a shake of her head. "It's best I go home."

"Best for whom? Have dinner with me, Jenna, otherwise I'll have to dine alone." He stepped in front of her, making her stop walking. "Besides, I can't ask anyone else. Word might get back to Chelsea."

She was grateful for the young child that ran into them right then. Adam's words were a reminder that she couldn't let herself soften toward this man. For a moment she'd forgotten that their being together was for Stewart's sake, on her part at least.

"Jenna?" he reminded her, once the mother had rescued her child, leaving them alone in a dwindling crowd of people heading for the exit gates.

She faked a smile. "Okay, why not?"

He must have sensed the subtle difference in her attitude because his eyes narrowed slightly, but she didn't give him the chance to talk. She stepped around him and continued walking, and he fell into step beside her.

They ended up playing roulette at the casino for a couple

of hours. Jenna wasn't a big gambler but surprisingly she enjoyed it. Her ex-boyfriend, Lewis, had brought her here a couple of times and had once got himself half-drunk and caused a small scene. Being with Adam was different. He had total control of himself, and he seemed delighted in her excitement when she won a small amount at the table.

Around seven they strolled up the stunning black marble staircase to one of the lavish restaurants, the sound of the fountains near the entrance echoing high up the stairs. It was early and the restaurant was just starting to fill up, but the maître d' knew Adam and welcomed him with deference, then took them to an intimate table in the corner. No doubt Adam had brought many women here. But Jenna wasn't really one of them, and that was another reminder this was all a farce. One she shouldn't forget. She was wallpaper for him, that's all.

Adam nodded to someone at a table across the room, then smiled back at Jenna like she was his everything. "Good. Word should get back to Chelsea now."

She smiled tightly. "Perfect."

They ordered the meal, and once alone again he gave her another smile. "I've enjoyed spending time with you today, Jenna."

She knew this was an act for the benefit of others. "It was a nice day," was all she could manage.

His gaze rested on her. "I mean it."

She tried to steady her breathing. "Don't get comfortable with me, Adam. I'm only here with you because of my brother."

He leaned back farther in his chair, his mouth thinning slightly. "Ahh, bring it all back to that. It's good protection."

"I don't need protection from you. I can handle myself."

"Don't challenge me, Jenna."

She wanted to dare him, but something…the way he narrowed his eyes…said he was waiting for her to do just that and he didn't care right then that they were in a roomful of people.

"I wouldn't give you the satisfaction," she said, pasting on a smile when she saw the waiter returning with their drinks.

After a delicious meal that she couldn't do justice to, he took her home at a fairly early hour, insisting on walking her to her door. She felt obliged to invite him in for coffee, but her tone said she'd prefer he didn't accept.

He accepted.

"You have a nice apartment," he said, as she put the coffeepot on.

"Thanks." She turned away, concentrating on preparing the brew. He'd been here last night before the ball, though he hadn't looked at anything but her.

And then there had been that kiss….

"You own it?"

She hoped he thought the flush in her cheeks was from annoyance. "Now is that a polite question to ask?"

"I doubt I was trying to be polite," he mused.

"Yes, I forgot who I was talking to for a minute there," she scoffed, then admitted, "Yes, it's mine."

No need to tell him the loan was almost killing her in repayments. Her job paid well, but interest rates had gone up recently. If only she'd known Stewart was going to need money *before* she'd put her life savings down as a deposit. She would have rented for a while longer until her brother was paid back the money owed to him by the Roths.

She shook off her thoughts, and they had their coffee while Adam told her a story about an interior decorator he'd dated who'd once painted huge daisies on his living-room wall—in bright orange.

"You didn't like it?" Jenna joked.

His lips twisted. "There's a moral to the story. Don't break up with a woman until she's finished the decorating." He drained his cup and put it down on the table. "Now, it's Sunday tomorrow. What will you be doing?"

"Absolutely nothing." She'd already decided tomorrow was her own. "And I intend to keep it that way. Surely we can give the issue of the money a rest for one day?"

He stared hard and for a moment she thought he might argue.

Her chin lifted. "I need some time to myself, Adam," she added, not to soften him, but merely to point out why she wouldn't back down.

He took a moment to nod, then he pushed to his feet. "Okay. I understand."

She blinked in surprise. "You do?"

"We all need space sometimes." He leaned toward her, kissed her cheek and headed for the door. "I'll call you." He shut the door quietly behind him.

She was alone.

"I'm sure you will," she murmured in the silent apartment.

On Monday morning Adam was just finishing up some work when Dominic's personal assistant announced Todd was there to see him. He groaned inwardly. His friend didn't stop by the Roth offices too often. "Send him in, thanks, Janice."

Todd strolled in, looking the easygoing but confident businessman. "I see you're still doing Dominic's job."

"He's not due back from his honeymoon for another ten days."

Todd shook his head in bemusement. "Your brother only got married a couple of months ago and already he's taking another honeymoon. Sounds like things are turning out well for him."

Adam agreed. Yet it hadn't been so easy for his older brother. "I know, but things were...awkward between him and Cassandra at first. Now they've found they love each other, they wanted some time alone together with Nicole."

Todd's face sobered. "Yeah, I know. Liam's death certainly made an impact on everyone." His friend didn't know the half of it, Adam mused, knowing he couldn't tell him about Liam's involvement with Stewart Branson. The less anyone knew the better. "So I'm helping Dad run the show. He and Mum should be back from Brisbane tomorrow, as well."

"Good. That'll give you a clear weekend coming up."

Adam grew wary. "Why?"

"Chelsea and I are having a housewarming party at our new vacation home in the Grampians. We want you to come for the weekend. I assume you'll bring Jenna. Actually, Chelsea *insists* on you bringing her. Chels really liked her."

Adam had to bite his tongue. "Did she?"

"You know how Chels is. When she takes a liking to someone she almost kills them with kindness."

Adam *really* had to bite his tongue. "Yes, I know."

Todd looked pleased. "So you and Jenna will come?"

"I'm not sure," he began, seeing disappointment dawn in his friend's eyes. "Jenna may have something else planned," he said, more to give himself time to think about this. Spending a whole weekend with him might tip Chelsea over the edge, and that thought was far from egotistical.

"You and Jenna *have* to come, Adam," Todd said quickly,

then grimaced. "I think Chelsea needs to be around people she likes right now."

Adam went on full alert. "Why?"

Todd shrugged. "She's been a bit down lately."

"About?" God, if Chelsea had put her marriage at risk...

He seemed to hesitate. "She's had some...problems. It's just women's stuff, but you know how it goes."

Adam had the feeling there was something more to this, though suddenly he didn't get the impression it had anything to do with *him*. Thank God! Were Todd and Chelsea having marriage problems? Was the openness between them simply for show?

Todd cleared his throat. "I'd really like you there, Adam."

Adam considered his friend. If this was important to Todd, then he'd go. He nodded. "I'll see what I can do."

Todd's relief was evident.

After he left, Adam sat at the desk and twirled the gold pen in his fingers. He remembered Todd coming around to his apartment after Maddie died, making sure he was okay, then forcing him to get up and get dressed, forcing him to eat. Todd had been there for him every day when he'd been at the lowest point of his life. No one else had been able to get through to him. Todd had been the only one.

All at once he knew that even if there was something going on between Todd and Chelsea now, he wouldn't tell Jenna just yet. Otherwise she might think that he'd accept her as his companion for less than the agreed month. Whether the money issue was resolved between them soon or not, whether the issue with Chelsea was resolved quicker than expected, he still wanted to have his full month with Jenna Branson. And that's what he would have.

* * *

"Well, well, you're a dark horse, aren't you?" Marco Conti murmured, coming into the room where Jenna was working on Monday morning.

She tried not to react to the slimy glint in his eyes. How on earth Roberto and Carmen Conti had parented such a son, she didn't know. Love was certainly blind in this case. In their minds, Marco could do no wrong.

"What do you mean, Marco?" she asked, picking up a small pair of pliers and continuing working.

"First you dump me at the races last weekend, and then I hear you attended the Mayoral Ball with none other than Adam Roth. *Then* I hear you were seen at the flower show with him on Saturday."

"So?" This guy had been busy.

"There's more to you than meets the eye, *cara mia*."

She looked up. "Marco, who I go out with is none of your business. And I didn't dump you at the races. I *wasn't* your date."

Something dark crossed his face, then vanished. "You could do worse than catching a Roth."

"I don't think Adam would appreciate that comment," she said without thinking, and was surprised to see Marco cringe.

He recovered and gave a smarmy smile. "I was only joking, Jenna. That's all I was doing." A tiny pause. "You have no need to tell him what I said."

So…Marco was actually intimidated by something. Interesting.

Jenna could care less. She just wanted Marco out of her hair. "No, he doesn't need to know." An impish urge took hold of her. "But I'd appreciate if any gossip you hear you don't pass on here at work. I don't want people to feel awkward with me. I'm sure Adam would appreciate knowing you're helping me."

Marco drew himself up. "Of course."

She breathed a deep sigh of relief when he left. Not only had she got him off her back, but to him he had saved face by conceding to a Roth. She felt pleased with herself to have outwitted him.

Her self-congratulations didn't last, though, not when everything seemed to keep coming back to Adam. She was on edge about her next "gig" with him, whenever that would be. No doubt she would have to accompany him to a whole series of events he needed to attend over the coming weeks.

It didn't help that her mother had called yesterday morning to ask if she'd enjoyed the Mayoral Ball. Jenna had tried to sound enthused, while evading saying too much about the man she'd attended with. It hadn't helped that her parents had been about to head out to the flower show, which left no option but to admit she'd been the day before. With Adam? Yes, Jenna had replied. The brief silence that had come down the line had been telling, and she'd hurriedly reminded her mother not to say anything to Stewart.

This was all getting very trying very fast. Please God, let the money be settled soon. Then she'd be able to break it off with Adam, and her parents wouldn't be too concerned if she told them he hadn't been the one for her, and that would be the end of it.

Around seven-thirty that evening, Adam dropped by her apartment. He didn't kiss her hello, but her heart still thudded when she opened the door to him.

"Would you like to go out for a drink somewhere?" he asked, stepping inside.

She closed the door behind him. "Do I have to?" He

turned around with a wry look and she wrinkled her nose. "Sorry, I didn't mean it quite like that. I'm a working girl. I don't party during the week." Actually she didn't party much at all, not even on the weekends. She must be so different from his other women friends. *Mistresses,* she corrected, reminding herself that she wasn't his mistress and didn't intend to be, so being different in this case was a good thing.

A shadow of relief crossed his face. "That's okay. I'm not really up for it myself. I just thought *you* might like to go out."

His consideration softened something inside her, even more so when she saw that he looked tired. He must have a lot to worry about right now, with his brother and father away so much, not to mention all this business about Liam. She tried not to let it get to her.

"You've just finished work by the looks of things."

He loosened his tie a little. "Yes."

"Have you eaten?"

"Not yet."

She hesitated. "Me, either. I made spaghetti bolognese and there's plenty to share if you want to stay and eat with me. It's nothing fancy."

He eyed her quizzically. "You don't mind?"

"You've been feeding me a lot lately. I guess I can repay the favor," she said wryly.

He smiled. "With an invitation like that, how can I refuse?"

She smiled back at him, then spun toward the kitchen. "Would you like a glass of wine?" she asked, pleased that at least her voice sounded normal, even if her racing pulse wasn't.

He followed her and stood in the doorway. "No thanks. If

I had alcohol right now I'd probably fall asleep." His voice lingered. "Of course, then you'd have to put me to bed."

She peered at him, not smiling now. "Why do you say things like that? We don't have an audience."

"I like making you blush."

"I don't embarrass easily. If my cheeks are red, it's from anger," she fibbed.

The gleam in his eyes said he knew better. "I enjoy knowing I'm affecting a woman…like she affects me."

She felt heat burst into her cheeks. "Adam…" she warned.

"Do you realize you blush on and off for me? I kind of like being the switch that turns you on."

"And off," she flipped back at him. She handed him some cutlery and place mats. "Here. You can set the table over there."

He chuckled, then took the items and did as he was told. With a silent sigh of relief, she turned away and finished preparing the food. Soon they were sitting down to eat.

In contrast, Adam didn't talk much while they ate.

"That was delicious," he said, finally, putting his napkin aside after he'd cleaned his plate. Then he leaned back in his chair with an inward look. "You can be quite calming to be around."

"I can?"

His mouth tilted. "Sometimes."

"You're just tired."

He acknowledged that with a nod of his head. "I wanted to tell you something and was waiting until we'd eaten."

Her heart jumped into her throat. "You've got the money?" she said, hope rising inside her. It would solve all their problems if—

His mouth turned down at the corners. "No."

"Oh." That was somewhat disappointing, despite it still being early.

"My guys are on it now."

She nodded. It was a letdown to realize he'd kept to his word and hadn't even started looking for the money until she'd attended the ball with him. It said how much he *didn't* trust her. Of course, she didn't trust him either, so why would he be any different? There was nothing between them to trust anyway.

She held herself stiffly, preparing for what he was going to say. "What do you want to tell me then?"

"Todd stopped by my office to see me today. He and Chelsea are having a housewarming party this weekend. He wants us to come."

She considered that. "I guess it would be okay," she said slowly.

"It's in the Grampians, at their new vacation home."

"What!" She thought ahead. "That's a long drive."

"Around three hours. It'll mean staying overnight."

"In the same bedroom?"

"Yes."

"Same bed?"

"More than likely. Unless Chelsea decides to keep us apart and give us a room with twin beds, and that could be very likely," he said cynically. His gaze caught hold of her. "Would it be so awful sharing a bed with me?"

Her stomach rolled with nerves. "That's not the point, Adam."

"At least you don't deny you want me."

"I—"

"We're both adults, Jenna. We won't be hurting anyone if we take this further and sleep together."

"Making love was not part of our bargain." He was a man who'd have plenty of lovers. He had to realize by now that she didn't sleep around. "I'll come for the weekend, and I'll even share a room with you…" God help her. "But I'm *not* sleeping with you."

He gave an indifferent shrug. "Oh, well. I tried."

She didn't know if she was more disappointed that he had given up so easily, or dismayed that she was disappointed. Then she eyed him speculatively. Or had he given up? They still had to share a room together this weekend, didn't they? He was probably just playing with her.

Adam pushed to his feet. "I thought I'd drive us there myself on Saturday morning instead of Friday evening, and we can come back after lunch Sunday. That way we only have the one night to worry about sharing a bed." He smiled down at her. "Not that it's a worry to me."

After he left, Jenna lay awake until the early hours. She rather thought even one night with Adam Roth might be too much.

Way…too much.

Five

Jenna grew more apprehensive the closer they got to the Grampians National Park. She should be enjoying the richness of the deep blue sky and the picturesque rural view on either side of the highway, but being under Chelsea's watchful eyes at the Mayoral Ball a week ago had been exhausting. She couldn't shrug off the feeling that a weekend of Chelsea might prove too much.

"I'm not sure this is such a good idea, Adam."

He shot her a sideways glance. "Relax."

Relax? This wasn't just about Chelsea. With him looking so handsome in gray trousers and a black polo shirt, a woman would have to be dead to be able to relax next to him.

"Couldn't you have just told Todd no?" she had to point out. "Or said we had other plans? Perhaps you could have said you had to work. Better yet, that *I* had to work."

"You agreed to do this."

"I know, but—"

"Accept it, Jenna."

She sighed. "I suppose so."

Soon after, Adam needed a break from the driving so they stopped at a small café for coffee before getting back on the road again. They drove through historic gold-mining towns and the many wineries in the area, and the journey would have been exciting if her stomach hadn't been tied in knots. Not even the peekaboo glimpses of the Grampian Mountains in the distance eased her anxiety.

Finally, the mountains were growing closer and they were turning onto an unassuming dirt road outside one of the main towns. They traveled along it for a short distance before turning into an open gate sided by two stone pillars. The place was certainly secluded.

Jenna's eyes widened as she looked ahead to where the road ended about half a mile in the distance. "Good grief. That's their *vacation* home? That's a mansion with a capital *M*."

He looked faintly surprised. "They do a lot of entertaining."

She gave a hollow laugh. "So do lots of people, but not everyone has a vacation home like this. Most families are lucky to have one house, let alone two."

His jaw thrust forward. "I know it."

Something made her push. "I don't think you do." Undaunted, she continued, "Doesn't your family have a vacation home? Somewhere you get away from the city? Didn't I read that your family has a yacht?"

He didn't look pleased at the inquisition. "The *Lady Laura* is named after my mother." He paused. "And we have a vacation home in far north Queensland. It's on a secluded beach so that we can have some privacy."

"A tropical retreat," she mocked. "How nice. Everyone

should have one." She knew it was nerves, but she couldn't seem to stop herself from running off at the mouth.

He shot her a dark glare as he pulled up in front of the mansion. Then he cut the engine and turned to her fully. "You seem to have a problem with anyone who has money."

She went on the defensive. "When it's built on other people's money, I do."

His mouth tightened. "I know you're on edge, but do me a favor. Try not to pick an argument in front of the others."

"Or?"

"You won't like the result."

"Is that a—"

Adam's door flew open and Chelsea stuck her head in the car. "Welcome, Adam," she said, a glowing light of excitement in her eyes as she put her hand on his arm and practically pulled him from the seat.

Todd opened the passenger-side door. "Yes, welcome to our humble abode, Jenna," he said, smiling at her. "Here, let me help you out."

Jenna quickly pulled herself together and took advantage of his outstretched hand. "Thank you, Todd." Once on her feet, she glanced across the roof of the car and saw Chelsea hanging off Adam's arm like some sort of expensive accessory. Jenna had dressed in a pantsuit she thought was becoming, but up against Chelsea she felt like she should be ushering people to their seats. The only thing she was missing was a flashlight, she mused with self-derision.

Todd tucked Jenna's arm in his. "Did you have a good trip?" he asked, as the other two came around the car.

"Yes, it's a lovely drive in the country." She shot Adam a quick look that harked back to their conversation about the rich. His eyes narrowed in reply.

"Is everything okay?" Chelsea asked, evidently catching the tension in the air, looking from one to the other.

Adam smoothly extricated himself from Chelsea's clutches. "Jenna gets a little carsick at times," he explained. "Are you feeling better now, darling?" he asked with fake concern.

Jenna was sure Chelsea gave the tiniest start at the endearment, as she did herself. Goodness, if he was using endearments now she really *was* going to feel woozy.

She cleared her throat. "A little."

Chelsea soon recovered with a hopeful smile. "Perhaps you'd like to take a quick lie down before lunch then, Jenna? We won't eat for a few hours yet. We'll look after Adam, so don't you worry about that."

Jenna rather thought it was more Chelsea who would look after him. Still, she smiled gratefully and avoided Adam's eyes. "Yes, I think I *would* like to lie down," she said, needing some time away from him…from them…*all* of them. "That's if you really don't mind, Chelsea?"

The other woman beamed at her, friends for life right at this minute. "Of course not!" In one swift movement, Chelsea moved her husband aside and slipped her arm in Jenna's. "Some of the others arrived earlier, but don't feel obligated to rush. Take as long as you need."

In next to no time, they were inside the magnificent foyer and Jenna was handed over to the housekeeper. Then Chelsea and Todd took Adam off to another part of the house to meet the other guests. If she'd cared, Jenna would have smarted a little at being dumped so expertly. As it was, she could only be thankful that she was being shown to a suite with a sitting room plus a small private balcony, and that she had it to herself for now. It served Adam right for threatening her back there in the car.

Then she looked at the king-size bed.

Oh, heavens.

"Time for lunch, Jenna."

Jenna's eyelids flew open and she looked straight into Adam's eyes. She became instantly aware that his irises were blue and darker somehow. Had he been watching her? She blinked in panic and sat up, and he straightened away from the bed.

"You could have let me sleep longer," she grumbled, trying not to let him see how he affected her.

"No chance. You got away with sneaking in here before. Now I want you by my side."

She quirked an eyebrow in wry amusement. "Chelsea being a handful?"

"You could say that."

All at once she felt guilty for not being there with him. She'd agreed to help keep Chelsea at arm's length and that's what she had to do.

She swung her legs off the bed. "What's on the agenda for this afternoon?"

"Lunch and a lazy afternoon beside the pool."

Her head snapped toward him. "We're not swimming, are we? I didn't bring my swimsuit." She'd been thinking more along the lines of them all sitting around the drawing room, than prancing around the pool. She should have realized the pool would be more Chelsea and Todd's style.

"I'm sure one can be supplied."

"That's okay. I think I'll give the swimming a miss today." An imp of mischief reared its head. "Besides, I'm still feeling a little carsick from the long drive here."

He passed her an ironic look. "Then I won't swim, either. I don't want to encourage Chelsea."

Jenna nodded, relieved not to have to worry about

seeing Adam in his swimming briefs. It was just as well for Chelsea's sake, too. The other woman would eat him alive with her eyes. And Todd might notice.

"I'll just go freshen up." She went into the bathroom, having already unpacked. She'd left Adam's things for him. She wasn't any man's servant.

He had unpacked by the time she came out, and was sitting on the edge of the bed, waiting for her. She'd taken off her matching jacket before lying down, but now she wondered if she could leave it off altogether.

"Is this okay to wear?" she asked, indicating her sleeveless knit top, pants and strappy low-heeled sandals.

"You look lovely," he said huskily, pushing to his feet and coming toward her, an intent look in his eyes.

She put up her hand to stop him. "Don't even try it."

He stopped. "Try what?"

"Kissing me."

"I wasn't about to." He placed his hand on the small of her back and led her to the door. "We'd never get out of this bedroom otherwise."

They went downstairs together.

Jenna was relieved to see another six couples had been invited for the weekend. Everyone seemed very nice, and lunch in a shaded area by the pool ended up a chatty affair.

Chelsea and Todd were excellent hosts, though Jenna suspected Chelsea had brought in the other couples so no one would notice she had a thing for Adam. Jenna noticed. And a couple of times throughout the lunch, she even thought Todd was looking at his wife with an odd bleakness in his eyes. Yet he didn't appear to be watching Chelsea with Adam, and that was a relief. Something wasn't right between the other couple, but she couldn't put her finger on it.

Adam had been attentive at the Mayoral Ball, but now he took it to a new level. It wasn't exactly overkill but he made it clear to the others they were supposed to be lovers.

"Darling, here we go. Finish this off for me," he said, holding a fork up to her mouth with a small piece of Tasmanian salmon.

"No, I'd better not. I'm really quite full." She couldn't quite bring herself to use an endearment.

"But it's delicious, darling."

She could see he was enjoying paying her back for her earlier desertion. "I know. I had some already." She was aware of the others watching them.

"But I hate to waste it."

Then perhaps you could choke on it, she wanted to say, even as she gave in and let him place the fork in her mouth, somewhat surprised her gritted teeth didn't chew right through the metal.

"Good girl," he said as he withdrew the fork, his mockery for her eyes only, but also a sensuality in those depths that sent ripples under her skin.

He continued in the same vein with his dessert, then with the cheese and crackers. The hardest part for Jenna was *not* flinching whenever he touched her, and *not* blushing whenever he talked to her in that lowered voice. Crazily, after a while it gave her a strangely warm feeling having a man pay her attention like this. Lewis had been less than attentive at times.

After a suitable break, some of the others decided to go for a swim in the pool. Chelsea, with her fabulous body in front of Adam, teasingly tried to get him off the lounger to go change for a swim, while everyone laughed at her antics.

"No, I'm just too lazy today." He reached over to Jenna

lazing on the other lounger beside him and picked up her hand. "Jenna and I are just fine here."

Chelsea smiled and seemed to accept it, but Jenna thought she gave a rather childish flounce as she left to dive into the deep end of the pool. Jenna freed her hand from him as soon as she could without anyone noticing, but of course *he* noticed.

The afternoon whiled away. The staff put up large umbrellas to provide shade from the warmer autumn sunshine, and there was plenty of food and drink available. Jenna stuck to nonalcoholic drinks and she was pleased to see that Adam did, too. She had to say she enjoyed herself, and even he appeared to be relaxed…at least until Chelsea came to sit on a spare lounger near Adam and started vying for his attention in a way that could be construed as merely being sociable.

Jenna knew better.

And so did Adam, if the slight tension around his mouth was anything to go by.

So it was a relief when in late afternoon everyone got up to go and prepare for the dinner party. Of course, as Jenna followed Adam into their suite, she realized there were still some hours left before they had to go back downstairs. Suddenly, she was wary of how he might suggest they keep themselves occupied until then. Sharing that bed was out of the question.

He flopped onto the mattress and fell back against the pillows with a groan. "God, that woman exhausts me."

It dawned on her then that despite relaxing around the pool all afternoon, he hadn't really had a break from people since they'd left the city this morning. He'd been on the go all this time. "Take a nap," she suggested, feeling guilty because she'd been thinking only of herself.

He opened one eye. "You don't mind?"

"Not at all. I might go downstairs and see if I can find a book to read."

He opened two eyes. "You can't."

"Why?"

"We're supposed to be lovers. And I can tell you right now that I wouldn't be letting you out of my sight if that were true. We'd be making love."

Her stomach gave a quiver. "Then I'll go in the sitting room. There's some magazines on the table in there."

Something lurked in his eyes as he leaned up on his elbows. "You can join me here if you like."

"I don't like." She started toward the other room on legs that shook slightly.

"Pity." He collapsed on the pillows.

She glanced back at him as she left the room, seeing his eyes had closed. She was sure he was asleep as soon as the word was out of his mouth.

Instead of going straight to the magazines, she went out on the balcony and stood taking in the afternoon sun glinting on top of the hills. Her pulse took a while to settle, but eventually the superb view and sheer peace and quiet on this side of the house gave her a welcome respite after the nonstop chatter at the pool.

Whether it was the different surroundings or not, her hands began to itch and suddenly she was bursting with a new design for a pendant. If only she'd thought to bring her sketchbook, but she'd assumed she'd be too busy keeping Adam company.

Then she remembered the writing pad and pen she'd seen next to the magazines. She hurried back inside to the sitting room and sat at the small table, needing to draw while it was all so fresh and vivid in her mind.

How long she sat there she didn't know.

Not until Adam spoke behind her from the doorway. "What are you doing?"

She half twisted around to face him, sucking in a quick breath at the sight of his slightly tousled hair. He looked almost boyish...no, make that *playboy*-ish.

"I had an idea for a design."

His gaze went to the papers spread over the table. "Looks like you've drawn more than one," he said, coming into the sitting room and walking toward her.

She shrugged. "I guess I did sort of get carried away."

"Show me."

She looked down at the design she'd almost finished, then up at Adam again. "They're only rough," she said, remembering how uninterested Lewis had been in her designs.

"I'd still like to see them."

He seemed sincere, so she nodded. "Go ahead."

For the next minute he stood there studying them. She tried not to care what he'd think, but she knew she did. Finally, he looked at her with admiration. "These are really terrific."

Pleasure filled her. "You think so?" she said warmly.

"Absolutely. Roberto is very lucky to have you working for him."

"Thank you," she gushed, unable to stop herself, but it meant a great deal to hear him say that. Oh, she had full confidence in her designs, but this man had discerning tastes and she appreciated that.

Right then she caught an odd light in his eyes. She jumped to her feet. "I think I'll go take a shower." His eyes darkened and she saw his mouth open. "Alone," she preempted him.

His lips stretched into a smile. "I was merely going to say I would take a shower after you."

He might *say* that, but it wasn't what he'd been thinking, she knew, sending him a wry look before gathering up her designs and heading back into the bedroom.

Seeing the imprint of his body on the comforter made her steps falter. The intimacy of all this was quite overwhelming, and suddenly Stewart's money wasn't the issue between them. This was only about her and Adam. As fast as she could, she put her designs in her overnight case, then made for the shower.

When she came out of the bathroom ten minutes later, she was still feeling weird about sharing a room with a man she didn't know. Adam was sitting up against the pillows reading a magazine about yachting, but he lifted his head when the door opened. A thick bathrobe covered her from head to calf and she carried her day clothes, but he was actually looking at her bare face. She'd pulled her hair back in a ponytail and washed off her makeup, and he was assessing her in a way that pleased her. He didn't seem to be cringing, so she figured she didn't look too bad.

Going over to the chaise lounge, she began folding the clothes in her hands, giving herself something to do. "Chelsea told me there are some local dignitaries coming tonight," she said to cover up her nervousness.

He closed the magazine and put it aside. "I'm not surprised. Chelsea and Todd like to socialize."

"Well, I'm glad I brought a selection of clothes with me."

"I'm sure you managed to find something decent from…" He lifted a brow. "Now, where was that place? Vinnie's?"

She knew he was teasing her, and it turned her mouth dry. The temptation to smile at him and see where it would lead was almost irresistible.

Instead, she pursed her lips and played it cool. "I don't

always shop there, you know. I just wanted something special for the ball, that's all. I've got plenty of my own clothes for this sort of thing."

"You'd look fantastic in anything." He came off the mattress. "Or in nothing."

She stilled as he walked around the bed. His eyes were hot and she held her breath.

He kept walking…straight into the bathroom, and closed the door.

A pang of disappointment flooded her, embarrassed her. Damn him. He'd known what he was doing. He was toying with her, leaving her to wonder if he was ever going to kiss her again.

The sound of the shower being turned on released her feet from their fixed position. She hurried into the walk-in closet before he could come back out. Then as fast as she could, she dressed in a long black skirt and silky lilac top, applied her makeup in the vanity mirror and topped it all with a pair of dangling earrings she'd designed herself.

She was ready.

But she *wasn't* ready for the sight of him coming back into the bedroom with only a towel wrapped around his hips. The blood rushed in her ears as she swallowed hard and avoided his eyes, hurrying into the bathroom and closing the door. She definitely didn't need any blush for her cheeks after that, she decided, rubbing the steam from the mirror and staring at her heated reflection, then not leaving the room until she'd cooled down.

He was putting on his dark dinner jacket, dressing in front of her as if they were lovers, the action making her even more aware of them sharing a room together.

He turned to look at her and his eyes darkened. In three strides—one for each thump of her heartbeat—he was in front of her.

His head descended, and with the next beat of her heart she couldn't stop herself from opening her mouth to him. His tongue found hers, almost making her dissolve as he took her and teased, drawing her deep into a delicious well of sensation that was all about being with this man and no other. It was a kiss to die for.

Finally he let the pace slow, stopping and leaving her trembling. She swallowed the taste of him, then somehow managed to croak, "Let me guess. That's so people downstairs will think we're lovers."

"No, that one's for me."

Six

Downstairs, Adam watched Jenna from across the room as she talked to one of the couples they'd met this afternoon. By the darting glances she gave him and the slight flush under her skin, he knew she was aware he was watching her. Satisfaction filled him. After that kiss in the bedroom, he had no doubts she would be his lover before the night was over. He knew when a woman was on a losing battle. She might be able to say no to him, but she couldn't say no to herself.

"Adam, don't you think what William is saying is *so* interesting?" Chelsea enthused, drawing his attention back to her and the other man at her side.

He smiled politely at them both. "Of course." Chelsea had taken him away from Jenna on the pretext of introducing him to this bore of a person, but it had just been an excuse to separate them. God, he was so sick of this woman. If it wasn't for Todd he'd have no hesitation in setting her straight. He didn't like being held to ransom like this.

"William has quite a collection," Chelsea said.

"Does he, now?" Adam said, not the least interested in the other man's collection of butterflies. He'd prefer to collect women himself...and Jenna was one of them. And at least he'd set her free afterward, he mused.

Just then Adam saw the couple at Jenna's side go off to talk to someone else, leaving her standing alone. He was about to go to her when another man moved in, as if he'd been waiting for that exact opportunity, and she turned to him as though he was a lifeline in a sea of faces. Adam's hand tightened around his glass. That smile should be for *him*.

As fast as he could, he excused himself and moved to her side. "There you are, darling," he murmured, slipping his arm around her waist, feeling her give a start of surprise as he pulled her hip to hip. He sent the other man a definite look that she was *his*.

"Er...this is Franklin," Jenna said, looking wary.

"How do you do, Frank?"

The man's mouth pursed. "It's Franklin, actually."

"Franklin, then." Adam smiled briefly down at Jenna. "I see my lady has been keeping you company."

Franklin stiffened, clearly getting the picture. "We've just met." His eyes darted away. "If you'll excuse me, I see someone over there I know." He rushed off.

"Did you have to do that?" she whispered.

"Do what?"

"Scare him off like that. I might have wanted to get to know him better."

"Not on my watch, darling," he growled, taking a sip from his glass, his hand still holding her hip against him.

"Stop it. You don't have to call me that in private."

"But I'm only playing a part." Just as *she'd* been playing when she'd made her escape as soon as they'd arrived this morning. Of course, he'd made her pay at lunch when he'd offered her the food from his fork. Oh, that mouth of hers...

"You're going overboard with this stuff. I was merely talking to the guy and you're acting like a jealous lover."

He lifted a brow. "Isn't that the point?"

She blinked, then sighed. "Yes, of course."

Another couple came up to them then and the rest of the evening passed without incident. Adam refused to leave her side, not even when Chelsea tried to steal him away again. Neither woman had any chance of getting their wish.

Eventually the local guests began to depart, and Chelsea and Todd were kept busy seeing them to the front door. He saw Jenna look around at the six other couples staying here overnight, panic in her eyes, but it was a panic that was self-induced. He would never force a woman to do anything she didn't want to do. But if she *wanted* to do something...

He firmly took her by the arm. "Come on, darling. It's time we went to bed."

"Oh, but—"

"She's such a night owl at times," he joked to the others. "Good night, everyone." He led her from the room with a chorus of good-nights following them. It might be good-night for those people, but as far as he was concerned this was just the beginning.

Jenna wasn't sure how she managed it, but as Adam went to reach for her inside the bedroom, in her panic she sidestepped him to move a few feet away. "You can sleep over there," she said, jerking her head toward the chaise lounge near the window.

"No."

"You're *not* sleeping with me," she said, aware she was struggling to remain unaffected. He'd been stirring chords of longing in her all evening...all day—ever since she'd met him, actually.

"So you're not sleeping in the bed, then?" he mocked.

She watched him work his tie loose, and it was as if they were lovers coming home and getting ready for bed. As if they did this each night.

She swallowed hard. "You should be a gentleman and sleep on the lounge."

"Sorry. I like my comfort too much." He took off his jacket next and threw it over an upholstered chair. "Anyway, this bed's big enough for both of us."

"The *suite's* not big enough for both of us," she muttered, perhaps unwisely, she thought when she saw him moving toward her.

He took her by the arms. "You want me, Jenna," he said silkily. "I know you do. Let me show you how much."

Her stomach dipped. She wasn't sure why she was fighting this so hard. Perhaps because he expected her to cave in, and she wasn't going to let herself become one of his women. She'd fallen into bed with Lewis, and only ended up a number.

She lifted her chin. "I wouldn't appreciate it tomorrow."

With the speed of light the lines of his face turned rigid and he twisted toward the bathroom. "I'm going to brush my teeth, then I'm getting into bed. You sleep where you want."

The door closed and she stood there for a minute, her breathing unsteady, her knees shaky. She'd done the right thing, she told herself. This way at least she wasn't a statistic.

Knowing time was passing, she grabbed the comforter

and one of the pillows and dropped them on the chaise lounge. Then she quickly collected her makeup remover and hairbrush from the vanity and her night things from the dressing room. As soon as he came out of the bathroom, she went rushing past him, catching an unnerving glimpse of bare chest exposed by his undone shirt.

Her hands shook as she changed into her negligee and robe, then completed her toilette, but she held her head high as she came out of the bathroom. Damn him, he was sitting up in bed, his arms crossed behind his head. She almost stumbled when she saw the light from the bedside lamps spilling across his naked chest.

"Don't worry, I'm wearing the bottom half of my pajamas," he pointed out with a touch of sarcasm.

"Good."

Something in the air changed, and a deliberate pause hung in the room. "Not that I usually wear them. I generally prefer—"

"I never gave it a thought," she cut across him, not wanting to hear him say out loud that he generally wore nothing in bed. The picture was too vivid in her mind right now.

She placed her folded skirt and top on the chest of drawers, then went to the chaise lounge and began plumping up her pillow. She could feel his eyes on her.

"Don't you think you're being ridiculous?"

She placed the pillow back down and straightened. "No."

"You won't get a good night's sleep on that thing," he pointed out.

"And I will over there with you?" she scoffed, picking up the comforter next, intending to spread it over the lounge.

He smiled appreciatively, then it faded and his face took

on a serious note. "Look, we can put some pillows down the middle, if it'll ease your mind."

She halted, surprise rippling through her. "You would really do that?"

"Yes."

Then she made a face. "Ah, but can I trust you?"

"Of cour—"

Tap. Tap.

They both froze.

"Adam." Chelsea's voice came through the door. "I'm just checking that everything's okay."

A second passed, then Adam threw back the sheet on the other side of the bed. "Come and get in next to me," he whispered. "And take off that robe first."

Jenna heard the words but it was taking a moment to register. Get in bed with him? Take off her robe?

"Come on, hurry up," he said in a low voice, irritation crossing his face when she still didn't move. "Don't spoil it now," he rasped.

His words finally penetrated her mind. She dropped the comforter and did as he said, and soon he'd half dragged her across the sheets and into his arms before she could think or catch her breath.

"Adam?" Chelsea called out, louder this time, but not enough to disturb the other guests.

"Chelsea, everything's fine," he called out.

The door opened and she peeped around it. "I was just checking—" Her eyes flew to Jenna enfolded in the crook of his arm. There was no sign of Todd.

Feeling uncomfortable, Jenna tried to push herself away from Adam a little, but his arms tightened around her, keeping her firmly against his naked chest. She realized she was only making it look as if Chelsea had interrupted something.

A small flush rose in Chelsea's cheeks and she quickly looked away. Then her gaze rested on the pillow on the chaise lounge and the comforter on the floor next to it, and Jenna felt Adam tense beneath her.

Chelsea frowned. "You don't want the comforter?"

"No, we'll be warm enough," Jenna said quickly, and heard a rumble of laughter in Adam's throat. She looked up at him and saw the amusement on his face. Her cheeks heated up, playing right into his hands. She looked away again.

"Oh. Okay then." Chelsea still hesitated. "Well, let me know if you need anything."

"We will," Adam said.

There was an awkward silence.

"Good night, Chelsea," he said with more firmness this time.

"Good night." She closed the door and left them alone.

Jenna immediately went to push away, but his arms tightened. "Shh, stay there. She hasn't gone yet."

She stilled, waiting and listening. Half a minute passed. "Do you think she'll come back?"

"Who knows with Chelsea?"

"We should lock the door."

The words fell in a hush.

She felt the muscles of his chest flex beneath her palm and realized she was resting her hand on his bare skin. In fascination, she tilted her head back to find his eyes dark and deep and firmly on her. "Good idea," he murmured.

But he didn't move.

She wet her lips. "Er…the door," she reminded him, and waited for him to release her.

He stayed still. "Do you really want to sleep alone tonight, Jenna?"

Looking into his eyes, smelling his warm male scent and intently conscious of the side of his body against hers, it was hard to think coherently. "Um…I should."

"Should what?" He started to run his finger lazily down her bare arm. "Do you know how beautiful you are?"

Her heart started to race as she sensed something turn in the air. "Don't."

His finger drifted to a stop. "I want to make love to you."

Hearing him say it out loud in this tiny space between them made her gasp and had a red flag waving "Danger" in her mind. She had to get out of his arms before it was too late. She went to push back.

"Jenna?"

She stopped. His husky voice was working its way through her, draining her resistance. Who was she fooling? She didn't want him to let her go. She wanted this as much as he did.

The red flag turned white. She mentally let it drop in capitulation. "I want you, too," she heard herself whisper. *Surrender.*

Something deep ignited in his eyes. "No regrets tomorrow?"

She shook her head. "No regrets tomorrow."

He paused a second longer. "Don't move," he said, and eased away from her to slide out from under the sheet.

He went to lock the door, then came back toward her in a pair of pajama pants that left nothing to her imagination. He was aroused, and it turned her into a mess of bones, especially when his hands went to the waistband, intent on taking the pants off.

"Not yet," she whispered, startling herself, aware she was suddenly afraid of losing total control. She'd never felt this way before with a man.

"I don't usually make love with my pants on," he teased.

Her throat felt blocked. "I'm not used to a...situation like this," she admitted. And she wasn't. She'd had a couple of lovers over the years, but they'd been men she'd thought she'd been in love with. And amazingly it hadn't felt as powerful as what she was feeling for this man—whom she didn't love.

His amusement disappeared. He wasn't teasing now. "Do you want me, Jenna?"

She took a deep breath. Did she really need to think about this? "Oh, yes, Adam. I do."

He turned the lamplight off. "Then when you're ready, *you* can take my pants off," he said in a low voice, and slid back into the bed beside her.

Jenna shuddered as Adam drew her into his arms. She was grateful he had turned off the lamp, more than thankful it left them in a privacy of moonlight. They could see each other, but it was her eyes she wanted to hide from him as much as possible. In the dark he would not be able to see into their depths.

Of course, concealing her body's reactions from him was impossible—nor did she want to—but that was all she wanted him to see. If he discovered that he affected her more with one touch of his finger, one crook of his smile, than any man had ever done before him, he might just use that against her when it came time to resolve their family issues. She couldn't allow him that.

Lord, she was thinking too much, she decided, gladly welcoming his kiss, pushing all thought to the back of her mind. His mouth enticed her to open her lips fully, and she slid into a moan as his tongue swept in...and swept her breath away, the effect no less than searing.

Then he took his time playing with her tongue, but soon he must have needed air, too. He broke off the kiss and sucked in a solid gasp of oxygen before grazing along the top of her shoulder, his fingers pushing the thin strap of her negligee aside, letting it fall partway down her arm, baring her skin for his warm lips. He did the same to the other side, then moved back to gaze at the sight of her bare shoulders lashed by the silk material.

He groaned and kissed her again, his hand working its way down to her hip, sensually caressing every inch he touched through her nightgown. The blood in her veins turned syrupy and pooled low in her belly. Her nipples ached for him to lower his head and suck their throbbing tips, and she eagerly awaited his mouth on her breasts. Instead, he got on his knees and lifted the hem of her nightgown, sliding the silky fabric up and over her head, leaving her only in her panties. His gaze glittered through the moonlight, burning a path over every single inch of her. The impact made her head whirl.

And then he was running his palms over her breasts in an outward circular motion, making her take a shaky breath as he targeted her sensitized nipples. Her head pressed back on the pillows as she let him have his way for long, glorious moments, his touch wonderful.

Suddenly, she wanted to see him, too. And to touch him. Normally, she wouldn't feel so forward. She'd never had such a strong urge to reach out for a man…to know every inch of him…. It should be scaring the hell out of her, but she couldn't think past the moment. She pushed herself to her knees, bringing them face-to-face.

She was first to reach out, surprised a little that he'd let her take the lead. Her palms tingled as she moved over his hot, dampening chest, her fingers prickling at the heavy beat of his heart beneath the smooth skin and wisps of masculine hair.

"You surprise me," he said gruffly, as her hands advanced over his rib cage. "I thought you might be shy."

She stroked his firm stomach. "You thought wrong."

A challenge flew from his eyes. "Wrong?" He reached out and slid a finger down under her panties with exact precision, through her curls, parting her. She almost came undone when he began a delicate manipulation, her head falling back as he continued the action, her bended knees weakening. She wasn't sure how long they would hold her up.

He laughed low in his throat. "No, I don't think I was wrong at all."

From somewhere she found the strength to straighten up. This had suddenly become a game of who would succumb first. Oh, she knew she couldn't win—not the way he was making her feel—but she'd give it a damn good try....

"Then you'd better think again," she murmured, deliberately slipping her fingers under the waistband of his pajamas, slowly pushing them down to his knees. She took in the sight of his manly hips, the arrow of curly hair, his shaft hard and fully erect, ready to take, to conquer and to totally consume her.

Reaching out, she slid her hand around his thickened length, then proceeded to stroke him. "Oh, yes, dead wrong."

Without warning, he flipped her backward onto the mattress.

Her eyes widened. "Hey, that's not fair."

"Tell it to someone who cares," he drawled.

Then he shed his pajamas, and her panties soon disappeared. His kisses became deeper and hungrier as she returned each one. He ran his hands over her, touching places that came close again to making her lose her head. Hot on her trail.

"Adam, please," she begged, when he rubbed himself between her thighs, then moved away, leaving her wanting. "I need you."

"Shh." He reached over to the night table.

She turned her head on the pillow and watched him take a condom from his wallet. "You knew I'd sleep with you?" she said half to herself, but she wasn't angry with him. She couldn't be. She just wanted him inside her.

"I was hoping." He sheathed himself before slowly entering her, and then he began the heated thrust of his body. It was slow, it was deliberate, and it sent shock waves of sensation pulsing through her veins.

And when she finally did lose her head, Adam did too, locking them together on an unstoppable journey until they exploded their release.

Seven

The next morning Adam lay in bed beside Jenna, watching her sleep in his arms. It amazed him that he wanted her again so soon with so much hunger. Sure, he was a man with a healthy sexual appetite, but when he woke in the morning with a woman in his bed it always felt like he was dining on a light breakfast. Of course, more often than not he usually *wanted* something light anyway.

But with Jenna, it was as if he was being offered a wholesome breakfast…as if it filled him…completed him even…as if she satisfied something substantial in him.

Last time he'd felt like that had been with Maddie.

Bloody hell!

He dropped his eyelids again, pushing all thoughts of his late wife to the back of his mind. This wasn't the time or place to be thinking about the woman who had introduced him to love.

When he opened his eyes again sometime later, Jenna was looking at him. "I see you're not an early riser."

He gave a low chuckle and pushed himself forward against her. "I wouldn't say that."

She blushed. "You know what I mean."

"No, show me."

Her hand touched him and he was instantly lost. Afterward they showered together, made love again, then dressed and headed downstairs.

Adam had to admit he was surprised by her. Other women wanted to talk and decipher everything, sometimes wanting a declaration of love or commitment, yet Jenna seemed to be happy to just be with him.

And when they walked into the breakfast room to find Todd and Chelsea there alone, Jenna didn't gloat, like the other women he knew would gloat at being made his lover. In a way he wished she would, rather than being sensitive to Chelsea's feelings. It was what they were here for after all.

Yet how could he fault Jenna when her actions were showing him a depth of character he was only now beginning to appreciate?

"Good morning," he said, holding a chair out for Jenna but smiling at Todd and Chelsea. For a moment the other couple sat there in a kind of stony silence, making him suddenly aware of the tension in the air.

Then Todd put on a forced smile. "Good morning. Did you both sleep well?"

Adam sat down next to Jenna, but he watched Todd. "Yes. What about you two?"

Todd's smile was tight. "Terrific. This country air has me sleeping like a log."

"I'm glad someone did, then," Chelsea snapped, much to Adam's surprise. He felt Jenna startle, too.

"Chels…" Todd said in a warning tone.

For a second Chelsea looked as if she would snap at him

again, but then she seemed to realize she had an audience. She pulled a face. "Sorry about that. I've got the beginnings of a headache."

Adam remembered what Todd had said about Chelsea's female problems, but her excuse just now didn't gel. It had been too glib.

"Perhaps you should go lie down," Jenna said sympathetically.

Antagonism flared in Chelsea's eyes, then banked, and she put on a bright smile for everyone to see. "No, I'll be fine."

At that point Adam suspected that Chelsea's ill health was more likely due to her jealousy over seeing him and Jenna in bed together last night. For a brief second he wondered if he hadn't unwittingly dumped Jenna in the middle of something impossible, but then he remembered she was tough. If Jenna could handle *him,* she could handle Chelsea.

The arrival of the other guests in the breakfast room brought a flurry of chatter. Chelsea seemed to go into overdrive, her eyes extra bright as she turned into the perfect hostess. It didn't disguise the hint of hostility in the air, though after watching her send one or two dark glances at her husband, Adam had to wonder if this was more about Todd than not.

"So this morning we have a lot of activities to get through," Chelsea said now. "There's tennis, horseback riding and swimming to choose from, or you can choose all three—if you're game," she joked, with a wink. "And after lunch I've arranged for a tour of a local winery. I can guarantee you'll love it," she enthused just a little bit too shrilly.

Adam saw Jenna dart a look at him, and he knew

instantly what she was thinking. He agreed. He didn't want to stay any longer, either.

"I'm afraid we can't stay, Chelsea," he said, placing his napkin on the table. "Jenna and I both have to get back to the city for another commitment that's come to light."

"But you can't!"

He stiffened in anger. No one told him what he could or couldn't do, especially not someone who had no claim to his time.

Chelsea seemed to notice she'd made a mistake, but that didn't quite stop her. "Surely you can stay, Adam," she said in a pleading tone. "Please say you will."

Her comment irritated the hell out of him. It would have irritated him whether he and Jenna were lovers or not, but she appeared to be ignoring Jenna, and that was the height of bad manners. "Sorry," he said, not sorry at all.

"But—"

Todd pushed to his feet then, sending his wife a hard look before turning to their guests. "How about we all go change into something more casual so that we can start the activities? Chelsea has arranged a selection of sports gear for anyone who may need it." He glanced at Adam and smiled. "Let me know when you and Jenna are ready to leave, Adam," he said, silently indicating he had no problem with their early departure. "I'll see you off."

Adam nodded, then cupped Jenna's elbow and pushed both of them to their feet. "I will. Thanks. We won't be too long." He led Jenna out of the room, but another couple followed and conversed with them as they went up the stairs.

In the bedroom he was still disgusted by Chelsea's actions. "Let's get our stuff together," he said, striding away.

A couple of seconds passed, then she said, "Chelsea was upset."

He turned at the entrance to the walk-in closet and saw she hadn't moved. "It's because she knew we'd made love last night."

Jenna blushed a little, even as she looked baffled. "Didn't she already believe we were lovers?"

"Yes, but seeing us in bed together must have finally hit home."

She nodded, then a sigh escaped. "I'm glad we're leaving soon."

"So am I," he said pointedly, growing fascinated by her pink cheeks. Thoughts of Chelsea faded from his mind.

As if trying to ignore her own embarrassment, Jenna tilted her head. "Do you really have a commitment in the city?"

This woman was enthralling. "Yes." Casually he leaned against the doorjamb, slowing things down for a few moments. "I'm committed to making love to you all afternoon."

Her eyes flared with pleasure. "I see."

He loved the little pulse that started throbbing at her neck. If he hurried back to her, he could put his lips against it…no, then he wouldn't want to stop. He'd want to pull her into his arms and make love to her again.

"Come on," he said brusquely, pushing himself away from the wooden frame. "Let's pack our things and get out of here."

Todd was waiting at the bottom of the stairs when they came down. "Chelsea asked me to give you her apologies. She and some of the others have gone to the stables."

Adam was relieved not to be seeing her again so soon. "That's fine, Todd. Please give her our thanks."

Jenna smiled. "It's been a lovely weekend. I've really enjoyed it."

"I'm glad." Todd's expression seemed strained. "And I'm sorry about things this morning."

Adam looked at his friend with concern. "Is everything okay between you and Chelsea?"

Todd waved a dismissive hand. "Don't take any notice of Chels. She's just on edge with…everything."

Adam wanted to ask if the "everything" involved *him,* only he couldn't. If he was responsible for Chelsea's bad mood, he certainly didn't want Todd to know it.

Just then, two of the male guests came out of the drawing room and saw them standing in the entrance, preparing to leave.

"Hey, there's the man who'll remember," one of the men said, coming toward them. "Adam, what was the name of the guy your father had convicted of fraud? It was about five years ago. Burke something or other…"

Adam froze, then he said tightly, "Milton Burke."

"Oh, yeah, that's the guy's name. He ended up doing a couple of years in prison, didn't he?" The guest didn't wait for an answer. "Yeah, old Milt was a professional con man. He—"

"We're leaving," Adam cut across him, not caring if he appeared rude. Taking Jenna by the arm, he turned away and strode out the front door of the mansion to where his car was waiting. Their overnight bags had already been put in the trunk, and after a brief farewell to Todd, he drove off the estate.

"Er…are you okay, Adam?" Jenna asked once they were on the road.

He glanced at her. "Never better," he quipped.

After that he concentrated on the driving, making it clear he didn't want to talk. He wasn't angry with her, just with the way things were. The mention of money and fraud back there had called to mind what stood between him and this woman who was now his lover. Stewart Branson was back between them again like a brick wall, though truth be told that wall had never really fallen down.

Dammit, between Jenna's brother and Todd's wife, life was getting far too complicated.

And he didn't like it one bit.

By the time they reached the city just after lunch, Jenna was trying not to worry. Adam had been remote from the minute the mention was made of the guy who'd gone to prison for fraud. It was a powerful reminder that the Roth family was far from lenient if they were wronged.

Not that Stewart had done anything wrong. Far from it. *He* was the one wronged.

But with Adam so quiet beside her now, she couldn't stop from worrying about *their* relationship. Was he having misgivings because they were back in town? Had it merely been the country air? A mistake on his part?

"Do you regret making love to me, Adam?" she had to ask as soon as they stepped inside her apartment.

"Time's too short for regrets," he muttered, then swung her up in his arms and headed for the bedroom. She wasn't exactly sure why his words didn't thrill her, but she was soon preoccupied enough not to think about it just then.

He left late afternoon with the promise to call.

After he'd gone, Jenna wondered about the state of their relationship. They hadn't spoken about being faithful to each other, but would he be committed to her while their affair lasted? She had to remember Adam had no ties to her. He owed her no loyalty—except the loyalty of a lover. To her, that was everything. To him, it might not be.

No, she had to believe that he *would* remain faithful. He wasn't like Lewis. Already she knew he had more integrity in his little finger than Lewis had from head to toe. She only had to see how Adam *hadn't* slept with his best friend's wife. It was admirable.

And yet—in spite of knowing that Adam would treat her well—she couldn't help but admit something was bothering her. She was now another man's mistress.

Again.

At least with Lewis she'd thought she loved him and that they had a future together. She had no long-term future with Adam. Their divided loyalties ensured it would never work between them anyway.

And that prompted the question—why had she changed her resolve and become Adam's lover? She'd been so determined not to get involved, yet now in one brief overnight trip she'd slept with him. She could only think those very loyalties that stood between them showed a man who put himself second when it came to the people he cared about. She found that very appealing, especially in a successful businessman whose spare time was limited.

So here she was.

A mistress.

Again.

Perhaps she should just enjoy being his mistress while she could—even if it didn't change the facts.

Later that evening Jenna's telephone rang and she raced to pick it up, hoping it was Adam. "Hello," she said, her heart thumping.

No answer.

She blinked, then listened hard, but there was only silence. "Hello?" she repeated, thinking it could be a wrong number and the other person had been caught off balance.

More silence.

She began to feel uneasy now. "Who is this?"

Another couple of seconds passed, then she thought she heard a woman's sigh just before the person quietly ended the call.

Jenna shivered with apprehension as she replaced the handset. If it *had* been a wrong number, then surely the person would have simply hung up straight away. If it had been family or friends, then…

Chelsea!

She wasn't sure how she knew it was the other woman. It just…fit. It hadn't been a threatening silence, more disconcerting. Could Chelsea have been checking to see if Adam was still with her? And did that mean Chelsea had tried Adam's apartment and received no answer? He was probably catching up on work and didn't want to be interrupted.

And how the heck had Chelsea gotten her phone number anyway? She grimaced. It wasn't really surprising, considering who the other woman was.

The question for Jenna was whether she should tell Adam about this. If she did he might put his relationship with Todd at risk, when there was no proof it had been Chelsea at all. It would be best to wait and see how things panned out first.

Half an hour later, the phone rang again. Jenna cautiously answered, thankful this time it was her mother, and pushed aside her disappointment that it wasn't Adam.

Joyce Branson was her usual cheery self, talking about the championship game of tennis that was coming up and whining a little about Jenna's father being home and in the way now that he was retired. She didn't ask anything about Adam.

Then her mother mentioned how she'd seen Vicki and the children, but said how she was still worried about Stewart being so far away from his family. That refreshed Jenna's worry. It was amazing how on the surface everything seemed normal—even if it wasn't. It pained her to keep secrets from her parents.

At work the following morning she found herself checking her cell phone in case Adam called. Constantly. There were no calls, but she was eternally grateful that Marco didn't make an appearance. She didn't think she could have stood the questions she'd have to field about her and Adam's relationship.

Normally, she loved her job, but the day dragged and she was grateful to arrive home, eager to see if Adam called that evening. She tried to persuade herself that he probably wouldn't for a few days, and when the phone didn't ring over the next few hours she had to accept it. He had other priorities, she told herself, but to no avail. Her heart was just about convinced she'd hear nothing, when the doorbell rang around eight.

It was Adam.

His eyes drank her up as he stepped inside and kicked the door shut. Without a word, he caught hold of her hips and brought them flush up against him, his hardened body making her gasp. It was clear he'd been wanting her before he'd even reached her door. The thought of it made her feel more feminine than ever before.

Then he pressed her back against the wall and kissed her, and he kept right on kissing her until her toes curled in her shoes and her knees threatened to buckle. He stopped for a breath, but not for long. His fingers went on the move, working open her blouse, undoing her trousers.

"Why can't I get enough of you?" he murmured, with a darkening look of desire in his eyes, his lips creating havoc as he bent his head and began to lavish each nipple through her lacy bra. Then he kissed down her stomach…farther down until his fingers lowered the front of her panties so he could access her with his mouth...to where she was more than ready for him.

She held his head to her while he pleasured her, until tremors started to shake her body and her breath came as fast as the upwelling explosion.

After she climaxed, he stepped her out of her panties and swept her up in his arms, carrying her over to the couch, where he sat her down. With her heart in her throat and barely able to catch her breath, Jenna watched as he stood there and undid his trousers in front of her. Her hand tingled to—

"Not this time," he muttered, preempting her touching him as he ripped the wrapper from a condom and sheathed himself. Then he sat next to her, pulled her on top of his hard length and entered her.

"Adam!" she cried out as he groaned and filled her with all that he was. She grew hot. Instinctively, she lifted herself an inch...then slid down on him. She did it again and he caught her by the hips, holding her so that she could easily fall into a rhythm that was beautifully exquisite. Their eyes on each other, they soon climaxed together.

"Oh, my God," she muttered when they'd finished and their foreheads were resting against each other while they caught their breath. Then she dragged in some air and lifted her head away from his. "Is it always like this?" she whispered, half in wonder, but regretting it the instant the words were out of her mouth. "No, don't answer that." She didn't want to hear his response. To him, this was a regular occurrence.

Adam put his hand under her chin and made her look him in the eyes. "No, it isn't always like this."

Her heart tilted sideways. "Oh."

As if he'd said enough, his face turned blank and he lifted her off him and went into the bathroom. She sat there for a moment, telling herself she wouldn't be normal if she didn't feel thrilled at his words.

And yet as she tidied her clothes, she was concerned. In the long run it would have been better if there hadn't been this intense attraction between them. In the long run she'd have to survive without him…without *this,* she decided, fully aware she'd never be able to look at her couch again without thinking of the two of them here. Suddenly, she felt an odd pain at the thought. Maybe after this was over she'd get a new couch. Hell, she might even sell this apartment and buy a new one. Start afresh. She had the feeling she might need to get totally away from memories of Adam.

"Have you eaten?" she asked, when he came back.

He sent her a dry look. "Yes."

"I'm talking about dinner."

"So am I," he teased, then nodded. "Yes, I've eaten. I had a business dinner."

She was surprised. "You finished early."

"I wanted to see you."

He had? Why? Had he discovered she'd been telling the truth about the money? Why else would he come here after a long day at work? She swallowed. And why didn't she feel happier than she did? She should be ecstatic for Stewart's sake.

"Um…about anything important?" she asked, trying to sound idle.

"Yes. I needed to make love to you." He pulled her up close. "And I did." Then he kissed her briefly. "I have to go. I have some work to finish up tonight for an early morning meeting."

Relief ribboned through her that the money clearly wasn't his main concern right now, then she felt bad for her family's sake. She couldn't be selfish enough to take her happiness at their cost.

So it was a good thing that Adam wasn't staying the night, she told herself as she walked him to the door. He was respecting her space as she respected his. It kept the lines divided.

"I'll call you."

She nodded, but as she closed her door she wondered if this was how their relationship was supposed to work from now until their time was up. Was she to wait around for his call all the time—at his whim—like a mistress who dropped everything for his pleasure and had no life of her own?

Something inside her flattened at the thought.

Over the next few evenings the same thing happened. Adam never promised to see her, but invariably he'd turn up around eight and make love to her. They even made it to her bedroom most of the time and she'd hope he would stay the night, but after a while he would take himself home. It made her think even harder. Was he actually giving her some space?

Or himself?

Eight

Adam hadn't intended to visit Jenna again so soon, but somehow on Thursday evening he found himself heading for her apartment. Every night this week he'd aimed to go straight home after work, only it hadn't quite worked out that way.

It was disconcerting to realize he'd never physically wanted a woman so much as he did Jenna. The need to be inside her thickened his blood and stirred his pulse. He'd constantly had to put thoughts of her aside throughout the day. He'd be in the middle of a meeting and picture her gasping her climax. Or he'd be reading a report and his mind would wander to untying her silky bathrobe and kissing her all over.

Tonight on his arrival he did exactly that. She tasted good. She felt good. And she was damn good in bed. But as he was dressing to go home, he suddenly felt as if he should be offering her more—though more than what he wasn't sure.

"Can you make dinner tomorrow night?" he heard himself ask.

One elegant eyebrow rose as she slipped into her bathrobe. "Another function?"

"No. It'll just be the two of us."

"Alone?"

He had to smile. "The two of us alone, yes. Well, as alone as we can get in a restaurant."

It took her a moment to think about it. "So this isn't for Chelsea and Todd's benefit, then?"

"No." He hadn't heard from the other couple since last weekend, and right now he didn't give a damn.

Jenna flashed him a smile. "That would be lovely."

That gorgeous smile rocked something inside him, and suddenly he was scrambling to put them back on a physical relationship. "Bring an overnight bag."

"A...bag?"

"You'll be spending the night at my place."

She looked pleased, but as he drove home he was glad she didn't know his thoughts. Perhaps he'd made a mistake in narrowing it all down to just the two of them. He didn't want her getting the idea that anything further could develop...and yet he didn't have the heart to cancel. Besides, it was only a matter of time before their relationship began to wane anyway.

And then there was the money issue between them.

It was just as well he had a meeting arranged with the forensic accountant. The guy was still checking it out, and so far there was nothing to report, but Adam still wanted an update in person first thing Monday.

And that prompted the question—what if the money couldn't be found?

* * *

The following evening Jenna was thrilled to be dining alone with Adam—until Lewis Carter showed up with his latest girlfriend on his arm as they were finishing their dinner. She saw him a split second too late.

"Jenna?" He stopped as he passed by their table.

She pasted on a smile, more aware of Adam's interest than she wanted to be. "Yes. How are you, Lewis?" Not that she cared one way or the other.

Lewis's eyes darted to Adam, and he gave a nod of recognition before returning to her. "Totally heartbroken you didn't return my calls."

He made it sound as if she'd been the one at fault, and not the other way around. Ooh, how typical of the man! It would serve him right if she reminded him of his unfaithfulness.

And revenge was sweet….

She reached across the table and slid her hand over the top of Adam's, giving the dreamiest smile she could muster before looking up at Lewis. "Now you can see why."

There was a moment when Lewis's smile stretched like a piece of elastic. Then he bounced right back. "You're still quick off the mark, Jenna, my love."

"And you're still—" *a jerk* "—the same."

Lewis's date started to fidget from lack of attention. "Honey, can we go sit down? I'm starving."

He laughed and winked at them. "She has quite the appetite."

With a bad taste in her mouth Jenna watched them walk away.

"So you dated Lewis Carter."

"Don't remind me," she muttered, turning back to Adam, a little surprised he hadn't already investigated her previous relationships, especially considering her claim about Stewart. "Obviously you know him. He recognized you, too."

"We've met a couple of times."

Her lips twisted. "Lucky you."

Adam looked amused. "At least he appreciates your wit."

"It's about the only thing he did appreciate."

His amusement faded. "What happened?"

She picked up her glass of wine and took a sip before speaking. Better to say it and get it out in the open. She had nothing to hide. "I met Lewis when we both backed out of our parking spaces at a shopping center one day. There wasn't a lot of damage, but he insisted on taking me for a drink to calm my nerves. We exchanged names and addresses for our insurance companies and—" she gave a wry shrug "—it went from there."

"How long were you his girlfriend?"

"About six months."

"I'm surprised Carter could remain faithful for that long."

"He didn't. I thought he was getting serious, but he was *serious* only about cheating on me."

His gaze intensified on her. "I would never cheat on you, Jenna."

"Thank you," she murmured, meaning it.

But a second later she couldn't help thinking it would be easy for him to remain faithful for the short period of time they had left together. As quickly, she chastised herself. That wasn't fair of her. She'd already decided Adam wasn't like Lewis.

He studied her some more before speaking again. "Carter didn't like your designs, did he?"

Her eyes widened. "How did you know that?"

"You were self-conscious about showing me your

drawings back at the Grampians. It was almost as if you expected me to criticize them."

She was touched by his perception. "I'm glad you didn't," she said softly.

His eyes stayed on her for a few beats, the blue irises darkening with desire before he pushed back his chair and held out his hand. "Let's go."

She had no argument with that. She was more than ready to concentrate on her and Adam again—and more than ready to forget Lewis Carter.

Adam took her back to his apartment, and they made love over and over during the night—as if they hadn't seen each other all week—as if they hadn't touched each other at all in that time. Lewis was far from her mind and yet she knew he was partly responsible for the intensity of their lovemaking. Seeing her ex-lover again reminded her that what she had with Adam was very special. And Lewis would hate to know that.

They slept until late Saturday morning, when Adam groaned and rolled out of bed. "I've got to go. I've got a meeting with a business acquaintance in half an hour."

Jenna lay on the pillow, sleepily distracted by the sight of his naked torso. "You're working today? It's Saturday."

He strode toward the bathroom. "It was supposed to be on Monday, but something came up and now the guy's going to be out of town then." He stopped to look at her with an odd smile she couldn't decipher. "You stay here and I'll be back in a couple of hours."

Jenna dozed lightly while Adam showered and dressed, but after he left, she pushed herself out of bed and headed for the shower, too.

She was enjoying her second cup of coffee and thinking about making herself a late lunch when the concierge called up to say that Adam's mother was here to see him. She held her breath. Obviously the man had only started his shift recently, or he would have known that Adam had left earlier.

Her breath started up again as she tried to think. What was the protocol here? Would Adam want his current lover to meet his mother? Shouldn't she just say Adam wasn't home and let Laura Roth come back later?

Then she remembered.

Liam Roth.

Didn't *she* want to meet the mother of the man who had cheated her brother? "Please tell her to come up," she said, curiosity getting the better of her.

Then she checked herself in the mirror to make sure she looked presentable before going over to wait at the private elevator. Soon the doors were sliding open and an elegant woman stepped out. Jenna hesitated a moment, forgetting the money issues, taken slightly aback to be greeting such a prominent person.

And sleeping with her middle son.

In the end, Adam's mother spoke first. "Hello, I'm Laura Roth," she said with a warm smile, offering a manicured hand.

Jenna was surprised by her warmth. She pulled herself together enough to shake her hand, though she rather felt like she should curtsy. It was natural to be formal with such a woman. "Hello, Mrs. Roth."

"Call me Laura."

Jenna didn't think she could do that. "Please, come right in," she said politely, and led the way farther into the living room. She should dislike the woman for what Liam had done to the Bransons, only she wasn't getting that feeling. "I wasn't sure whether to ask you to come up or not. Adam's gone out, you see. He had to meet a business acquaintance."

"On a Saturday?" His mother tutted. "I shouldn't be surprised."

Jenna noticed a curious light at the back of the other woman's eyes, but at least his mother was too well-bred to ask outright if she was her son's mistress. "He'll be back soon if you want to wait."

Laura shook her head. "I can't. I'm off to lunch with a friend in the city, and I just thought I'd stop in and see Adam as I was passing. I wanted to ask him to pick up his cousin when he comes to lunch tomorrow. Logan's car is in the shop getting a minor repair and I told him not to bother about using one of our drivers. It's not out of Adam's way."

She nodded. "I'll make sure he gets the message."

"Thank you."

Just then, the elevator pinged open and Adam strode in wearing a frown. "Mum, you should have let me know you were coming," he scolded as he kissed his mother's cheek.

"That's okay, darling. Jenna's been looking after me."

"Has she, now?" Adam turned to look at Jenna, a warning in his eyes, telling her she'd better not say anything about Liam or Stewart. Jenna didn't want to use the situation for her own benefit, but remembering her brother and his wife and how close they were to losing their home, she defiantly lifted her chin a little at Adam.

He noticed.

"I have to go," Laura said after glancing at her slim gold watch. "I have a lunch date."

Adam's gaze returned to his mother. "With Dad?"

Laura smiled as she headed for the elevator. "No, with Della." She pressed the button, then turned around. "Jenna, you should come to lunch tomorrow with Adam. Now that Dominic and Cassandra are back from their second honeymoon, we're having a family get-together."

Jenna darted a look at Adam and saw the alarm in his eyes. "Laura, thank you, but I don't want to intrude."

"Do you have a previous engagement?"

"No, but—"

"Then I insist." She stepped into the elevator. "See you both tomorrow. Don't forgot to collect Logan, darling."

The doors slid closed.

Silence echoed through the apartment.

Jenna stared at Adam. She could see he wasn't pleased. "I'm sorry. I'll come up with an excuse and you can give my apologies."

"No."

Her forehead crinkled. "But I thought—"

"We're going." His tone brooked no argument.

She considered that. He definitely didn't want her near his parents, yet he was making her go?

"Aren't you worried I'll say something about the money?" It would be the perfect time to take advantage of being near his family, especially his older brother and his wife. After all, Cassandra had been married to Liam before she'd married Dominic. She would be the one who could know something.

"No, I'm not worried. I can easily repay the favor, or have you forgotten that?"

Her stomach clenched. When it came down to it, he didn't trust her. And it stunned her to think that it should even matter. They were lovers in one aspect of their lives, but enemies in another. "I know exactly where things stand, Adam."

As if he suspected more than she was saying, his glance sharpened. "I'm thinking this will work out with Chelsea.

If she hears I took you home to meet my parents, she might finally give up trying."

So that was why he'd agreed. She should have realized. "Or it might make her even more desperate to get your attention," she pointed out. "Chelsea's a very determined woman. Don't underestimate her."

"I don't underestimate any woman."

Her chest felt tight. "There you go, then," she said, turning away to go into the kitchen and fix them a light lunch, giving herself something to do.

After that, Adam was quiet as they sat on the balcony and ate in the sunshine. He wasn't as relaxed as he'd been previously. It wasn't that he was rude, but there was a withdrawal in the air that suddenly made her ache inside.

Jenna wasn't comfortable staying the rest of the day, and when she made an excuse about needing to go and work on a design, she caught a glint of relief in his eyes. She pretended not to notice as he offered to get his driver to take her home.

"No, I'll catch a cab."

"But—"

"You don't need to see me home," she said firmly, knowing she had to get out of here and away from him. Her company wasn't wanted right now and she could feel it all the way through her bones.

He took a long moment to nod. "I'll collect you tomorrow around noon."

She shot him a quick look. "I'm sorry if it's making things awkward for you. I really could cancel, you know. Just this once we could forget all about Chelsea."

A muscle ticked in his cheek. "No, my mother invited you, Jenna. You have to go, whether we like it or not. We may as well use the situation."

It wasn't the answer she wanted to hear and she turned

away to collect her things, disheartened. She hadn't taken a step when he pulled her up close and kissed her. At least he still wanted her physically.

But in the cab home she suspected that somehow she'd just crossed her own personal line. Adam had chosen her because he'd trusted she wouldn't get emotionally involved with him. Too late she realized she might already have done exactly that.

Adam stood at Liam's bedroom window at his parents' mansion and looked down on the terrace below where his family sat around a poolside table after Sunday lunch. There was much teasing and joking today. It was so damn good hearing laughter in this house again.

It was clear to everyone now that Dominic and Cassandra were meant to be together. Adam was convinced Liam had known it when he'd secretly asked Dominic to supply sperm to give her a baby. Poor Dominic had suffered a great deal because of that, knowing he had fathered a child he'd been unable to acknowledge until after Liam had died. But now everything was fine and out in the open, and Adam knew that Liam would be happy up there in heaven with the way things had turned out. For Dominic anyway. For himself, he was wondering what the hell Liam had dragged him into.

"Adam, what are you doing in here?"

Startled, he turned around, glad of a respite from his thoughts. "Nothing, Mum. I just had the urge to come up here, that's all."

His mother's face softened as she took a few steps inside the bedroom. "You miss your brother, don't you? We all do, darling."

He searched her face. "Are *you* okay?" he asked with concern. "It hasn't been that long. Not really."

"Three months. And I miss him with an ache that leaves

a hole in my heart, but I think I'm finally accepting that he's gone." She eased into a smile. "I have so much to be thankful for."

He watched her. She was right, yet his heart still ached for her. To lose a child…

"And you, darling?" she said gently. "This week is going to be hard on you."

His chest tightened. "You remembered."

"Of course. Maddie's death left a big hole in all our hearts, but none more than yours. We wouldn't forget her, not on the fifth anniversary of her passing, not even on the twenty-fifth anniversary. She's in our hearts, darling."

"Thanks, Mum," he said gruffly. He was aware his mother didn't know the full story, and he was glad she'd been spared. For his mother to know she had lost an unborn grandchild as well as a beloved daughter-in-law wasn't something he'd ever let her discover. He'd keep that from her forever.

"And now you have Jenna," she said gently.

His head went back. "Why do you say that?"

"I like this one. I think she's a keeper."

He didn't want to get into this discussion. He didn't need this right now. Yet he couldn't stop himself from asking, "Why?"

"She's a brunette."

He raised an eyebrow. "So?"

"You always go out with blondes." She hesitated. "Ever since Maddie, that is."

He stiffened. He hadn't realized. "Don't make the mistake of thinking there's more than there is. Jenna and I aren't serious. Everything else is a mere coincidence."

"Darling, you—"

"Mum, don't try and marry me off," he snapped, then saw her flinch. He winced. "Sorry, I don't mean to sound harsh, but I don't intend to marry again. Not for a long time, if ever. I'm happy with my life these days. I intend to keep it that way."

She stared then slowly nodded. "Whatever makes you happy makes me happy, Adam."

He cleared his throat. "I know."

There was a burst of laughter from downstairs and he was grateful for the interruption. He turned back to look out the window, seeing Dominic's contented face as he chased his toddling daughter around on the lawn.

Then his gaze slid over to where Jenna and Cassandra were laughing as they watched the little girl and her father, and something lurched against his ribs. He knew Jenna would keep her word and not say anything to his sister-in-law about the money, but it hit him then how hard it must be *not* to say anything. Jenna was as protective of her family as he was of his. He admired that in her.

"I'd better get back downstairs," his mother said behind him. There was a pause. "Are you coming?"

"Give me a few more minutes. I won't be long."

He heard his mother leave but he was more tuned in to Jenna right now. She was so beautiful it made him catch his breath.

Yet it was more than that gorgeous smile and that tinkling laugh floating up to him. He'd been watching her over lunch and she seemed to fit right in with his family. She didn't gush at anyone, like one or two of his women friends had when they'd run into members of his family while out on a date. Jenna had even been a little on the shy side with them at first, but his mother and Cassandra soon had her discussing jewelry designs and it was like a flower opening, the petals peeled back to reveal the warmth of the woman inside. A warmth that held a true sincerity as she in turn asked questions of them that indicated a real interest in others. Her warmth melted something hard inside him.

Oh, hell.

Mentally, he pulled himself back at the thought and reminded himself that as much as he was coming to admire Jenna…as much as he wanted to keep on spending time with her…their being together was mostly about Chelsea, and about the money. Everything else was a bonus.

And that reminded him what his contact had said yesterday. So far there had been no hint of the money that Stewart Branson had said Liam had conned from him. It was still a mystery. And that meant no one could discount anything just yet. They had to continue trying other avenues. The money may well be tied up somewhere less obvious.

Yet as he turned to go back downstairs, he found himself wishing that he and Jenna had some sort of future together. One that was longer than his usual relationships anyway. He'd be more than happy with that.

Jenna was fully aware the moment Adam walked back out onto the terrace. He'd been quiet throughout the meal, his eyes shifting constantly to her, but not with desire or pleasure. Afterward, he'd gone inside on the pretext of getting something or other, but she had the feeling he'd needed to be alone. She hadn't followed him for that very reason.

His mother had slipped inside shortly after that, and Jenna had to wonder if Laura had gone looking for him. The other woman had only been away ten minutes or so, and on her return Laura had smiled at her, but there had been a suggestion of worry in her eyes. For Adam? And was *she* the problem? Or was she being too sensitive because Adam hadn't wanted her here today? She had to admit that if *her* family was at risk of being thrown a bombshell, she'd be on edge, too.

And yet it still hurt. Did he really think she would tackle Cassandra, his mother, or any of the other family members about Liam? She had as much to lose by doing that as he did. Besides, she'd taken a shine to Cassandra today, and would have to think hard before spoiling the other woman's happiness. Cassandra wasn't to blame for her late husband's actions.

Just then Adam came to sit beside her, and a new apprehension began to gnaw at her stomach. Surely this couldn't only be about the money? He wouldn't have left her alone with his family if that were the case. He'd have stayed by her side without fail, making sure she said nothing out of place.

So what about her being here was troubling him? It didn't take long to come to the conclusion that Adam didn't like her keeping company with his family. She was his temporary mistress, after all. And his family was the highest echelon of Australian society.

It made sense now. Hadn't he been a little remote from the moment he'd collected her before lunch? His cousin had held the door open for her, but Adam hadn't even kissed her hello when she'd slid onto the passenger seat. She'd put that down to Logan being with them. Logan Roth was another male in a family that seemed to produce men with extra good looks, charm and money, and she'd suspected his presence might have curbed Adam's actions. At least, that's what she'd told herself.

As quickly as her thoughts rushed at her, they bounced confusingly back in the other direction. She knew Adam fairly well by now. He was a man who wouldn't let anyone stop him from doing what he wanted. If he'd wanted to kiss her in front of Logan, he would have. If he had minded her being here as his mistress, he'd have refused to let her come. No, there was something not quite right going on here.

"And now I want you all to join us in a celebration," Dominic Roth said, popping open a bottle of champagne, drawing Jenna from her thoughts.

"This sounds interesting," Michael Roth teased, smiling as his eldest son began filling some glasses on a tray and passing them around.

"It's more than interesting, Dad."

"The suspense is killing me, Dominic," his mother said.

"Hang on, Mum." He finished pouring the last drink, snatched up his own glass and gently tugged a glowing Cassandra to her feet. He slipped his arm around his wife's waist. "We're going to have another baby."

It had been clear what the announcement would be, but there was still a moment's delightful surprise. Much congratulations and lots of toasts followed. Jenna felt moved that she'd been here to see all this. For all their money and connections, Adam's family was as close as her own family and with the same values. It was a comforting thought that no matter who you were, the old-fashioned ideals of love of family were still so important.

And then Jenna glanced at Adam. He seemed as glad as everyone else, yet she got the strongest feeling he was off balance about the news. Why? He loved his family more than anything. She only had to see how instinctively he'd defended Liam, and how protective he was about them not knowing about the money.

On the way back to her apartment a few hours later, he kept up an emotional distance. Logan had stayed behind, so it wasn't that his cousin was in the way this time. She felt hurt that he was putting up walls. As far as she knew, nothing had changed between them. He'd seemed happy enough yesterday before his mother's visit, but now it was like part of him wanted to keep her close, another part didn't. As if something—she didn't know what—was holding him back and it was so deep, so intense, he couldn't let himself face it.

In a way, she understood. There was something about Adam that touched an elemental piece of her, drawing emotions she didn't want to acknowledge. Her feelings were strengthening for him and she'd crossed the line, but she wasn't in love with him, thank heavens. Yet. It would be a blessing when this was finally over. Perhaps now was even the time to suggest that very thing….

Back at her place, she started edging to what was on her mind. "I'm sorry, Adam. It might have helped the situation with Chelsea, but I shouldn't have gone with you today. You didn't want me there. I know it and so do you."

There was an interminable pause. "It's not that. It's…" The line of his jaw flexed.

"Yes?"

"I've got some stuff on my mind, that's all."

"Maybe I can help?"

He stood there a moment longer, then, "Come here," he muttered, pulling her into his arms to hold her tight.

"Adam, I—"

He silenced her with a kiss.

And she let him.

They made love, but during it all he still kept up some sort of barrier between them. She tried to reach him on an emotional level, but he was in a place she couldn't follow. He was satisfying her, no doubt about that, yet it was like he was being driven to take her, not driven to make them one, like the previous times they'd made love.

Afterward he went into the bathroom and she tried not to think at all. She needed to regain her sense of balance, but she couldn't do that when thoughts of Adam and this demon that suddenly seemed to be riding him were on her mind.

When he came back out of the bathroom, his face was as white as the towel he'd wrapped around his hips.

She sat up. "What's the matter?"

"The condom was broken."

"What! How?"

"I'm not going into bloody detail. It broke."

"Oh, my God," she whispered.

He just stood there.

Then it started to hit her. She was terrified and yet...she felt the tiniest of thrills. "I could be pregnant already."

"Don't say that," he grated harshly, throwing off the towel and reaching for his pants, bringing her back to reality. His movements were jerky. He was clearly upset.

Jenna got off the bed and went to him. "Look, don't worry about it," she said, trying to stay calm herself. "It'll be fine." She put her hand on his arm.

He tossed it off like he'd tossed away the towel a minute ago. "You know that, do you?"

She was taken aback. "No, I don't know that," she said firmly, aware one of them had to keep their cool. "But I do know that panicking about it won't help the situation."

He gave a hesitant pause that was so uncharacteristic of him. "You're right, of course," he muttered, then continued to finish dressing.

Clearly he was going home and she had no problem with that. But was he going because he had something to do? Or because he wanted to get away from her? The latter filled her with dismay. Did he think so little of her that he'd hate her to have his baby? The reminder that she was only a warm body in his bed brought a hard lump to her throat.

She'd been a fool to think it had been anything other than sex. God, she shouldn't be surprised.

"I'll call you," he said, giving her a brief, hard kiss with a slight lashing of gentleness, as if he just couldn't quite let go of her...yet.

After he left, she sat there and wondered if he really would call her this time. And would it be because he wanted to? Or because she could stir up trouble for his family?

Driving home, Adam felt sick at the thought of the broken condom. Dammit, he should have taken more care, only he hadn't really been concentrating on that. He'd just wanted Jenna and had been trying not to think about anything else. He'd wanted to bury himself in her body and forget that it was coming up to the fifth anniversary of losing his wife and child. He wanted to forget that Dominic and Cassandra were now having another child and that he really was very, very happy for them, but that it only served to remind him he'd lost so much himself.

And now look what his lapse had done!

Jenna could be pregnant.

She could be carrying *his* child.

He couldn't go through that again. A loss like he'd had wasn't something a person could overcome. He could still see Maddie's ecstatic face telling him she was pregnant and the lump of emotion the thought of her carrying his child had brought. She'd been such a lovely person. She'd only wanted to be a good wife and a good mother. And she would have excelled at both.

If she'd been given the chance.

At the next intersection, he turned his car around and headed toward the cemetery.

Nine

Jenna went to work the next day but there were no calls from Adam. Her heart sank that evening when he didn't drop by her apartment, either. He finally phoned her at home, but their conversation was stilted. He was distancing himself from her. Everything had been heading toward this, but clearly the broken condom had been the final straw for him. Whether he'd want to continue the facade for Todd and Chelsea's sake, she wasn't sure.

And if she was pregnant?

She fought not to stress about it. Maybe it was burying her head in the sand, but right now she had too much else to worry about. Nor would she let herself think about what Adam's reaction would be if he were to become a father, though if it was anything like his reaction now she didn't think he was going to like it. Nonetheless, she took comfort that Adam was the kind of man who took his responsibilities seriously. She would worry about it *if* it happened. Not before.

Keeping busy after that was a necessity, especially when he didn't call her at work the next day, or the next evening, nor were there any messages left on her cell phone. But on Wednesday evening her doorbell rang and her heart jumped in her throat. Adam was here! She raced to answer it.

She could feel her face fall with disappointment when she saw her sister-in-law at the door.

Vicki wrinkled her nose. "You look like you were expecting someone else. Sorry, I should have called first."

Jenna summoned a smile. "You're welcome here anytime, Vicki. Come on in."

"I won't stay long if you've got someone else coming soon," she said, stepping into the apartment.

Jenna realized it was fortuitous that Adam wasn't here. It was best to keep them all apart, not because she thought Adam might say something about the money, but because she didn't want Vicki seeing how her relationship with him was falling apart. Right now it was just so personal.

She shook her head and tried to appear unconcerned. "No, I'm not expecting anyone else." She gestured for Vicki to take a seat on the couch. "So, what have you done with the children?"

"I dropped them off at Mum and Dad's place." Vicki's parents had died when she was a teenager, so she considered the older Bransons her parents now. "I told them I wanted to go to the library and get some books and that it was best if I didn't take the kids."

Jenna had an uneasy feeling. "This all sounds rather mysterious."

"It is."

"Would you like a cup of coffee first?" She was starting

to get heart palpitations that Adam might arrive now, but she couldn't be impolite.

"No, thanks." Vicki took a letter out of her handbag. "You might be able to help me figure this out, Jenna. The quarterly bank statement came today for our mortgage and I'm confused. It says that we're behind on payments. Worse, that we still owe three hundred and fifty thousand dollars." Her forehead creased. "Last year we only had fifty thousand dollars left on the loan, so I don't know why this extra amount has been added. And such a large amount, too."

Jenna lowered her lashes, trying to appear as if she knew nothing. "Let me see the statement." Vicki handed it over, but Jenna already knew what she'd find. "Yes, that's what it says."

If only Stewart had thought to have mail from the bank sent directly to him. Of course, he'd been a mess when he'd left the country and no doubt it hadn't occurred to him. Anyway, Vicki had said "quarterly" bank statements. Just their luck the end of the quarter had been now.

"It has to be a mistake, right?" Vicki said.

Jenna tried to appear unconcerned. "I'm sure it is."

Vicki looked relieved. "That's what I thought. I didn't get to open the letter until tonight. Otherwise I would have phoned them to check."

Thank God she hadn't. "Did you mention this to Stewart?"

"He's only contactable via email at the moment, but no, I didn't want to worry him when he's so far away. And I didn't want to worry Mum and Dad, so I didn't tell them, either."

Jenna nodded, greatly relieved on both counts. "Good thinking. No need to worry any of them."

Vicki's brows drew together. "The trouble is it's my turn

to help out with the lunches at the school tomorrow and I'll be busy all day with that. I won't be able to phone the bank in private." She paused. "Do you think you could phone them for me tomorrow sometime?"

Jenna knew instantly that the bank wouldn't speak to her about it, but she needed time to think about this latest development. "Sure, leave it with me. I'll see what I can find out and give you a call tomorrow night." If she could just stretch things out, give Adam time to end the investigation and put the money back, then perhaps Vicki need know nothing of what had transpired.

"Come for dinner after work," Vicki said. "It would be lovely for the girls to see you again. They've missed you."

Jenna's heart softened. "I've missed them, too."

Vicki left after that and Jenna sat on the couch and worried herself crazy. She had Stewart's email address, so she should probably contact him about it all, but that would only upset him, being so far away from home and unable to explain it all to Vicki in person.

Damn her brother for letting himself get involved with Liam Roth. And damn her brother for getting *her* involved in this, as well. It was affecting too many lives now. Perhaps destroying them.

An hour later Jenna couldn't stand it any longer. She'd been debating whether to go see Adam tomorrow morning at his office about what Vicki had told her, or to go see him now. She chose the latter, unable to sleep not knowing what was going on with him, both personally and with the money.

She didn't phone him first though, frightened he might put her off coming. It was only on the way over in her car it occurred to her that another woman might be there with him. Her heart constricted at the thought. Well, then, at least she'd know it was officially over.

The concierge was pleasant, but he insisted on phoning the penthouse first, and she was fine with that. In the quietness of the foyer, she could hear Adam's voice as he answered. There was the slightest pause when he heard who wanted to see him, though Jenna was at least grateful the concierge didn't seem to notice. Or he was probably too well trained to show it.

"Go on up, Ms. Branson."

Adam was waiting when she stepped out of the elevator. Her step faltered as she walked toward him. He looked as gorgeous as ever, but his face was slightly pale and that caught at her heartstrings. Was the thought of her being pregnant making him look like this?

She frowned. "Adam, are you okay?"

He avoided her eyes as he leaned down and kissed her, not on her mouth but on the *cheek*. "I'm fine." He gestured for her to take a seat on the couch, but she preferred to stand.

She surreptitiously glanced around, noting the papers spread on the dining table where he'd obviously been working. She was intensely relieved not to see any signs of another woman's presence. "I'm interrupting your work."

He grimaced. "The last couple of days have been... hectic."

"I see," she said slowly. Then she took a deep breath. "Adam, my sister-in-law came to see me tonight." She explained about the bank statement. "So I was wondering if you knew anything more about the money?"

His face shuttered. "No, I'm afraid not. It's still being investigated."

"Oh." She frowned. "It's taking a long time, isn't it?"

He shot her a glare. "That's the way it is sometimes."

"I see." She drew herself up straighter. Clearly she wasn't going to get anything more out of him about this right now. "Please let me know if you find out anything."

"I will."

He was like a stranger, and she couldn't stand it any longer. Her niggling doubts suddenly took over. "Look, Adam, if we're finished please tell me now."

"What the hell!" His brow knitted together. "What gave you that idea?"

She faced him fully. "Oh, just a little matter of you not wanting to be with me, that's all."

And the kiss on the cheek before.

And the condom breaking.

His gaze held hers. "I *do* want to be with you."

She didn't let herself acknowledge relief. "Really? You're very good at putting up walls."

A curious look passed over his face. "What are you on about?"

"You've stayed away all this week, yet last week you couldn't get enough of me."

"I still want you," he growled. "Don't doubt that."

"Then why aren't you showing it?" she challenged, relieved but not.

He heaved a sigh. "Look, with Dominic back in the office we've had a lot of work to catch up on. We're working on something new, too. It's eating into my evenings."

She searched his eyes, wanting him to tell her the truth even if it wasn't what she wanted to hear. He seemed sincere, yet… "Do you realize you've never stayed overnight at my apartment?"

He stiffened. "So?"

"It's your way of keeping your distance, isn't it?"

His brows drew into a straight line. "I've let you stay here overnight. How can that be keeping you at a distance?"

"Don't try and confuse the issue. This is about *you* staying with *me,* not *me* staying with *you.*"

He gave a short laugh. "There's a difference?"

"You know there is." She would stand here until he acknowledged it. "See, you're doing it even now. You're trying to twist things around so I won't notice that you're holding yourself back from me."

Another short laugh. "Obviously, it's not working."

"Don't make fun."

He sent her a sharp look, then ran his fingers through his hair. "What do you want from me, Jenna?"

"Honesty, Adam. Just plain old honesty."

Several seconds crept by.

"So you want honesty?"

She braced herself. "Yes."

He expelled a breath. "Yesterday was the fifth anniversary of my wife's death," he said, making her gasp. "*That's* why I've stayed away this week."

Her breath deserted her for a couple of seconds. "Oh, Adam, I'm sorry. I didn't know."

"I didn't expect you to know," he said in a low voice.

She felt a twinge that he had shut her out, but then, he didn't owe it to her to tell her this. It was such a private thing. She just wished… "I've made it worse for you."

He took steps toward her and pulled her close. "You didn't," he muttered into her hair. "I've been trying to keep busy and work through it all."

Her heart ached for his ache.

"Tell me about your wife." She felt him startle against her and she frowned as she eased back. "You don't want to talk about her?"

"No, it's not that. It's just…no other woman has asked me to talk about Maddie before."

Her heart swelled. "I'm glad I'm the first."

Squeezing her hands, he stepped back and went to stand a few feet away near the dining table, putting distance between them, but this time she understood his need to stand alone.

He lifted his shoulders. "Where to begin?"

"What sort of person was she?" Jenna asked, helping him out, curious all the same.

"Beautiful." He smiled at himself, then inclined his head. "A beautiful person. She loved life and it showed. She used to giggle a lot. A schoolgirl type of giggle. She was such a practical joker."

"She sounds like she was great fun."

"She was. The day she was…" his eyes filled with pain "…killed, she had all these balloons in the car. I assume she was bringing them home to plant around the house as a surprise. The police don't know why she swerved into a light pole, but we think it might have been because of the balloons. A witness said she saw Maddie trying to push one over the backseat just before the accident." He took a shuddering breath, looking bleak. "God, it seems like only yesterday she was here with me. Yet at the same time it seems like forever."

A lump welled in her throat. "Oh, Adam."

He gave a hard laugh. "Did you really want to hear all this?"

She went to him then, slipped her arms around him and hugged him tight, wanting to take away his pain. "Yes," she whispered, leaning up and kissing him tenderly on the mouth. "Adam, I'm so sorry for your loss."

"I know."

"Would it be wrong of me to make love to you right now?"

His eyes darkened. "I think it would be very right."

She kissed him again, then took his hand and led him

into his bedroom where she stripped the clothes from both their bodies and made love to him, needing to help him forget his pain.

They both fell asleep, but in the early hours of the morning she woke and lay there curled up beside him, thinking about what he'd told her. Until now she hadn't really had time to reflect on Adam being a widower. She'd had so many other things of concern that thinking beyond any immediate problems hadn't really been an option.

Now she at least knew what was going on with him. Their relationship wouldn't lead anywhere in the long run, but she was pleased she at least understood some of his actions. He'd lost the love of his life and he wasn't about to settle for second best. Sadly, to him all women were considered second best…and that included *her*.

At the thought, she knew she needed some breathing space. Careful not to wake him, she slid out of bed and dressed quietly, then crept out of the apartment, leaving him sleeping heavily.

It was only as she drove home that something occurred to her. Adam had said nothing about the possibility of her being pregnant, and she hadn't brought it up, either. It was as if he'd shut it out of his mind. Thinking back on the terrible week that he'd had, there was no way she'd remind him now.

By midmorning Jenna was over her need for time-out and was eager to see Adam again, so she was delighted when he called her at work on her cell phone.

"How about lunch today?" he asked. "Can you get away around noon?"

"That would be wonderful."

He sounded pleased to be seeing her again, and she felt the same. She'd decided to take this moment by moment, but it made her feel good to know he was putting in an effort to be with her.

Except that when Jenna entered the restaurant, she was dismayed to see Adam wasn't alone. He was sitting at a table with Todd and Chelsea.

He pushed to his feet as soon as he saw her and weaved through the tables, his eyes set on her face. "Sorry," he muttered, kissing her briefly on the mouth. "They were already here and I couldn't ignore them. Now smile."

She pasted on a smile as he guided her to the table, but Jenna was wondering if Chelsea had known Adam would be here today. It might only have taken a well-placed phone call to his personal assistant to find out.

The other pair welcomed her in a friendly manner, but she couldn't help notice the friendliness didn't reach Chelsea's eyes. Then the other woman's gaze flickered down over Jenna's pants and top that until this moment had felt more than passable. Now she felt like something the dog had dragged in.

No one had ordered yet, and while they made their decision Chelsea seemed to go into overdrive again. She laughed loudly at something on the menu, pointing it out to Adam in a flirtatious way, then asked the waiter for another glass of wine as she tossed back the remains of her half-empty glass in a way that actually made Todd's mouth tighten. At that point Jenna suspected the other pair's presence hadn't been by design. They really had been about to lunch together, and now Chelsea was thrown by the appearance of her and Adam.

And then from over at another table in the corner, a baby suddenly started to cry and Chelsea seemed to freeze a moment before her eyes flew to her husband's face. Something passed between them.

"Chels, don't—" Todd began.

Chelsea pushed to her feet. "Shut up, Todd," she choked in a low, pain-filled voice. "Just shut up!" Grabbing her purse, she rushed out of the restaurant.

There was a stunned silence at their table.

Todd surged to his feet, but paused to look at them both. "I have to go," he muttered, then twisted around and hurried after his wife.

Adam and Jenna sat in a pocket of silence for a few seconds, their gazes following Todd. The noise in the restaurant remained static, so it didn't appear that others had noticed anything out of the ordinary.

"What the hell was that about?" Adam finally said.

"I'm not sure."

Outside the restaurant, they saw Chelsea flag down a taxi and almost fall onto the backseat. Todd reached it just as the vehicle drove away. Like a defeated man, he stood and watched as his wife slipped out of sight, then he slowly turned and came back into the restaurant.

He was pale as he flopped down onto his chair. "I'm sorry you saw that."

Adam frowned at his friend. "What's up, Todd?"

Todd winced. "I didn't want to say anything before but…" He lowered his gaze and took a deep breath before looking up again. "About two months ago we found out Chelsea was pregnant," he said, making Jenna gasp. She felt Adam stiffen beside her. "We were both thrilled. Then…she lost the baby and…" His eyes held anguish as he focused on Adam, sharing his pain with his friend. "Things haven't been the same since. That baby crying just now tipped her over the edge."

Jenna tried not to think how *she* would feel in the same circumstances. Not when she might be pregnant herself. Oh, God, she wasn't going there.

Surprisingly, Adam didn't speak. Could he be thinking

about *her* carrying his child? Or was he silenced by his friend's heartache?

She dared not look at him as she stepped in the breach and said sympathetically, "I'm so sorry, Todd."

The other man inclined his head. "Thanks." Then he looked back at Adam. "I didn't want to say anything to you, Adam." He paused. "You can see why, can't you?"

Adam seemed to pull himself together. "Yes, of course," he said somewhat abruptly, but he looked pale, and Jenna was reminded how seriously to heart Adam took this friendship with Todd. They were very close.

"Chels hasn't been the same since it happened," Todd was saying now. "She seems to have gone off track somehow. We've both been putting on a brave face, but I know it's eating her up inside."

A couple of seconds ticked by and no one spoke, but both men looked extremely worried. Jenna had to admit Chelsea didn't seem like a stalker now, just sad. The other woman had a wonderful husband who loved her and hopefully many more babies in their future, but first they had to get through this.

"Have you tried talking to her?" she asked, wanting to help.

Todd gave a short shake of his head. "No. Every time I do she starts to cry and I feel helpless, so I end up letting her be."

Jenna's brows drew together. "She needs you, Todd. You really should go after her."

"She'll only start crying again."

"Then let her cry." She tilted her head at him. "And perhaps you ought to have a good cry right along with her. It might be the only way to deal with this."

Todd blinked.

Adam cleared his throat. "Jenna's right. You both need to work through your grief before you can move on."

There was a pause. "I guess we do have to start somewhere." A determined light grew in Todd's eyes as he rose to his feet. "Thanks, you two." The sincerity in his eyes encompassed them both before he left the restaurant.

Jenna silently wished the pair well.

Then her gaze returned to the man beside her. "Looks like we've got our answer why Chelsea has been acting so strange."

Adam was trying to cope with the shaft of pain in his chest. Todd and Chelsea had lost a baby? Todd had gone through the same thing *he* had gone through? He could understand why his friend hadn't wanted to tell him. Todd would be remembering Adam's darkest days.

Of course, Todd would also be aware of one big difference. He at least still had a wife to help him get through this.

Unlike Adam.

Thank heavens he'd thought to cut Todd off before he'd said anything more in front of Jenna. No one knew about Maddie having been pregnant when she'd died. No one except him and Todd and the hospital staff. Todd had promised he'd never tell a soul, not even Chelsea. Adam fully believed that he'd kept his word. Chelsea wouldn't be acting so foolish toward her husband's best friend if she'd known they had losing a baby in common.

A baby.

Jenna could be pregnant.

"I suspected there was something more going on between them."

Jenna's words jolted him back into the moment. He scowled at her. "You didn't say anything to me about that."

She lifted one slim shoulder. "It was a hunch, nothing more. It wouldn't have helped the situation. We couldn't do anything about it."

He thought about that, and admitted, "Yeah, I got the same hunch when Todd invited us to their vacation home. He told me Chelsea had some sort of female problems. He didn't say it was something serious."

Jenna began to chew her lip. "I think she might have phoned me once. It was the evening we came back from their vacation home."

"What!"

"When I answered, no one spoke. It was quiet for a few seconds, then they hung up. I still think it was Chelsea. I suspect she was trying to see if you were with me."

"Why the hell didn't you tell me?"

"It was nothing. Not really. And I had no proof." She sighed. "Poor Chelsea."

He took a calming breath. "Yes." Chelsea's grief had made her look foolish, that was all.

"I guess you were just a distraction from her losing the baby." There was compassion in Jenna's voice. She considered him. "I don't think she'll be after you anymore, do you?"

She was right. "No, I don't think so, either." And that was a great relief. "But she probably still needs to see us together for a while longer. At least until she gets her head in a good place."

"Good idea."

He suddenly felt the need to say more. "Anyway, I don't plan on giving you up just yet, Jenna." And she'd better not think otherwise. To make sure, he reminded her, "This isn't only about Chelsea. We need to get the money sorted out with your brother." There was no escaping that fact. "That's the reason we came together in the first place."

Her gaze faltered. "True." She moistened her mouth. "So, this means I owe you two more weeks of my time. While you find the money for Stewart, that is."

His jaw clenched and he wanted to say that as far as he was concerned, finding the money wasn't for Stewart. It was to clear his own brother's name, if he could.

And one of them was going to lose big-time.

Just then, he caught sight of the waiter coming their way. "Let's have some lunch."

She hesitated. "Actually, Adam, I'm not very hungry right now. I hope you don't mind."

He realized he'd lost his appetite, too. "I'm not hungry, either." He pushed to his feet and helped her out of her chair. "Come on. I'll walk you back to work."

As they left the restaurant he noticed his cell phone had a couple of messages from the private investigator. He didn't mention it to Jenna, but his heart had just slammed right into his ribs.

At Vicki's place that evening, once they'd had dinner and the children had gone to bed, Jenna relayed the information she'd learned from the bank. To make herself feel better about deceiving her sister-in-law, she'd phoned the bank this afternoon, and as suspected had been told they would only deal with their customer. Jenna had mentioned that Vicki would call tomorrow then, and was told that the account was in Stewart's name and only Stewart could discuss the account with them.

"Really?" Vicki said with dismay. "They won't talk to me about it? It's *my* house, for goodness' sake!"

"Yes, but the account is in Stewart's name only."

Vicki frowned. "We never realized it would be a problem."

Jenna wondered if Stewart had done that deliberately.

Of course, he really couldn't have known he would lose his money. No person in their right mind would put their house up as collateral if they thought they were going to lose it.

Vicki nodded, still clearly worried, but trying not to show it. "Thanks for checking for me, sweetie. I appreciate it."

"That's okay. I'm glad to help."

"I'll email Stewart tonight and tell him there's a problem with the account," Vicki said. "He can email the bank himself and give them permission to talk to me while he's out of the country. Once he's back we'll have to see about putting the house in both names."

"Sounds good," Jenna said, though she suspected Stewart's first action would be to call or email *her* about it. He didn't know she had forced Adam to help sort this out, and he would be frantic when he received Vicki's email in case his wife discovered the truth about the money.

No doubt he would come up with a plan for delaying the inevitable. Knowing her brother, he'd soon realize he only had to pretend to Vicki about putting her name down as a contact. Once he returned to Australia, he'd be hoping to replace most of the money himself, though he had no idea the money might still be repaid out of Liam's account—and she wouldn't tell him. She didn't want him to get his hopes up on something that may not come to be.

And why the heck was she being so considerate of Stewart at the moment? She didn't feel too kindly toward him right now. Either way he'd have covered his own butt.

"So you're telling me you can't find any trace of the money?" Adam ground out. Today had been one shock after another. First Todd and Chelsea at lunch, now the forensic accountant was meeting him here in his penthouse before dinner rather than risk him coming to the office. He wanted his family knowing nothing about this.

"That's right, Mr. Roth. And believe me, I've had my people check thoroughly. They know all the tricks and all the places money can be hidden in secret accounts, and there's nothing to be found. Absolutely nothing."

It was as he'd suspected. "So Stewart Branson didn't give any money to my brother?"

"No."

"So it's a con job," he said, his lips flattening with anger. And Jenna was in on it, along with her brother. He should have listened to his gut instinct from the beginning.

"It certainly looks like it. I have some pretty damning evidence."

Adam scowled. "Evidence? But I thought you just said you couldn't find anything?"

"I didn't. But I *have* discovered something very interesting. Did you know that Stewart Branson…"

By the time Adam finished listening, he was more than angry. He was ice-cold furious. He latched on to the feeling, taking pleasure in the pain, knowing it was far better than thinking about any other matter with Jenna that might be totally out of his control. *Nothing* was going to be out of his control again where she was concerned. Not ever again.

Ten

Jenna left Vicki's house fairly early with the excuse that she had to work tomorrow. There had been no calls on her cell phone, and she wanted to get home now to see if there were any messages from Adam on her answering machine. After what had happened at the restaurant today, she thought he might have contacted her to talk more about Todd and Chelsea.

Adam was waiting at her apartment door when she stepped out from the elevator. Joy swept through her.

She smiled as she came toward him. "Have you been waiting long?"

"Long enough," was the curt reply.

She looked at his set face, and her smile slipped. Perhaps she'd heard wrong? It could have merely been the acoustics here in the hallway. Or maybe something else had cropped up with his friends?

She smiled again. A smaller one this time. "I didn't know you were coming. I've been out to dinner."

His mouth tightened, but up closer she could see something flicker in eyes that had a definite hardness to them. "Just open the door," he said in a clipped tone.

She did.

Something was seriously wrong. Was he angry because she hadn't been home waiting for his arrival? That made her even angrier with herself now for hurrying home. She wasn't going to pander to him, she decided, going over and putting her handbag on the couch.

"So, what's up?" She angled her chin as she turned to face him. She might be his mistress, but she wasn't about to take the brunt of his bad mood.

"You are," he snapped. "You're a real piece of work, lady."

Air rushed into her lungs. "Wh-what do you mean?"

His top lip curled. "So innocent. You play the part well."

She stiffened. "What are you talking about?"

"Remember how I met with that business acquaintance last Saturday?"

"Yes."

"It was about the money."

A light dimmed inside her. He'd said his appointment was business, and she supposed it was…but to not mention it had been about the money was deceiving.

She drew herself up. "Tell me."

"That guy had been through everything and checked everywhere to see if your brother had given Liam any money. Up until last Saturday there was still no trace of any transaction, but we decided to keep on trying. By this afternoon he'd exhausted all avenues and concluded no such transaction had ever taken place."

Her brain stumbled. "That can't be," she whispered.

"Can't it?"

She thought for a moment, then something occurred to her. "Just because you found nothing doesn't prove a thing."

"No, but I found out something very interesting in the meantime. Your brother has a gambling problem."

She could only blink. Her mouth tried to work but wouldn't.

His lips twisted. "You're surprised? Or surprised that I know?"

"Wh-what?"

"You and your brother have been caught out, Jenna. Admit it. Your brother lost the money gambling, and you both concocted this scheme to get me to give you money so that he can put it back in his bank account for the mortgage. It was brilliant. A dead man can't talk, can he? Liam can't deny the charges and I can't prove conclusively that the money *didn't* change hands. Not yet anyway."

She was trying to get her head around this. He was saying that Stewart had gambled the money away and hadn't given any money to Liam to invest at all? That he had made up all this to get the grief-stricken Roth family to replace the money? And worst of all that *she'd* planned this with her brother?

"You're not serious," was all she could manage.

"Dead serious, my sweet."

And he was.

She shook her head. "Apart from knowing I've done nothing wrong, I don't believe what you're saying about Stewart. You're just trying to get out of paying. You're making it all up."

He ripped some papers from his jacket pocket and thrust

them at her. "I have it all in writing. Read it and see. You can't dispute it."

Her hands shook as she took the paperwork and began to read. She could feel the blood drain from every cell in her body. It was all there in black and white.

"Your brother has been gambling under an assumed name so that no one would trace it back to him. He's been living another life. Stewart Branson is as clean as a whistle and that's why it took so long to discover this."

She shook her head. "I don't believe it," she muttered, more to try and convince herself that the paperwork in front of her was a bunch of lies. How could it *not* be?

"I'm sure," he said sarcastically. "Hell, you probably increased the amount and asked for more money than he needed, intending to put the money back in his account *and* pay off this fancy new apartment you've bought yourself."

That last bit brought her up short. "I took out a mortgage on this apartment." She was proud of buying this place from her earnings. It was all aboveboard and honestly earned.

"Which you could still have paid off early and no one would be the wiser." A second ticked by. "You've been caught out, Jenna. Admit it."

How could she admit to something she hadn't done?

"What if I told you I didn't know anything about Stewart's gambling? What if I believed he was telling me the truth?"

"I'd say you were lying."

"You *want* to believe that, Adam."

"No, I *have* to believe it. This scam is serious business. Three hundred thousand dollars is a lot of money."

"I don't want any money that doesn't belong to Stewart, Adam."

"You've suddenly found some principles, have you?"

"Obviously you'll think what you want." She steadied her breathing, then considered him. "You believe I lied to you, but you lied to me too, Adam."

That brought him up short. "When?"

"When I asked you last night you said you didn't know anything further about the money. You didn't mention what the appointment last Saturday was about, nor that there were further questions about not being able to trace anything."

Nothing on his face relented. "Rule Number One. Don't tell your enemy your game plan."

Hurt sliced through her. "So I'm your enemy now, am I?"

"Were you ever anything else?"

She gave a soft gasp. "Thanks very much."

For a split second he looked pained, then he glared at her. "You used me, Jenna. You used me to try and get money out of me to help your brother, and probably some for yourself, as well. So don't try and make it sound like *I'm* the one who did anything wrong."

This man in front of her was a stranger, his face hard, his eyes like steel. He wasn't about to relent. He was totally convinced of Stewart's guilt.

Of *her* guilt.

"Are you going to the police about this?" she asked, not in fear for herself, but for Stewart. If he really did have a gambling problem…if she'd inadvertently made demands of Adam Roth on his behalf…where would it lead?

A light of triumph entered his eyes. He thought she was guilty and running scared. He gave a sharp shake of his head. "No, I want to spare my family any further pain."

Her shoulders sagged with relief.

"But if I'm pushed, then I *will* go to the police," he warned. "Don't doubt that. So I suggest your brother gets some help. He's been dealing with some unsavory types and next time he may not be able to pay them off. If he lands in debt with them again, they'll no doubt sort him out."

"Oh, my God." Her voice quavered from deep inside. This was getting worse every minute. It sounded as if Stewart's life could be in danger in future.

There was a pause, and Adam almost looked sorry for her. "He needs help with his addiction, Jenna."

"I know," she murmured, finally admitting out loud that it must be true about Stewart.

"And you need help, too. You can't go around conning money from people."

She thrust out her chin. "I only wanted repaid what I thought belonged to Stewart."

"So you say," he mocked. "By the way, I said I'd merely look into the money. I didn't say I'd pay it back. Ever." A vein pulsed near his temple. "I owe you nothing."

"And I don't know you at all, do I?"

"No, you don't." He twisted away and slammed out the door.

Jenna sank onto the couch, a sense of pain so intense, so acute she could feel it like a very real punch in her heart. And there was only one reason for it. For the first time she knew.

She loved Adam Roth.

Bile sat in Adam's throat as he drove home. He should have known Jenna was too good to be true. All that pretending to be concerned about her brother losing his home. And her concern for her sister-in-law and nieces. It had all been lies. Sure, she'd been concerned, but only because she was in on it with her brother. Her sister-in-law might even be a part of it, too. How many others had the Bransons tried to scam?

God, what a fool he'd been. He'd actually thought she was like his mother and Cassandra. He'd actually thought Jenna had integrity, even if it had been misplaced with her brother.

He'd been wrong.

Totally.

It would never happen again, he decided, hardening what was left of his pride. No woman was ever going to get the slightest chance to make a fool of him again. He was a playboy through and through, and that's the way it was going to stay.

And whenever he thought of Jenna Branson in the future, he'd imagine a mere notch on his bedpost...even if it killed him.

Jenna wasn't sure how long she sat there after Adam had gone. Time didn't matter. Not when her heart was breaking. How could Adam think this of her? How could he believe she would have anything to do with deceiving anyone, let alone him? It hurt to think about it.

And then there was Stewart.

No wonder her brother had told her to let things be when she'd first suggested approaching the Roths. He'd known he hadn't given Liam Roth any money. How fortuitous for him that Liam's funeral had been on the television the day he'd come to her apartment. It had given him the excuse he'd needed to justify both his wan appearance and his newly increased mortgage. He'd put on a thoroughly convincing act.

The only good thing now was that Stewart must have used the mortgage money to repay his gambling debts. Otherwise they'd be after him...perhaps even Vicki and the children. The thought made her feel sick.

God, Adam had been right that it would happen again

if Stewart didn't get help. Gambling was an addiction. She hadn't had personal experience of it until now, and she wasn't exactly sure what it all meant, but she suspected he wouldn't be able to control it without some sort of outside assistance and support. Knowing Stewart, he probably wasn't about to do that unless pushed.

Her mouth firmed with determination as she jumped to her feet and went to turn on her computer. Her brother was going to get one hell of an email from her right now. She wasn't going to mention her affair, but she would tell him everything else that had occurred since the day she'd met Adam at the races. It seemed another lifetime ago now instead of mere weeks.

And then she wanted answers.

She did that, then changed into more comfortable clothes before making herself a cup of coffee. She waited. An hour later her telephone rang.

It was Stewart.

"Jenna, what the hell have you done?" he demanded down the line, sounding as if he was in the room with her and not in the Middle East.

She wished he was. She'd box his ears, as well as give him an earful. "Me? Good God, Stewart! You're the one who lied and cheated. Why on earth did you concoct such a story?"

She heard him curse. "It would have been okay if you hadn't confronted Adam Roth. I had it all worked out. I've made some money, and I was about to bank a lump sum, but now you've got us implicated in some sort of elaborate swindle."

She couldn't believe he was blaming *her*. "Maybe you should have been honest with me in the first place," she said through gritted teeth.

"And what about Vicki?" he said, ignoring her comment.

"Did you tell her anything about this? Is that how come she got her hands on the bank statement?" he demanded, his words telling her Vicki must have already emailed him tonight about him making it a joint account.

This so wasn't fair. *She* was getting blamed from all angles. "The bank sent the quarterly statement to the house because *you* forgot all about it."

There was a pause. "I can't be expected to think of everything, you know."

"Well, you should have preempted that and had the statement sent to the Middle East, or even to me. It's fortunate for you that the account isn't in joint names, or Vicki would be frantic by now. And no, she doesn't know about any of this. I've only just found out myself." And she wasn't over the shock of it.

"You're not going to tell her, are you?"

"No. *You* are."

"Don't be ridiculous, Jenna. It's sorted out now. You said in your email that Roth wasn't going to press charges. I'll be making enough money over the next few months to put it all back on the mortgage. Vicki doesn't need to hear about this. Let it rest."

It was tempting to let things ride, but she knew she couldn't do that to her brother. She loved him too much.

"You're fooling yourself, Stewart. You've got a gambling addiction and it isn't going away. Eventually you'll get the urge to gamble again and who knows what will happen next time? Some of those people might decide to play dirty if you don't pay up."

He gave a hard laugh. "You've been watching too many gangster movies."

"Have I?"

There was dead silence.

"It'll be fine, Jenna," he said tightly. "Trust me."

"I'm sorry. I can't. Next time you might lose the house. And you might lose Vicki and the girls. They deserve better."

The words hung in the air.

He made a sound like a groan. "I can't tell her, Jenna."

"You don't have a choice," she pointed out, then heard herself say, "If you don't tell her, then *I* will."

"You wouldn't!"

"Yes, I would." But surely he wouldn't let her. When it all came down to it, if Vicki had to know, then he had to be the one to tell his wife.

"Okay, you win, sis. *You* do it."

"Wh-what!" Jenna almost dropped the phone.

"Look, I'm thousands of miles away, and telling Vicki this in a phone call isn't the way to go. You're absolutely right that she deserves better. She deserves to hear this directly. If you do this, you can answer any questions she has and judge how she is taking it. I don't want her to do anything silly."

She blanched. He'd well and truly called her bluff... and yet she wasn't beyond a bit of manipulation herself. "Okay, I'll do it. But only if you promise to get help for your addiction as soon as you get home." She took a moment to let that sink in. "And I'm going to tell Mum and Dad, as well."

"You can't do that!"

"They deserve to know, Stewart," she said, making sure her tone held no nonsense. She wouldn't relent on this. "I tell them as well, or I don't say anything and I let *you* sort it out when you get back, and by then you'll probably have Vicki frantic with worry. She might even hop on a plane and come and see you."

He swore. "Okay. Do it." He paused, then muttered, "I never knew you were such a hard person, sis."

Not hard enough apparently, she decided as they finished the call and hung up. A thank-you would have been nice.

The next day Jenna took the day off work, asked Vicki to leave the kids with a babysitter, then she met them all at her parents' place where she told them everything about Stewart and Liam Roth. She left out any mention of her and Adam's relationship, and she definitely didn't tell them she was in love with him. She'd leave it for a while, then let them think things had cooled and died a natural death. At least she was no longer a mistress.

Of course, telling her family about Stewart was one of the hardest things she'd ever had to do. The enormity and complexity of Stewart's gambling problem upset everyone. After the shock had worn off, it was clear they were all going to support him. Her parents had fifty thousand dollars they offered to put into their son's mortgage account, but that was their retirement money and Vicki flatly refused, stating that Stewart had to take responsibility for all this. Jenna had always loved Vicki, but at that moment she admired the other woman for everything she stood for.

Mother and wife.

Later, Jenna decided to leave them to talk. She'd had enough of it all and just wanted to go home and lie down and *not think*. She'd spent such a restless night going over what she had to say. It was upsetting.

As she walked to the front door, Jenna discovered her mother saw more than she'd realized.

"Adam Roth," Joyce began. "He seems a good man."

She tried not to react. "He is, Mum. Very good."

Her mother searched her face. "He doesn't hold your brother's gambling problem against you, does he?"

She winced inwardly. "No, of course not," she lied,

then kissed her cheek. "I have to go. I've got to finish up something at work." She moved to leave.

"Jenna?"

Her steps stopped. "Yes?"

"You're a good sister. Thank you for helping Stewart."

Love rose inside Jenna's chest. She hugged her mother one last time. "Thanks, Mum," she murmured, warmth staying with her until she arrived home at her apartment.

Then it suddenly all felt so empty.

Just like her.

Eleven

Over the next few weeks Adam threw himself into his job. He'd stayed in Melbourne to help his father run the business while Dominic had been away on his second honeymoon, but now he went back to traveling interstate. He'd often come home to Melbourne a couple of times a week, but then was off again the next day, checking on his family's department stores all over the country. It kept him busy.

As did the women he dated.

Not that they gave him much satisfaction anymore. He pretended to enjoy their company and he even tried to enjoy a good-night kiss, but whenever he tried to take it further something held him back. He just didn't want any of these women.

He wanted only Jenna.

Damn her.

But what was the use of wanting someone who was a liar and a cheat? Someone who had tried to con him and his family out of money they had nothing to do with? Dammit, when he thought about Jenna approaching his parents about Liam…telling them their dead son owed money…he could feel his blood boil.

And he refused to think about her being pregnant. Okay, so that was something he couldn't lay blame on her for. The broken condom had been an unfortunate incident, that's all. Beyond that he couldn't think about it—*wouldn't* think about it. It just wasn't going to happen.

He was at the office the following week when his PA announced he had some visitors. He groaned to himself as Chelsea and Todd came into his office. He'd spoken to Todd a couple of days after Chelsea had run out of the restaurant all those weeks ago. Things were going well for them now and they were trying for another baby.

Since then, he'd returned Todd's calls a couple of times and acted as natural as possible, but he had heard the worry in his friend's voice. Todd had remembered it had been the anniversary of Maddie's death, besides realizing Adam wasn't seeing Jenna anymore. Adam hadn't elaborated on the latter.

"We were just walking by and decided to stop in and see you," Todd said, his eyes sharpening as he did a quick study of Adam. "So, how have you been?"

"Busy." Adam gave him a wry smile as he gestured for them to sit down.

"We've just had two weeks in Paris," Chelsea bubbled.

Something inside Adam relaxed as he sat down on his chair. Happiness had eluded him, but he'd never wish the same for his friends.

He smiled across the desk at her, his first genuine smile for Chelsea in many months. "You're looking very happy."

"I am," she said, reaching out and taking hold of Todd's

hand beside her. "It was so romantic. Todd really knows how to sweep a girl off her feet."

"She's as light as a feather," Todd quipped, winking at Adam, not looking the least embarrassed. He'd earned his right to romanticize his wife.

Then Todd's eyes narrowed. "Everything okay with you?"

"Sure." Adam appreciated his friend's concern, but he didn't really need it.

Just then, Todd's cell phone rang. He was instantly all business. "Excuse me. I have to answer this." He got up and was speaking into his phone as he went in the outer office.

Chelsea immediately sat forward on her chair, not smiling now. "This is awkward for me, Adam," she said, keeping her voice low. "But I want to apologize to you. I know I made you uncomfortable. I went a little crazy there. I lost the…baby…and it seemed like Todd didn't care."

Adam's heart constricted for her loss. "It's okay. I understand."

"Please don't tell Todd how I…harassed you. I really do only think of you as a friend."

It was a relief to hear her say that. "I won't."

She held his gaze, reading the sincerity in his eyes. Then she sat back on her chair. "Todd said you're not seeing Jenna anymore."

He could feel himself freeze up. "No, I'm not."

"I'm sorry. She seemed very nice."

"Yes, she did, didn't she?"

Thankfully, Todd came back and the conversation turned to more mundane things. They didn't stay long after that and left with his promise to visit them soon.

No sooner had they left, than his mother came marching into his office, parental purpose in her elegant steps. Adam swore under his breath. Was this some sort of conspiracy or what? So far he'd managed to avoid her these past two weeks.

"You haven't been returning my calls, Adam," Laura Roth said.

"I've been traveling around. Didn't Dad tell you?"

"Of course he told me. So did Dominic, but that doesn't make up for not hearing your voice myself."

"Mum, I've been busy."

"Yes, I know. I've seen the women you've been busy with in the papers."

He stiffened. "You have a problem with that?"

"What happened to Jenna? She was lovely."

How could he tell her anything close to the truth? Liam had been innocent of the crime, but why give his mother something more to think about in her grief? It was unnecessary that she know.

"It didn't work out. Sometimes that happens. Not everyone is compatible."

His mother shook her head. "No, you two were definitely compatible." She watched him steadily. "I think you're just scared after Maddie."

He felt the pain, then pushed it away. In any case, perhaps it was best she believe that. It would save any further hassle.

He shrugged. "I can't help what you think, Mum."

She held his gaze. "I really thought you might find happiness with Jenna."

"Did you?"

She made a face. "I can see you don't want to talk."

"No, I don't. I'm a busy man." Then gently, he said, "I'm sorry."

She didn't say anything for a moment. "So am I, Adam.

Sorry you're going to end up old and alone with no one to love you," she said, not appeased.

He raised an eyebrow at her. "So that means *you* won't love me when I'm old and alone?"

She gave him a light smack on the arm, then kissed him and left. His mother had said Jenna was a keeper the day they'd all lunched together at his parents' place. She'd been wrong about that. Laura Roth was the one to keep.

At least he could relax now that his mother had caught up with him. And maybe now she would rest easier knowing she couldn't do anything more. He prayed she'd leave it alone anyway. There was nothing anyone could do. He missed Jenna, but he would learn to live without her. He'd learned to live without Maddie, hadn't he? And Maddie had been the love of his life.

So the last person he expected to see coming out of a movie theatre in the city one evening was Jenna. He'd just been to a business dinner in a nearby restaurant, and was about to cross the road to where his driver was waiting in the car when he literally ran into her.

"Adam!" she exclaimed softly.

He reached out to steady her as something deep inside steadied, too. He wanted to hold on, not let her go, as if she was the balance he needed to subsist.

Then he remembered what she'd done.

He dropped his hands and broke free. "Hello, Jenna," he said, unable to quite tear his eyes completely away from her, despite the anger still smoldering inside his chest.

Then someone coughed.

It was the woman beside her.

Jenna seemed to recover. "This is my sister-in-law, Vicki."

Stewart's wife.

Curious, he inclined his head at the other woman, but

received a hostile nod instead. Clearly he was persona non grata to the Branson family. Not that he cared. He'd come up against less friendly people in the boardroom and won.

His eyes were drawn back to Jenna. "You look good," he said, and meant it.

She moistened her lips. "So do you."

Time took a pause.

In the streetlight he was suddenly aware that she'd lost weight. There was a hint of dark circles under her eyes, too. His chest lurched as he wondered if he was to blame, but as quickly he knew he wasn't. She and her brother had caused all this from the start. He wouldn't feel sorry for her.

And then something hit him. God help him, but if she'd lost weight then at least she shouldn't be pregnant. If she was, surely she'd be putting on weight by now? A powerhouse of relief washed through him. He could not have handled knowing he was to become a father again. It would have been the ultimate cruelty.

Vicki slipped her arm through Jenna's in a protective manner. "Come on," she said firmly. "We have to be going."

Jenna hesitated. "How's Todd? And Chelsea?"

He allowed that she did have some genuine concern for others. "They're doing okay. They worked it out."

Her face relaxed a little. "I'm glad."

"Yeah, me, too."

Vicki tightened her arm. "Jenna, let's go."

Jenna nodded. "Yes, we should."

The two women went to turn away.

"How's Stewart?" he found himself saying.

They both stopped.

"He's coming home in a couple of weeks." It was Vicki who spoke in a curt tone before she guided Jenna away.

He turned and crossed the street to where his driver waited in the car. There was nothing else to say. He doubted he'd ever see Jenna Branson again. And that was just as well.

Jenna didn't think she could have driven them back to Vicki's house, so she was grateful her sister-in-law insisted on doing the driving. She felt sick after seeing Adam.

Oh, God, he'd looked so gorgeous that her heart had ached for him. And it ached even more when she remembered all the women he'd been seen dating recently. The newspapers had even commented on how hard "the playboy had been playing lately."

"Come inside for a drink," Vicki said, bringing the car to a stop in the driveway of her house twenty minutes later.

Jenna pulled herself together. "Thanks, but no. I should be going home. I've got work tomorrow." It was a weeknight, but Vicki had insisted Jenna needed to get out and relax and that it couldn't wait until the weekend.

Vicki frowned. "Sweetie, I can see you're upset. Come inside for a little while." She put her hand up when Jenna opened her mouth to refuse. "No. I insist."

Jenna knew when to give up. "Okay."

Once they were inside the babysitter left to go home next door, then they checked that the girls were sleeping before she and Vicki headed to the living room.

"How about a glass of sherry?"

Jenna's stomach turned. "Do you have any mineral water?"

"Sure. Or I could make coffee or a hot chocolate. Or how about—"

Jenna felt nausea rise in her throat. "I'm sorry, I—" She

ran for the bathroom, where she was sick. She didn't realize Vicki was there until she finished throwing up.

"You're pregnant, aren't you?"

Twelve

"You son of a—!" a male voice growled down the telephone line.

"What do you want, Branson?" Adam cut in, scowling. When his PA had said Stewart Branson was on the line, he hadn't expected this. He'd only seen Jenna last night. What the hell were they up to now?

There was a low curse. "You couldn't help yourself, could you? You just had to have her."

Adam's hand tightened around the phone. He didn't discuss his sex life with anyone. "Look, I'm heading out of the office to catch a plane. Perhaps we can continue this fascinating conversation another time."

"Don't hang up or you'll regret it," the other man warned.

"I don't take kindly to threats."

"No, you just like to give them."

Adam's jaw tightened. "Branson, *I'm* not the one who tried to get money under false pretenses."

"It wasn't supposed to go so far. Jenna wasn't supposed to—"

"Scam me?" Adam scoffed. "Come on. I'm not the lowlife who left the country, then used his sister to do his dirty work."

There was an abrupt pause. "It wasn't like that."

"Frankly, I don't care what it was like. It's over, Branson." Another moment and he'd hang up. He wanted to get on with his life, not listen to this guy justifying actions that had been criminal in the first place.

"I admit I have a gambling problem," Branson said quickly, as if knowing the call was about to end. "And I'm going to rectify that when I get home. But leave Jenna out of it. She knew nothing. She thought she was helping me."

Something in his tone stopped Adam from putting the phone down there and then. "You're just trying to scam me again, Branson." The man was probably trying to get him back with Jenna…and an unending supply of Roth cash. And if not cash, then the Roth connections were certainly a drawcard. He wasn't falling for it.

"I wish to hell it *was* a scam," Stewart muttered.

Adam stiffened. "What does that mean?"

"What I did was wrong, Roth, but what you did in getting my sister pregnant and not taking responsibility is far worse."

Adam's breath stopped dead. "What did you say?" he croaked, not caring that he was showing the shock rolling through him. He felt as if someone had sliced his chest open.

"Jenna's pregnant. And I expect you to do something about it."

Adam shuddered, then inhaled some air and started to

breathe again. This couldn't be. Jenna had lost weight. She would have said.

Or would she?

"Roth? Did you hear me?"

Adam swallowed. "Leave it with me," he managed to say.

"So you'll go see Jenna and fix things?"

"Yes."

"Good." There was a pause. "No one else knows yet, Roth, except me and my wife. I'm giving you time to make things right." The other man disconnected the call.

Adam sat there and stared at the hand piece before slowly putting it down to rest. Usually, he would never let another man hang up on him or threaten him. It was a measure of his complete and utter shock. Yet he had to admire Stewart Branson for taking a stand for his sister.

Jenna.

She'd once told him she was his worst nightmare. Right now he had to agree. She was pregnant…having his baby… and he doubted Stewart Branson was going to like the outcome.

After seeing Adam last night, Jenna hadn't been able to face going to work today so she'd called in sick. And she *was* sick—with morning sickness. She'd started feeling off-color a few weeks ago, but this morning she'd been feeling light-headed and nauseous, the morning sickness seeming to hit her with all its force. It was as if now that she'd acknowledged it, its very strength had intensified.

She'd suspected she was pregnant after she'd missed her last period. She just hadn't wanted to take the test. But after she'd been ill last night at Vicki's place, her sister-in-law had taken that out of her hands and had gone out to the local pharmacy and bought a pregnancy kit. It had confirmed her worst fears.

She was pregnant.

But was it really her worst fear? For all the problems ahead of her, she wanted this child more than anything. How could she *not* want the child of the man she loved? With new wonder she touched her stomach again, aware of a life beating beneath her heart. It was the most glorious feeling on earth.

Of course it didn't discount the fact that she had some heavy-duty thinking to do. She'd made Vicki promise not to tell Adam. He wanted nothing to do with her and seeing him again last night had merely confirmed that. His eyes may have eaten her up for that initial moment when they'd run into each other, but they'd soon hardened again. He thought she was a dreadful person. He would not want her to have his child.

On the other hand, she couldn't quite let the feeling go that a man had a right to know he was going to be a father. She would be distressed to *not* tell Adam. It would feel dishonest, and if he found out the truth later wouldn't it confirm his low opinion of her?

Yet with all his wealth, he might even try to take her baby away from her and raise it himself. The thought made her feel more than physically ill. It made her feel heartsick. Could she really believe he'd do that? Could she afford to believe he *wouldn't?* And if that were the case, wouldn't it be stupid of her to tell him about the baby at all?

Oh, God, her head was spinning.

Right then her doorbell rang. She jumped. No one knew she'd stayed home today, except the people at work. She hoped to high heaven it wasn't Marco. She really couldn't stomach him right now and would probably be rude.

Hopefully, it was only Vicki. Her sister-in-law might

have called her at work and learned she'd stayed home, and had decided to check on her. The phone had rung a couple of times this morning, but she hadn't answered. And she'd turned off her cell phone, too. She hadn't wanted to see people today.

The doorbell rang again and this time the person kept their finger on it. Already she had a headache and the sound went right through her, making her head swim. She rushed to answer it. Vicki would be worried about her, but all the same—

"Adam!" Her knees turned weak when she saw who it was, and she had to grab the door handle to hold herself up.

He stepped past her into the apartment without any greeting whatsoever. This was obviously not going to be a friendly visit.

Heart thumping with dismay, she slowly closed the door and turned to face him. The last time he'd been here was over a month ago. He'd been angry and upset then. Looking at him now, she knew nothing had changed. He *still* looked angry and upset, a pulse beating in his jaw, his nostrils flaring. Outside the movie theatre last night may not have happened. Clearly, she'd been wrong that he might have been glad to see her, if only for a heartbeat.

And then something occurred to her. Could Vicki have told him? She instantly dismissed that. Her sister-in-law had promised she wouldn't. Vicki knew she needed time to think about this.

"Adam, why are—"

"I owe you an apology, Jenna." He cut right across her in a hard voice.

She blinked. It was the last thing she expected him to say. "You do?"

He stood there watching her, his whole body tense,

telling her something was terribly wrong in spite of the apology. "You weren't trying to scam me about the money for your brother. I know that now. I'm sorry I accused you of something you didn't do."

She frowned. The words coming out of his mouth didn't match the angry look of him. "How do you know all this?"

"Stewart told me the truth," he said curtly. "He phoned me."

She was trying to get her head around that. "Stewart?"

Her brother was going to get help for his addiction as soon as he came back to Australia, but where Adam was concerned Stewart had been more than pleased to let sleeping dogs lie. She swallowed, suddenly getting a bad feeling about this. If Stewart had told Adam the truth, then why was Adam still looking so furious? Surely he'd be relieved she'd been telling the truth.

She could feel a mounting sense of panic. "I don't understand. Why would he call you now? It's over and done with."

"He wanted to abuse the hell out of me."

"For you not believing me?"

"That—" a pulse ticked beneath the taut skin of one cheek "—and other things."

She swallowed hard. Dear God. "Oth-other things?"

He stood in the middle of the living room. "You should have told me, Jenna," he grated harshly. "You should have said something."

A shiver went through her. What was he talking about? Was this merely about—

"You should have told me about the baby."

In an instant the air was sucked from the room.

"You know?" she whispered, unable to move, unable to do anything but try and get through the next seconds.

He gave a hard jerk of his head. "I know," he rasped. "Your brother blasted me about you not more than half an hour ago."

"Oh, God." Her feet moved then, and she made her way to the couch, sinking onto it before she fell down in a heap. Adam knew she was carrying his child. He was here to see her about it. She wasn't prepared. She didn't know what she was going to do...or say to him. It was all so new to her.

She moistened her mouth and looked across at him. "Vicki promised she wouldn't tell you, but I didn't think about her telling anyone else." Another thought came to mind and she groaned. "Oh, God, he's probably telling my parents right now."

"No. He said only he and Vicki know at this stage." His lips twisted. "Your brother's giving me the chance to make things right."

That was something at least.

"You weren't going to tell me at all, were you?" he said icily, drawing her focus back to him.

"Um...I don't know. I only found out for sure last night." She explained about returning to Vicki's and becoming sick. As she finished speaking she suddenly noticed how white he was around the mouth.

Through anger?

Or angst?

"You're not pleased about the news." It wasn't a question. She could see it was a fact.

He stood there, not moving. "No, I'm not pleased."

In spite of everything, the words caught at her heartstrings and she hugged her stomach. "I won't get rid of my baby, Adam. Don't ask me to."

His face turned pale. "I didn't...I wouldn't."

Her shoulders sagged a little. There was no way she'd have an abortion, but she was glad to hear him say it.

"But this is the one time I can't do the right thing, Jenna," he said, his jaw tightening with absolute firmness. "I have strong feelings for you, but I can't marry you. And I can't be a father to the child."

She managed to lift her chin. "I don't think I've asked anything of you yet, Adam."

"I know, but I want to assure you I'll still set you and the child up for a life. I'll even acknowledge in writing that the child is mine. It's just that…" He swallowed. "I can't be involved with it at all."

Her nerves tightened. "That 'it' you refer to is your own flesh and blood," she choked, unable to let him get away with this one thing. This was *their* baby they were talking about.

His head reeled back, and he heaved in a breath then slowly expelled it. "Yes, you're right." He pushed a hand through his hair. "Look, I need to explain something. I don't want you thinking…" He stopped for a second, his eyes turning dark with inner pain. "My wife was pregnant when she died in the car accident."

Jenna gasped. "Oh, my God, Adam."

His eyes said he appreciated her sympathy. "We'd known for a few weeks, but we hadn't told the family. We were going to tell them that night at a dinner party."

She knew immediately. "The balloons. Your wife was bringing them home for the party, wasn't she?"

He nodded jerkily. "We didn't get to tell the family the news about the baby, and I didn't tell them afterward, either. Only Todd knows. I almost drank myself to death after that, but he came around and made me get up and start living again. He was relentless. He wouldn't let me be." He took a shuddering breath. "I owe him a bloody hell of a lot."

Now it made sense why Adam had been so determined not to encourage Todd's wife.

"Adam, I'm *so* sorry." She wanted to get up and go to him, but she sensed he couldn't handle her touching him right now. He was holding on to his control by mere threads. Her being pregnant had brought all this up again for him.

"I loved Maddie and I loved my unborn child," he said with full sincerity. "Losing them almost killed me. It *did* kill a part of me. I'm not capable of going through that pain again. I'm sorry, Jenna. I really am."

Jenna's heart broke for him. She could only imagine what it was like to lose his wife, his child, his whole world. If anything happened to him—to *their* child—she knew she wouldn't have a life without them. She'd merely exist.

As Adam existed.

In her heart of hearts she knew what she had to do. She'd let him pay for the upkeep of his child. She'd even let him pay for some of her own expenses, so that she could look after their child properly. But what she would never do now was tell him she loved him. She wouldn't burden him in such a way. It would only add too much guilt to a man who already felt far too much responsibility for his family and friends. A man who'd already been through so much…lost so much more.

Her eyes stung and she blinked the tears back as she pushed herself off the couch to stand up. "Adam, I—" Suddenly she felt dizzy. She stopped to get her balance, thinking she'd gotten up too quickly.

"Jenna, are you okay?"

"I—" She vaguely heard Adam's voice just before everything turned black.

"What the hell!" Adam watched Jenna begin to topple over. He lunged forward before she could fall to the floor, and she collapsed unconscious in his arms like a rag doll, her face white.

He felt the blood drain out of him. "Oh, my God," he said hoarsely, and stretched her out on the couch, putting a cushion under her head. Then he knelt beside her, tapping her face. "Jenna, wake up."

She just lay there.

His lungs were tight. He could barely breathe. He swallowed a lump of fear in his throat and tapped her face again. This time she began to come around. "Thank God," he murmured, falling back on his heels with relief.

But only for a moment. An instant later he surged upward and moved to sit beside her. "Jenna?"

She opened her eyes and blinked. "What happened?"

"You fainted."

Her forehead wrinkled. "Fainted?" She went to get up, then lay back down. "I feel so dizzy." She swallowed. "My ear is really sore now. I'm starting to feel nauseated again, too."

He shot to his feet. "Stay there. I'll get you a bucket or something, then I'm calling my doctor." He strode into the kitchen and found a small bucket under the kitchen sink. It would do. He took it back into the living room, along with a towel, and put both beside her on the floor.

She had her eyes closed and seemed to be resting. His hands shook as he flipped open his cell phone and called the family doctor. Oscar was in a consultation, but Adam insisted on speaking to him and the receptionist immediately put him through.

Adam told him the problem in a rush then ended with, "She's pregnant, Oscar."

A pause came down the line. "Is she hemorrhaging or having any other problems with the baby?" Oscar asked sharply.

Adam had already thought of that. "No, I don't think so. She's just dizzy."

"To be on the safe side, I'll call an ambulance anyway. Now give me the address. I'll meet you at the hospital."

Fear jumped inside Adam's chest, but he managed to tell the doctor the address.

"And Adam, it'll be fine. It's probably more to do with morning sickness than anything else."

"I hope you're right, Oscar." Adam hung up. He could hear the understanding in Oscar's voice. Apart from Todd, only the medical people at the hospital had known Maddie had been pregnant. Oscar had been one of them.

He crouched back down beside Jenna, his chest so tight watching her lie there with her eyes still closed. "Jenna?" he said gently, touching her arm. "The doctor's going to send around an ambulance."

She lifted her eyelids, fear flickering in her eyes.

"There's nothing to worry about. It's only a precaution. My doctor thinks it may just be some morning sickness."

Her hand went to her stomach in a protective fashion. "It's probably best."

Something twisted inside Adam as he sat on the floor next to her, not caring about his clothes, not caring about anything but Jenna right then. He wouldn't let himself think about the baby. This was about Jenna. He had to get her well again.

Time ticked by.

"Adam?"

"Yes?"

"I think I'm a little scared."

"Don't be." But his heart was thudding almost out of his chest. He felt so helpless. "Would you like a drink of water or something?"

"No." She swallowed. "Just you."

"I can supply that." He held her hand, realizing she felt

hot. She must have a temperature, too. Oh, God, that didn't sound like morning sickness to him.

"Adam, I'm sorry."

"For what?"

"For doing this to you. I'll be fine. I really will."

"I know you will. And there's *nothing* to be sorry for." He touched her cheek. "Now rest. They'll be here soon."

They were, but it wasn't soon enough for Adam's liking. He would have read them the riot act if he hadn't been so damn relieved to see them.

The paramedic seemed to think the baby was fine, but Adam didn't relax until the doctors at the hospital had thoroughly checked her over and diagnosed an ear infection. Then they gave her some antibiotics that were safe for early pregnancy to stop any further infection, and something for the dizziness that had a mild sedative effect, and said they were keeping her in overnight. He felt much better about it all once Jenna was tucked up in bed in the private room he'd insisted they give her. He would pay. He didn't care about the money.

"I think I should call your parents," he suggested, as she was nodding off.

Her eyes burst open. "Don't let them find out about the baby."

He squeezed her hand. "I'll make sure no one tells them."

She sighed and closed her eyes. "Thank you," she murmured, then her eyelids fluttered open briefly. "Vicki might tell them. Don't let her," she ended as she fell asleep.

The thought of calling her parents wasn't pleasant, but the thought of calling Jenna's sister-in-law gave him an on-the-spot headache. The woman had despised him last night. Still, he had to speak to her first so that she wouldn't inadvertently mention the baby.

Thankfully he'd had the forethought to grab Jenna's keys, handbag and cell phone from the side table as they'd left her apartment. No doubt her parents' telephone number and Vicki's would be on speed dial.

Jenna's sister-in-law was upset, then cold with him, but he got an assurance she would say nothing about the baby. "For Jenna's sake, not yours," she snapped. She suggested that she call her in-laws, but Adam felt he should do it himself. She hung up after saying she'd be there soon.

Then he called the Bransons, who were alarmed, naturally, but he assured them Jenna was fine.

After that, he sat by the bed and waited.

They all arrived half an hour later, and once they saw for themselves that Jenna was okay, they turned their attention more fully on him. Vicki couldn't quite hide her hostility, but Jenna's parents seemed very nice and were grateful he had been there for their daughter. No doubt her parents thought Vicki's attitude was because of Stewart. They, at least, didn't appear to hold their son's addiction problems against him.

But all of them had a question in their eyes that he couldn't answer. He knew they were wondering why he'd been with Jenna today. It was obvious her parents knew about their previous relationship. No doubt he'd be considered the worst kind of person once they learned of the baby, especially once they knew he wouldn't marry their daughter. Hell, he felt disgusted in himself, too. He couldn't blame them.

"I have to go pick up the children," Vicki said, looking at her watch half an hour later.

"Yes, you go do that, love," Joyce Branson said. "We'll stay with Jenna until she wakes up."

"There's no need for you to stay," Adam said firmly, and

received a speculative look from the others. "I'm happy to call you when Jenna wakes up."

"Thank you, Adam," Joyce said, "but I wouldn't feel right leaving my daughter."

Adam glanced away before they could see his irritation. He wanted to be with Jenna by himself. Time was running out for him. He and Jenna didn't have much longer to be together.

"Of course..." Tony Branson said, drawing Adam's eyes to Jenna's father, "Joyce and I could really do with a cup of coffee. I'm sure there must be a cafeteria around here somewhere."

Adam nodded at him. He knew what the other man was doing and he was grateful.

Once they left, Adam felt the tension ease inside him. Jenna was still sleeping, and he was happy to sit by her side for now. Just him and Jenna together.

But as he sat there, as the minutes ticked by, it began to sink in that it wasn't fair to Jenna for him to stay too long. He'd have to leave eventually.

For good.

At the thought, he dropped his head into his hands, everything weighing heavily on his mind. At least he knew Jenna's family would help look after her and the baby. They were decent people. He would provide what he could with monetary assistance, but that's all he could offer her. She and the baby deserved better than a man who'd lost a large chunk of his heart five years ago.

Taking a shuddering breath, he lifted his head. God, how could he have been so wrong about her? She looked so peaceful lying there, so beautiful. She was a person who touched other people. A person who touched *him*.

And then it hit him.

He loved her.

Like an exorcism, his inner demons left him in that instant, taking his grief with them, repairing the hole in his heart and filling it with a new, stronger love.

He loved Jenna.

He loved their baby.

He couldn't let either of them go.

Thirteen

Jenna opened her eyes to a dimly lit room. She blinked as she tried to adjust to where she was, then she saw Adam sitting in the chair beside the bed and everything came rushing back. She was in hospital!

"The baby?" she whispered, her heart filling her throat.

Adam was on his feet instantly. "It's okay. Our baby is fine."

She sighed with relief. Then she realized something. Had he said "our" baby? Maybe she was hearing things because of the ear infection?

"How are you feeling now?" he asked.

She lifted her head and tried to sit up. "I'm not as dizzy anymore."

"The medication must be working." He gave her a gentle smile as he helped her get more comfortable against the pillows. "You'll be better in next to no time."

There was something different about him, but she couldn't quite pinpoint it. Then she remembered, and panic rose inside her. "My parents? And Vicki? Did they come? Are they here? Did Vicki tell them about the baby?"

His smile warmed even more. "Yes, they were here. And no, they still don't know about the baby. That's up to you to tell them when you're ready."

Her shoulders slumped with relief. At least she didn't have to face them over that just yet. "That's good, then."

He nodded. "I convinced them to go home for a few hours. I said I'd call them once you woke up."

"Thank you." Then she bit her lip. "You didn't have to stay with me, Adam."

"Yes, my love, I did." He placed his lips on her forehead. "I want to stay with you the rest of my life."

"Wh-what?"

He eased back and looked into her eyes. "I love you, Jenna. I'm not letting you go. Not now. Not ever."

"But—" She tried to get her head around what he was saying. "What about Maddie and the baby?"

He didn't flinch at all. "Maddie's at peace and so is our child. And for the first time since their deaths, I'm truly at peace, too." He kissed her hand. "I have no doubt I would have had a good life with Maddie, but it wasn't to be. You and I were meant to be together, darling."

She looked at him and her heart dared to hope. "Are you really sure?"

"I've never been more certain of anything in my life. Maddie was the love of my youth, Jenna, but *you* are the love of my *life*."

She thrilled to the words. "Oh, Adam."

"And you love me, too, don't you?"

"I'm that obvious?"

He leaned down to gently seal a kiss on her lips. "Love recognizes love, my darling. Will you marry me?"

"Yes!"

"Good. Your mother is already planning our wedding." He smiled as she blinked in surprise. "I had to get your parents out of here somehow. Otherwise I'd never have gotten you alone."

"So they're happy about it?"

"Definitely. And I'm sure they'll be even happier when they learn about the baby."

Jenna's heart rose with sheer happiness. Everything was falling into place now.

Adam was right. It was meant to be.

Epilogue

Babies abounded everywhere at Christmas later that year. Cassandra and Dominic had welcomed their second daughter, Eli, a month previously in November. Chelsea had joyously given birth to a baby boy only a week ago, making Todd a very happy father. And even Vicki and Stewart were expecting their third child in a couple of months' time.

For Jenna and Adam, their son, Christian Liam Roth, was born on Christmas Eve. They decided to name him "Christian" to celebrate their Christmas baby, and "Liam" in honor of the uncle he would never know, but who had brought his parents together. Laura and Michael Roth were the proudest of grandparents, as were Joyce and Tony Branson.

Jenna was allowed to come home from the hospital on Christmas Day, on the condition that she only go to the Roth family lunch if she took things easy. It had been Adam's one condition. He'd even arranged for her family to be at the lunch too, not that the Roths had minded sharing on this occasion. Considering that Adam had barely left her side the whole pregnancy and would make sure she didn't lift a finger today, she found his concern both amusing and touching.

She watched him check their sleeping son again in the bassinet, and she smiled with love. "You can relax now, darling."

He grinned ruefully. "I'll try."

As a new mum, she felt nervous herself, but this was more than that. She knew he'd never fully be able to relax and not worry about them. And she understood. She felt the same. She could only imagine what it would be like for him to let himself love so much when he knew the pain of loss so well.

Looking at their son now…looking at her husband…she wasn't so sure she would be quite as brave to love again. She thanked God that Adam had been able to open his heart. He loved her and Christian with an intensity that took her breath away.

"Did I tell you that you're my idol, Mr. Roth?"

He smiled adoringly at her. "I seem to remember you called me something entirely different when you were giving birth to our son yesterday."

She chuckled. "Don't let that fool you. I'm usually a very polite person."

He gave her a soft kiss. "Sweetheart, you fooled me the moment I met you. I didn't see you coming at all."

Jenna looked into Adam's eyes, her happiness true and complete. Love had found a way to heal all wounds, and now they could fully focus on the future.

And that looked very bright indeed.

* * * * *

& 🌹 A sneaky peek at next month...

Desire

PASSIONATE AND DRAMATIC LOVE STORIES

2 stories in each book - only £5.30!

My wish list for next month's titles...

In stores from 16th December 2011:

☐ Have Baby, Need Billionaire — Maureen Child

& The Boss's Baby Affair — Tessa Radley

☐ His Heir, Her Honour — Catherine Mann

& Meddling with a Millionaire — Cat Schield

☐ Seducing His Opposition — Katherine Garbera

& Secret Nights at Nine Oaks — Amy J. Fetzer

☐ Texas-Sized Temptation — Sara Orwig

& Star of His Heart — Brenda Jackson

Available at WHSmith, Tesco, Asda, Eason, Amazon and Apple

Just can't wait?

MILLS & BOON®
Book Club

Save up to £31

Join the Mills & Boon Book Club

Subscribe to **Desire**™ today for
12 or 6 months and you could
save up to £31!

We'll also treat you to these fabulous extras:

- **FREE L'Occitane gift set worth £10**
- **FREE home delivery**
- **Books up to 2 months ahead of the shops**
- **Bonus books, exclusive offers… and much more!**

Subscribe now at
www.millsandboon.co.uk/subscribeme

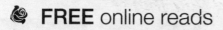

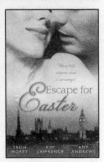

F